HOW TO WRITE A MYSTERY

A HANDBOOK FROM

MYSTERY WRITERS OF AMERICA

Edited by

Lee Child

with Laurie R. King

SCRIBNER

New York   London   Toronto   Sydney   New Delhi

Scribner
An Imprint of Simon & Schuster, Inc.
1230 Avenue of the Americas
New York, NY 10020

First Scribner trade paperback edition April 2022

For information about special discounts for bulk purchases,
please contact Simon & Schuster Special Sales at 1-866-506-1949
or business@simonandschuster.com.

The Simon & Schuster Speakers Bureau can bring authors to your live event.
For more information or to book an event, contact the Simon & Schuster Speakers Bureau
at 1-866-248-3049 or visit our website at www.simonspeakers.com.

1 3 5 7 9 10 8 6 4 2

Library of Congress Cataloging-in-Publication Data has been applied for.

ISBN 978-1-9821-4943-7
ISBN 978-1-9821-4944-4 (pbk)
ISBN 978-1-9821-4945-1 (ebook)

Contributor permissions appear on pages 309–313.

Contents

CONTENTS

Other Mysteries

CONTENTS

The Writing

CONTENTS

CONTENTS

Introduction

LEE CHILD

Let's get the jokes out of the way first: "Every successful mystery novel must have two specific attributes. Unfortunately, no one knows what they are." "What's the difference between a thriller and a mystery? An extra zero on the advance." And so on, and so forth.

In fact, the attributes a successful mystery must have are many and various, and the successful mystery writers in this book explore them in depth. The question of definition is equally complex. What actually *is* a mystery? The word means different things to different people. Publishers, editors, reviewers, and genre buffs tend to infer an exact specification, narrow enough to be precise yet broad enough to include several even more precise subcategories. By contrast, I have known several older folks, all very well educated, who call anything south of, say, Haruki Murakami a "mystery."

Publishers, editors, and reviewers need to be precise, and genre buffs like to be, but writers don't have to join them. I write without a plan or an outline. The way I picture my process is this: The novel is a movie stunt-man, about to get pushed off a sixty-story building. The prop guys have a square fire-department airbag ready on the sidewalk below. One corner is marked *Mystery*, one *Thriller*, one *Crime Fiction*, and one *Suspense*. The stuntman is going to land on the bag. (I hope.) But probably not dead-on. Probably somewhat off center. But biased toward which corner? I don't know yet. And I really don't mind. I'm excited to find out.

I think most writers are like that. And they should be, because most readers are. Or, nowadays, most *consumers*. Mystery Writers of America was founded around the slogan "Crime doesn't pay. Enough." We acknowledge commercial realities, because we're all subject to them. The demand for story is still huge. But the supply is growing. In the old days, movies and TV competed with books for leisure time, but they didn't really scratch the same itch. Now, quality long-form narrative television gets dangerously close.

Therefore we need to write better than ever. And we should feel free to use the whole airbag. "Mystery writers" is a noble and evocative term, but we shouldn't think it limits us. Far from it. From day one, MWA was all over the map. We need to keep it that way, fluid and flexible—and better than ever.

You can make a start on figuring out how by reading this book. It's all here. I'm deeply grateful to all the contributors—and I think you will be, too, eventually—and to those who worked hard behind the scenes. A lot of people gave up a lot of time. Why? Because they want you to be them, twenty years from now. Hopefully even better. They're telling you how. Weird, I know. Maybe that's one of the attributes. A successful mystery novel must be written by a good human being. Plus one other thing. Unfortunately, no one knows what it is.

The Rules and Genres

Neil Nyren—The Rules—and When to Break Them
Carved in stone or gentle suggestions: what are the rules in the mystery genre, why do they matter, and when don't they matter?

Meg Gardiner—Keeping It Thrilling
Nine things your thriller needs to be lean, mean, and exhilarating.

Naomi Hirahara—Insider, Outsider: The Amateur Sleuth
The point, and point of view, of your accidental detective.

Rachel Howzell Hall—Finding Lou: The Police Procedural
Are you a cop, or do you just play one on the page?

Alex Segura—The Mindset of Darkness: Writing Noir
It's about character: the flawed protagonist and letting your characters fail.

Charlaine Harris—Crossing the Genres
Mixing your mystery with a vampire, a talking cow, or a love interest?

Jacqueline Winspear—The Historical Mystery
Time, place, and the past.

Tess Gerritsen—The Medical Thriller
Playing on the reader's real-life fears and hunger for insider knowledge.

Gayle Lynds—Researching the Spy Thriller
Or: Why can't I just make it all up?

The Rules—
and When to Break Them

Carved in stone or gentle suggestions:
what are the rules in the mystery genre,
why do they matter, and when don't *they matter?*

NEIL NYREN

Everybody loves lists, and the crime fiction world is no exception: the ten books if you love historical thrillers; the twelve books for fans of Agatha Christie; the five psychological suspense novels you need to read *right now*; the best books of the year, of the decade, of the *century*. And, of course, the lists of rules for how to write them all.

W. Somerset Maugham famously said, "There are three rules for the writing of a novel. Unfortunately, no one knows what they are." That hasn't stopped people from making them up anyway. In 1928, American detective author S. S. Van Dine published "Twenty Rules for Writing Detective Stories." In 1929, British author (and theologian) Ronald Knox created his "Ten Commandments for Detective Fiction," later known as the "Decalogue." In 1973, suspense writer Brian Garfield produced "Ten Rules for Suspense Fiction." In 2001, Elmore Leonard provided *his* ten rules of writing to the pages of the *New York Times*.

The lists are useful for writers of crime and suspense fiction, and well worth absorbing, although some of the earlier ones are, let's say, problematic (Knox's rule number 5 reads: "No Chinaman must figure in the story." What?). They're useful because if you're just starting out, you need to have some sense of what you're doing—what the conventions are, what the subgenres are, what generations of crime writers have found that works or doesn't work. The rules and conventions give you a solid footing. After *that*, though, anything goes. Anything? Yes. Because they're not holy writ (the "Commandments" notwithstanding). The beauty of being a writer, the pure joy of the creative act, comes when you take those conventions and smash them, reinvent them, twist them into brilliant pretzels.

We'll get to that, but first you need to figure out just what the heck it is you're writing, so let's look at some of the subgenres of crime and suspense fiction and see how they sort out.

The most basic division—and the question that comes up all the time—is: Just what *is* the difference between a mystery and a thriller? The latter term is thrown around all the time, sometimes indiscriminately, because publishers feel that thrillers tend to have the bigger market, and so they're happy to slap it on all kinds of books, but at the very core, the difference is this:

Mysteries are about a puzzle. A crime is committed, usually murder, and the protagonist has to weave their way through clues and suspects to finally arrive at a solution. It's a more cerebral endeavor, and the key question is "Who did it?"

Thrillers are about adrenaline. Something bad happens, with the certain promise that more—and probably even worse—bad things will happen unless the protagonist can prevent them. The stakes can be intimate (one person's life) or huge (the fate of the world), the protagonist can be an ordinary person or a superhero. Whatever the case, it's the suspense that drives the book, the chase, the scramble, and the key question is "What happens next?"

Many books are pure mystery, many books are pure thriller—but as you know from your own reading, it's much more common for a book to have elements of both. Traditional mysteries can be filled with suspense, headlong thrillers can be tied to enigmatic puzzles—there's your first lesson on how the genres explode.

All the subgenres flow from there. Here are just some of them:

The crime novel: Some people use this term more broadly to mean any novel involving crime—in the UK, "crime" encompasses pretty much anything in the realms of mystery, thriller, and suspense—but more specifically as a subgenre, it's a novel more about the criminal than the law enforcer, and often told from the criminal's point of view. It can be light

(Donald Westlake) or grim (James M. Cain) or nestled nicely in between (Elmore Leonard).

The police procedural: This is the cop book, whether that cop is alone, part of a team of police, or in an even broader law-and-order network of detectives, medical examiners, sheriffs, ADAs, and the like. The police procedural looks at how a cop solves a crime and sometimes at the protagonist's home life as well, which is often not a bed of roses. Many great writers inhabit this territory—Ed McBain, Joseph Wambaugh, Michael Connelly, and Don Winslow, just to name a few, plus the classic Scotland Yard cops of Ngaio Marsh, Ruth Rendell, and P. D. James; the Navajo cops of Tony Hillerman; the South African cops of James McClure; and, of course, more Scandinavians than you can shake a stick at (not that I'd advise shaking a stick at them—many, many terrible things happen to the people in Scandinavian crime novels).

The hard-boiled detective and *noir novels*: These are two distinct subgenres, though often inhabited by some of the same characters and tropes. The *hard-boiled detective*—think Chandler, Hammett, and Ross Macdonald, and their spiritual children Sue Grafton, Sara Paretsky, Walter Mosley, and Robert B. Parker—often has unorthodox methods that suit them well, and is not averse to bending or breaking the law in pursuit of justice. That's the critical point, however: deep down the protagonist has a very moral center, and is trying to do the right thing, often against steep odds. In *noir*, however, everybody is compromised, criminal and cop alike; the system is corrupt; and no matter what you do, the outcome is often lose-lose. It's a bleak world, which I find intoxicating, but, hey, to each their own taste. Jim Thompson, W. R. Burnett, James M. Cain, Dorothy B. Hughes—try any of them.

The psychological thriller: This subgenre is very big. There's crime and there's violence, often within families or small groups, but the stakes are often more mental and emotional than physical. The protagonist may be the victim or the perpetrator or both, but she (it's more often a she) is a little or a lot unstable, often an unreliable narrator, and the trick is often to uncover just what is *really* happening to whom. A subgenre of this subgenre is the *domestic thriller*, which is purely within the family—secrets and lies between a married couple, siblings, parents and children, and so forth. Patricia Highsmith's *Strangers on a Train* and Megan Abbott's *Dare Me* are good examples of psychological thrillers; Gillian Flynn's *Gone Girl* and B. A. Paris's *Behind Closed Doors* specifically of domestic thrillers. And for a devilish twist on the domestic thriller, check out Samantha Downing's ridiculously entertaining husband-and-wife murder team in *My Lovely Wife*.

The traditional and *cozy novels*: These are also separate subgenres, though with similarities at times. The *traditional* mystery is in the classic format—a crime, usually murder, disturbs a community; a police officer or amateur sleuth investigates, searching for clues, interviewing witnesses and suspects, and narrowing down the field until the killer is unmasked and the community restored. This is the territory ruled over by the greats such as Agatha Christie, Dorothy L. Sayers, Josephine Tey, Ellery Queen, Ngaio Marsh, and many others. In the *cozy*, the setting is usually rural or small-town, the violence most often occurs offstage, the sex and profanity are minor to nonexistent, and the investigator is usually an amateur and most often a woman whose interests lie elsewhere—knitting or baking or antiques, say. See Joanne Fluke, Diane Mott Davidson, M.C. Beaton, and Katherine Hall Page.

The international and *spy thrillers*: These genres often overlap. The action is on the world stage, something big is at stake, an individual (sometimes a professional, sometimes an ordinary person) or group of individuals must penetrate to the heart of the plan, often against a ticking clock, often against overwhelming odds. The situation is sometimes black-and-white, good versus evil. Other times, there are considerably more shades of gray, with the outcome more ambiguous, the protagonist often disillusioned (if they had any illusions to begin with). Masters at all this are too many to count, but I'll single out John le Carré, Daniel Silva, Len Deighton, Ken Follett, Alex Berenson, Eric Ambler, and Frederick Forsyth. The *political* thriller could be grouped in here, too—there is a governmental power struggle or scandal or corruption or conspiracy. The protagonist may be an outsider who unravels it all, or an insider fending off a power grab or worse—assassination, overthrow, a false flag provocation for war—from outside. See Vince Flynn, Brad Thor, David Baldacci, Fletcher Knebel. You could also put in this general category the *military* and *technothriller* novels, featuring international military action and potential conflict of all kinds, suffused with a deep knowledge of hardware, tactics, and the military heart and mind. Tom Clancy is the king here, but he has a host of troops, including Dale Brown, Stephen Coonts, Larry Bond, and W.E.B. Griffin.

We haven't even touched upon so much else. *Historical mysteries* and *thrillers* constitute a rich and varied field that stretches from Steven Saylor's first-century-BC Rome, to Ellis Peters's twelfth-century England, to Laura Joh Rowland's seventeenth-century Japan, to Anne Perry's Victorian England, to the various twentieth-century wartimes and interwar periods of Jacqueline Winspear, Charles Todd, Philip Kerr, and Alan Furst. There are the *medical* thrillers of Robin Cook and Michael Crichton; the *legal* thrillers of John Grisham and Scott Turow; the *financial* thrillers of Paul Erdman, Christopher Reich, and Stephen Frey; the *ancient conspiracy* thrillers of Dan Brown; the *technological* wonders and warnings of writers such as Daniel Suarez, Ernest Cline, Andy Weir, and Crichton again (nano and cloning and AI, oh my!); the *romantic suspense* of Jayne Ann Krentz, Nora Roberts, Linda Howard, Sandra Brown, and Julie Garwood; the *forensic* cases of Patricia Cornwell and Kathy Reichs; the *environmental* and *eco-danger* territory that has been explored by Carl Hiaasen, Karen Dionne, Douglas Preston and Lincoln Child, Nevada Barr, and C. J. Box.

Name a subject, and there's a subgenre for it. Each of them has its own rules and conventions—and all of them have had authors who have gaily subverted them, combined them, reimagined them, and created something altogether memorable.

If you were asked to name the most classic murder mystery author of the twentieth century, many of you would immediately think of Agatha Christie—yet Christie was delighted to break the conventions when it suited her. One of S. S. Van Dine's twenty rules was "There must be but one culprit, no matter how many murders are committed." In *Murder on the Orient Express*, however, Christie made *everybody* the culprit, a whole group of murderers taking revenge on a criminal.

The number one rule in Elmore Leonard's ten was "Never open a book with weather"—but Tony Hillerman's brilliant *Listening Woman* opens with a 247-word *aria* of weather, describing the howling wind as it crosses the landscape and swirls around three key characters. It's incredibly compelling, and draws you into the book just as swiftly as any gunshot or murder.

One of the primary rules for many of us in publishing when considering a crime novel submission has always been "Someone has to be likable, or else the reader can't identify." Then *Gone Girl* came along and absolutely obliterated that dictum. Tell the truth: Did you actually *like* either the husband or the wife in *Gone Girl*? No. How about the girl in *The Girl on the Train*? No again. Those books seem to have done all right, though—and they forever changed the category of psychological suspense.

Other writers have mashed the subgenres up. Rex Stout combined the traditional mystery-solving of Nero Wolfe with the hard-boiled private eye narration of his legman, Archie Goodwin. Tana French's Dublin Murder Squad books have taken the police procedural and imbued it with all the character complexities of psychological suspense (as did P. D. James and Ruth Rendell before her). Carl Hiaasen combines the environmental thriller with comic noir. Lyndsay Faye's trilogy set in 1840s New York City gives us the police procedural as historical thriller. Tom Clancy took the military thriller, wedded it to the political novel, filled them both up with technology, and the technothriller was born.

Still other authors have gone a step further and mashed up entire genres—crime fiction with science fiction, horror, or the paranormal. Charlaine Harris mixed mystery with the supernatural and the romance novel to create the Sookie Stackhouse series. Andy Weir's *Artemis* blends science fiction with the heist novel. Stephen King's *11/23/63* is a political thriller by way of time travel. Lauren Beukes's *The Shining Girls* does the same for the serial killer novel—that's how the man finds his victims. One of the most compelling books of recent years, Ben H. Winters's *The Last Policeman*, is a police procedural that follows a local detective's murder investigation under the shadow of an asteroid due to wipe out Earth in six months—a circumstance that changes everything. One of my favorite books, Martha Grimes's *Send Bygraves*, depicts a Scotland Yard detective trying to solve an extraordinarily spooky series of small-town murders—in a 108-page illustrated poem. Stuart Turton's ingenious 2019 novel, *The 7½ Deaths of Evelyn Hardcastle*, depicts a very traditional Christie-like isolated-manor-house-with-many-suspects mystery with one key difference: the protagonist is stuck in an endless time loop, and every day he wakes up in the body of a different suspect. How did the author even think of that? I don't know, but I'm glad he did.

Mind you, cross-genre books can be tricky. Those categories exist for a reason. Publishers know how to pitch them, bookstores know where to shelve them, reviewers know if the book's in their preferred wheelhouse, consumers know if it's a kind of book they've always liked.

But when a cross-genre book works, when *any* rule-breaking book works, there is a special exhilaration to it. *Did she just do that? Is there more? Can I do it, too?*

Yes, you can.

I'm often asked at writers' conferences for my best advice to a writer. You'll find other people's answers scattered throughout this book, but here're two of mine. The first one is obvious: If you're a writer, then you must write. Sit yourself down in a chair every day and turn out some pages—it doesn't matter how many, just as long as you're doing it. When Sue Grafton spoke at conferences, she'd sometimes ask, "Who here wants to be a writer?" Naturally, a sea of hands would go up. "Then what are you doing sitting here?" she'd say. "Go home, go back to your room, go write!"

The second piece of advice goes hand-in-hand with the first: You must write—but you also must read. Read everything. Read the genres you like and those you've never tried. Read the authors you admire and those you've never heard of. Read the authors who contributed to this book—they're here for a reason. Read them all, absorb them, see what works, figure out *why* it works—and then use everything you've read to create your very own style.

Surprise yourself. Surprise us all.

Make brilliant pretzels.

CAROLYN HART

A traditional mystery is about the struggles of ordinary, everyday people who sometimes succumb to evil. The traditional mystery reveals the truth of relationships. When the detective sets out to discover who committed a murder, the detective is actually discovering what fractured the relationships among the people involved in the story. The ultimate aim is to uncover truth. . . .

One might ask, aren't mysteries all about murder, guns and knives and poison, anger, jealousy and despair? Where is the good?

The good is in the never-quit protagonist who wants to live in a just world. Readers read mysteries and writers write mysteries because we live in an unjust world where evil often triumphs. In the traditional mystery, goodness will be admired and justice will prevail.

—*Publishers Weekly*, 2009 Mystery Issue

Keeping It Thrilling

Nine things your thriller needs to be lean,
mean, and exhilarating.

MEG GARDINER

So, you crack your knuckles and sit down at the keyboard to write a thriller. You're eager to create a gripping story in which the protagonist tries to stop something dreadful from happening. You want to cause delicious anxiety and apprehension that keeps readers on the edge of their seats, turning the pages in dread and exhilaration. How do you create work that lives up to the name and *thrills*?

Nine Things a Thriller Needs

1. Minimal Weight

Thrillers must read lean and mean. Fluff and padding dull their impact. Cut needless words, scenes, and characters.

(By way of example: I originally titled this list "Ten Things a Thriller Needs," but condensed it to nine.)

2. Powerful Conflict

Every story is a journey, told through conflict. The protagonist wants something. The antagonist seeks to prevent them from achieving their goal. That's plot: obstruct desire.

With thrillers, the story needs a compelling main character, a devastating antagonist, and a sharp hook for the plot. The hook catches the protagonist's world and yanks it radically out of balance. That kicks off the protagonist's quest to put things right. Ideally, the hook involves the antagonist and the threat they present.

Protagonists must actively drive the story forward. They can't sit back and watch events unfold. Passive protagonists will suffocate a thriller; your heroes and heroines need to be in the thick of the story, making stuff happen. Of course, they face incredible opposition: antagonists who are formidable adversaries. Weak, unintelligent opponents aren't scary or dangerous, so give your antagonists power, skills, charisma, and overpowering drive.

In a thriller, the story is about the choices the characters make when facing deadly threats, under increasing pressure, often with time running out. The only real way to find out what characters are made of is to crack their world in half. Then you learn whether they can fight their way clear of the debris, rescue people who need help, and rebuild from the wreckage. Give your characters strengths, weaknesses, and dreams. Heroic courage and desperate flaws. Give them a past. A family. Baggage. (They were raised by thieves. They were orphaned in the woods and adopted by badgers. They were taught to fight, or to be quiet and demure.) How will that past haunt them and those around them? Will they escape it? Embrace it?

And give them a future. Give them two: one they strive for at the story's outset . . . and a different future they find after they complete their quest. To sharpen conflict, drill deep into the characters' lives—their drives, fears, and desires. Then set the characters against each other. The protagonist and antagonist each seek vital goals. Those goals clash. Their conflict will drive them to an irrevocable confrontation at the climax, where they resolve the issue between them . . . with talk, takedowns, or fire.

Bottom line: Trouble builds character. Go deep. Dig into your characters—intellectually, morally, emotionally, and spiritually. Then throw them into a struggle that puts them to the test. That's Thriller Writing 101.

3. High Stakes

The *stakes* in a story are what will be won if the protagonist succeeds and lost if they fail. Does your protagonist face embarrassment? Professional failure? Maybe at the start. *Maybe.* But in a thriller, the stakes need to escalate until, at some point, death must be on the line. Perhaps it's a metaphorical death—the end of a career or relationship . . . No, you're writing a thriller. It's physical death.

You need danger. Characters that readers care about should be in jeopardy. A sense of threat should hum through the story, like a jet engine that has a gremlin inside, *Twilight Zone* style, and might blow at any time.

4. Suspense

Suspense involves a state of anxious or excited uncertainty over how events will turn out. That uncertainty creates apprehensive doubt. It causes literal nail-biting. It jabs readers with pins and needles as they wonder what will happen next.

It keeps them turning pages.

As a writer, you cause that uncertainty by creating curiosity about what's going to happen and concern for the characters.

So: Raise a question—and don't immediately supply the answer. Pose a problem but don't reveal the solution. Withhold information from the reader—and from the protagonist. Make getting that information vital to the protagonist's goal, then parcel it out slowly, and force them to struggle for it. Stretch out the time it takes to resolve the uncertainty, and dangle the answer just out of reach. Have well-laid plans go awry. Let a character's deepest fear become reality. Create a looming sense of danger. Have a crisis erupt that requires an immediate response.

Then make it impossible for your characters to immediately respond.

The writer's job is to create a problem that demands fixing, then veer in another direction. Prolong and worsen readers' desperate desire for resolution.

Add in concern for the characters, and suspense is exponentially amplified. Compassion and sympathy deepen readers' connection with the people on the page. They guarantee that readers will remember the story long after it's finished.

5. Tension

Tension is distinct from suspense. For thriller-writing purposes, consider tension equal to excitement. Dole it out in bursts. Suspense can be sustained over an entire novel. Tension spikes like a Geiger counter at a meltdown. It tightens the screws (or reveals that the screws the gremlin loosened in the jet's engine are about to fall out). It's a shot of adrenaline.

How can you create tension in a story? Insert moments of danger, friction, and confrontation. Set a deadline. Nothing ups the stakes like a timer ticking down. The bad guys are rolling into town on the noon train. The hurricane is due to hit at sundown, and the last boat off the island leaves in twenty minutes. A boys' soccer team is trapped in a cave with water rising. The hero's unit has been poisoned and will die in six hours without the antidote.

Think of tension in terms of minutes or seconds of peril. Or an explosive confrontation. Which can involve a volcanic eruption, or the deadly showdown with Brenda from HR.

6. A Swift Pace

Thrillers *move*. They rumble, roll, race. They don't lumber. And they never tread water. The story should advance on every page. Give it energy. Make sure it never sits still. Your story is the 82nd Airborne, diving out the door of the plane while the sergeant shouts, *Go, go, go!*

Of course, the characters—and readers—do need breathers. They need moments to exhale, reflect, and rest up. But the story as a whole is like the Pony Express. Someone's always got to be waiting to take that handoff and *ride*.

You can write scenes where characters take a languid midnight swim in the ocean. Give them a chance to banter and blow off steam.

Or to walk the dog, cook dinner, and make love. Nonstop action isn't what makes books feel relentless. Books feel relentless when the action slows but unanswered questions lurk in the background.

The pace can relent, but the suspense never should.

Let your characters have a moment of zen, or ecstasy, or pie. Let them laugh. There's nothing like a splash of humor to give characters—and readers—a lift. But keep tension and unsettled issues churning away in the story, and in the reader's mind and gut. Mysteries remain unsolved. Clocks tick down. Bad guys scheme, and load weapons, and creep nearer. And each lighter scene can feed into the main plot. Beasts lurk beneath the placid surface of the ocean where the hero swims. The heroine's dog slips the leash and dashes into darkness, where a killer lurks.

7. Action

Because the ultimate stakes in a thriller are life and death, even slow-burning stories of psychological suspense will eventually feature physical action. And physical action—including violence and chase scenes—works best when it combines tension with emotional stakes.

A note on violence: Explicit brutality doesn't make a story more frightening. Gore doesn't necessarily up the tension. In fact, what often increases fear and tension is a threat that remains partially veiled in mystery—because readers' imaginations will create terrors more frightening than authors can portray. The theater of the mind is more powerful than a bucket of blood.

Simple, visually clear action descriptions work most effectively. You don't need to analyze every muscle twitch involved in a commando's silent leap from a rooftop, or describe the exact angle at which the villain cocks her fist before walloping somebody. And always remember: Action should reveal and amplify conflict, suspense, tension, and character. Mere blows don't land in a story any more than they do in a video game.

Chase scenes likewise must be visually clear. Beyond that, they must be even more emotionally powerful than equivalent scenes on the screen. Readers don't get the visceral sensory impact that viewers receive from watching a chase scene, so you need to deliver other kinds of punches. And for a chase scene to excite readers, it has to avoid every cliché pulled from other chases you've seen or read. *Bullitt* is iconic. Try to duplicate it, and you'll write a predictable knockoff.

Elements that go into a chase scene include:

Setup. Build in suspense, tension, and questions from the beginning. The hero must get to Buenos Aires or Terrible Thing X will happen. The heroine must escape from Moscow with the Tiny Thing the Spies Want, or the truth will die with her. Give the character a goal. Lay out the stakes.

Buildup. Create a vital goal: freedom, rescue, justice, survival. Then start throwing obstacles in the character's path. Add time pressure. The flight is canceled. The replacement flight is diverted by a medical emergency. Or it's brought down in the wilderness by a flock of geese, and now the hero must escape on foot.

Climax. Add emotional pressure. Up the stakes. The Tiny Thing the Spies Want starts ticking. The Cub Scout troop that's leading the hero out of the forest betrays him to the conspirators. The hero finally eludes the cops and arrives at the convent with seconds to spare . . . only to discover that Sister Mary Margaret has been taken hostage by the bad guys.

Ingenuity. Think of unexpected twists and build them in from the beginning. In *The Dead Pool*, Clint Eastwood is chased across the hills of San Francisco, à la Steve McQueen in *Bullitt*—not by hit men, but by a tiny remote-controlled car that's packed with explosives. It's simultaneously an homage to a classic and a fresh, clever take.

Never forget: Chase scenes should be designed to illustrate, reveal, or develop character. Make us care about the people on the page. Show us how and why they do what they do . . . and how the action affects them and others.

8. Twists

A plot twist is an unexpected turn in the story that dramatically shifts the direction or expected outcome of the narrative. Twists turn stories upside down. They surprise readers who think they know what's going on.

Twists can involve a discovery, a revelation—say, of a secret—a betrayal, a declaration of love, a mistake, a failure of courage . . . the possibilities are wide open.

Writers can withhold information or mislead readers with ambiguous or false information. This is a classic technique in mysteries, where uncovering information—and the killer's identity—is the goal of the story. You can toss in red herrings or an unreliable narrator. You can create misdirection: Make readers think the big, bright explosion on the mountaintop is the important development. Get them to look away from what's bubbling in the harbor.

But no matter how you plant a twist, it should be earned, or the reader will feel burned. Use twists to ramp up tension, suspense, the stakes; to reveal and change character.

Yeah, you're wondering. *But . . . how do I think up a twist?*

Write down all the wild ideas that hit you. Play with them. Think about what happens if you put your wild idea at the story's beginning. Or its midpoint. Or at the climax. Work both forward and backward in the story from those possibilities.

When you're coming up to a major scene or a turning point in the story, ask yourself: What's the most obvious next step for the story to take?

Do the opposite.

Or if you have a scene, sequence, or act that develops in a straight line from beginning to end, redesign it. Deliberately build in a minefield for your characters. Turn that straight line into a physical, emotional, or moral assault course.

Use twists to reveal something about character. Go deep. Dig into the characters' needs and desires. Play on your characters' strengths, wants, fears, and flaws. And on their pasts. Their lies. Their relationships. Use twists to expose and affect your characters, and thereby to shift the course of the story.

Any twist should ideally do more than shock. Slapping readers with a huge surprise won't be enough, on its own, to get them to love the sudden turn the plot takes. A twist should deepen and enrich the characters and the story.

The best twists are surprising yet inevitable. They create moments when readers gasp and mutter, *No way...* but, on reflection, think, *Yeah, of course.* And those moments arise out of character and conflict. Those twists lead to stories with emotionally rich, satisfying conclusions.

9. A Breaking Point

In thrillers, there often comes a point where:

- the magnitude of the challenges the protagonist faces drives her toward taking a dark turn—not to break bad, but to jump some fence and plunge across a border. The line can be moral, physical, or emotional: breaking the law; abandoning a personal code; surrendering to an obsession . . .
- the hero has his back against the wall. Out of ammo, out of allies, out of room to run. At the mercy of the antagonist. It's John McClane—bloody, beaten, hands up, seemingly defeated— facing Hans Gruber at the end of *Die Hard*. Your job as a writer is to push the character up against that metaphorical wall, then figure out: How does your protagonist find the ingenuity, strength, and courage to overcome seemingly hopeless odds and triumph? (Or die trying . . .)

Either scenario can happen, or both. Your job as a writer is to drive the story to this point. Or, to put it another way: *Raise the stakes and make it hurt.* In a thriller, this point has to involve a defining physical and moral trial. What turn of events would really test your characters? How can you ratchet up the conflict and present your protagonist with a challenge that will make or break them?

Of course, taking your protagonist to the edge—smashing apart their world and forcing them to face wrenching dilemmas while staring down the threat of annihilation—is easier to design in a standalone novel than in a series. But in every thriller, ideally someone finds themselves on such a precipice. And by the climax, the protagonist should have developed a personal stake in that character's success and survival, and be crucially involved in the showdown with the antagonist. That's the delicious challenge for a writer.

With every item on this list, I keep coming back to one thing: character. The story grows from characters who desperately want something and who, to get it, face off against each other in deadly conflict. Start, continue, and end with that, and you'll be on the right track. And you'll keep readers coming back for more.

BETH AMOS

Homicides and other crimes come with a built-in level of suspense, but that's often not enough on its own to keep readers interested and invested in the story. The pace of suspense should be a roller-coaster ride—first the build-up, then the exciting plunge, then another build-up.

Insider, Outsider:
The Amateur Sleuth

The point, and point of view, of your accidental detective.

NAOMI HIRAHARA

Unlike police procedural or private investigator stories, the amateur sleuth finds the writer, not the other way around. No other mystery genre reveals more about the author's inner, work, or personal life. In some ways, amateur sleuths are the ultimate insiders, because they originate from inside us or from a very specific community. However, they also are definitely outsiders, as they are the main crime solvers outside the work of established law enforcers or professional detectives.

As the amateur sleuth is not paid for investigative services, the most daunting challenge for a writer of this subgenre is to justify the involvement of their protagonist in the story line. And if this is a continuing series, believability can be particularly strained. It's up to the writer to create a convincing and captivating world for the reader. Writing an amateur sleuth novel requires a strong point of view that has to delight, thrill, or comfort.

First of all, why this particular sleuth?

Many writers, especially for their first series, create a character similar to either themselves or someone in their own lives. There is nothing wrong in this. The writer has inside information about a certain occupation, lifestyle, historical time, geographic region, or community. The challenge is to determine what essential, concrete details need to be integrated in your book to make your sleuth fly and not be weighed down by unnecessary minutiae. And perhaps even more important, to determine the organic motivations for your sleuth to solve the crime.

First, you should consider what draws you to a particular type of character. Who do you root for? I'm attracted to underdogs and invisible people, individuals who are often ignored. Who do you feel is misunderstood? The pretty, popular young woman who is often depicted as an airhead? The older single woman? The stay-at-home dad?

You might seek to make heroes out of the people around you. Do you want the office drone to finally find agency? How about a lawyer who in the real world is buried by the inefficiencies of the legal system? Or perhaps you want to find joy and meaning in an everyday life filled with delicious baked goods and crafting. All of these sleuths can find their place in a mystery—it's your job as a writer to make it happen.

Amateur sleuths need to be pungent and vibrant from the minute you meet them. This pungency can be represented in their appearance, speech, point of view, or relationships. Whether you choose to write in the first or third person, the narrative has to be laden with this fresh perspective and personality. I used to advise writers to pretend to interview their protagonist to help them build characters, but now I think writing an amateur sleuth mystery requires more than this superficial questioning. We need to dig deep inside ourselves and find themes and rhythms that distinguish us from other people.

If you are writing in third person, explore the fullness of metaphors and similes from your main character's point of view. Take what's important to your sleuth and examine the world from their eyes. Ultimately it may be precisely those details that lead the sleuth to solve the crime.

A longtime fan of the cozy mystery subgenre, the late Don Cannon, told me once that he likes learning about occupations in these novels. Stephen King, in his book *On Writing*, also observes that readers are fascinated by the subject of work. (This may be more of an American phenomenon.) If you are stumped with where to begin, why not start with your sleuth's job? The beauty of the amateur sleuth mystery is that the main character does something besides detecting. Get immersed in that job or lifestyle. If you don't have much firsthand experience, go visit an actual workplace and note the mundane aspects of the job. How do the workers carry themselves? What kinds of equipment, special tools, or clothing are involved? When do the employees take breaks, and are those on- or off-site? A deep dive into the profession will give you insights into how your sleuth differs from the thousands of other ones out there.

Naming the Sleuth and Likability

I am big on finding the right name for your sleuth. I've encountered other writers who can commit to going forward with their tale with *xxx* as a temporary character name, to be filled in later. But for me, the drive to write a story doesn't go smoothly without the proper moniker.

I look to the classics—Arthur Conan Doyle's Sherlock Holmes, for instance. Do you know that the names Sherrington Hope and Sherrinford Holmes were under consideration? Do you think Doyle's stories would have reached their epic heights with those choices? Both Doyle and Agatha Christie found inspiration for character names from friends, local police detectives in the news, and neighborhood buildings.

Again, be mindful of what you may encounter in your everyday life. Make sure the rhythm and sound of the name rings true. If it's an ethnically specific name, check whether it's authentic and spelled correctly. In these modern times, you should also Google the name to see whether anyone has the same name. If no one pops up, you are probably safe. Check your fellow authors' books, too. You may be surprised to see how many mysteries feature a sleuth with a similar name. As I wrote my Officer Ellie Rush bicycle cop series, I was surprised to see how many Ellies were featured in other mysteries. In response, I experimented with different first names, to no avail. Sometimes you can't avoid the repetition. Own it and go on.

There's also the question of likability. Rather than worrying whether readers will like your amateur sleuths, you need to consider whether the characters are compelling and entertaining. (Truth be told, I gravitate toward cranky curmudgeons.) And as I once heard veteran writer Jan Burke advise, if you have an unlikable protagonist, add a likable sidekick. If this sidekick finds something redeemable in the sleuth, then readers will expect to, as well.

Inciting Incident

For many of us writers of amateur sleuth mysteries, the inciting incident—the discovery of the dead person—usually involves a loved one as either the victim or, more likely, the prime suspect. This makes sense for the first mystery or standalone, but how about for subsequent mysteries? Most skeptics point to the Jessica Fletcher quandary—why are so many people killed in the seaside village of Cabot Cove?

Regarding this conundrum, I point to any other mystery subgenre except perhaps noir. There's a level of fantastical thinking in the creation of most of these works. Most real private detectives don't have exciting, action-filled cases; most of their time is spent sitting in cars, or on the computer. Homicide investigators rarely discharge their weapons. Usually the most obvious suspect from the get-go committed the crime. The country of Iceland, which produces some of the most harrowing popular murder mysteries, has very few homicides in a year.

In comparison to these other genres, amateur sleuth mysteries are unfairly accused of being the number one offender in straining credibility. The writer needs to keep one eye on this, but what's more important is to create a world where the reader doesn't care if the body count is realistic or not. The incidents happened in your magnificent creation, and that's all that matters. You might encourage your character to move around geographically, so the pool of potential victims is much larger. Or your amateur sleuth can begin to get a reputation for crime solving, which may bring people to their door. It's a delicate balance, but one that all writers of series fiction must address.

Relationship with Law Enforcement

Of course, since we are dealing with murder, law enforcement has to have a presence in your book. But it can be anywhere from fairly limited to very close, such as an intimate or romantic relationship. Some have chosen to make their sleuth a former covert agent or crime fighter whose latent skills surface in dangerous situations. (Their connections can also be useful during the investigation.) Depending on your worldview, police officers can be depicted as either friend or foe. The more pressing question is how an amateur sleuth is going to detect and solve a crime that the professional investigator cannot. The answer lies in the sleuth's "superpower"—whether that's a special expertise related to the job, a relationship, or an underestimated personal characteristic.

I've leaned on clues to develop one of my mystery series; in fact, after determining the theme of a certain book, I then figure out what specific clues will be the bread crumbs for my sleuth. These bread crumbs will be ignored by the authorities because they lack the cultural or horticultural awareness that Mas Arai, my aging Japanese American gardener, has. It's a delight to select these clues, the physical objects that mean so much more than even the reader realizes.

The Changing Sleuth

Rex Stout's Nero Wolfe is a great example of a literal armchair detective who doesn't change much over time. He rarely leaves his New York brownstone and has a dependable assistant, Archie Goodwin, who also is unchanging. Yet Wolfe, with a plus-size body and a love for orchids, is definitely memorable, and his eccentricities keep the reader engaged.

It's still possible to successfully create this kind of static amateur sleuth who doesn't have much of an emotional arc or backstory. During the early part of the twenty-first century, however, readers gravitated more toward the evolving sleuth who is able to reconcile the past and go forward by entering into new relationships and identities, such as by getting married or having children. Yet these trends ebb and flow with the times, and who knows—perhaps we will once again crave a hero who is more consistent and unsurprising. The more important issue is who you want to spend extended time with. Because when you give birth to an amateur sleuth, chances are that both of you are in it for the long haul.

Questions to Ask When Developing a Sleuth

Who do you personally root for?
What kind of people do you root for?
How do you or people around you feel misunderstood?
What is your character's superpower?
What is your character's Achilles' heel?
What is your character's biggest fear?

For Right Brainers Who Crave Lists

I'll be honest, I'm not an analytical writer. I didn't learn how to write in a journalism or master of fine arts program. I learned by doing and writing, and writing from my heart.

But I know some of you want more prescriptive advice, or at least more analysis. So here's a rundown of different kinds of amateur sleuths, at least how I see it. This list, of course, is not comprehensive, and I hope new categories will continue to be created over time.

Elderly Person

Superpower: Their invisibility is their strength. Also life experience can provide more reference points to solve the crime.

Challenges: Because of physical limitations, how can you make them compelling to follow?

Advantages: Usually retired or semiretired, so they may have time on their hands. Also, they may rely on old technology, which can provide more opportunities to actually talk with suspects and witnesses.

Examples: Agatha Christie's Miss Marple; Mas Arai

Proprietor of a Brick-and-Mortar Business

Superpower: Expertise in their field, standing in the community

Challenge: They need to be attached to their business, so how can they leave it?

Advantages: The small business can be an interest point.

Examples: Joanne Fluke's Hannah Swensen; Cleo Coyle's Village Blend; Jenn McKinlay's Fairy Tale Cupcakes; E.J. Copperman's Haunted Guesthouse; Abby Collette's Crewse Creamery; Jennifer Chow's Hollywoof; Carolyn Hart's Death on Demand; Vivien Chien's Ho-Lee Noodle House

Lawyer or Legal Personnel

Superpower: Understanding of law
Challenge: Law can get boring.
Advantages: Lawyers have plenty of opportunities to get involved with law breakers.
Examples: Sujata Massey's Perveen Mistry; Michael Nava's Henry Rios; Lisa Scottoline's Rosato & Associates; Alafair Burke's Samantha Kincaid; Paul Levine's Jake Lassiter; Sue Ann Jaffarian's Odelia Grey

Journalist

Superpower: Reason to be nosy and ask questions
Challenge: Traditional journalism is a dying profession.
Advantages: Access to law enforcement, criminals, witnesses, lawyers, etc.
Examples: Hank Phillippi Ryan's Jane Ryland; Michael Connelly's Jack McEvoy; Jan Burke's Irene Kelly; Jill Orr's Riley Ellison; Denise Hamilton's Eve Diamond; Karen E. Olson's Annie Seymour

Parent of Young Children

Superpower: Caretaking
Challenges: What to do with the children as the sleuth investigates? And how to write realistic children that are not too precious or cloying?
Advantages: Many opportunities to interact with different people connected to their children. Also, if they are full-time caretakers, their time is (somewhat) their own.
Examples: Donis Casey's Alafair Tucker; Ayelet Waldman's Juliet Applebaum; Victor Gischler's David Sparrow

Service Provider

Superpower: Physical mobility
Challenge: If it's a mundane service, how to make it interesting?
Advantages: Travel from customer to customer. The writer can also explore underclass issues.
Examples: Kate Carlisle's Shannon Hammer; Barbara Neely's Blanche White; Laura Levine's Jaine Austen; Elaine Viets's Helen Hawthorne

Resident in a Small Town

Superpower: Intimacy
Challenge: Why are all these people dying?
Advantages: Everyone in a big city dreams of living in a small town. The supporting characters, who are as important as the sleuth, provide fun writing opportunities.
Examples: Donna Andrews's Meg Langslow; Hannah Dennison's Island Sisters; my Leilani Santiago

Medical Professional

Superpower: Knowledge about how to kill people
Challenge: Overload of scientific details
Advantages: These doctors, coroners, nurses, and midwives have constant access to life-and-death situations.
Examples: Tess Gerritsen's Maura Isles; Charles Todd's Bess Crawford; Colin Cotterill's Dr. Siri Paiboun; Edith Maxwell's Rose Carroll

Young Person

Superpower: Optimism
Challenge: As technology and youth culture change rapidly, how to keep your character current?
Advantages: Young people have more energy, more free time, and fewer responsibilities than a middle-aged person with a family.
Examples: Alan Bradley's Flavia de Luce; Mark Haddon's Christopher John Francis Boone

Royalty / Wealthy Person / Celebrity

Superpower: Fame, fortune

Challenge: How to create a rich, successful sleuth that people will want to root for.

Advantages: Access to any kind of resource. And the public likes reading about royalty and rich people.

Examples: Tasha Alexander's Lady Emily; Rhys Bowen's Lady Georgiana Rannoch; Dorothy Sayers's Lord Peter Wimsey; Rex Stout's Nero Wolfe

Nature Worker

Superpower: Knowledge of the great outdoors

Challenge: Lack of regular human interaction

Advantages: If you are good at physical description, you make this setting come alive.

Examples: Nevada Barr's Anna Pigeon; Dana Stabenow's Kate Shugak; Sandi Ault's Jamaica Wild

Professional / Office Worker

Superpower: Keen sense of seemingly trivia details

Challenge: How to make the professional interesting?

Advantages: If it's your present or former profession, you may not need to do much additional research.

Examples: Adam Walker Phillips's Chuck Restic; Dianne Day's Fremont Jones; Dianne Emley's Iris Thorne; Patricia Smiley's Tucker Sinclair

Clergy / Religious Follower

Superpower: Access to people's innermost secrets.

Challenges: Issues of confidentiality and limits of religious practices

Advantages: Faith communities, with their special rituals, represent an insular world that readers may either identify with or desire to know more about.

Examples: Julia Spencer-Fleming's Clare Fergusson; Faye Kellerman's Rina Lazarus; G. K. Chesterton's Father Brown; Michael Lister's John Jordan

Academic

Superpower: Knowledge of facts and history
Challenge: How to place the eggheads in harm's way
Advantages: Travel to other locales or world-building at a university
Examples: Elizabeth Peters's Amelia Peabody; Gigi Pandian's Jaya Jones; Cynthia Kuhn's Lila Maclean; Dana Cameron's Emma Fielding

LINDSEY DAVIS

Lindsey's Top Ten Essentials for Aspiring Writers (of which there have always been eleven)

1. Word processor—dump the beat-up Remington and the green ink
2. Sensible chair—protect your back
3. Mortgage as long as a telephone number to make you finish
4. Fixed deadline and fear of missing it
5. Scary agent
6. Absolutely *no* routine
7. Workplace sobriety—don't drink and type
8. Thinking time—let the brain do the work
9. Warm room—thinking leads to hyperthermia
10. A synopsis—write it, then ignore it
11. A Good Idea—this really is a good idea!

Finding Lou:
The Police Procedural

Are you a cop, or do you just play one on the page?

RACHEL HOWZELL HALL

I'm not a cop. I'm not a lawyer. I'm nowhere close to working as a first responder.

I write—fundraising proposals, gift acknowledgments, donor update reports, mystery and suspense novels.

But I live in Los Angeles, a city of four million people. A native, I grew up in this city—and not the parts of L.A. you saw on television. Not the shiny and bright L.A. in Randy Newman's "I Love L.A." music video. Not the slick and sexy L.A. filmed for *Real Housewives of Wherever* and *Keeping Up with Whothehellcares*. My Los Angeles is south of the 10 freeway but still close enough to the Pacific Ocean that the aroma of salt and sea mixes with the smell of fried chicken and cigarettes. Palm trees rustled in the courtyard of my family's apartment in the Crenshaw District. The Hollywood sign, white and bright, sat on a hillside just a few miles away—I could see it from our kitchen window. That icon never felt like a thousand miles—even in South Los Angeles, we knew celebrities. Little Richard and Rerun sometimes came to my church for services. Ice-T frequented the same car wash on Crenshaw Boulevard that the rest of us patronized.

So. Not a cop. But my neighborhood saw a helluva lot of them. Heard sirens and police helicopters all the time. As a child, I didn't know that Black cops existed. That women cops existed. The Black women cops . . . I believed more in crop circles and magic beans than in the possibility that a Black woman cop worked somewhere in Los Angeles. And these unicorns sure as hell weren't heroines of crime stories.

I'd loved reading Michael Connelly; though he didn't write about my part of the city, with its barbecue and fried-fish joints on every corner and brown skin on everybody (not just the pimps and cousins/lovers/aunties of the suspect or victim), he still wrote about this town I loved.

And I'd loved reading Walter Mosley; though he didn't write about contemporary L.A., with its crowded freeways and gentrification and women not always being femme fatales but simply . . . women, he still wrote about this town I loved.

Where were the L.A. stories of crime-fighting Black women? Women connected to their families, pissed off by the fools in their neighborhood who made it worse for everybody, committed to serving and protecting their beloved community, the same community that taught them how to love their skin, their hair, and the curves of their hips and lips?

If you can't see it, you can't be it—and if you don't know it, how do you write it?

Before I started the Elouise Norton series, I had work to do. First, find that character in preexisting work and see how the author pulled off that magic trick. I knew that my request was narrow and that the results would be close to nil. But then . . .

Paula L. Woods. *Inner City Blues*. LAPD detective Charlotte Justice. The riots. Yes! Dear reader, I consumed those books like they were Funyuns. There it was! My Los Angeles. There was Charlotte, a woman I saw walking around Westwood in the eighties. She went to my same hairdresser and stood behind me in the long line at Phillips Bar-B-Que. She knew Albertsons grocery store made the best fried chicken in the city. I knew Charlotte, and her presence encouraged me. Her presence also depressed me—there were only four novels in the Charlotte Justice series, and I had a sinking suspicion why.

So: I'm not a cop. I don't look like most cops. I'm an English/American literature major drawn to nonprofit communications. I love a genre that, up until recently, didn't publish or feature Black women. The few writers who did publish saw their series stuck at three or four books at the most.

Like a foolish romantic, I still struck out to write my own Black homicide detective story.

Why did I do that? That's another essay. How did I do it? That's the point of *this* essay.

Step 1: *Read.* Consume those stories that you'd want to write. First, for pleasure. Then forensically. What do you like about that story? What don't you like about that story? Read the reviews—good and bad—so that you can address the points they raise as you write. As for my reading list: of course, Connelly, Mosley, and Woods. But also David Simon, Miles Corwin, and for Los Angeles, Ryan Gattis, Naomi Hirahara, Gary Phillips, and Gar Anthony Harwood. Include screenplays in your reading, but not crappy ones. Again, David Simon.

Step 2: *Attend conferences.* This one may be difficult because it requires money. Save up for one conference, then. As my first conference, I chose the California Crime Writers Conference, sponsored by the Southern California chapters of Sisters in Crime and Mystery Writers of America. Dedicated to helping writers, this conference features experts—from cops to FBI agents to forensics specialists, the megillah. Also, it's small and intimate, so there are your favorite crime and mystery writers standing next to you. This was my first conference and I will love it forever. My second-favorite conference that I attended as I was getting started: Writers' Police Academy. Some conferences will let you volunteer to receive a discount rate. Others provide scholarships and grants. Check out the websites for Sisters in Crime and Mystery Writers of America.

Step 3: *Ask questions.* But mind what you ask. I'm sorry, but yes, there *are* dumb questions. If you're blessed to have an audience with an expert, don't ask stupid questions. Time is precious—ask those questions that you cannot answer with Google. I ask about biology, since my cop and PI is female—from peeing to periods (and if those words squick you out, maybe you shouldn't write crime), I ask women in law enforcement how they handle those things. Sex, cramps, bras beneath bulletproof vests . . . can't find any reliable answers on the interwebs.

Step 4: *Watch TV.* I watched a lot of *The First 48.* Not for the cases, mind you, but to look at the world being filmed. From the station with its coat rack filled with different neckties to the family picture stuck in the visor of the detective's car. Hearing the cadence of people being questioned, the clothes they wear, the tattoo on the detective's wrist. I rolled down the streets in these episodes—from New Orleans to Tulsa to Detroit. I saw the different types of uniforms worn by cops in the same department—the blue wool but also the khakis and polo shirts. I wrote down things that struck me, atmosphere and details I wouldn't otherwise have access to.

Step 5: *Subscribe.* Get thee into the Metro section of the newspaper. *Los Angeles Times* has always had a great Metro/California section. Growing up, my first section of the paper was Metro and then Comics. Death and crime lurk in these pages. On the web, reporters have incredible series, following a case from first victim to needle in the arm. My hometown paper also lists homicides that occur each day. It's macabre, but then you didn't choose to write romance, correct? Follow the paper on Twitter. Follow those reporters on Twitter. Get to know the underbelly of the city you're in.

Step 6. *Shoot past the stereotypes.* Not all cops drink whiskey and play jazz. Not all cops yearn to pull out their gun and fire. Not all cops have broken marriages and kids who resent them. Not all cops are good. Not all criminals are flat-out evil. Not all criminals are poor. Not all criminals live south of the 10. Not all criminals are violent. Not all victims are noble. Not all victims are women. Not all victims had a secret. Not all victims are easy to love. Not all victims were at the wrong place at the wrong time.

Step 7. *Don't give up.* When I was submitting to houses for the first Detective Lou Norton novel, *Land of Shadows,* some editors told my agent that Lou wasn't special. This was 2012, and oh sure, there were *thousands* of novels starring Black women homicide cops [insert eye roll]. You will hear that: *This is nothing special.* You will ignore it. You will ignore it because the story that you're writing comes from the community that's being overpoliced, because your cop was told girls can't play, because your cop actually listens to the community. You will ignore it because you've actually listened to how people speak, what scares them, and you will write it without being a bigot and a racist. You dig?

Step 8. *Hold on to that day job.* First, I'm editing this as the world is in quarantine. My day job is paying for the electricity that keeps this laptop charged—and if I get sick with coronavirus, my health insurance covers my treatment. So there's that. Also, jobs are a great resource. Your coworkers? They're nuts. And they're related to other strange people. You may experience that wackiness firsthand or hear a story that may just make one of your scenes more interesting. Collect these stories and use them, maybe not now, but someday. My brother once told me about this hooker who put Visine into a john's drink and took money out of his wallet while he was on the toilet with diarrhea. See, Visine is a laxative and this is the real way she came into money. Great stuff.

Does any of this help?

I certainly hope so.

You're starting off in a better place than I did—with this book and collection of essays, you have gold in your hands, my friend.

LINWOOD BARCLAY

When I write a book, I feel as though I am building a house. I'm the carpenter. I am banging this thing together, one stud at a time. If literary writers are the gardeners, crime writers are the contractors. A genre in which a well-constructed plot is critical demands practitioners who know enough to measure twice, cut once.

The second draft—and, as is often the case, several drafts beyond that—is when the finishing touches go in. Trim, wallpaper, paint. I hang a few pictures on the walls. Family pictures are stuck to the fridge with magnets. It's those subsequent drafts where I add in all the details I failed to include as I got the story down.

I'm not a big believer in "writer's block." I think it's adorable that of all professions, we have an actual condition to justify not getting our work done. But in any line of work, there can be times when we need to take a break, to clear our heads. Go for a walk. Cut the grass. Build a Lego kit. That's often when the solution to our problem will come to us.

The Mindset of Darkness: Writing Noir

*It's about character: the flawed protagonist
and letting your characters fail.*

ALEX SEGURA

"Noir," as it's used to describe prose, can be interpreted in many ways—almost to its own detriment. Some see it as a genre, others as a style. Some drill down to classify it even more precisely. For my money, noir is a mindset—but before we can get into that, we have to discuss what we know noir to be.

The term "noir," of course, comes from film noir, which literally means "black film" in French, and refers to an era of Hollywood cinema that boasted a number of stylish crime dramas, predominantly in the 1940s and '50s. But parallel to its cinematic counterpart, noir grew to prominence as a subgenre of crime fiction during the '40s, often confused with its sibling, hard-boiled crime fiction. So what sets noir apart? Well, it depends on who you ask.

Some will say noir stories have to feature a sense of looming failure or darkness, or excessive sex and/or violence. Many will point to some of the cinematic tropes, like the femme fatale or the bleak, dour ending. Many works of modern noir define themselves based on a nihilistic point of view. Though hard-boiled private eye novels—like those of Raymond Chandler, Ross Macdonald, and Mickey Spillane—and noir works are often confused or thought interchangeable, one could easily argue that the best, most lasting stories in the hard-boiled genre are heroic in nature, with a tainted-knight-style hero circumventing the law and defying "the system" to reestablish a greater sense of equity, allowing for the scales of justice to return to balance by story's end. Noir films and novels, on the other hand, are about moral ambiguity and base emotions, with characters driven by lust, greed, fear, and often hate. These are pessimistic works about messed-up people who've made dodgy choices in life.

Megan Abbott, one of my favorite modern crime writers and a shrewd student of noir in particular, had this to say about the two subgenres and what sets them apart:

> The common argument is that hardboiled novels are an extension of the wild west and pioneer narratives of the 19th century. The wilderness becomes the city, and the hero is usually a somewhat fallen character, a detective or a cop. At the end, everything is a mess, people have died, but the hero has done the right thing or close to it, and order has, to a certain extent, been restored. . . .
> Noir is different. In noir, everyone is fallen, and right and wrong are not clearly defined and maybe not even attainable.

I tend to use Megan's description as my own internal definition of noir—and it influences how I approach the genre. For my money, noir stories involve people painted into corners, forced into desperate, often illogical actions to try to bring balance to an imbalanced and unfair world. More often than not, that imbalance is their own fault, and their panicked actions are a by-product of their own selfish, lustful mistakes—whether it's a lurid affair, a money scam gone wrong, or murder.

It's through that filter that I can get to the heart of this piece—which is "writing noir," which raises the question: How do you write noir? My own novels are first and foremost private eye stories, starring a down-on-his-luck ex-journalist, Pete Fernandez. So they can't be noir, right? Wrong. As noted above, PI stories are about a heroic figure, even if flawed, who pushes back on the establishment to do the right thing. But that doesn't mean PI novels can't be noir—quite the opposite.

The key to writing noir can be learned from any Jim Thompson novel, if you want a shortcut. The one most critics would rightfully point to is Thompson's seminal *The Killer Inside Me*, about a small-town sheriff who finds his life quickly unraveling as the reader discovers the true monster hiding beneath the police uniform. It's a jarring tale propelled by Thompson's terrifying and unreliable narrator, and leaves the reader shaking in disbelief and surprise. Dorothy B. Hughes's *In a Lonely Place* features a similar twist, if executed differently—both novels evoke the same "not everything is as it seems" tone, and that makes for immediately unsettling reading, a tenet of great noirs. Generally, Thompson's noir novels are stories about bad people doing bad things who are forced to do worse by circumstances they can't control. You can inject these same kinds of characters into any type of story, which is the secret flexibility of the term. Noir isn't only noir when it's all-consuming. You can inject noir elements into any kind of story, as long as you're clear on what noir is—to you and to the reader.

In many of my novels, there's a key character who serves as the noir protagonist—but it isn't necessarily the story's main protagonist, Pete the (sometimes amateur) private eye. In my third novel, *Dangerous Ends*, the twist reveals that someone the reader (hopefully) considered an ally was, in fact, spending years trying to hide a deadly mistake—one that cost them the life of their own mother. The twist—which I'll do my best not to spoil—does what all good twists should, which is that it makes you reconsider everything you've read that's come before, and while damning the character, it also creates sympathy for an admittedly "evil" person. That's noir—when we can have some feelings of remorse for a character's terrible, murderous actions, because deep down, we fear that in the same situation, we'd probably make similar choices. Noir is an emotional tone— it comes from a primal state of being. The best noir characters may be calculating and cunning, but they're also propelled by basic emotions, and end up paying the price for their instinctive reactions.

Many crime fiction series, especially procedurals and PI novels, are what I like to call "evergreen." That means that while you may see some incremental changes from book to book, for the most part, the character you meet in the first novel remains consistent until the end. Ross Macdonald's Lew Archer is a good example. In the first Archer novel, *The Moving Target*, Archer makes reference to a past career as a cop. It's a carbon copy of Chandler's Philip Marlowe, and Archer remains a Marlowe clone for the first batch of novels. But the point is, we don't learn about Archer's (or Marlowe's, for that matter) past, nor do we see either character change much from book to book. Whatever development happens is in service to the plot, whether it's Macdonald's deep dive into the meaning of villainy or Chandler's twisty, often meandering but beautifully written character puzzles. While these kinds of novels are superb, and prime examples of how to do serialized stories that are more plot-driven and procedural in nature, they're not conducive to being works of noir.

The root of noir is in character—and to fully experience a noir story, you have to see the character go from their norm, whether buttoned-up businessman unhappy with his job or bored housewife, to their rock bottom: the businessman completely penniless and wanted for murder; the former housewife on the run with the gardener who killed her husband. See what I mean? And while these kinds of characters can exist in a PI novel or procedural, as I noted above, if the series is more evergreen than "evolving," it's harder to label the work as noir. (Though there is some precedent for an evergreen PI, in this case the film version of Mickey Spillane's Mike Hammer, existing in a noir tale—check out 1955's *Kiss Me Deadly*, directed by Robert Aldrich, a powerhouse noir that, in many ways, destroys the idea of the battered, heroic private eye.)

Exceptions aside, noir hinges on change—actualizing change and showing change—and that is the core of what I like to call the "evolving" PI novel or crime series. Some examples are George Pelecanos's Nick Stefanos novels, or Dennis Lehane's masterful Pat and Angie series. While each book spotlights a specific case our heroes must solve, we're also in the trenches with them—and seeing them change from book to book, often for the worse by the end of it, adds a jolt of noir that many evergreen series lack. You'll notice, too, that most evergreen series can run indefinitely. For example, while Michael Connelly's Bosch character does change from time to time over twenty-plus novels—partners die; he's shunted to different departments—his basic elements remain, making for a Bosch who is almost Holmesian in his consistency, yet giving the reader the impression of change on the protagonist's journey toward solving the crime. On the flip side, with characters like Stefanos or Pat and Angie, by the end of their respective—and relatively brief—series, most readers could not imagine them going on any further. Their stories are over, and the characters are spent. That's an element of noir, believe it or not.

This is a long-winded way of saying noir can be many things, and there are many ways to write it—but at its core, noir is about character, whether it's your protagonist, your supporting cast, or your villain. It's about the evolution of character, more precisely—and the fallout of the decisions characters make under duress and how they react when things start to go south. Take, for example, the 1944 Otto Preminger film noir masterpiece, *Laura*, an elegant and unforgettable work that feels miles away from the grimy and bloodstained streets one would expect to find in the pages of a crime novel or in a mystery film. Yet it is noir, as we discover the truth behind Gene Tierney's mysterious Laura and just what happened to her.

The primary challenge in writing noir is the ability to let go—to allow your characters, through their own actions, to dig themselves deeper into the holes they've created, and to allow them to fail—and to understand that a dour narrative arc can still be engaging, emotionally challenging, and even more realistic than the tidy, well-plotted narratives we've come to expect from mainstream cinema and literary blockbusters. Noir is also not always about bad people doing even worse things—it's often stories about inherently good people tempted by evil, or innocents dragged into the darkness by forces outside of their control—like Burt Lancaster's murdered ex-boxer in Robert Siodmak's *The Killers*, based on Ernest Hemingway's short story.

Noir is not a place for happy endings or convenient resolutions. It feeds off the gray areas and darkness in the world, and man's (and woman's) primal urges, whether they be sexual or other vices—think of Frank and Cora as two of the three points on the love triangle that's central to James M. Cain's classic noir novel *The Postman Always Rings Twice*. When writing noir, the most impactful character—though not always the protagonist—is the presumed innocent, the normal person going about their daily life who finds themselves yanked into something big and dangerous. Suddenly out of sorts, the personal imbalance leads our character to make rash decisions, and the consequences of these choices help shape who the character will become. *Queenpin*, the noir masterpiece by Megan Abbott, is a prime example of the trope: we follow a young woman's slow descent into the underworld, watching as she gradually becomes an expert at the game of deception and double-crosses, unseating her mentor and boss. The novel deftly flips noir tropes, because of Abbott's own expertise in noir, and serves as a showcase in how to invert the elements of noir while still holding true to the general tone and feeling that noir requires—a dark, despondent, and desperate energy that only increases as the characters spin out of control, unable to hang on, but unsure of what happens if they don't.

THE MINDSET OF DARKNESS: WRITING NOIR

The best advice I can share with someone looking to write a true noir, not just a crime novel and not just a hard-boiled tale featuring bad people, is to immerse yourself in film noir and the noir works of past masters like Cain, Thompson, Hughes, and modern neonoir believers like Abbott, James Ellroy, and Scott Phillips. On a technical level, as we've discussed, noir plots follow the same arc—things are okay, temptation arises, temptation is taken, bad decisions are made, things get worse, things get out of control, the end. It's not a clean, three-act structure and it's certainly not one that concludes with everyone sated and every thread tucked in its place. Noir is messy, noir is dark, noir is sexy and painful, and noir is real. In a dangerous world that's more gray than black or white, noirs reflect our darkness—creating an eerie beauty that can arise only when all hope is gone.

HANK PHILLIPPI RYAN

You stare at your blank page. You type *Chapter 1*, simply so there's something there. You think: *I have no idea what comes next.* You reassure yourself it's fine, there are many other people who write without an outline. But how do they do that? Here's the secret. Writing "without an outline" is not really quite true. You *do* have an outline. You're writing a book. A book is a story. A story has a format and an arc: beginning, middle, end. A story has a character you care about, with an escalatingly high-stakes problem that demands to be solved. The good guys should win, and the bad guys get what's coming to them. And in the end you want some form of justice, and to change the reader's world. And what makes it even more logical, you're writing a certain genre: a mystery, a thriller, a police procedural. When you type the words "Chapter 1," even though you don't know what will happen in the *plot*, you know what *kind* of book you're writing. With that crucial decision, you're making a contract with yourself, and with your readers, that a specific type of book is on the way. Now. Tell that story in the way it needs to be told.

There's a moment in the writing process when you wonder: *Am I finished? Is this manuscript as powerful and polished as it can be?* Then you worry: *How can I be sure?* Try this random walk method of editing. Pick a page of your manuscript, any page at all. Remember, even though you're writing a whole book, each page must be a perfect part of your perfect whole, and that means each individual page must work. So, page by random page, use this quick checklist of what to look for: First, is something *happening*? Is there forward motion? Or are you reading an entire page of people yammering, or someone mulling something over, or an elaborate description of turning left on Maple Street then turning right on Elm? Next, check the page for intent and motivation. Ask yourself: Why is this scene here? What work does it do? Does it advance the plot or reveal a secret or develop the character's conflict? Do your individual characters behave the way a real person would behave? Are they true to themselves?

Then examine your technique. Too many dashes? Repeated words or clichés? And finally, look for poetry. Does the rhythm of the sentences change and flow? Is your writing as seamlessly naturally beautiful and specific and strong as it can be?

And here's a final secret. I always know when I'm finished, because I forget I'm editing, and realize I'm simply reading the story. It's not *my* story anymore, it's its own story. And then I think—*done.*

Crossing the Genres

Mixing your mystery with a vampire,
a talking cow, or a love interest?

CHARLAINE HARRIS

Though the blending of mystery with fantasy, science fiction, and/or romance is done quite often now, this multipronged approach was rare and held in deep suspicion only a couple of decades ago.

Mystery writers were warned about a list of things they must not do:

Don't kill a child.

Don't kill a cat.

Don't let the detective solve the mystery by supernatural means, and don't let your sleuth, professional or amateur, use supernatural means in the investigation of the crime. If there was a supernatural clue, perhaps delivered in a séance, there had to be a human agency behind it . . . à la *Scooby-Doo*.

If a writer did use supernatural elements, perhaps the appearance of a ghost or a creature that rose from the dead, the book was slotted into the category of "woo-woo." (Like the sound a spirit makes, "*Wooooo . . . wooooo.*") If you wanted to be a serious mystery writer and keep the respect of your peers, that categorization was something to be avoided at all costs.

But writers will be writers. Our minds don't stand still but keep freewheeling through the universes in our heads. It's possible to love mysteries and yet get tired of (or bored with) the rules, whether they're Father Knox's Ten Commandments or S. S. Van Dine's Twenty Rules. There may come a day when you want to keep yourself entertained by introducing a vampire to the mix of characters—or a sorcerer, or a talking cow.

Though this may sound like spontaneous fun—a lot of us write to keep ourselves entertained—you had better put in some serious work beforehand if you want to make other genres blend harmoniously and richly with your mystery.

Don't experiment in adding elements to the mystery genre because you think the supplemental genre is "hot" right now. That way lies madness . . . or more usually, a lot of mediocre books. When I first decided to take the plunge, there was no such field as "urban fantasy." And my first cross-genre book was a hard sell; my excellent agent worked on selling *Dead until Dark* for two years. (Thirty-second printing now—neener neener neener.) Pushing a cross-genre book these days is much easier, as long as you've taken a fresh approach.

Decide on mixing genres because you have read and respected books that are not mysteries. And you should have read a *lot* of them, whether westerns or sci-fi, horror or romance.

Especially when it comes to the romance genre. Don't assume that you understand the rhythm of a romance novel unless you've read ten, or twenty. The course of true love never runs smooth, and you should know where the bumps in the road are going to make their presence known. There are numerous specialized romance niches, too: Amish love stories, gay love stories, men who fall in love with women who have babies by other men. The romance field has embraced the paranormal world with fervor. Lions and tigers and bears (oh my!) get together and get it on. Lonely vampires meet their human mates. Aliens abduct human women all the time, and find them irresistible.

No matter the genre, do your homework. If you've become interested in fantasy, watching a few vampire movies is not enough research. You need to familiarize yourself with the lore behind the mythic creature, examine that lore, make it your own. For example, in their earliest written adventures, vampires could not cross running water. In these days of cars and buses, you'd better think about that particular bit of myth very carefully. That's not to say you have to follow all traditions blindly—not at all. But if all your vampires love to swim, you'd better have an explanation ready.

If you're fascinated by hard-wired science fiction, and you decide to set your whodunit on Mars, learn everything about Mars you can. If your characters are humans, they have to have some credible way to survive in the Martian environment. Create your own history of the Mars colonization, the culture that grew there afterward, the way people must live to make the new planet work. Industries? Banking? Justice system? Go in depth to make this world believable, or there's no point at all in setting your book there. The cool factor lies not in setting a mystery on another planet, but in making it the *only* place your story could have had the same ending.

Just a note: You can go overboard on planning your world and its society. I knew a woman who'd worked on her world for five years . . . and hadn't written a word of the book all this world-building was for.

I am often asked what the next big thing will be in the bookselling world. The writers who ask this want to jump on a preexisting bandwagon. I don't scorn any way a writer gets published. If you can see a wave cresting and you can produce a great book that has all the trademarks that are popular, good for you. In general, books that are written to cash in on a trend are not as successful (in the sense of being fresh and original) as the books that started that trend, which were books written from the heart. This is as true in cross-genre novels as it is anywhere else.

To promote what you've written, you'll need to attend conventions you've never been to before. Science fiction conventions are different from mystery conventions. Romance conventions are different, too. If you have a low tolerance for cosplay and filking, or if you don't believe in highly organized writing panels or discussions about alien sex and three-ways, at first such gatherings may strike you as strange or ludicrous. Get over it. Mystery conventions will feel like the staid middle-aged ladies who wear pearls and pumps in comparison.

So: Love the genre you want to include in your work. Learn the lore. Do your due diligence. Create your own bandwagon.

I just wrote some books set in an alternate-history America, specifically in the west. I *then* found out there was a whole subgenre called weird west. And that was what I was writing. And I was welcomed into a fold I hadn't even known existed. I felt like the first person landing on a strange planet who gets off the spaceship to discover there are already footprints in the dust.

And finally . . . know where you're going. Are you writing a mystery that has elements of the weird and eerie? Are you writing horror with an underlying puzzle? Are you working on a romance where sparks fly up while an investigation goes on? Are you examining another world via a trip through its criminal justice system? You should have a fixed goal. It'll help you enjoy the daily fun house that's the life of a novelist.

KATE WHITE

An agent friend of mine, who once worked as an executive at a major publishing house, says she's always blown away by people who decide one day that they want to become an author but think it's just something you *do*, rather than something you have to learn *how* to do. "People who've had success in one field," she explains, "like law, or medicine, or true crime writing, often have a hard time accepting that if they're going to write fiction, it means starting at zero again. They don't think they should have to." But they do.

The Historical Mystery

Time, place, and the past.

JACQUELINE WINSPEAR

I'm always amused when I see the novels of Jane Austen included in lists of "best historical fiction," because Jane Austen was not a writer of historical fiction. If she were she would have been writing stories set in the Stone Age, Medieval Britain, or the reign of Elizabeth I. Jane Austen was a popular contemporary novelist with a sharp eye and a dagger wit who used her insightful observations of others to inform her novels, peppering the narrative with colorful characters, revealing dialogue, and insightful social detail. She just happened to have lived a couple of centuries ago, leading us to confuse the history and the writer—yet Jane's skills as a social commentator and expert storyteller give us a good starting point when discussing the historical mystery. The best historical mysteries are written as if the author were of the time, not simply looking back.

The historical mystery is a narrative form that brings together the historical novel and the mystery novel. Both are successful literary traditions in their own right, offering the writer a broad landscape for developing an engrossing story that blends a great idea with a personal interest in a given historical era—most writers of fiction craft their stories based around something they've observed, overheard, read about, or experienced that has given rise to a certain curiosity that I think of as the "kindling" for their story. That kindling, the raw material with which writers of historical mystery start the fire, is no good on its own. It needs fuel, a match and a good blast of air to get it going. Research gives us the fuel, elevating our characters and a sense of time and place with detail, while at the same time underlining the integrity of the narrative—and if there's one thing that readers of historical fiction look for and want to feel as they read, it's a certain underpinning of authenticity in the story. Slap a Band-Aid™ on a character at a time before adhesive dressings were commercially available and no matter how many dates you might have right, someone will let you know about the one incorrect detail. In addition, getting that snippet right gives you a golden opportunity to enhance a sense of time and place with a description of dressing a wound in, say, the 1800s. As writer Rhys Bowen says, "The most important thing with any historical mystery is to get everything right."

Mastering the "historical" is crucial, because if you want to write mystery and you have a sense of what it means to weave a compelling plot, get the details right and you're home and dry. Oh, but the devil is in those details, and a successful historical mystery depends on engaging, realistic characters along with a balanced amount of period detail—and that includes dialogue—drawn together in a plot that is not only believable but reflects the era. In other words, your job is to render the reader a curious, attentive, excited, and emotionally involved time-traveler.

As writers, we can base the research component of our fire upon what marketing people call "primary" and "secondary" research—primary we do ourselves, and secondary is the work of others, perhaps a book or an academic paper. My primary research has involved walking miles across London to trace the path of a killer in a story I was working on. I have pored over old maps to get details right, and though the city has changed dramatically, I have learned that much can be gleaned from remembering to look up as I make my way along the street—I might be alongside a modern retail outlet, but if I cast my eyes above the plate-glass windows, I can see the telling architectural details from, say, the 1930s. Primary research might involve speaking to people who lived through a certain era, whereas secondary research could be listening to audio of people recounting their experiences during that same time period. Whether in print or through headphones, I am immersing myself in an authenticity of locution. My grandmother would not have said, "See you in a minute." She would have said, "I will see you presently." Small details, yes, but all building blocks of character, time, and place. If you've only ever used a cell phone, it would behoove you to get an old or reproduced telephone with a dial and a receiver and feel what it is like to try to make a call in an emergency. Feel what it's like if you have found that dead body and you want to call the police, or to try to stop a crime happening—and you're dialing away and it seems to be taking ages . . . yet perhaps not really, because you don't expect a faster service; after all, you're in 1925 and you're used to this type of telephone. And if the telephone hasn't yet been invented, feel the terror when you cannot summon help and there is a dark stranger lurking outside the back door.

If your story isn't set within living memory and you cannot find your "live" research subjects, then you must go to the research of the day—novels, poems, old paintings, and photographs. Author Laurie R. King suggests, "Diaries and letters give a better picture of actual life and language than memoirs and biographies, because they're immediate." With mystery, especially, we want that immediacy, and certainly it can be gained from our own experience, but with a caveat—you must remember the old adage "The past is another country."

Imagine this: It is a few days before Christmas in late 1970s England, on a dark, clear, freezing-cold evening. I can feel my cheeks glowing and my fingertips getting colder inside my gloves. I am losing the feeling in my toes, but I am happy—thrilled and excited by the season and this evening. I am twenty-three years old and warm inside, because I am walking along the street with my boyfriend, an army officer who has just arrived home on leave from a war zone. We are on our way to a gathering in the town, the community coming together to sing carols and drink a hot toddy or two while sharing the blessings of the season. We are laughing, joking, at last together after months apart, when a car backfires on the street as it passes. In a split second I am flat on my face behind a parked car and he is holding me down to protect me. I can feel his whole body shaking, and in that moment I realize that he is no longer with me on the way to a cheery holiday sing-along but guiding his men as they patrol a street where they could be cut down and killed in an instant. His automatic reaction has shocked me into the world he keeps from me with his cheeky smile and wicked sense of humor. I will remember this moment, and several decades later, long after we have both moved on in life and wouldn't know each other if we passed in the street, I will dredge it up from my past to get inside the head of a character who has been to war—though his soldiering was during a different time and a different conflict.

Imagine this: I am in my car sitting in stopped traffic on a major motorway close to London's Heathrow Airport. It is half past five on a Friday evening and I am on my way home from work. I have left a good two cars' distance from the vehicle in front of me, a brand-new Mercedes-Benz. I am not sure which came first, the crashing sound that seems to be all around me, or the realization that my car has been shoved at speed into the Mercedes-Benz and is crumpled back and front. Without a second's delay, I know I have to get out because I can smell gasoline—I filled my tank after leaving work—yet my door is jammed, so even though my neck really hurts, I clamber over my briefcase and a bag of shopping on the floor of the passenger seat. The drunk driver behind me—on his way to Heathrow following a liquid lunch—did not see the stationary traffic and was speeding at over seventy miles per hour when he hit me. One year later I am walking along a street when I hear a car skid, the sound of brakes shrieking behind me. I am suddenly out of my own skin, my heart pounding as I clutch my neck. I remember this day when writing a scene in which a young woman has to return to a place where she has seen death of a most terrible kind, and I am trolling through my memories trying to recall what it feels like to relive terror. And not for the first time I ask myself, *How would I feel if . . .* while grappling with a completely different event at a different time—which works when I bring together knowledge gained in research and season it with a visceral response to craft a painful scene.

The essence of how those experiences were used is in a melding of experience and research, which is at the heart of character. I am not trying to give my characters exactly the same experience that I had—how could I, for we exist decades apart?—yet I can take a certain sensation and, with my understanding of the past, develop authentic time-appropriate responses to a given situation. I bear in mind that behaviors are often different when the vast changes in society across centuries and cultures are taken into account. Consider the following example, whether you are setting a story in fourteenth-century Rome or nineteenth-century New York.

Research conducted by medical historians during the Iraq War revealed interesting differences between the responses of soldiers to death in World War I and in the contemporary army. It was the sort of study that provides a lesson for the writer of historical fiction. In the early 1900s, even small children were accustomed to seeing dead people, because loved ones often died at home with the family gathered around the bed to bid farewell and bear witness to the passing. Death in childbirth was not unusual, and it was also somewhat common for people to die in domestic accidents, or on farms and in factories. However, though many young men had seen death, they hadn't seen lots of blood and gore, so trench warfare and the realities of the battlefield were psychologically wounding—soldiers expected the death, but not the torn bodies. Fast-forward to 2003. Most of the soldiers had been raised on TV, film, and video games where they saw a lot of blood and gore. The problem for the young soldier was that witnessing the blood and wounds on the battlefield wasn't quite as shocking as it had been for his great-grandfather, because in his experience, actors blown to pieces on the screen turned up again in another movie, or the game character could be made to resurrect several times over. The on-screen battlefield had not led to death—yet it did in the reality of modern combat, and thus grave wounds leading to never seeing that person alive again became a source of PTSD in young soldiers. This example demonstrates that we mustn't assume that the response of a person to an event two hundred years ago or even fifty years past is going to reflect our twenty-first-century perspective.

Examining your motives for writing the historical mystery can spotlight many avenues for exploration as you craft the narrative. Your curiosity will reveal plot points and opportunities to ground your story in its time—a sense of wonder is a powerful attribute for the writer of the historical mystery. "I sort of backed into historical fiction," says Laurie R. King, adding, "I wanted to write about a young woman who became apprentice to Sherlock Holmes, and his author finished with him in 1914—so I rapidly started learning about the years during and after the Great War." And for Rhys Bowen, the call came from family connections. "I was raised by my grandmother and great-aunt and heard stories from them of the Great War, Edwardian times, the twenties. They all sounded exotic and interesting."

For every historical mystery published, there is an author who could be lost under a mound of papers and books gathered for research purposes, and having spent a small fortune on those materials, plus traveling to walk the streets of another city and hotel bills along the way, becomes determined to use all accumulated material. But here's the key to a balanced historical mystery—just because you did the research and spent all that money and gave all that time does not mean you have to use every single piece of acquired information. Not every bloom clipped should make it into the vase. I believe research should be a bit like an iceberg—only 7 percent of it should be visible above the surface. And the rest? Trust me on this one—it will inform every single word you write. Research included with a mindset of "I've got it, so I'll use it" will become a speed bump in the story, causing reader interest to evaporate under a surfeit of architectural detail as the historical provenance of every single street is recounted on your protagonist's route as she roars through 1800s Boston. Think: "Balance." And how do you know when you have that balance? Read sections aloud and be honest with yourself regarding the places where the pace slows, and then be prepared to kill your darlings—arguably the most useful assassination in your mystery. All facts quoted should be correct, with names and dialogue appropriately reflecting the era—but use your research as if it were a powerful spice you're about to add to soup. Taste often to ensure ease of digestion.

The historical mystery is one of the most popular literary forms published today, offering the writer an opportunity to explore the human condition across the ages, through different cultures and while characterizing people in conflict with themselves and each other—and for writers who like comedy, there is always humor to be found in times past. Rhys Bowen has observed, "Historical novels are popular now because there is much to feel uneasy about in the present." As a writer of historical mysteries, I could not agree more, and in my own experience, readers are looking to the past not only for a sense of power over events, but also to observe qualities of endurance and resilience and an ability to come through troubling times, so all is well that ends well. Which brings us back to Jane Austen.

As writers of historical fiction, we ply our craft as if we are in the midst of the action, as if we are right now, in this moment, wearing those hobnail boots, or that tight whalebone corset, or the scratchy bloodstained uniform with lice along the seams. We must write as if we are personally facing the eight-course Edwardian lunch or the meager meal of unleavened bread and water in an Egyptian slave's quarters. Immersed in that other time and place, we take our match to the fire. And we write.

SUZANNE CHAZIN

"I write because I want to have more than one life," novelist Anne Tyler was once quoted as saying. I agree. When I sit down to write, my fun comes not from looking into a mirror, but from peeking into someone else's window.

The Medical Thriller

*Playing on the reader's real-life fears and hunger
for insider knowledge.*

TESS GERRITSEN

Many of us are afraid of doctors and hospitals—so afraid that the stress of just being in a doctor's presence can make our blood pressure soar. The phenomenon is so well known that there's a name for the syndrome: white-coat hypertension. As a physician, I know these fears are sadly justified because a hospital is the most dangerous place many of us will ever find ourselves, a place from which we might not make it out alive.

Medical thrillers play on these very real fears, and they've been scaring readers for half a century, ever since medical doctors Robin Cook (*Coma*) and Michael Crichton (*The Andromeda Strain*) introduced the genre. Doctors or nurses usually play prominent roles in these stories, but the central character of your thriller needn't be a medical professional. What *is* necessary to your plot is a theme that focuses on medical science or ethics, as well as medical settings or situations.

While it helps to be familiar with this world, you don't need to be a doctor to write a medical thriller. Just by being a patient, you may have experienced something that frightened or unsettled you, and that experience may be enough to launch your story. Although I'm a medical doctor, it was my experience as a patient that inspired *The Surgeon*, my first Jane Rizzoli novel. While I was having my blood drawn for routine lab tests, it occurred to me that blood is the most intimate thing we routinely hand over to a stranger. Those blood tubes can reveal many secrets about you—whom you're related to, which illicit drug you last ingested, what disease you're likely to succumb to. What if your blood sample ends up in the wrong hands? What if that person decides, based on your blood test, that *you* will be his next murder victim? That became my premise for *The Surgeon.*

If you're searching for a story about medical ethics, you'll find inspiration just by reading the newspaper. In the U.S., where medical care is expensive, you'll find heart-wrenching stories about families desperate to keep a loved one alive. When a lifesaving drug is scarce, which patient should get it? Who gets to live and who is simply allowed to die? These life-and-death decisions are the dramatic engine of the genre. Imagine the desperation of a parent with a dying child. Think of how far you'd go and what rules you'd break to save your kid's life. This desperation can inspire any hero—or villain.

Brave new science, and its unintended consequences, is another common theme in the genre. What are the consequences of cloning? What if you could edit the DNA of babies to make them more "perfect"? What if a pharmaceutical company's new miracle drug has a fatal side effect—one they're desperately trying to hide? I've found ideas for my stories in journals such as *Discover, Science,* and *Scientific American,* where cutting-edge discoveries are first reported. My novel *Life Support* was inspired by an article about a form of mad cow disease that was transmitted by human growth hormone harvested from cadavers. That scientific tidbit made me wonder: If we found a medical fountain of youth, what could possibly go wrong?

Pandemics are another perennial theme in medical thrillers, and no wonder; whether it's Ebola or some new strain of bird flu, pandemics threaten us all. The infectious agent need not even be terrestrial. Crichton's *Andromeda Strain,* about a deadly extraterrestrial organism, raised the stakes even higher by putting the future of all humanity at risk.

I should add a cautionary note about topics that seem difficult to sell. No matter how well written and well publicized they are, thrillers about cancer or HIV or Alzheimer's seem to have a tough time on the genre market. Perhaps these subjects are just too close and too painful for us to contemplate, and readers shy away from confronting them in fiction. (I confess I do.) If your medical thriller about cancer keeps getting rejected, it may be because you've chosen a subject no one wants to think about.

My literary agent once told me that readers choose medical thrillers because they're hungry to know secrets. They want to know what doctors know, how they think, and what *really* goes on behind the doors of the operating room and the morgue. You may not need to be a medical professional, but since your story most likely features medical professions and settings, you need to be familiar with the world in which doctors and nurses work. What does a doctor's average day look like? How do they evaluate a patient in crisis? When things go horribly wrong in the hospital (and too often they do), how do professionals react?

You also need to know how one becomes a doctor. The most common mistakes I've come across in the genre, both in novels and in film, spring from ignorance about the process of medical education. In the United States, it's a lengthy journey that starts with a college degree. These four years in college are often referred to as "premed," but you're not actually learning any medical skills yet, so never have a premed character perform an appendectomy. Your undergraduate degree can be in any major (mine was anthropology), but to apply to medical school, you must complete a year of college biology, a year of physics, two years of chemistry, a year of English, a semester of biochemistry, and mathematics through calculus. Most medical schools also require applicants to take the Medical College Admissions Test, a daylong multiple-choice exam that tests your skills in science, critical thinking, and psychology. Since only about 40 percent of applicants are accepted to any U.S. medical school (and some elite schools have acceptance rates as low as 3 percent), you'll need both a high college GPA and a good MCAT score to compete against the approximately 53,000 other college students who are also applying to medical schools.

While getting into medical school is a challenge, once you're accepted, you've made it through the most difficult part of the winnowing process. Medical schools want their students to succeed, and the vast majority of medical students will graduate (although misconduct or significant underperformance will certainly get you expelled). These four years of focused medical studies include classroom and lab work as well as hands-on rotations in hospitals, operating rooms, and clinics. This is when you truly learn the art of being a doctor. You also learn what it's like to go thirty-six hours without sleep, to feel the warmth of splattered blood in the operating room, and to watch the life drain from a patient's eyes. It's a grueling, challenging, sometimes heartbreaking four years, and it takes grit to make it across the finish line to graduation. And since more women than men are now enrolling in medical schools, these brand-new doctors are more and more likely to be female.

But even with your freshly minted medical degree, you're *still* not ready to practice medicine. Postgraduate training (otherwise known as a residency) still lies ahead. Depending on which specialty you choose, this can add three years (for internal medicine, family practice, or pediatrics) to five years or longer (surgical specialties), with some subspecialties such as neurosurgery requiring a whopping seven years of postgraduate training. These various specialties and subspecialties can be confusing to laypeople, and novelists sometimes mistake "neurologist" for "neurosurgeon" or "cardiologist" for "cardiothoracic surgeon." Learn the difference before you describe a neurologist (who doesn't wield a scalpel) as a neurosurgeon (who does).

The eleven-to-fifteen-year educational marathon from college through residency requires intelligence, stamina, and determination. In a thriller, these are the qualities you'd find in a hero . . . or a formidable villain. But doctors are also human, and the profession suffers from higher rates of suicide, depression, and substance abuse than does the general public. A flawed and emotionally vulnerable doctor is believable in a novel; a truly stupid doctor is not.

If you're not in the medical field, how do you find the details and anecdotes that will give your story the all-important aura of verisimilitude? Talk to a doctor or nurse. Ask them what their average day is like. Ask them about their worst day and their best day on the job. Ask them about their triumphs (they'll be happy to share these) and their mistakes (which could be harder to pry out of them). But don't make this visit a fishing trip; before you take up a professional's valuable time, know what you need to ask and have a list of questions prepared. Prior to the meeting, do enough research to already be familiar with the technical vocabulary specific to your plot. By now you should already know the bones of your story and many of the crisis points. If the crisis is an internal abdominal hemorrhage in the operating room, then look up the basic anatomy of the abdomen and which major blood vessels might rupture. Know the surgical instruments that would be on the OR tray and what each one is used for. Know the difference between a scrub nurse and a circulating nurse and the role of each member of the OR team. Prepared with that knowledge, you will save both your time and the doctor's when you sit down and ask: "Your patient's blood pressure is crashing on the table. What's the first thing you'd do?"

A large part of making your story believable is using authentic lingo. If your MD character says to another MD, "The patient had a heart attack," your story loses credibility. But if he says instead, "The patient had an inferolateral MI" (a specific type of heart attack), suddenly the dialogue is believable—even if your readers have no idea what "inferolateral MI" means. The television series *ER* gave viewers a real taste of the characters' world because the writers didn't dumb down the dialogue. Their fictional doctors talked like real doctors, even though the audience probably understood only half of the medical terms being batted back and forth. Emotional context was crucial. It didn't matter that viewers didn't know the meaning of "V-tach"; all they needed to hear was a panicked character saying "Oh my god, he's in V-tach!" and they understood that V-tach was a very bad thing.

Your use of medical lingo, while essential to authenticity, is a delicate balancing act for writers. Without it, the thriller loses its verisimilitude, but use too much and the reader will be frustrated by all the incomprehensible words. One way to make the terminology easy to understand is to include an everyman, a lay character who's as new to these words as the reader is. He needs other characters to explain things to him, and whatever he learns, the reader learns. Another strategy is to simply let the emotions of the scene do most of the explaining, the way *ER* did. They didn't stop to define every medical term, yet it didn't take long for viewers to learn what "stat" means. If a character says in an urgent voice, "I need those results, STAT!" its meaning becomes clear.

Dry medical details become far more fascinating when they're consequential to a character. In my novel *Harvest*, my hospitalized heroine has a 16-gauge IV inserted in her arm. The gauge of the IV seems irrelevant to the reader—until Abby yanks out the IV to make her escape, and the hole left by the big-bore IV dribbles a trail of blood as she flees. Suddenly, that detail becomes relevant—and disturbing.

Powerful emotions can propel readers through even the most technical details of a story. In my novel *Gravity*, a medical thriller set aboard the International Space Station, I needed to explain the complex protocol an astronaut needs to complete before going on a space walk (otherwise known as an EVA, an acronym for "extravehicular activity"). It's not a matter of simply donning a pressurized suit and popping out of a hatch. It requires a daylong period of depressurization, followed by an hour's prebreathe of pure oxygen. Only then can the astronaut exit the hatch and float into un-pressurized space. These details were crucial to the plot, but I ran the risk of boring readers with all the technical information. How could I make it more palatable?

I did it by giving it emotional context. While my astronaut heroine, Emma, is going through her EVA checklist, she's also thinking about what goes wrong if she *doesn't* adhere to the protocol. She thinks about what it would be like to die of decompression in the vacuum of space. She thinks of the first symptoms when nitrogen bubbles form in your bloodstream: Your chest aches. Your eardrums burst. Your lungs explode from expand-ing gases. Your blood boils and, in the next instant, it freezes solid. It's a horrifyingly agonizing way to die, and that fate is on her mind as she prepares for her EVA. Suddenly the "boring" details become far more interesting because the reader understands the terrible consequences of making a mistake.

In writing *Gravity*, I had another tough decision regarding technical language. All my characters were NASA personnel, so there was no handy everyman who could help readers understand the acronyms and aerospace jargon. I had to choose between making my characters understandable to readers and making them speak like real astronauts. Should Emma say: "I've put on my space suit and I'm ready for my space walk"? Or should she say "I've donned my EMU and am ready for EVA"? I opted to keep the dialogue as authentic as possible and have my astronauts speak like astro-nauts. To help readers with the NASA lingo, I added a glossary at the end of the book. It's not the best solution. It's challenging for readers to absorb all the new vocabulary, and some found it too intimidating, but it was the only way to thoroughly immerse them in the experience of orbital space.

Be careful not to go overboard with technical details if they're not vital to the plot. You may think that including all that esoteric information makes you look brilliant, but you risk overwhelming readers and losing sight of the story. Doctor-novelists seem especially prone to this mistake, perhaps because we're trained to educate patients and, darn it, we want to *explain* things. But in a novel, too much explanation leads to the dreaded crime of telling, not showing. Don't do this. Technical details should serve only to enhance the plot, not overshadow it.

Whether or not you're a medical professional, you'll need to keep a few basic reference books handy. Invest in a comprehensive medical dictionary (such as *Stedman's*) as well as an illustrated atlas of human anatomy. New medical textbooks can be pricey, but used copies will serve your purpose just as well, as long as they're not too far out of date. Your story may also call for more specialized information. If your character is a pathologist, you'll need a pathology textbook; if she's a general surgeon, consult a surgical textbook. Used booksellers are a fantastic resource for finding obscure medical references. While hunting for reference materials for my historical medical thriller *The Bone Garden*, I found an 1812 surgical textbook available for sale online. The book laid out, in chillingly matter-of-fact detail, how to cut off an arm without anesthesia. It was the same edition that Civil War surgeons referenced when they performed battlefield operations, and that book added gruesome authenticity to my amputation scene, right down to how to immobilize a screaming patient while you're sawing off his arm. I didn't need to embellish the gore; just having my character watch over the surgeon's shoulder and hear the rasp of the bone saw was horrifying enough.

Doctors and nurses are witnesses to the beginning of life and the end of it. In matters of life and death they serve on the front lines, and this inherent drama makes the medical thriller an enduringly popular genre. If you're not a medical professional, these stories may seem challenging to write. You'll need research skills, a few vital textbooks, and a source who's willing to tell you what you need to know. But most of all, you'll need what every writer needs, whatever the genre: a sense of the dramatic. All the research in the world can't fix a thriller that's not thrilling.

GIGI PANDIAN

Don't compare your writing and publishing journey to anyone else's. In this strange and wonderful profession, there's no straight line to success. "Success" doesn't even mean the same thing from one author to the next. You can define it for yourself.

Researching the Spy Thriller

Or: Why can't I just make it all up?

GAYLE LYNDS

Whether you're an intelligence-community veteran or a civilian who's never set foot inside any of the alphabet agencies, you've no doubt discovered as you plan and write your novels that there are things you don't know—or maybe you think you know, but you're not sure.

So you Google whatever you're wondering about, or you check your files, or perhaps you make some phone calls. If you're allergic to the word "research," you probably wouldn't use it to describe what you've just done. Maybe you'd call it "looking stuff up."

Why Research?

As you no doubt know, there are writers who say they hate research, and yet they want to create page-turning espionage novels. To accomplish that worthy goal, their work must contain authentic spycraft, memorable characters from low and high places, and plots and subplots that are, at the very least, plausible.

In other words, don't put a manhole in the middle of Fifth Avenue in New York City with a Belarusian spy arising silently out of it at midnight to head west to break into the high-security United Nations building. Just don't. What's wrong with the scene? The direction the spy is heading; the fact that the writer hasn't checked to make certain a usable manhole is located there or at least could be; and that even the much-maligned Belarusians mustn't be portrayed as dumb, not if the novel's characters and plot are to be taken seriously. Besides, there are much better ways to get inside the UN, even at midnight.

Over the years, readers and interviewers often asked Robert Ludlum where he'd worked for the CIA. Surely he'd been undercover? His standard answer was allegedly given with a conspiratorial smile: "No, I was never a spy. But I have friends . . . and an imagination."

Bob's second novel, *The Osterman Weekend*, is the story of a clandestine CIA operation to uncover Soviet assets, a humdinger of a covert-action tale. But there was a problem: Bob set the story in New Jersey. This alarmed Bob's editor and publisher because it was illegal for the CIA to work domestically, and they were concerned about bad fallout: reviewers might jeer, Bob could disenchant his audience, and maybe the feds would come after him (and the publisher).

Bob fought back and refused to change the plot, and the hardcover was published in March 1972. Unsurprisingly, the book was a hit. And then, three years later, in 1975, Bob was vindicated. During the Church Committee congressional hearings, James Jesus Angleton, who'd been chief of CIA counterintelligence, admitted to a shocked nation that he'd directed "a widespread program of domestic spying and surveillance by U.S. intelligence agents" (as summarized by the *Los Angeles Times* in his obituary on May 13, 1987).

Of course, inquiring thriller minds want to know how Bob had found out what the CIA was secretly doing here at home. One of Bob's contemporaries recounted all of this to me with personal touches and great gusto, but he hadn't been able to pin Bob down about how Bob had known—or guessed. So most likely either one of Bob's sources had let it slip, or Bob had deduced it from what he'd read or heard.

Either way, his research paid off.

How Does One Use Research?

More than any other field of fiction, spy thrillers tend to have revelatory or predictive qualities. Why? It's not by magic or accident. Notice how important research becomes in the next example, too, and how it can lead to an exciting and surprising conclusion.

Sometime around 1999 I began to wonder whether there was a highly placed mole in the FBI. As an espionage novelist, I was of course keeping up with the news and analyses about CIA moles as they were uncovered throughout the decade. In particular there was a lot of heat about Aldrich ("Rick") Ames.

But why were there so many in the CIA and none in the FBI? Statistically, it didn't make sense. And it didn't make sense politically—U.S. secrets were high-value targets for Russia even back in the early post–Cold War era. Also, there were a lot of Russians in the United States. In fact, more ex-KGB officers lived in the Washington, DC, area than anywhere else except Moscow, and the Russian embassy and consulates housed undercover agents specifically to recruit, bribe, blackmail, or steal U.S. technical and political information. To a Russian spy, controlling an FBI special agent would be gold.

Maybe there really was a major mole in the agency, I thought.

I focused my research, which included written material as well as chats with men and women active or retired in the intelligence field who were generous with their insights and observations. Everything I gathered was in the public domain.

I learned about blown NOCs (spies with nonofficial cover), deeply buried American assets overseas who had vanished or been executed, and foreign operations that had fallen apart. Some of the incidents couldn't be explained away by what Rick Ames and other CIA officers had revealed to the Russians, and before them to the Soviets. In fact, the CIA hadn't had all of the information that seemed to lead to some of the clandestine tragedies and deaths. But what the CIA hadn't known, the FBI could have.

None of this information was in one place or from one source. Over several months I put together bits and pieces, hints and facts. I wasn't certain, but it seemed to me I had enough that it was worth taking a chance . . .

A rule for writers: Something doesn't have to be probable, but it should be plausible. Research can help you decide.

The result was that I created a highly placed FBI mole I called Robert ("Bobby") Kelsey for *Mesmerized*, the spy thriller on which I was working. Then in February 2001, while the manuscript was at the printer, Special Agent Robert Hanssen was arrested. In headlines around the globe, the FBI man was being called the most damaging traitor in U.S. history.

I was gobsmacked. My deductions about an FBI mole had been right. Later I learned I'd even accurately postulated some of the clues and steps that had led to his unmasking. Thank you, research.

As for my naming my FBI mole Robert, that wasn't because I knew it was also Hanssen's given name . . . it was just dumb luck.

Research + Creativity

I often use words similar to Bob Ludlum's when I deny having been a spy. "I know people, and I have an imagination." And then I smile, because research and one's imagination not only work together, they drive and feed each other. We love our imaginations and our inventions, whether characters, plot twists, or a particularly clever way to kill. Research can make our writing lives better, our books better, and our nights more fully slept.

On the other hand, if you have to force yourself to do necessary research, you might ask yourself whether you're really interested in what you're writing. Sometimes the secret to a writer's wanting to do research is to find a situation, a character, or a subject that intrigues you. If you're fascinated, you have a greater chance not only of fascinating your reader, but also of motivating yourself to dig deep and productively into research that will help bring your book to fire-breathing life.

Here's an example of a classic espionage thriller set in World War II whose bones I find compelling, and so did millions of readers: What if a Nazi spy discovered that the airfields in England being secretly prepared for a Pas-de-Calais landing were really filled with plywood airplanes and tanks, and the actual Allied invasion was to be at Normandy (*Eye of the Needle* by Ken Follett)? You as the writer must've already done some research to know about this real-life situation, or perhaps you remember reading about it in a history class.

Here's another fiction classic, this one set in 1960s Europe: What if disgruntled French military officers hired a professional assassin to kill President Charles de Gaulle (*Day of the Jackal* by Frederick Forsyth)? You as the spy writer are already familiar with intelligence agencies, so you decide that in your novel, all the spy shops are going to be ignorant of your killer. He's not in their files. They've never heard of him and have no way to identify him. You're delighted, because this limitation will enhance the suspense of your novel. Then you research de Gaulle and discover an interesting fact—he's the world's most heavily guarded man. You are inspired! He's going to be nearly impossible to kill, which will increase suspense even more.

Now that you've made those two creative decisions about the anonymity of the Jackal and the difficulty of assassinating de Gaulle, you realize you get to figure out the steps the anonymous assassin must take to pull off the job and what the heroes can do to find and stop him. You have exciting research ahead, and you're well on your way to writing a riveting book.

What Is Research? How Do I Know
Whether Something Is Research?

Most of us do research every day. We look into the refrigerator to assess its barrenness, a particular issue when on deadline. We stand in the driveway or the alley asking our neighbor about her trip to San Francisco, or Kiev, or the Yucatán Peninsula. We study our checkbook to see whether we have funds to get through the month. We go to our child's (or grandchild's) school for the holiday concert of songs from around the globe. All of that is research, often part of our everyday lives and pleasurable or at least tolerable—and sometimes very useful to a writer.

For instance, there's mold on the oranges in the refrigerator—what kind of mold? Can it be used to create an antibiotic—or an epidemic? In the checkbook we find what looks like an error ... hmm, could an accountant see something similar and suspect money laundering? And those songs from different cultures ... an education in themselves. If one or more are from countries in your new novel, jot down the songs' names and make a note to yourself describing them. It's research.

The spy novel on which I'm working is set largely in Moscow, and I'm already fascinated by the culture, the beauty, the depravity, the generosity. I want to research that and more. Sights, odors, colors. People. Spassky Gate. The bridges illuminated by twinkling lights. Busy Komsomol Square, where three rail terminals converge and a tall statue of Lenin stands nearby, watching, holding the lapel of his coat with one hand while the other reaches for a back pocket. Lenin appears to have just realized his wallet has been swiped. That's Komsomol Square. It's reality. It's powerful.

Here are research samples I particularly like and find useful:

- History: ". . . parades in the Soviet Union were not something
  you watched, they were something you participated in. The only

71

observers were the members of the ruling Politburo atop Lenin and Stalin's tomb in Red Square and a few invited members of the diplomatic corps in the bleachers alongside." —Loren R. Graham, *Moscow Stories*

- Traffic: "I soon learned that an ambulance stopping to pick up a fare in Moscow wasn't unusual. Every vehicle was a potential taxi. Private cars, dump trucks, police cruisers—everyone was so desperate for money that any and all would take fares." —Bill Browder, *Red Notice: A True Story of High Finance, Murder, and One Man's Fight for Justice*

- Vladimir Putin in 2005: ". . . Putin pulled a pack of 3-by-5 cards from his inside jacket pocket—the Americans called them his 'grievance cards'—and began lecturing [President George W.] Bush about . . . well, about how fed up he was being lectured to by the Americans." —Angus Roxburgh, *The Strongman: Vladimir Putin and the Struggle for Russia*

- Oligarchs at a swank nightclub: "New arrivals were greeted by women who were beautiful on a surreal level. The interior design was out of Somerset Maugham, all dark woods and lazy ceiling fans. Here a man could sip Johnnie Walker Blue, light a Cuban cigar, sip a brandy, unwind, and make more money." —Martin Cruz Smith, "Moscow Never Sleeps" in *National Geographic*

Could you have made up any of the above excerpts? I couldn't. I'm thrilled my research turned up such vivid illustrations of life in Russia in various eras. Do I steal and pretend I wrote what I found? Of course not. Instead, I sit back, close my eyes, and allow the words to create moving pictures in my mind. Soon the pictures and thoughts meld into other research, and my imagination kicks in. A scene begins to form. Characters arrive. I must write now. I want to create moving, vivid pictures for readers.

General Research Advice

There are many ways to discover the kind of rich detail that brings a novel to life and in which the reader is so deeply immersed that they have entered your world to experience and believe. And there are caveats, too. . . .

How much is too much? Never confuse the reader. Including too much research in your book can do that, mislead simply by the preponderance of words, descriptions, and explanations. Another way to look at it is: don't throw in a bunch of stuff that's pointless, even though you like it. In the end, we novelists use perhaps a tenth of a percent of the research we've done for any one book. That's a sobering but realistic figure. Love your research. Know a lot of it is background enabling you to create a believable fictional world, and only a tiny fraction of the details will actually make it into your book.

How can I organize my research? One of the biggest challenges is remembering where you put your research so you can find it easily again. There are software programs that enable you to scan printed documents into searchable files that can also contain saved online documents. Some authors sort their printed research into labeled piles on tabletops and shelves or even the floor. I label manuscript boxes into which I toss clippings, notes, and printouts. Other writers use index cards and file folders. Arrange your research books by subject matter on shelves or in stacks on the floor. Most of us flag the pages of books to remind us what's inside that we may want, or we scan the pages into searchable files.

Is it necessary to travel to research scene locations? Yes and no. Go if you can. But even if you do, you'll likely want guidebooks, flyers, and insider accounts and descriptions either printed or online for reference, and also to prepare you to take advantage of your on-site research. I use AAA books and maps a lot, as well as *National Geographic*, travel magazines, travel blogs, and travel websites. My best research finds often come in the comments sections of websites and from the people I talk to before I go or after I arrive. CIA.gov has an open-source library with a lot of information about foreign countries. I'm often asked whether I visit every location in my books. The answer is I travel to some, but I seldom reveal which. It seems to me I'm doing my job well if readers and fellow writers believe what I've written and can't tell the difference.

Where can I find insight and analysis about politics, power, and espionage today? Read current news reports, of course. I particularly like to compare different perspectives, different sources. One can deepen and broaden one's understanding of the forces at work that way, and doing so feeds the imagination and the ability to create subplots and characters of differing opinions. Asking yourself as author how we got to this point in politics and global dynamics is also a valuable question, and that means history, culture, and geography, too. That sort of deep analysis usually is found in books. But there are also valuable online intelligence-gathering resources like Stratfor.com.

Don't get lost in your research. You'll be tempted to. It's not only easy but seductive to discover one interesting situation or detail after another. Also, research provides an excuse to procrastinate. Trust the voice that comes into your mind and announces, *Enough is enough. Get back to writing.* You may not be finished with the research, but you have enough to push forward in the book. Also, look at your calendar. When is your deadline? That sobering question is sometimes enough to jerk oneself back into reality and resume writing. And finally, some of us often experience an escalating desire to write, wanting to get back to the story, feeling the pull of imagination, the demanding joy of creativity. Yes, it's time to write!

And finally . . .

For me, writing in the spy field is a lifestyle, a constant intake of information, finding one nugget and pursuing it as it dies a natural death or explodes into more nuggets. I read. I listen. I watch. Most of all, I enjoy. Still, for all of us authors, our ability to work waxes and wanes during writing. We get exhausted, or are beset by fears that the work is no good. It's all part of being a professional writer—we learn the emotional depths as well as heights of our highly creative pursuit.

When your energy is low and you wonder why you ever thought your current manuscript would be any good, fall back on your research; it can rekindle your interest and remind you why you hungered to write the book in the first place.

And also, there's a bonus to all of your research: you've become something of an expert, which means you've got interesting topics, experiences, and insights to talk and write about as you do publicity and make appearances.

Research is a chance to satisfy your curiosity.

Research is an adventure into the unknown.

Through research, you discover and expand not only your thriller but yourself, the writer.

STEPHANIE KANE

Writing what you don't know forces you to go out and learn it, an excitement that translates onto the page. Being too familiar with the culture in which you write limits your capacity to bring it to life. Fresh insights elude jaded eyes, and it's easy to overlook the kinds of details a stranger would find telling. In researching settings, don't just go there; watch how people act.

Other Mysteries

Susan Vaught—Mysteries for Children: An Introduction
*The kids' mystery, from picture books to YA—
expectations and some hints.*

Chris Grabenstein—Unleash Your Inner Child
*Middle-grade mysteries: you, too, can become
a rock star for ten-year-olds.*

Kelley Armstrong—The Young Adult Mystery
*Complex, authentic stories for the young adult—
emphasis on adult.*

Dale W. Berry and Gary Phillips—Graphic Novels
*The mystery within the panels: your conversation
with words and pictures.*

Art Taylor—The Short Mystery
*What do the characters (and readers) want
in your mystery short story?*

Daniel Stashower—Ten Stupid Questions about True Crime
Building a vivid page-turner, out of nothing but facts.

Mysteries for Children:
An Introduction

The kids' mystery, from picture books to YA—
expectations and some hints.

SUSAN VAUGHT

I want to write for children. What are the rules?

Sooner or later, all authors who write books for children get a version of that question—and then they get a version of the confused look produced by the answer:

There aren't any, and they change all the time.

No, seriously. There isn't a style guide or set of bullet points we can hand you, but we can tell you this much: there are conventions, and these shift like slang, rapidly and unpredictably. You need to know the conventions so that if you decide to break them, you're making an informed choice. Oh, and you'll have to keep up with the landscape, but here's the big secret:

It's a lot of fun!

The label "children's book" refers primarily to the audience for the story, not the story's complexity, vocabulary, or concepts. Children's writing encompasses books for a wide range of ages, conventionally viewed as birth to eighteen years. However, these lines have grown very fuzzy, and the upper numbers often sneak toward the mid-twenties. Most people who buy children's books are adults, purchasing either for a child or for themselves. Roughly a quarter of any children's book readers will be grown-ups.

Currently, there are four basic divisions in children's writing, rooted generally in age and reading level, but also in the characters and themes presented.

Picture books. Picture books (including their younger siblings, board books) are geared toward children eight years of age and younger, and generally are designed to be read to eager little minds. Ages of characters in picture books vary widely, especially when considering nonfiction and biographical pieces. Currently, picture books average 500 or fewer words, and most do not rhyme. For reference, *Goodnight Moon*, still selling well after 48 million copies and seventy-three years, contains 131 nonrhyming words. But before you think about sitting down on a weekend to whip out a few sentences that will handily support several generations of your family, remember that you have 500 or fewer words to introduce an unforgettable character and lead readers through a compelling situation with a satisfying beginning, middle, and end. Most children's writers agree that picture books are the hardest stories to do well, for just that reason.

So, can you write mystery-themed picture books? Absolutely! Check out Jon Klassen's award-winning *I Want My Hat Back*, or *Alphabet Mystery* by Audrey Wood. Scholastic has a list of excellent mystery-themed picture books here: https://www.scholastic.com/teachers/articles/teaching-content/books-support-mystery-genre-study/

For picture book mysteries, lost items and mysterious (often ultimately funny) situations predominate, and for the most part these books avoid violence, darkness, and crime or theft (by humans—animal thefts are common, though possibly overdone).

Side note: Most authors do not illustrate their own picture books. Artists are chosen by publishers and share equally in the book's profits.

Early readers and chapter books. There are many subdivisions within these categories, encompassing books that serve as stepping-stones from picture books to independent reading of text. Aspiring or early readers, stories for emergent readers, and increasingly less illustrated chapter books are usually geared toward children six to eight years old, and range from 1,000 to 2,500 words. As with picture books, the number of words should be what is needed to tell the story—but they still need to be exactly the *right* words. Typically, characters in these stories are eight to ten years old, and themes in the stories relate to the basic developmental tasks of this age group: exploring the world, making new friends, dealing with being nervous or mad or having other big emotions, being scared of new things, and other earlier childhood growth edges. Mystery stories for kids really get rolling at this level, from timeless classics like Gertrude Chandler Warner's *The Boxcar Children* to more modern offerings like Doreen Cronin's J.J. Tully mysteries. From gross and hysterical to slightly spooky, these books give readers a few more challenges, but mystery situations still tend to revolve around missing items, strange happenings, and other situational, non-crime-based conundrums. Violence and darkness are not prominent, although children can face some actual peril.

Middle grade. Conventionally, middle-grade books have a target audience of children ages seven or eight to twelve years. Target word count is 35,000–45,000, though this varies widely (and yes, several of the doorstop Harry Potter books are considered middle grade). Most children still seem to enjoy "reading up," or reading about characters slightly older than themselves, so many middle-grade protagonists are twelve or thirteen years old. Booksellers can be very rigid with classifications, and push any story with a teen character toward young adult shelves, which has resulted in fewer tales featuring kids ages twelve to fifteen. Developmentally, themes of sampling identities, finding "who you are" at a basic level, dealing with next-level emotions like terror or even infatuation, lying versus truth, basic ethics—all game at this level. Mysteries are one of the most popular genres for this audience, and puzzles and clues and searching for solutions can be deeply satisfying to young readers. Murders and violence still aren't prominent for this age group, though. Middle-grade conventions (and the virtues of poop and underwear) are discussed in excellent detail in Chris Grabenstein's contribution following this chapter, and I encourage everyone to suck in a bunch of air for fake burps and give it a read.

Young adult. Typically, young adult novels are 45,000–70,000 words, and target readers ages thirteen to eighteen or nineteen. Most YA characters are sixteen to nineteen years old and dealing with issues of autonomy, coming of age in a modern sense, and real-life stressors ranging from grief, to gender identity, to sex, drugs, and rock and roll—basically anything at all writers want to write and readers want to read. No, really. Trying to figure out what "can't be written" in a YA novel is basically just tempting the forces of the universe to be sure a book on just that topic becomes a bestseller less than a week after you decide the concept is too risky. Also, it is very important to remember that today's adolescents are a diverse and globally connected group, pushing older artists to provide them with works that truly represent them and their experiences, and that are free of tropes and stereotypes. Traditional crime, homicide, global conspiracies—you can do it all for teens. Very successful YA writer Kelley Armstrong addresses these and other conventions related to YA storytelling expertly in her essay later in this book, and I wish it could be required reading for aspiring YA writers.

C. M. SURRISI

If you are writing a mystery for kids, remember that your protagonist can't drive and has a curfew, and no one will believe them or let them be involved.

Unleash Your Inner Child

Middle-grade mysteries: you, too, can become
a rock star for ten-year-olds.

CHRIS GRABENSTEIN

Underpants. Poop. Fart.

If any of those words made you smile, you might be ready to write mysteries for upper-elementary/middle-grade readers!

I started my author career in 2005 writing mysteries and thrillers for adults—including the Anthony Award–winning *Tilt-a-Whirl*, the first in my John Ceepak/Jersey Shore series. In 2007, however, an editor was looking for a middle-grade ghost story. One of the (several) rejected manuscripts stacked on my bookshelf was a Stephen King–ish ghostly thriller for adults called *The Crossroads*.

The editor thought it would make a good ghost story for kids *if* . . .

I got rid of all the grisly violence.

I cut the adult language.

I made the kid in the story the protagonist.

And . . . if I cut the manuscript from 110,000 words down to about 40,000 or 45,000 (yes, that's the length of all of my children's books).

I did all of those *if*s and *The Crossroads* was published as my first book for young readers in May 2008. It also won an Anthony Award, plus an Agatha. Since then, I have published about fifty different books for kids (including two dozen with James Patterson), had a few number one bestsellers, and filled my bookcase with three more Agatha Awards and lots of children's choice state book awards instead of just rejected manuscripts.

I've also never made it back down the shore for another Ceepak adult mystery. I'm having too much fun writing for kids. Your fans treat you like a rock star. They come to book signings hugging your books. They laugh at all your fart jokes.

What follows will be my random ramblings, trying to piece together what I think I've learned over all these years. Take what you like and leave the rest.

So how do you write mysteries for eight-to-twelve-year-olds?

The same way you write them for adults.

Start with a great main character. After all, that's the only thing anybody, kid or adult, really remembers a year or so after they read your book. For instance, I read all the Sherlock Holmes short stories. I vaguely remember a few plot points. A snake slithering down a rope (or was it a bedpost?). A league of redheads. But I distinctly remember Holmes, Watson, and the Baker Street Irregulars.

Give your young readers an interesting sleuth, one they can see themselves in.

Kids love a good puzzle. Teachers love mysteries because, in addition to teaching reading skills, they also encourage deductive reasoning. Logical thinking.

So, first and foremost, make sure your mystery makes sense. Give the kids a fair play problem with real, workable clues. A mystery they might've solved before your sleuth if your sleuth weren't so darn clever. Don't just slap on a solution at the end. Your readers should see clues (and red herrings, of course) and be able to solve the riddle.

Kids know when they're being cheated or, worse, talked down to.

Make the game fun and fair.

A big difference between kid and adult mysteries: No dead bodies. Especially no dead pets. There are plenty of other crimes to deal with. There's no need for killing folks or animals. Your stories, of course, can be gruesome and gross and full of slime and nasty body odors. Just no corpses.

Another tip: Try to remember how you felt when you were eight to twelve. That's *how you felt*, not what everybody was wearing or the most fascinating and memorable thing you did when you were a fifth-grader. Kids today want stories about kids today. Of course, there are exceptions to every semi-rule—kids love historical mysteries and time travel stories. But, in general, kids who are kids today want to read about kids today. Resist the urge to write your memories.

But, as I said, remember what it *felt* like to be eight to twelve. This is when kids start separating from their parents and begin the sometimes painful process of turning into their own persons. This is often the age when kids wonder how their parents could possibly be their parents. It's one of the reasons why *Harry Potter and the Sorcerer's Stone* (the first book in the series) is probably the best example of a mystery written for this group of readers. Of *course* Harry is an orphan who's really a wizard! Eleven-year-olds always think they must be orphans (even if they're not) because their parents suddenly seem so strange and alien. And, yes, all eleven-year-olds have superpowers that dumb adults just haven't realized yet.

How you felt when you were in third, fourth, fifth, or sixth grade is exactly how kids at that age feel today. The emotions have remained the same. But the props and window dressing have changed. For instance, don't put a chalkboard in your classroom scene. Nobody uses chalkboards anymore. They are dusty relics. Do try to remember how it felt to be in front of a class, unable to solve a math problem because, oops, you didn't do your homework.

The feeling is the same.

The props are different.

Another tip? Travel back in time. When I first started writing for younger readers, I dug up my old fifth- and sixth-grade class photos. I looked at my friends. Tried to remember their names and all the goofy, stupid, and sometimes dangerous stuff we did because we were growing up. I listened to music by the Monkees, because "Daydream Believer" was huge when I was in the sixth grade. It was a time when friends were, for the first time, becoming more important than family. I remember more about hanging out with my buds and raiding a slumber party or pulling pranks on Halloween than I do about where my family and I went on vacation during those years.

And then I thought about the bullies who picked on me. The girls I had a crush on before I even knew what a crush was. The confusion about who I was and who I wanted to be—a person separate from my parents and my family.

If you can tap into those feelings, you can tap into the emotions of the kids currently going through all the things you've already gone through.

More random ramblings:

Don't try to be cool by playing to trends that are hip with tweens. You don't want to be the obnoxious Uncle Morty dropping down to the rumpus room to rap with the kids about all the groovy things they're doing. (Nothing is groovy anymore, Uncle Morty. Nothing.)

Remember Silly Bandz? Of course not. And you're not alone. But a few years ago, Silly Bandz, those brightly colored and multishaped rubbery bracelets were all the rage in every school I visited. So much so that some schools banned them because the lunchtime Silly Bandz swap scene was getting a little too intense in the cafeteria.

Now nobody knows what Silly Bandz are. I am very glad I never built a whole plot around them.

Same with fidget spinners. They were everywhere. They, too, were banned in many schools, the same way Super Balls were when I was a kid. Now fidget spinners are nowhere (except on the floor of the United States Senate).

Ditto for slang, daddy-o.

"She's so extra" in 2020 means she's over-the-top. By 2021, who knows. It might mean she's a background player in a movie.

"Fire" is now something cool. In a year or two, it'll probably just mean a roaring blaze or a Bruce Springsteen song.

I have found two words that have withstood the test of time: "cool" and "awesome." That's about it. Okay. Maybe a few more: Bogus. Random. Lame. Wimp. Weenie.

Watch out for current cultural references. I once had to push back against an editor who wanted me to describe my red-headed hero as a shorter version of Shaun White, the professional snowboarder and skateboarder. Back in 2010 (which is literally a lifetime ago for your young readers), "the Flying Tomato," as he was known, was the coolest, hippest red-haired ginger dude going. Today? Not so much. A fifth-grader would read that reference and go, "Huh? Shaun who?"

You don't want to include anything that will dramatically date your book because here is one of the many beauties about writing for this audience: There is a new group of fifth-graders every year. Your mystery has a chance to live a very long shelf life if kids, teachers, and librarians fall in love with it. My number one bestseller (other than the books I write with Mr. Patterson) was and still is *Escape from Mr. Lemoncello's Library*. It came out in 2013. Most of its first readers are in college now. But every year, thousands of new kids discover it. Don't make it hard for the children of the future to fall in love with your mystery.

When writing for eight-to-twelve-year-olds, I encourage you to write "up." There is a reason that most of my protagonists are twelve. Eight-year-olds will gladly read about someone slightly older. A nine-year-old will not read about somebody slightly younger. (Because "Eight-year-olds are such babies.")

Speaking of characters, make your cast as diverse as you possibly can. That's the real world real kids live in. "Own Voice" stories are being snapped up by publishers all over the kidlit world today. If you write about a cultrual group other than your own, it pays to have what are being called "sensitivity readers" check your manuscript. They will advise you about issues of authenticity. I've been very fortunate that my publishers use this technique to vet my work prior to publication.

Have fun. Remember, kids love to laugh. Poop, fart, and underpants weren't arbitrary choices for the start of this essay. I once attended a Society of Children's Book Writers and Illustrators conference—and yes, you should join SCBWI if you're serious about writing for kids, the same way you joined MWA because you're serious about writing mysteries—and heard the very witty, very smart Marvin Terban give a talk entitled "Laugh It Up! Why Humor in Children's Books Is Essential, and How to Make Your Books Funnier." According to his research (yes, he really did research), "poop," "underpants," and "fart" are the funniest words for kids in our target audience. Hmmm, I wonder if that's why *F-A-R-T* was featured so prominently in the short story I wrote for MWA's *Super Puzzletastic Mysteries* collection.

A few more things:

Adults shouldn't help kids solve the mysteries. Where's the fun in that?

Avoid yucky stuff. When I first started writing for kids, I told everybody I was doing YA, young adult. My editor said, "No, this is MG. Middle grades." (Today, I might drill down even further and say that the vast majority of my books are upper elementary—third through sixth grades, not seventh or eighth.)

I asked my editor, "What's the difference between young adult and middle grades?"

He told me something I'll never forget. "In middle-grade books, the boys and girls like each other but they don't *like* each other."

Every once in a while, we might sprinkle in a hint of romance or a crush, but we avoid all the mushy stuff, like kissing. I sometimes say I write "prehormonal" stories.

When writing for kids, I try to remember taking my nephew Sam to see *Star Wars: Episode I—The Phantom Menace*. He was nine or ten at the time. Sam loved all the chase scenes and the exciting space battles and the cool gizmos. When folks started smooching? He stood up, turned around, and banged his head against the seat cushion until I advised him the yucky stuff was all done and we were back to the explosions.

Which reminds me: Kids have video games and apps and YouTube videos and a world of fast-paced entertainment at their fingertips. Do not be boring. Do not describe things like dew droplets clinging to blades of grass. Cut to the chase scenes and space battles and cool gizmos, metaphorically speaking. As Elmore Leonard so famously said, leave out the parts nobody wants to read. That goes double for kids. A lot of kids don't want to read at all. You have to hook them with your first sentence and take them on a ride. Your mystery has to be as exciting as a killer game of *Fortnite*. (If *Fortnite* is still a thing when this essay is published. See above: *do not write to trends*.)

Finally, I leave you with the same words I tell kids who ask me on school visits how they can become a writer: Read, read, read. Write, write, write.

Somebody on Twitter recently said you need to read at least one hundred books in a genre before you dare attempt to write one. I'm not into numbers. But I do recall that when that editor gave me the challenge of turning my creepy adult thriller *The Crossroads* into a spooky story for kids, the first thing I did was head to the bookstore. I picked up Louis Sachar's *Holes* and Carl Hiaasen's *Hoot* and the first Harry Potter book. I read them, and more important, I studied them. I tried to figure out what made their particular clockworks tick.

As I continued to write for children, I went to the books that were winning children's choice state book awards, because kids were the ones voting for those winners.

If you really want to write for kids, read what kids really want to read. Avoid the broccoli books. The ones that are "good for children."

And think about the books you liked to read when you were young. How they made you feel. The friends you found between their pages. For many adults, the books we read when we were eight to twelve are the ones we remember all our lives.

So wake up your child. Not the one sleeping in the next room—that's just bad parenting. No, I'm talking about the one still hanging around inside of you.

I'm guessing that child is eager to come out and play.

And maybe even help you solve a mystery.

ELIZABETH SIMS

Occasionally I talk to schoolchildren about writing. I create suspense by asking them how many sheets of paper it takes to write a novel. They guess, and suddenly they very much want to know how many sheets of paper it takes to write a novel. No matter what they guess, they're always shocked and horrified when I unveil the foot-high stack of handwritten pages of rough draft of one of my novels. They've just experienced suspense and a payoff, though they don't realize it.

When I ask what you need to write a story of suspense, inevitably one kid yells, "Put in a bad guy!" Good advice, if obvious. Readers must stick with you to the end, and suspense is the foremost element that keeps them turning pages.

The Young Adult Mystery

Complex, authentic stories for the young adult—
emphasis on adult.

KELLEY ARMSTRONG

Perhaps the biggest question YA writers get from aspiring writers is "What *can't* I do in YA?" I was once on a panel where an audience member asked that question, and another author said there were only two things you can't do in young adult: bestiality and boring. Someone then mentioned a YA romance with shape-shifters and on-the-page sex, and she revised her answer to "Boring, then. You just can't do boring."

I've used that anecdote many times, because it accomplishes two things. First, it establishes the cardinal rule of YA: "Don't be boring." Second, if a writer is shocked by the bestiality joke, they may need to read more young adult fiction and divorce themselves from any idea that it is "for children." Let's start with that: the reading level and expectations of teenagers.

Teen Reading Level

The concept of teenagers is a relatively recent one. The word is first seen in the early 1900s, but the concept of a truly separate stage between childhood and adulthood didn't really catch on until the mid-twentieth century. For most of history, teenagers have been considered young adults, and that's the term we use for fiction aimed at readers in their teens. That's also how we need to think of them. As young *adults*. Not old *children*.

When I ask writing students to guess what grade level they write at, most say "high school." They're college educated themselves and proud of their writing ability. Yet their work rarely exceeds grade seven or eight. Most newspapers are written at a grade-five level. Commercial fiction averages only slightly higher. That isn't an insult to the writing level—it's proof that we underestimate how young readers are when they reach full reading comprehension. Teen readers have reached that stage. Therefore, you do not need to simplify your writing for them.

Teens are capable of reading a mystery as complex as any written for adults. Indeed, many of us *were* reading adult fiction when we were teenagers. I was devouring Agatha Christie and Stephen King before I reached my teens, and that is not uncommon among readers of my generation, when there was little available for teen readers. What today's teen thriller reader expects is a fully complex story about fully complex characters . . . who just happen to be teenagers, like them. You should not feel the need to complicate your prose or raise your vocabulary (and please, don't raise it to "teach" them) but neither do you need to simplify.

Young Adult Readers

So, who reads young adult mysteries? The obvious answer is "young adults," but it's a little more complicated than that. The target audience is teenagers, but it's estimated that at least half of YA readers are adults. While there is "young YA" aimed at middle-grade and early high school readers, most major publishers are looking for crossover appeal.

What that means is, again, that we do not want to simplify our prose or story complexity. Adults who read YA are looking for a unique reading experience, not "an easy read." What it *doesn't* mean, though, is that we focus on the adult audience. These mysteries are intended for teens, to reflect their lives in a way adult fiction does not. Write with those teens in mind and just remember, if you're tempted to "write down," that half your readers may be adults.

Diversity

While diversity is making ripples in adult fiction, a proper understanding of the issues—and respect for them—is essential to entering the mainstream YA market. Diversity is a huge concern in YA, and I expect that will not change until we see a YA bookshelf that accurately reflects the diverse teenage population.

Diverse books reflect the world teens see around them. For most, that is a population rich in variety of all kinds—race, religion, sexual orientation, gender identity, neurodiversity, and ability. That does not mean that YA writers have a checklist for characters. Instead, we naturally write the world in all its complexity because that is what teens see, and we're striving for authenticity. If you're new to this mindset, look at your character cast. How many are white, cisgender, heterosexual, able-bodied, and neurotypical? If it's "most" or even "half," take a closer look at the teen community you're trying to reflect.

Now that you have a diverse cast of characters, do your research to portray them accurately, just as you would do research to make sure you portray a lawyer or FBI agent accurately. Then make sure your critique partners, beta readers, or editors include people from the communities you've written about to ensure you haven't made errors. If you have a major character from a community that is not your own, consider hiring a sensitivity reader.

(Note that in this section I've used terms common in discussions of diversity. If any of them are unfamiliar to you, researching them is an excellent place to start forming a groundwork of knowledge. If an editor asks whether there are, for example, any neurodiverse characters in your book, you'll want to be able to answer authoritatively.)

Own Voices and Cultural Appropriation

In adult fiction, the validity of concerns about "Own Voices" and cultural appropriation is debated, often with discomfort and disconcertment. It's much different in YA, where they are considered valid and serious issues.

Own Voices means that an author comes from the same marginalized community as their protagonist. It is used only for marginalized characters. When an agent says they want Own Voices works, they do not mean white protagonists from white authors. They mean marginalized protagonists from authors who share that marginalized identity, such as a Black protagonist from a Black writer or an autistic protagonist from an autistic writer.

Cultural appropriation can occur when a writer writes from a perspective that is not their own. Currently, in adult fiction, doing so is generally considered cultural appropriation only if the book is intended to tackle issues of that identity. For example, if a straight non-Muslim writer wrote a book about a young Muslim man struggling with a secret homosexual relationship, that would be cultural appropriation. Young adult fiction is different.

Years ago, I wrote a YA trilogy with a part–First Nations protagonist. At the time, that was acceptable because the book wasn't about her heritage. In that era, the argument was that we needed more diversity in our main characters. While having a writer of that culture would be preferable, there was a lack of diverse published authors to tell those stories.

Now we recognize that the lack of diverse *authors* is the problem, not the lack of diverse *protagonists*. Authors from the dominant culture have traditionally been encouraged to tell their stories and found acceptance in a way that writers from marginalized communities have not. If we say we want diverse stories but we're fine getting those stories from any writer, regardless of cultural background, then there's no impetus to seek out Own Voices stories, which most of us can agree is the better option.

Whether you agree or disagree with the issues of Own Voices and cultural appropriation, as a YA writer, it is important to understand that publishers will want your story to be diverse but that your main character should be from a marginalized community only if you share that identity.

Gatekeepers

It's time to delve into those burning questions of maturity level. In other words, let's talk about sex . . . and profanity and violence. First, a quick note on gatekeepers. This is the term used to describe authority figures who stand between young readers and books. This includes parents, teachers, librarians, and others.

Gatekeeping can serve a very positive purpose. No writer wants their work finding its way into the hands of readers who are not yet emotionally prepared for the content. However, in some cases, gatekeeping is more about blocking books that the gatekeeper deems inappropriate in *general*, rather than blocking those inappropriate for a specific reader.

Teens are very capable of selecting their own fiction, being old enough to shop and have their own library card. Therefore, gatekeepers are less important in teen fiction than in middle grade, but they are still an issue because the library and school market is very important to publishers.

Maturity Level

My first YA came out in 2008, and it was considered older YA, rated on some sites as 16+ despite the absence of sexual content and profanity. Now those same books are considered more middle school than young adult. YA has become increasingly mature, in part because many YA readers are not actual teenagers, and in part to answer a question of authenticity—depicting experiences that teenagers can relate to, rather than a fantasy world where they never need to consider questions of sex or sexuality, where they never need to confront or experience darkness or violence. The teens themselves haven't changed, but they've become more vocal about wanting authentically mature fiction.

Is there room for "sweet" YA? Of course. But when I give writing advice, it is always aimed at the largest market and at traditional publishers, and unless they specifically target younger readers, they're looking for authentic teen voices and stories.

Profanity

When I tackle this subject in a writing workshop, I always jokingly give the "big secret" that teenagers—gasp—swear. The reaction is usually laughter. Most of us know this from our own teen years. Yet a mother once insisted to me that her seventeen-year-old son and his friends *never* swore. My response, as the mother of teens, was that they did . . . just not around her. My kids grew up in a rural, religiously conservative area. Their friends never swear in front of adults, but you'd better believe that their language is very different when they think we aren't around. As the author, you are not the adult in the room. You are another teenager.

If you would prefer to avoid profanity, you must find a way to make its absence unnoticeable. Avoid expletive substitutes. Please don't have your teens saying "darn" or "heck," unless your story is set in the fifties. If you have a fantasy world, you can make up your own profanity if you're more comfortable with that. You can also scale it, choosing a level of profanity you're comfortable with.

For most aspiring YA authors, though, the question is "Are there certain words I *can't* use?" The answer is: it depends. At one time, we were cautioned to avoid "the F-word" because apparently Walmart wouldn't carry YA books with it. That's no longer the case. I've polled teens on their word choices and "the F-word" is tied with "shit" at the top of the list, with softer profanity (like "hell" and "damn") running a very distant second.

You absolutely do not need to use strong profanity, but you may feel free to do it and open that dialogue later with your editor.

Violence

When I was a teenager, I worked in a movie theater box office. It never failed to astound me how many parents, when considering whether an adult-accompaniment movie was appropriate, were uninterested in the violence level. (What they did care about is in the next section.) That was thirty years ago. As someone who wrote a horror/fantasy trilogy with serious violence, I can attest that this has not changed.

When it comes to violence in YA mysteries, it is neither necessary nor discouraged. You make the choice depending on the story you wish to tell.

Sexual Content

So, what did parents care about all those years ago at the movies? Sexual content. Even mild nudity was enough to make many change their minds about bringing their kids. That remains largely true for the book gatekeepers.

I mentioned my older-YA horror/fantasy trilogy. While I do not hear about the violence, I have fielded complaints about the sexual content . . . which is one non-explicit scene of respectful and consensual exploration. All those complaints have come from gatekeepers.

Explicit sex is still rare in young adult fiction. It's more commonly found in new adult, which is a term given to fiction with college-aged protagonists. When it comes to YA mysteries, I can't recall having seen any on-page sex, though I'm sure it's been done.

While explicit sex is rare, having characters dealing with sex is very common because it's part of portraying realistic teen experiences. For example, if you have two characters who have been dating for months and have never even *discussed* the subject, that is inauthentic to the modern teen reader. Your characters certainly may have decided not to have sex, but they need to have discussed that, even if you only include a passing reference to their decision.

Didacticism

As I've said, YA can be mistaken for "children's" fiction. That leads authors to believe they need to impart a lesson or "teach teens something." Don't. Remember yourself at that age and think of how much you enjoyed having adults lecture you.

If YA "teaches" anything, it does so obliquely, by providing examples of characters making mistakes and dealing with difficult situations. While readers may learn from that, instruction is not the author's goal. Instead, this is a positive side effect of handling issues carefully and sensitively, and of having characters learn or model coping strategies.

"Getting" the Teen Voice

How do authors long past their teen years capture the voice of teenagers? Well, first you need some teens to study in their native environment. If you lack teens in your everyday life, I wouldn't suggest kidnapping any. Highly illegal. Instead, take advantage of natural situations where you are around teenagers—perhaps at a neighboring table in a coffee shop—and pay attention to their conversation. Trust me, if you're over the age of twenty—and not an authority figure—you're invisible to them.

You may be surprised that their conversation is as varied and thoughtful as any adult one. Sure, there's goofing around and silliness, but they talk about *far* more than school and dating and cruel parents who won't let them stay out past midnight. One of my favorite unintentional eavesdrops involved a group of middle school boys debating how to make the best cup of coffee and discussing coffee bean origins. Another was the group of teen girls in Catholic school uniforms whose profanity proficiency impressed even me. What were those girls discussing with such vigor? Politics.

You can also watch movies or shows aimed at teens, but be aware that the actors are not teens and the screenwriters aren't, either. If those shows are popular with actual teens, though, it suggests that the story lines and characters resonate with them.

And, of course, you're going to be reading YA novels, right? Ones written in the past five years? *The Outsiders* and *A Wrinkle in Time* don't count (you'd be amazed how many people name these when I ask what modern YA they've read). Classic YA novels are excellent for understanding the origins of the genre, but to understand the current market, you want YA novels that are popular with actual teenagers (teen choice award winners, for example).

One more quick tip on the teen voice. When I started in YA, my daughter was a young teen. In my first book, she circled high-vocabulary words in dialogue. When I asked whether these were words teens wouldn't know, she said, "Oh, they know them—they just don't say them unless they're showing off . . . or talking to adults." It was a reminder to (a) not underestimate teen vocabulary, (b) remember to keep interteen dialogue casual, and (c) remember that many teens code-switch when speaking to adults.

Show a Little Respect

Before I close out, I have one final question for would-be YA writers. Do you genuinely like teens? Respect them? Find them interesting people, and enjoy the chance to hear their thoughts and listen to what they have to say?

I'm always shocked by how many would-be YA writers admit they don't really care for teens, don't understand them, and aren't interested in getting to know them. They only want to write YA because they've heard it's popular.

As someone who writes both adult and YA, I can tell you it is far easier to get published—and stay published—in adult fiction. Those who write

YA do so for the love of writing teen fiction. If this isn't you, then this isn't the age group you should target.

Final Words

When writing for teens, we don't dumb anything down. Nor do we censor ourselves to the point of being inauthentic to the teen experience. We write our casts to reflect the diverse world, but we largely stay in our cultural lane when it comes to narrative voice.

That's about it. Oh, except for my very first point, which is all-important: don't be boring. And have fun. This is a truly unique market with a truly unique audience, who will blow you away with their enthusiasm and their passion. As readers, we all look back on the unforgettable stories that shaped our young lives. Writing YA, you have the chance to tell that story. Take it.

PAT GALLANT WEICH

My mother was a writer. I was sixteen when she began her mystery novel. I knew when she got that glazed-over look that she was lost in one of the chapters. I asked to read them as she churned them out. I sat, mesmerized, begging for more, till finally, two years later, the book saw its way to a spellbinding conclusion.

Tragically, my mother got sick and died before being able to submit her manuscript. It was willed to me. I placed it in my closet, where it remained as the years wore on and circumstances changed. After eight years it was as if an alarm sounded in the closet: The birth of my son pushed me to my mother's manuscript. The moment my son was placed in my arms, I felt a continuum, a link to my past, present, and future that I had never before felt in quite the same way. And at that moment, I ached for my mother— I ached at *her* losses, for *my* loss of her, and for her to see my son. With those thoughts, the seed was planted: It was time to reread her mystery. I knew I'd be facing the pain of reading my mother's words and emotions, of witnessing lost dreams. It would bring me back, but it was a way I could be close to her again. I took out the manuscript and read all 325 pages in one sitting. I couldn't put it down. It was as good as I had remembered; no, it was better! I knew I couldn't leave it in my closet any longer. It was ready for a new home. But time has a way of running away. Another move, the baby, work . . . so, the manuscript was placed in yet another closet.

But I didn't forget. From time to time, the book would call out to me. I decided to submit it. *Everyone* I knew in the field discouraged me. There could be no second novel, and no editor would buy a mystery without the chance for follow-up books. I wasn't daunted. I stuck the manuscript in an envelope, said a prayer, and sent it off to Doubleday with a cover letter *not* mentioning that the author was deceased. I wanted to give it its best shot. Six months passed and I had forgotten about the submission. After all, everyone had said it didn't have a chance.

Then the doorbell rang. A messenger delivered a letter to me: Doubleday wanted the book! Just like that! Stunned, I ran to my grandparents' house to let them know a piece of their daughter, my mother, would live on. It was the first time their eyes had lit up (save for the birth of my son, three years before) since my mother had died.

Then came the nerve-racking ordeal of having to tell the editor who had accepted the book that the author was no longer living. I was afraid my mother would lose her dream once again. Terrified, I called the editor to thank her. "Who are you?" she queried, "an agent?" I didn't answer, asking only if we could meet and talk in person. Puzzled, she acquiesced, agreeing to a meeting the following day. My legs were jelly as I entered her office. Before I even sat down, I explained the situation. "I love the book," she said. "I still want it."

Living Image, by Gladys Selverne Gallant, was published by Doubleday in 1978. I notified everyone my mother had ever known. Fortunately, my grandparents lived to see the work published. It was printed in America, Canada, France, New Zealand, and Australia. It also ran as a condensed novel in *Cosmopolitan* magazine. My mother had given both love and life to me and, at last, I was able to give her something in return, something that, perhaps, gave her a touch of immortality.

Graphic Novels

The mystery within the panels:
your conversation with words and pictures.

DALE W. BERRY AND GARY PHILLIPS

DALE W. BERRY:

It should be a simple five-step process. You pencil pictures of the words, an inker darkens the pencils for print, a colorist paints it, a letterer pastes in captions and dialogue balloons, and you're done. *Voilà*, a comic book. Once upon a blissful time, perhaps, but no more.

Over the years, comic books have evolved from their humble beginnings as cheap, disposable reads into Big Business, able to power global entertainment franchises. But as intimidating as that might seem as a potential marketplace to many writers, there has also emerged right alongside this a wonderful by-product: a place for stand-alone works of every kind.

Developing parallel to their high-profile counterparts, independent, non-superhero comics have established themselves as diverse graphic storytelling vehicles that can elevate prose to sophisticated heights, where almost anything is possible.

Now read by all ages, the graphic novel format works and sells in any genre, any theme, and for any writing style. The reasons for the medium's coming of age are many, and already fill entire books by themselves. (As a solid jumping-off point to bring any curious writer up to speed on what graphic storytelling is, why it works, and how far it has come, I'd start with the fun and invaluable *Understanding Comics* and *Making Comics* by Scott McCloud.)

So, why do they work, and why do they sell? The addition of artwork to tell a story can help immerse the reader in the time and the place, the physical expression of the characters, and the emotions of the plot. At their core, by combining a script with all the visual tricks of sequential storytelling, plus the catalogue of illustration techniques currently available, graphic novels become a unique way to enhance a story's potential, generate added impact for the reader, and expand an author's footprint.

Limited, as ever, only by budget, labor, and imagination, even the most mid-range, black-and-white graphic novel can make for effective storytelling. And this is especially true when it features a strong, positive fusion of writer and artist. A book's success comes from the level of detail and depth provided by their two approaches.

In comics, roughly speaking, every panel on the page equals one story beat (though this varies widely). Each beat can be expanded or contracted by the number of pictures used to illustrate that action of the scene.

Because the pictures can show one thing while the captions say another, different—and multiple—levels of narrative can be told at the same time. As a scene switches, dialogue can continue in captions into the next scene. Writers can effectively create "voice-overs," continuing and overlapping narrative points of view, as needed. In this way, different moods can be evoked by contrasts in what you're seeing versus what you're reading.

GARY PHILLIPS:

The best advice I once received on how to write a comic book was to keep in mind that each panel on a page is frozen action, the single story beat, as Dale stated. Basically you describe one thing at a time, though more than one thing can happen in a panel. From panel to panel, as the story moves forward, the reader's mind will fill in what happens in between. Each page of a comic book consists of a number of panels, the sequentials. A given page is a series of shots taken as a whole; close-up, medium distance, pulled back, three-quarters downward-angled, and so on—the language of film and television applied to the medium of comics.

That's only natural given that storyboarding, where an illustrator draws the series of camera shots depicting the actions of the characters, has been utilized for decades in movies and TV. For just as television has given us the likes of *The Untouchables* to *Breaking Bad* on the small screen, and the

Godfather saga played out at the movies, the medium of comics and crime fiction have a long history together. The first issue of *Detective Comics* in 1937 (Batman wouldn't be introduced in its pages until the twenty-seventh issue) was an anthology featuring the likes of *Speed Saunders of the River Patrol*, Bret Lawton tackling the Peruvian Mine Murders, and Gumshoe Gus's case of the stolen Gotlotz Jewels. Ace Harlem, Bonnie Hawks, and Sally O'Neil are another three among many original investigators from various comics publishers who also faced down gangsters, mayhem, and murderers. Several literary crimefighters and criminals, from Sherlock Holmes, Sam Spade, Honey West, The Saint, Shaft, professional thief Parker, Perry Mason to Mike Shayne, have had their comic book or comic strip adaption outings as well. Even *I, the Jury*'s Mike Hammer was derived by Mickey Spillane from his unsold comic book character Mike Danger.

It's been observed the job of the comic book writer is akin to being a film director. Maybe. Of course, any fiction writing in general is intended to provide the reader with the pertinent aspects of the story, advance the plot, illuminate character, and hopefully have all three of these elements working in concert.

The main difference from prose is that in comics, the writer doesn't let the words get in the way of the art. The writing, no matter how evocative, is secondary to the images. Write, then chop and hone the words. Cut away with your figurative scissors. My personal style is a relatively minimalist approach to descriptions, and I write dialogue as if drafting a television script, pared down to the essence.

As my esteemed colleague Dale Berry has pointed out, the artwork is the vehicle upon which time and place, the expressions of the characters, and the mood and emotion of a given scene are conveyed. In a recent comic book produced by one of the Big Two (titles from Marvel and DC account for roughly 70 percent of month-to-month market share of sales), featuring the blind costumed vigilante Daredevil, I randomly opened the issue to a two-page spread of Jorge Fornés's well-composed sequentials.

In a particular sequence of just three panels, Fornés initially uses a three-quarters downward-angled shot to show a sedan driving along a Manhattan street. A word balloon is coming from one of the occupants of the car. It's established the action is taking place in a certain part of town, as we can partially see Chinese lettering on a sign. The next panel is a close-on shot of a younger man and an older woman in the rear seat of that car as they both gaze out at their destination. They do not look happy. The third panel is another three-quarters downward-angled shot of the two of them, now standing on the sidewalk outside the parked car. The woman shouts one word, the name of the gangster inside the building they've arrived at, a corner tavern. How do I know she shouted? Her word balloon is like an explosion, all pointed spikes, not round. And clearly a donnybrook has gone down in the bar, as glass, wood, a busted table, and debris litter the front of it, and the door to the place is missing. Light spills from within onto the sidewalk as well.

The other aspect to note is that panels one and three are a single tracking shot. The car is in different places, but when you take a second look, you see that the buildings and sidewalk shown in the first panel are part of the concrete landscape ending at the bar. In those three panels the artist has visually demonstrated what Dale wrote about. Don't get me wrong, I'm not taking anything away from the script by Chip Zdarsky, but the fact remains: the three panels have impact, conveying movement and the tenseness of the situation, amplifying what the words are communicating to the reader. Elsewhere in the story, captions are used to give us those multiple levels of the narrative. Clearly Zdarsky and Fornés, having worked together over a period of time on this series, have developed a shorthand for the look and feel, the pace of events they're portraying with these characters.

The writer in the script describes what the beat is. The artist interprets that to illustrate such in the language of panel-by-panel storytelling. How much or how little should the writer describe? Take the sequence below from *The Be-Bop Barbarians*, the graphic novel Dale and I produced about jazz, the Red Scare, and three cartoonist characters who will find themselves at odds with one another. One of our main characters, Ollie Jefferson, wakes from a nightmare, a harrowing replay of an incident from his soldier days in the Korean War. Written originally to be one page, it became two.

PAGE EIGHT OF BE-BOP BARBARIANS

Panel One

Medium down-angle shot as Ollie Jefferson comes awake and is sitting up in his bed after reliving this episode from the war. He is in boxers and

T-shirt, his sheet and blankets a jumble around his legs. He rubs a hand to his face. The lighting is blue and somber in his bedroom.

OLLIE: OH, MAN.

Panel Two

Close-on shot of his bare feet now on the side of the bed. There's a folded-over copy of the Communist Party's tabloid-style newspaper *The Daily Worker* on the floor.

Panel Three

Medium shot as Ollie, now in his robe tied at the waist, sits at his drawing board. He clicks on the swing lamp attached to his board.

SFX: CLICK

Panel Four

Now our POV is over his shoulder. He holds a pencil and on the drawing board is a sheet of paper with a very rough drawing of two cops using their nightsticks on a man on the ground. Ollie is reaching out with his other hand, clicking on the radio on a stand near the table.

VOICE OVER RADIO: . . . THE REVEREND WILMORE HICKS HAS CALLED ON POLICE COMMISSIONER KENNEDY TO ATTEND A COMMUNITY MEETING IN HARLEM TO ADDRESS POLICE AND NEGRO RELATIONS.

Panel Five

Reversed angle, closer in as Ollie fleshes out his pencils, though we can't see the page now.

VOICE OVER RADIO (off panel): AND IN OTHER NEWS, PRESIDENT EISENHOWER HAS ANNOUNCED A TWO-YEAR BAN ON NUCLEAR TESTING.

Here's the result:

Now, you'll note the section with the announcer coming over the radio is absent from that former page, as is Ollie clicking on his light over his drawing table—and no robe. All of this is now picked up in the latter page.

Dale felt the first part would work better if the initial sequence was silent. He was right. The combined pages worked so much better in establishing Ollie's mood after his harrowing dream. The published graphic novel is in color; a full pallet of hues playing its part in telling the story. The coloring I'd indicated for the first panel was laid in by our colorist J. Brown, which further relayed to the reader Ollie's state of mind.

DALE:

As you can see, the artist's job is to be interpretive—in a sense, to retell the story using pictures. So when working from an author's script, an artist has roughly two choices: interpret from a less specific, more generalized script (sometimes just an outline), or follow a highly detailed script to the letter. For the artist, both approaches bring certain challenges and rewards.

Working from a generalized script or outline, the artist has to fill in more of the blanks. This means not only designing all the scenery, the characters, the wardrobe, and the hairstyles, but also drawing everything the writer *hasn't* mentioned, while including everything they have. Not every written sentence needs to reiterate that a gentle snow is falling around the characters, but every panel of art will need to reflect it.

This sometimes dictates having to break down a script's otherwise perfect one-sentence description of a moment into several pictures in order to clearly express everything called for. Panels are added and subtracted. Beats are shifted. This can subtly change the rhythm of the story, and it's the responsibility of the artist to keep track of that rhythm when deviations occur. The artist is not just illustrating the script but storyboarding it, like a film.

The advantage of this approach is that it can create more impact for the reader and more successfully heighten the story's drama.

The disadvantage is that it can take longer to create. (Note to artists: don't go off-road if you don't know how to get back.)

On the other hand, say an author has written a highly detailed script, describing every element on the page in depth. Every beat, down to the lighting and "camera angles." The artist can then simply follow along and draw what's asked for.

This approach makes the overall production process fast, and for marketing and budgetary reasons can be especially successful for producing on a tight deadline. However, it can sometimes create an uninspired final product and a flat visual interpretation of the story. The end result can be a perfectly good product, but not great. And for some writers, this approach can hamper their voice, forcing them to slow down their own process by adding too much description.

So how much detail does a writer need to inject to give the artist enough information to work with?

My own rule of thumb is that it's always easier to write "Ten thousand horsemen came over the hill" than it is to draw it. So when scripting, I think writers should always describe as much as they envision, but leave some room for expansion/contraction by the artist. A good writer will leave just enough information to trigger the artist's imagination. (This is where working with such an experienced author as Gary is a bonus.)

The artist, for their part, must always do due diligence, making sure to lay out the story as accurately and emotionally "real" as possible, remaining true to the script or source material and evoking the right mood as needed. Research is essential to make sure every image and sequence looks and feels right.

(And as a side note to writers: Try to find the right artist for you. Plenty of people draw well, but not everyone will be able to express the mood or style your story requires.)

In the end, success depends on how simpatico the writer and the artist are with the material and with each other. This concept goes even further when you add the equally major contributions of a letterer or colorist. Every choice they make adds an important layer of interpretation and expression to the work.

This means there will always be give-and-take during the production process. Rewrites will occur, and pages will have to be redrawn, regardless. But the more the artist and writer are in sync with the "feel" of the material, the more dimension the story will have, the more the reader will get out of it, and the more effective a graphic novel it will be.

This inherently collaborative nature of the medium is what makes such a simple printed format become more than just an expression of the writer's voice or the artist's eye. The final result is a grand, entertaining synthesis of everyone's contribution (up to and including the reader). In this way, the modern graphic novel becomes one of those wonderful media where the more love you put into it, the more love you'll generate.

Plus, it's just a great way to tell stories.

DAG ÖHRLUND

When I teach writing classes and students tell me how difficult it is for them to write, I always stress the few things I feel are basic and necessary for successful writing: You must have a really good, preferably *unique* story. You must feel a burning desire to tell it, feel—actually—that few things are more important than doing just that. You must have fun, feel joy, while you are doing it. You must create interesting characters. You should write the kind of story that you, yourself, want to read. If you are into crime, skip the feel-good stuff.

The Short Mystery

What do the characters (and readers)
want in your mystery short story?

ART TAYLOR

What ingredients add up to excellence in short fiction within the mystery genre?

Reading the Edgar Award winners for Best Short Story might seem a good step toward discovering the "secret recipe" to success in this form. But even from the beginning, the range of stories on that list—diverse in genre, structure, and style—defied categorization. Before 1955, this award honored authors and full collections rather than individual stories, and Lawrence Blochman's *Diagnosis: Homicide*, the first book to win the honor, featured realistic, clue-driven mysteries, leaning heavily on the forensic training and scientific knowledge of pathologist-cum-detective Dr. Daniel Webster Coffee. The second book to win, John Collier's *Fancies and Goodnights*, couldn't have been more different, with stories that were determinedly surreal, absurdist, fabulist—four-hundred-plus pages and not a single traditional detective story in the batch.

For the balance of the 1950s and into the 1960s, the short-story Edgars spanned a similar variety: the realistic and the fantastic in alternating years, for example, or a plot-driven tale succeeded by a more deliberately paced character study. Even leaping forward to our latest decade, Doug Allyn's more traditional historical mystery "The Scent of Lilacs" stands in stark contrast to Gillian Flynn's half-gothic, half-noir "What Do You Do?"—and while both John Connolly's "The Caxton Private Lending Library & Book Depository" and John Crowley's "Spring Break" boast supernatural elements that might once have been considered unwelcome in the genre, even these two couldn't be more different in style or tone.

In short, analyzing more than six decades of award winners, I'd be hard-pressed to find one single solid model for how to write a short story. In fact, the only thing truly holding these tales together is their more limited word count—and what can you do with that common (and obvious) denominator?

Well, perhaps a bit, as it turns out.

For extra perspective on that point, we might need to go further back in Edgar history to . . . Edgar himself.

Poe believed that the short story was the pinnacle of prose compositions—the one that "should best fulfill the demands of high genius"—in part directly related to the form's brevity. Short stories, according to Poe, should be capable of being read in a single sitting, with "unity of effect" being both a goal and a challenge:

> If [the author's] very initial sentence tend not to the outbringing of this effect, then he has failed in his first step. In the whole composition there should be no word written, of which the tendency, direct or indirect, is not to the one pre-established design. And by such means, with such care and skill, a picture is at length painted which leaves in the mind of him who contemplates it with a kindred art, a sense of the fullest satisfaction.

No word written that doesn't serve the story's design? I imagine that strikes you, as it does me, as an unattainable ideal. However, if brevity is the defining characteristic of the short story and unity of effect the goal, then perhaps some of the qualities behind that sentiment—economy, efficiency, and unrelenting focus—should stand as guiding principles, whatever the subgenre or style of a mystery short story, and always with an eye toward entertaining the reader in the process.

Already anticipating that need for economy, efficiency, and focus, aspiring writers often circle back to several core questions in seminars or postpanel Q&A sessions: How many characters can you have in a short story? How quickly should the story get into the action? Can short stories have subplots? How important is a surprise ending, and how do you write one?

Rather than simple answers, some of these questions might depend on the story a writer is trying to tell. A woman unhappy with her husband and contemplating (or even carrying out) murder? That story can be told with two characters. Make it a love triangle, with jealousy leading to murder, and then you'd need three. How many for a clue-driven story? One victim, one detective, and three suspects might be just enough.

One piece of writing advice I think about regularly may help provide context to this question of characters as well as the ones on story beginnings and subplots. In her own quirky but insightful how-to book, *Plotting and Writing Suspense Fiction*, Patricia Highsmith talks about establishing lines of action or of potential action in the openings of stories and novels. What do characters want that they don't have? (That's one line of action a story might follow.) What conflicts or dangers do they face? Where do they connect with other characters or disconnect from them? Making sure that all characters have some role to play in those various lines of action will help determine whether each is integral to the overall design—or perhaps whether there are too many plotlines, or *subplot*-lines, to navigate successfully.

This idea of lines of action also offers perspective on a story opening. While conventional wisdom might advise writers, "Start your story in the middle of the action!" what does that mean? Not every story should begin with either a detective standing over a dead body or a killer running away from one. Instead, what conflicts will the story's characters navigate ahead, and how can you introduce some hint of those conflicts early and efficiently—laying down the lines of action that you'll then pluck and tighten consistently and with increasing intensity, to their breaking point or even beyond?

One of Highsmith's own stories, "The Terrapin" (a finalist for the 1963 short story Edgar), starts with a simple opening of doors, but everything that follows—emotional abuse, psychological turmoil, terrible violence— is presaged in that short opening paragraph:

> Victor heard the elevator door open, his mother's quick footsteps in the hall, and he flipped his book shut. He shoved it under the sofa pillow out of sight, and winced as he heard it slip between sofa and wall and fall to the floor with a thud. Her key was in the lock.

Lines of action might well be found crisscrossing a corpse, but they could as easily, as strongly, be established as internal anxieties or even at the level of the prose itself. Literally *nothing* happens in one of Poe's own most famous opening lines—"True!—nervous—very, very dreadfully nervous I had been and am; but why will you say that I am mad?"—and yet it's always struck me as gripping: the tone and the backward syntax, that question swung solidly at the reader, that disconcerting mix of exclamation points and em dashes . . . and the hints of insanity, too, of course.

After an opening that sets conflicts in motion, the prose throughout the story should be guided by economy, efficiency, and focus. Can a short story support lengthy descriptions, digressions, diversions? More on that in a moment, but in general, it's a solid rule to try to do more with less—and to trust your reader to fill in the rest. Suggest instead of describe; imply instead of explain. Rather than a long portrait of place, for example, highlight some telling specifics or emphasize a character's relationship to the setting.

This was the old house at Nyack, the same living room, the same Utrillo on the wall, the same chandelier glittering over his head. *The same everything*, he thought bitterly, even to the faces around him.[*]

Rather than an exhaustive inventory of character, frontload a key point or a distinctive bit of backstory.

I didn't stop giving hand jobs because I wasn't good at it. I stopped giving hand jobs because I was the best at it.[†]

And don't forget that voice distinguishes character, too—especially if established early and strong.

Here's the thing—I never took drugs in my life. Yeah, okay, I was the champion of my share of keggers. Me and The Pope. We were like, "Bring on the Corona and the Jäger!" Who wasn't? But I never even

---

[*] "House Party" by Stanley Ellin, Edgar winner for Best Short Story in 1954.

[†] Opening paragraph of "What Do You Do?" by Gillian Flynn, Edgar winner for Best Short Story in 2015.

smoked the chronic, much less used the hard stuff. Until I met Pope's little sister. And when I met her, she was the drug, and I took her and I took her, and when I took her, I didn't care about anything. All the blood and the bullets in the world could not penetrate that high.[*]

Wherever possible, let each sentence serve several purposes: a bit of dialogue, for example, that might reveal character (the character speaking, or spoken about, or listening, or all three) and push plot forward in one fell swoop.

"If I'd told him once, I'd told him fifty times never to talk to strangers or get into cars. But boys will be boys and he forgot all that when the time came. He was given sweets, of course, and *lured* into this car." Whispers at this point, meaningful glances in his direction. "Threats and suggestions—persuaded into goodness knows what—I'll never know how we got him back alive."[†]

And for clue-driven mysteries, if you're able to slip evidence into the predicate of the sentence or tuck it into a prepositional phrase—subordinating it, hiding it in plain sight—well, that's economical, efficient, and focused, too.

My father shook his head at me. "I don't like to hear ugly gossip coming out of your mouth, all right, Buddy?"

"Yes, sir."

"She didn't kill Hugh Doyle."

"Yes, sir."

His frown scared me; it was so rare. I stepped closer and took his hand, took his stand against the rest. I had no loyalty to that woman Papa thought so beautiful. I just could never bear to be cut loose from the safety of his good opinion.[‡]

Transcribing those previous lines, I recognize that they provide no

---

[*] Opening paragraph of "Amapola" by Luis Alberto Urrea, Edgar winner for Best Short Story in 2010.

[†] "The Fallen Curtain" by Ruth Rendell, Edgar winner for Best Short Story in 1974.

[‡] "Red Clay" by Michael Malone, Edgar winner for Best Short Story in 1997.

clear example to follow—not if you haven't read the entire story. But there's a key clue there—first scene of the story, and it's right there. And the necessity of reading the entire story proves this excerpt's success, too, since this passage lays the groundwork for the twists that follow, right up to the ending—a fine example of Poe's challenge that there should be "no word written, of which the tendency, direct or indirect, is not to the one pre-established design."

Which brings me to a couple of thoughts about endings.

Specific endings are notoriously difficult to analyze without (a) layers of spoiler alerts or (b) summarizing the entire story to explain how the ending earns its success. However, even generalities might help here, since some ending must be reached, for better or worse. A detective must unmask the killer and restore justice—or the killer must escape that justice. The jealous husband must kill the wayward wife—or be killed by her—or maybe by her lover—and husband or wife or lover must be caught or not caught or else the wife needs to turn on her lover, too, and. . . . In whatever direction events turn, a story needs to be complete—somehow.

But completion here doesn't necessarily mean overexplanation. As with "suggest instead of describe, imply instead of explain" above, short story endings are often most successful when they leave room for the reader to do a little work. A detective might unmask the criminal, but an author could sketch the outlines of a motive instead of scrutinizing it in depth and let the reader fill in the impact of this unmasking rather than belaboring the fallout on other characters or the wider community. And while husband and wife might reunite—the lover killed instead!—a sly side-eye at the end of the tale could hint at more betrayal to come.

Writers often (too often?) strive to sneak a plot twist into the final line. The ink was an exotic poison! The money was counterfeit! Those women were twins! But while such reveals can surely offer immediate pleasures, I would argue that *character* twists are often more effective. A new perspective on a character the reader has gotten to know, a secret desire that complicates motives, an unexpected action that nonetheless seems perfectly in character—these might provide the reader a deeper satisfaction.

But wait, aren't there exceptions to any of these guidelines? Because I've read a story in which . . .

Certainly. Absolutely.

Economy and efficiency have governed many of the examples I've chosen above, but that third word—*focus*—might well shift the balance in an author's approach. Long descriptions, digressions, and diversions? Those are possible, but they come with costs elsewhere.

A story about a criminal's motivations and psychology might focus more attention on character. Forget the key detail or bit of backstory suggesting great history. Instead, indulge in description! Luxuriate in backstory! But recognize that's the *design* of such a story—and that the luxury of such indulgences may come with the need for frugality in other aspects of the storytelling.

In a similar way, a clue-driven short story might skimp on developing three-dimensional characters while constructing an elaborately structured plot—or series of interrelated plots: several characters with straightforward motivations that collide in a perfect storm of actions and possibilities.

Stories can be all dialogue or have no dialogue at all. They can be all scene ("show, don't tell") or largely summary (because sometimes telling can still enchant and enthrall). They can unfold over the course of an hour or day or many decades. They can be flash fiction (under 1,000 words) or novella length (15,000 or more).

Based on the design being served, writers can choose to follow a wide array of styles and structures.

To bring us full circle—the way a strong story might, with a beginning that preps us for the end—I'd advise looking back at some of those Edgar winners to understand that range. Perhaps no single solid model will serve as a template, but so many stories can collectively open up a world of potential for the short form. Read Stanley Ellin for how to write luxuriant prose. Read Roald Dahl or Shirley Jackson for navigating tone and irony. Read Ed Hoch for plotting and for placing precise clues and Ruth Rendell for delving into psychological depths. Read Tom Franklin for working on a panoramic scope. And . . .

That list could go on, and it's not just these Edgar winners who can teach us, but so many fine short story masters at work today.

Despite a more limited word count generally, short fiction as a form has proven remarkably flexible. The models are myriad. The possibilities are, ultimately, endless.

CHARLES SALZBERG

It's something you hear over and over again as a beginning writer: "Write what you know." But what if you don't know anything? What if you're Emily Dickinson and the sum total of your knowledge of the outside world is what you see from your attic window? Is "write what you know" really that helpful? How about writing what you *don't* know?

I've never been arrested; I have no cops in my family; I've only been in a police station once; I've never handled a pistol; I've never robbed a bank, knocked over a 7-Eleven, or mugged an old lady. I've only been in one fight and that was when I was eleven. I've never murdered anyone, much less my family, and I've never chased halfway around the world to bring a killer to justice. I've never searched for a missing person and I've never forged a rare book. Yet somehow I find myself a crime writer who's written about all those things.

How, if I am supposed to write only what I know, is this possible? Easy. It's because I have an imagination, possess a fair amount of empathy, have easy access to Google, and like asking questions. If I were limited to writing what I know I'd be in big trouble because the truth is, I don't know all that much.

Ten Stupid Questions
about True Crime

Building a vivid page-turner, out of nothing but facts.

DANIEL STASHOWER

1. Is this a novel? Imagine yourself in a bookstore, standing beside a tall stack of copies of your new release. The title is *This Really Happened*. Above your head is a banner that reads: WELCOME TO THE TRUE CRIME SECTION. And perhaps you're wearing a T-shirt that says: I HAVE WRITTEN A BOOK ABOUT AN EVENT THAT OCCURRED IN REAL LIFE. Even so, the odds are good that the first person in line for a signed copy will ask, "Is this a novel?"

Space is tight. Let's assume, since you've made it this far into this handbook, that you've already come to grips with at least some of the basics of writing a book. We'll stipulate that you have a general understanding of structure and pacing, and that you're familiar with the challenges that lie ahead. For the sake of expedience, we'll zero in on the areas where writing a true crime book differs sharply from writing a novel.

There are several questions that true crime writers get asked over and over again. Some of them seem obvious—perhaps even a little clueless—but they're all good questions and they spotlight important distinctions about the genre. You should have an answer for each one before you dive in.

So, is your true crime book a novel? The answer may seem blindingly, hilariously obvious, but you'll be amazed at how many readers get confused on this point. A true crime story, by definition, is true. And yet, people will ask you this question *all the time*. Strangely, that means you did it right. When all is said and done, your story should have the shape and feel and narrative thrum of a tightly plotted novel. It should seem too good to be true. That's the challenge of it, finding ways to apply the structure and storytelling techniques of fiction to a real-life event without sacrificing factual accuracy or doing a disservice to the material. Truman Capote's *In Cold Blood* is often put forward as the prime example of the paradigm. "It seemed to me," Capote famously remarked, "that journalism, reportage, could be forced to yield a serious new art form: the 'nonfiction novel.'"

2. Where do you get your ideas? This is another perennial, as you're un-doubtedly aware, but there's no easy answer. "I am sorry to say that this question has become something of a bad joke among writers," Elizabeth Peters once remarked. "The only possible answer is: 'Everywhere.' You don't get ideas; you see them, recognize them, greet them familiarly when they amble up to you."

It's probably fair to add that fiction writers often look inward, drawing on their private experiences and imaginative instincts, while true crime writers, for the most part, pull from external sources such as newspapers, police reports, and the pages of history. Unfortunately, there's a great deal of random chance built into this equation. So, a better question might be . . .

3. Where did you get this *particular* idea? A handful of writers are drawn to the true crime genre as a means of coming to grips with a terrible event in their own lives. James Ellroy's *My Dark Places* and Ann Rule's *The Stranger Beside Me* are notable examples, along with Dominick Dunne's coverage of the trial of his daughter's murderer. These are extreme cases, of course, but few true crime writers are left untouched while excavating the details of a violent crime, even if the author has no personal connec-tion to the story. You should take a moment to reflect on this before you enter the arena. You'll be carrying around the details for many months, or perhaps years. The job requires you to walk a mile in the criminal's shoes, and to share in the agonies of the victims. Are you prepared to spend a year or more with a man who strangled his wife? With a cult leader? With a child predator? Plenty of writers have the ability to compartmentalize, which is all to the good, but the story is certain to get under your skin. On a related note . . .

4. When did all of this happen? Another glaringly obvious question, right? Surely the subject you choose will determine the time frame? If you decide to write about the Kennedy assassination, for instance, your research will be anchored in 1963. If that feels good to you—if you're willing to go wherever the story takes you—nothing more needs to be said.

Most of us, however, are happiest and most effective when dealing with a specific period of time, so it's a good idea to locate your comfort zone before you go looking for ideas. Many true crime writers are most effective in the present day, acting as investigative journalists, conducting interviews, and working with contemporary sources and documents. Do you feel at home with this type of legwork—even if it extends to knocking on doors and approaching the families of victims? Some writers look for opportunities to weigh in before the paint is dry, to offer commentary and interpretation of cases that are still in progress or have been left unsolved. A Scottish lawyer named William Roughead was a pioneer of the form with his essays on "matters criminous." In 1908 his work drew attention (including that of Arthur Conan Doyle) to a miscarriage of justice in the case of Oscar Slater, in which faulty evidence had resulted in an unjust murder conviction. Michelle McNamara's *I'll Be Gone in the Dark* is a cornerstone modern example, chronicling the author's determined efforts to shine fresh light on the Golden State Killer case.

Other writers gravitate toward historical cases where the outcome is firmly established. These stories often showcase some important forensic milestone or sociological turning point, or focus on a crime so dramatic and shocking that it rose to the level of "crime of the century," at least in its day. *For the Thrill of It*, Simon Baatz's account of the Leopold and Loeb case, is an excellent example, as is Douglas Starr's *The Killer of Little Shepherds*, tracking the search for Joseph Vacher, a notorious French murderer active at the close of the nineteenth century.

"Historical" is a pretty loose term here, flexible enough to encompass crimes that are, say, ten or more years in the past—old enough, at least, to have faded from the headlines. Each story of this type will present a distinct set of research challenges, and you should know what they are before you commit yourself. What are the sources? Books? Private papers? Old newspaper accounts? Can you access them? Is there enough material to support a book-length narrative?

In any case, if you haven't done so already, you should spend some time thinking about the types of crimes you'd like to explore, and the time frame that lines up best with your interests. Once you've taken your internal temperature on these matters, you'll have a better chance of finding something that suits you. It's comforting to learn that even Henry James struggled with this. The ways in which authors discover ideas, he once wrote, are really "scarce more than alert recognitions," like the discoveries made by scientists and explorers. The author "comes upon the interesting thing," he concluded, "as Columbus came upon the isle of San Salvador, because he had moved in the right direction for it." And speaking of the isle of San Salvador . . .

5. Did you have to do a lot of travel? Another popular question. Many readers, it seems, entertain romantic fantasies about this. They like to imagine that researching a nonfiction book involves travel to exotic locations in Gulfstream jets, and the uncovering of hidden scrolls by candlelight in the libraries of ancient monasteries. The reality tends more toward municipal parking lots, broken Xerox machines, and library collections that can be accessed only on alternate Tuesdays. As you weigh up the realities of any potential project, you should spend at least a couple of hours mapping out the research phase to get a handle on whether it's realistic in your circumstances. It often comes down to simple geography. If you live in Oklahoma and the materials you need are in New York, you're looking at a lot of flights and hotels. Those expenses add up fast, and the research always—*always*—takes longer than you expect. But maybe you have a friend with a guest room, or at least a couch? Take a look at the logistics ahead of time. Which brings us to . . .

6. How much research did you do? This may sound like cheating, but ideally you should not be able to answer this one. If your subject sprang from a natural area of interest, or a fascination with a particular crime or time period, you probably did a fair amount of background work before the project began. And even after you've finished writing, there will always be another book to read, another fact to chase down, another rock to turn over.

That's not to say that you shouldn't refine and focus your research plan ahead of time. You absolutely must have a strategy, even if you diverge from it along the way, to prevent wasted effort—especially if you're paying for a hotel room. Sometimes the path is clear from the beginning. If there are other books on the subject, or related topics, of course you should read them. But you may also want to poke around at the edges for material that will lend color. If you're writing a historical piece, for instance, it's interesting to read books and magazines from the period to pick up some of the flavor of the times. And of course you'll want to visit the scene of the action, if possible, to soak up local texture.

There will be traps along the way. You will likely come to distrust some sources as you become aware of false information and mistaken assumptions, all the more so when you start chasing material on the internet. Trust, but verify—you'll learn quickly which sources are reliable and which are not. You're also likely to see the same anecdotes and factoids repeated over and over again across various books and journals. Repetition doesn't make something true—whenever possible, trace the information back to the origin.

Another note of warning, at the risk of stating the obvious: When it comes time to write your manuscript, there will be a powerful temptation—almost a longing—to show off the long hours of research and overwhelm the reader with cheerful facts about train timetables and lace collars. It's good that you took the trouble to learn it, but that doesn't mean it's interesting. "What you need to remember is that there's a difference between lecturing about what you know and using it to enrich the story," Stephen King tells us. "The latter is good. The former is not."

Every time you reach for a fact, make sure it advances the story. Ideally it will also contain some mirror element of character, theme, or tone that exerts an emotional undertow, helping to move events along in ways that may not be obvious on the surface. If the train timetable establishes an alibi, go ahead and spend time on it. If the lace collar tells us something about a character's social station or fastidious habits, have at it. But sometimes a cigar is just a cigar, even if you boned up on hygrometers and stalk cuts. If the research isn't pulling its weight, leave it out.

For many nonfiction writers, research is the fun part and there's a strong temptation to keep at it forever. At a certain point, though, you'll have to hold your nose, jump in, and start writing. Don't despair; you will almost certainly find yourself doing more research to plug the holes as you go along.

7. Hey, wait a minute, wasn't there already a book about this story? Probably. In choosing a subject, nonfiction writers have to strike a balance between the obscure and the overfamiliar, to find the sweet spot between "it's been done to death" and "who cares?" Go to the bookstore, look online, find out what else has been written on your potential subject. If it's a famous case, like Lizzie Borden or Saucy Jack, do you have a fresh angle? If nobody's written about it, or if it hasn't been done anytime recently, can you find a hook that makes it relevant? Ask yourself . . .

8. Why should I read this book? You've probably noticed that most nonfiction book titles now feature a carefully crafted subtitle. You get the main title, a colon, and then a subtitle that serves as both a thumbnail summary and a sales pitch. *The Suspicions of Mr. Whicher: A Shocking Murder and the Undoing of a Great Victorian Detective. The Poisoner's Handbook: Murder and the Birth of Forensic Medicine in Jazz Age New York. Killers of the Flower Moon: The Osage Murders and the Birth of the FBI.*

By now you've likely heard more than you ever wanted to know about "elevator pitches," but they serve a useful purpose. It's a productive exercise to try to compress and refine the essentials of your idea into the title-colon-subtitle template. If you can't capture the essence of your idea in a phrase—if you can't quickly persuade a reader, an agent, or an editor that your idea has legs—you may need to dig deeper.

Let's also admit that a number of phrases and descriptors have become a little threadbare over the past few years—there can only be so many "Trials of the Century" and "Battles for America's Soul." In the early stages, for purposes of marshaling your thoughts, don't worry if you find yourself reaching for one of these clichés. It's a means to an end, and it will probably go through five or six revisions before you're finished.

9. Wait, you're saying this is all true? Every single word? The answer should be yes, but you will run across some dissent on this point. Much has been written about invented dialogue, composite characters, and other artistic liberties. Writers are very good at justifying their own choices, for both good and ill. One writer's "thought experiment" is another's horseshit. It probably boils down to this: if you stretch the truth, you'll be challenged on it. There's a guy in Peoria who's been collecting information on your story since the Nixon administration. He's out there and he's waiting for you.

10. My uncle once gave a shoeshine to John Gotti. I have a neighbor who served on the O.J. jury. My mother kept a scrapbook during the Patty Hearst kidnapping. Why don't you write a book, and we'll split the profits? One day, someone will come up with a polite answer for this one. Maybe it's you. If so, will you please get back to me?

CAROLE BUGGÉ

Often our best characters come from a place so deep within us, a force so universal, that it feels spooky, uncontrolled, eerie. Let it happen—if you have an experience like that, consider yourself lucky. More often, I suppose, characters are a hodgepodge of traits from people we know or have seen—or even other fictional characters. We imbue them with life by giving them the inner life of our own unconscious or conscious mind. . . .

Setting in a mystery story is never just setting. It is mood, foreshadowing, suspense, and anticipation—in some stories it is virtually a character in its own right. . . .

A lot of people seem to think that writing dialogue is a gift; either you have it or you don't. I disagree. I believe that perhaps more than any other skill in writing, you learn to create good dialogue exactly the same way you get to Carnegie Hall: practice, practice, practice. . . .

Anyone who says they find writing plots easy is either a liar or a fool. It's gritty, sweaty work, and it's what separates the men from the boys, the women from the girls, and the professionals from the wannabes. It goes by other names—structure, story, narrative through-line, story line—but it is the *single* most important element in the commercial (and often critical) success of a book in the crime genre. To paraphrase Vince Lombardi, plot is not the most important thing, it's the *only* thing. All the pretty prose, marvelous metaphors, and captivating characters in the world will not make up for the lack of a good story.

The Writing

Lyndsay Faye—On Style
The writer's voice, or, cooking with cadence, rhythm, and audacity.

Jeffery Deaver—*Always* Outline!
The why and the how of planning it out first.

Lee Child—*Never* Outline!
The argument for spontaneity.

Laurie R. King—The Art of the Rewrite
Turning your raw first draft into a clear, compelling story.

Deborah Crombie—Plot and the Bones of a Mystery
Bringing together all the elements of your novel so it stands strong.

Frankie Y. Bailey—Diversity in Crime Fiction
Enriching your novel by writing characters, not categories.

Allison Brennan—The Protagonist
Your hero: the one we relate to, the one who drives the story.

T. Jefferson Parker—The Villain of the Piece
Your hero in reverse: the forces that create a vivid villain.

Craig Johnson—Supporting Characters
The chorus of voices that backs up your protagonist.

Greg Herren—Writing the Talk
Dialogue that sounds true, reveals character, and draws in the reader.

William Kent Krueger—Setting
Your most versatile element: backdrop, player, and the all-pervading sense of place.

Catriona McPherson—Humor in Crime Fiction
Funny mystery, or mystery with fun: why, how, and when to stop?

Caroline & Charles Todd—Writing in Partnership
Two writers with one voice: how we learned to collaborate.

Max Allan Collins—Tie-Ins and Continuing a Character
Playing in someone else's sandbox.

On Style

The writer's voice, or, cooking with cadence, rhythm, and audacity.

LYNDSAY FAYE

Why Style?

To someone who doesn't read genre fiction, the notion of authorial voice in an airport paperback might seem superfluous. Aren't the simple mechanics of clues and deductions paramount? Why dither around with style when a mystery novel depends on plot twists? Isn't that like asking whether any one airport doughnut tastes significantly different from another airport doughnut? Aren't they equally formulaic to assemble and easy to swallow?

Devotees of both mystery novels and doughnuts know different. Take this hapless airport noob, lock him in a kitchen with whole milk, active yeast, sugar, flour, eggs, butter, and fry oil, and ask him to make something even approximating the quality of ten identical airport doughnuts. Then stick the chucklehead in an office with a laptop, relevant reference books, and a Wi-Fi password, and request he produce a bestselling police procedural. He'll have about the same amount of luck. It looks easy; it's the hardest thing in the world. We know that there are myriad doughnut flavors—and as many styles in the mystery genre as there are mystery authors writing them.

Naturally, the subtle hints and bald thrills sprinkled throughout your plot are crucial, the same way flour is essential in a doughnut. But try making a doughnut without sugar (or honey, or molasses, or erythritol if you're feeling particularly unhinged). You're going to have a lousy doughnut. Narrative voice is equally crucial. Writers can mistakenly suppose they are born with their own innate sense of style—doesn't that just mean the way I naturally sound? And sure, if you're the Mozart of historical thrillers, then please hang an oil portrait of yourself above your Carrara marble desk with my blessing. But let's assume instead what is far likelier: you're the Julia Child of the legal suspense novel world, and like Julia you published your first book when you were thirty-nine, after a great deal of practice.

It could take a thousand tries to perfect your doughnut recipe. It could take the proverbial ten thousand hours to find your voice. But both are achievable goals if you have passion for your craft.

If you take one piece of advice from my letter of encouragement, let it be this: You will find your personal voice only by writing. You can read style guides; you can sleep with them under your pillow for osmosis, commit genocide on adverbs and emulate your literary heroes. Your innate self, that lyrical rhythm that stamps *your* brainprint on your work, will emerge as you type and sweat and, yes, bleed on the page. I've been recognized as unmistakably myself in works that did not have my name on them at all, by people who heard my voice in them. But I've also, in the course of more than twenty years, written in the literal multiple millions of words.

Finding your style takes time. If your very first doughnut was the airiest confection in the history of baking, that, my friend, was a fluke. But here are some suggestions to guide you along the way.

Authorial Voice versus Character Voice

Your authorial voice, as mentioned, is the watermark by which we infer, *Aha!* You *and none other wrote this book*, the way you would recognize your mom's voice and speech pattern versus your boyfriend's on the phone. "I just love Laura Lippman novels" you might say, as opposed to "I loved *What the Dead Know.*" Or "My dream is to sound like Mary Higgins Clark," rather than "My dream is to create an updated version of *Where Are the Children?*" Once you've developed a voice, it's going to be vanishingly close to impossible for you to shake it. The science of writing style is called stylometry, and a computer program called the Java Graphical Authorship

Attribution Program provided weighty evidence that J. K. Rowling wrote *The Cuckoo's Calling* and christened herself with some shiny new initials.

Character voice, on the other hand, is the way your imaginary friends sound. While I intend to focus on authorial voice as the more ephemeral of the two—I mean, sweet baby in a manger, we all know that our characters need to sound distinct—there are many ways to enliven voices if you feel like you aren't writing a three-dimensional being. Such as:

- **Backstory:** Every character needs a backstory, no matter how minor they are. Well, that's not quite true. The dude pumping gas with a cigarette in his mouth while your protagonist flees to Tijuana can get away with saying "I didn't know anyone listened to the Stone Temple Pilots anymore" when your hero pays up, and we don't *have* to know anything about that guy's relationship with his invalid mom.
- **Specificity:** The reason I pulled off the above is because I actually used highly specific details to give Gas Station Man a voice *without* a backstory; he's careless about smoking around petroleum products but a snob about music, and a bit of a tool. He's probably a drummer. He isn't deep into customer service, so he likely hates his dead-end job. But for anyone with around five to ten lines or more, it's your job to know the basics of where they came from.
- **Observation:** Listen to the real humans around you, especially ones with distinct voices, and ask what makes their tones so memorable. As a professional actor for ten years, I was trained to do this so I could craft onstage characters; on-page characters are made richer by the identical process of observation and analysis. Take notes. What sort of slang did that barista use, and how? Are your stepdad's sentences short or rambling? Pointed or poetic? The school of human culture is much cheaper than a graduate degree: make use of it.

Pastiche, Fan Fiction, and the Sincerest Form of Flattery

Let's say I was completely mistaken and you *do* want to update Mary Higgins Clark's classic *Where Are the Children?* You have contractual permission from her estate and a deal with a publisher and you're raring to go. Or perhaps you want to write a Charles Dickens riff and have no fear of copyright law. Is it possible to emulate other people's styles to any degree of accuracy?

Yes. My first novel, *Dust and Shadow*, is a Sherlock Holmes pastiche pitting him against Jack the Ripper, and I've since written eighteen published short stories about Holmes. And this section is applicable to more than just imitative works; if you write historical fiction, you'll want to sound historical, just as we want our cops to sound like police officers and the wizards in our mystery-fantasy crossover stories to sound like real-life wizards.

There is a difference between what we *think* a heightened style sounds like and the way people actually talk. Both need to be incorporated for your Regency laundress heroine to work. Taking Sir Arthur Conan Doyle as my example, since I know him best, plentiful Sherlock Holmes stories written by modern authors assume that because the setting is Victorian, every sentence needs to sound relentlessly *nineteenth century*. They are in error. Granted, sometimes Sherlock Holmes talks like this:

> "My dear fellow," said Sherlock Holmes as we sat on either side of the fire in his lodgings at Baker Street, "life is infinitely stranger than anything which the mind of man could invent. We would not dare to conceive the things which are really mere commonplaces of existence. If we could fly out of that window hand in hand, hover over this great city, gently remove the roofs, and peer in at the queer things which are going on, the strange coincidences, the plannings, the cross-purposes, the wonderful chains of events, working through generations, and leading to the most *outre* results, it would make all fiction with its conventionalities and foreseen conclusions most stale and unprofitable."
>
> —"A Case of Identity"

That there paragraph was a sublime invocation of the complexity of London life, an ode to the bizarre, a prose poem, the declamation of a fully justified egotist, an opinion confided to a trusted companion, and a glancing reference to Shakespeare's *Hamlet*—all at once. It was, in short, a lot. However, sometimes Sherlock Holmes sounds like this:

"I'll be back some time, Watson," said he, and vanished into the night.

—"The Adventure of Charles Augustus Milverton"

Novices weaken their manuscripts by attempting to impose a particular style on each and every sentence, especially when emulating someone else or an era not their own. The reader's eye can't process too much embellishment; your already sweet doughnut has now been drowned in syrup. Conversely, being too timid with style, fearing criticism for attempting adventurous prose, will result in a baked good resembling a hockey puck. A short, unadorned statement will put a period on a rhapsodic passage better than any punctuation. And after a paragraph of clean, efficient exposition, we want to feel the sharp nails of the wind's fingertips brushing our necks.

Be audacious with your style. Be simple with your sentences, too. Just don't attempt to do either one constantly.

- **Anachronism:** Unless you're Hilary Mantel and doing it on purpose throughout, don't do it. Simply consult an etymology site if you're unsure, *et voilà*, your circa-1832 grandmother won't describe mauve drapes (mauve as an artificial dye was invented in 1859).
- **Regionalism in place and time:** There are as many versions of English as there are places it's spoken, and when mastering a foreign style, the devil is in the details. Narrator John Watson would far more likely write the attributive "said he" than "he said." A Brit would say "They took him to hospital," not "They took him to the hospital." A detective might use words like "vic" or "perp," but that depends on the person and the setting. Study texts from the place or time in question, write down the metaphors used, note linguistic quirks. This sort of research is hard work, a delightful pastime, and—once again—about as costly as a walk in the park.
- **Jargon:** It matters. We want people who are talking shop to sound authentic. If you're a retired Tennessee civil rights lawyer writing a thriller from the POV of an active Tennessee civil rights lawyer, then hot diggity, you're not going to have to work very hard. If *I myself* were embodying that narrator, conversely, it's my job to

read every book I can get my hands on written by Tennessee civil rights lawyers, and take heed accordingly.

Suppose you have no wish to *directly* imitate anyone. You want to create characters based on your personal history and passions? That's absolutely marvelous. But meanwhile, there is nothing wrong with trying on a beloved author's style like a designer coat and seeing where it gets you, or with being honest about hero worship. It gives you a starting point; it gives you a launchpad. There are going to be people who urge you to be pure, create your voice from some mystical combination of the void and your life experience. This is, to put it mildly, ripe horse pucky. Every novel written in the modern day is in some fashion inspired by a novel written in the past.

If you'd never read a novel or short story and adored it, why on earth would you want to do something as eviscerating as *write* one? The point is, the training wheels are going to come off at some point. They have to—eventually it's *your* heart that needs to be put through the meat grinder and smeared on your keyboard. But if you need that initial blueprint while you learn what works for you and what doesn't? Take it, and take it with pride.

As for the authors who might inspire you and whether they mind being imitated, it is their greatest privilege to galvanize a fledgling writer. If it isn't, then they are scurrilous cads, and ought to be writing apology notes to every novelist who ever lit a fire in their own souls.

On Music, Rhythm, and Humor

It's impossible for me to talk about style without talking about musicality and sense of humor. Both are supposed to be tied to your nature—you're either born funny or not, born with a sense of pitch or not. They're also supposed to be tied to your nurture—you're more musical if there was a piano in the house, you're funnier if you were forced to make people laugh so they wouldn't waterboard you in the toilet again.

Both are actually innate to every human on the planet, albeit in widely divergent forms. Both can also be honed.

When I talk about the musicality of style, I mean that both music and personal voice are based in sound and rhythm. Sentences vary in length, words can be mellifluous or grating, consonants and vowels can blend or clash, and you can hear *some* sort of tune in every sentence, even if they're not all Top Forty hits. Take a pair of sentences I wrote for copper-star policeman Timothy Wilde (sentences I still joke about, because it was my second novel and I peaked too soon):

Hope, I've discovered, is a sad nuisance. Hope is a horse with a broken leg.

—*The Gods of Gotham*

Timothy is a laconic little pessimist when he's not being an incurable romantic. These sentences, though, illustrate what I mean by musical rhythm and tone. The first flows in an easy, conversational way. If you broke it into emphases, it might look like:

ba, ba da-da-da, ba da da *da da*

It's not particularly memorable and serves to launch what comes after it. But the second sentence is extremely tuneful:

ba da da *da* ba da *da da da*

In fact, it's not far off from the ubiquitous "shave and a haircut, two bits" knock, is nearly identical to the verse beat of "Prince Ali" from the Alan Menken Disney classic *Aladdin*, and even alliterates with the symbiotic one-syllable words *hope* and *horse.* I'll never write a better set of independent clauses, so they make me furious.

Style is musical, and musicality can be learned, or at least improved. What kind of music do you enjoy listening to? Are you a Schubert fan? Radiohead? Carrie Underwood? There's no right or wrong answer, and isn't that glorious? *Why* do those sounds appeal to you? Are there others you dislike, and why might that be? What song lyrics do you admire most? Listen to some Elton John before writing your circa-1975 mob drama, or scour YouTube for basic music tutorials and pop music theory demonstrations. Following this advice, like my previous, is every bit as expensive as zoning out to your favorite band, be it the Beatles or They Might Be Giants.

Regarding humor, here is my unequivocal opinion: Whether your sui-
cidal bereaved father protagonist occasionally makes a witty remark about
smoking too much, or the cat solving your cozy is a laugh riot, humor is
essential. Our genre cracks open the cruelest acts of which humans are
capable, taking responsibility for shining light into dark crevices. So does
comedy. You needn't be Janet Evanovich to incorporate jokes into your
manuscript, and they needn't even be jokes. Wry observations, sarcasm,
creative insult—humor can be as heavy or as light as you choose. But writers who take their voice too seriously, without that crucial hint of self-
deprecation or clever viciousness, will rarely wind up with a memorable
result.

So you don't think you're funny? You're probably wrong. But you at
least know what makes *you* laugh. Expand the range of stand-up comedy
you enjoy, or watch a stand-up special for the first time. Write down bits
you admire and stare at their structure. Comics survive on twist endings.
A premise, a setup, and then *boom*, the punch line is the last thing you
expected them to say. What better education for a genre writer who relies
on the element of surprise? And as free an educational experience as a
breeze in June.

Doughnuts require a pinch of salt. Salt enhances the other flavors,
making them shine all the brighter—or the darker, as the case may be.

How to Read

A writer who hates to read would be like a pilot who detests flying—
possible, but highly unlikely and probably less competent. I'm going to
assume that you love to read. I'm going to further assume that what you
read influences what you write, if only subconsciously. In my final plea
that you take advantage of the world around you, even if you're concur-
rently spending tens of thousands of dollars being taught how to perfect
your art: when you read, *pay attention* to style. Style isn't some ineffable
quality possessed only by the brilliant. It's a learned skill that will eventually mold itself to fit the shape of you.

Meanwhile, identify aspects of your favorite novels that are deliberate
stylistic choices. Here is a passage that could have been written by no one
other than Raymond Chandler:

I looked at my watch once more. It was more than time for lunch. My stomach burned from the last drink. I wasn't hungry. I lit a cigarette. It tasted like a plumber's handkerchief.

—*Farewell, My Lovely*

And presented for comparison, one written by international suspense superstar Tana French:

That night. I know there are an infinite number of places to begin any story, and I'm well aware that everyone else involved in this one would take issue with my choice—I can just see the wry lift at the corner of Susanna's mouth, hear Leon's snort of pure derision. But I can't help it: for me it all goes back to that night, the dark corroded hinge between before and after, the slipped-in sheet of trick glass that tints everything on one side in its own murky colors and leaves everything on the other luminous, achingly close, untouched and untouchable.

—*The Witch Elm*

Chandler and French wrote vastly different passages above, but to say that one is *better* than the other would be senseless. Chandler is caustic, dry, amusing. French is lush, brooding, sensual. Chandler is playing a different song than French is; their humor will make itself known in different ways; and at the end of the day, because both are consummate professionals unafraid of revealing their true selves, we can point to these quotes and know exactly which author is which.

I've made an extreme contrast here. But my hope is that if you felt at a loss when people discussed "voice" before, you are more confident after having instantly recognized the difference. If you've been trying to master style for some time, please *keep trying*. It will happen, and the harder you work, the sooner that day will come.

Meanwhile, please buy yourself a doughnut. You're attempting to better your writing, which improves my chance of being able to read what you wrote one day. You've earned it just by picking up this book.

STEVE HOCKENSMITH

Dos and Don'ts for Wannabe Writers

DO write. That means putting words together to form sentences that you actually hope other human beings will one day read. (For the reason an explanation is necessary, see below.)

DON'T spend more than three months "researching" or "brain-storming" or "outlining" or "creating character bios" for your novel. All this might—*might*—count as work on your book, but it's not writing. (See above.)

DO read.

DON'T spend too much time reading about how to write. The best way to learn to write is to write. (See above again.)

DO keep reading this book. I didn't mean for you to stop reading *our* writing advice.

Always Outline!

The why and the how of planning it out first.

JEFFERY DEAVER

The first sentence can be written only after the last sentence has been written.

—Joyce Carol Oates

The world is divided into two kinds of authors: those who outline and those who don't—the "plotters" and the "pantsers," as in seat-of-the-.

Now, nothing is more subjective than writing, and if your technique works for you, wonderful. There are superb writers producing superb novels and stories by starting with a blank page or screen and seeing where the journey takes them.

I don't work that way. I am an ardent outliner, spending six to eight months planning a novel (or a week or so in the case of a short story). The outline is finished before I write a single word of the prose. I tell my students—that is, you, at the moment—that they don't need my obsessive level of planning, but I strongly encourage them to know where they're going, and in general how to get there, before they set pen to paper or pixel to screen.

I'm going to pitch my case for the outlining process now. There are four reasons why I'm a fan.

One, why should a work of fiction be any different than any other made object? We authors create products for consumers, don't we? Would you get into a car or board an airplane that has not been built according to carefully planned-out engineering diagrams? No. An outline is an author's manufacturing blueprint—geared to creating the best, and most appealing, end result we can, and allowing us to construct it in the most efficient way possible

Two, crime novels (maybe all novels) are about structure as much as fine prose. I'd even say structure is *more* important. Look at my favorite composer, Ludwig van B. His pieces are structured to elicit the highest emotional response within the listener (our goal, too, for our readers). For instance, you don't find two adagio movements together; the second one would put you to sleep. You don't see two andante sections side by side; the second one would lose excitement. You need to pace the symphony, just like you need to pace a tale.

Yes, one can create a smart structure on the fly, but that often means huge amounts of wasted time as you go back to rewrite what you've already generated to take into account a new direction you steer your plot in after months of writing. Outlining allows you to create an overview of the structure of the story in an easy and efficient way before writing.

Three, have you ever read a book that should not have been written? Yes, I guarantee you have. And one of the reasons for that unfortunate occurrence is this: Let's say you have an idea for a bang-up first chapter. You've thought up compelling characters and thrown them into a pressure cooker of action. Naturally, your energy up, you sit down to write. Out comes that scintillating chapter, in a matter of hours. Your juices are flowing, so you keep at it. You rip through chapter 2, then—a bit slower— chapter 3. Then you slog through chapters 4 and 5 and then, a month later, at 6, you're stuck in the mud.

You look at the two hundred pages you've written and consider the blank middle and, beyond that, the equally missing-in-action ending. You wrestle with the conundrum for a while. But you just can't see anything but a cliché-ridden middle and a contrived, deus ex machina ending.

You have two choices at this point. First, the intellectually dishonest, cowardly, and shameful approach (can you guess my opinion?): you write the bad middle and contrived ending and put it out for your readers. Or second, the courageous, noble, and honest thing: you throw the whole damn manuscript away and start over. (I've done both and they are equally painful.)

But if you outline, look at what happens. You *don't* write the first chapter. You stick a Post-it note on your wall, saying "Big Exciting Chapter 1." Then you step back and start filling in plot points on other Post-its. You'll realize within two or three weeks that what you've been working on isn't a book worthy of your—and your readers'—time. You pitch out a dozen Post-its and start on something else.

Finally, outlining greatly facilitates the process of writing the book itself. Let's face it, crafting fiction is an arduous, frustrating task. There are certain scenes that I dislike writing (action, for instance). Maybe I wake up looking forward to four or five hours at my computer, but the last thing I want to write that day is another car chase. Well, since the book is outlined, I don't have to write that scene, even if it comes next in the chronology of the story. I can put it off for as long as I like. I can, in fact, write the book in any order. Middle or end first, beginning last. And those violent action sequences? I can write those when I'm in the mood to kill somebody because, for instance, my cable's out and the company says they can't get anybody out to the house for a week. Die, cable guy, die!

Two caveats on outlining. First, such fine writers as George R. R. Martin and Lee Child reportedly don't outline, and we can see what superb books they produce. But in general I do believe that most writers will find it easier and more efficient to know where they're going ahead of time.

The second caveat: My own novels and stories are very fast-paced thrillers, which take place over a very short time frame and include several subplots. That's the sort of genre that benefits greatly from outlining. If, however, you write more character-driven stories, with less emphasis on plot, then you don't need much of an outline (but, Professor Jeff says, your job will still be easier and your final product better if you have *some*).

So, that's my case for outlining. Now let me turn to how I create an outline and what it looks like. By the way, I craft outlines manually, but I understand that software programs like Scrivener have outlining functions that can be quite good.

For a novel, I begin with Post-it notes and a blank wall or bulletin board. (Short stories don't require such expansive overviews; I create those outlines directly on the computer.) The Post-its represent everything that happens in the novel: character introductions and departures, plot points, backstory and flashbacks, research. Note that at this point they're not chapters or sections of the novel. Some examples might be:

- *Rookie finds victim.*
- *Victim's husband meets with his mistress.*

- *Mistress is revealed to be cop working with Sachs and Rhyme.*
- *Car chase that ends in deadly crash.*
- *History of tanning operations in New York.*
- *Subplot 1. Doctor tells Rhyme he has unexpected illness.*
- *Reveal: commissioner's son is on the take.*
- *Clue is found in trash barge, NY Harbor.*
- *Commissioner's son about to shoot Rhyme, but they've set up a trap. He's caught.*

I paste the notes up as the ideas occur to me, adding some, discarding others, and rearranging them constantly.

Over the course of, say, a month I will end up with about one hundred of these. Because I have several subplots in my books, I use a different color Post-it for each subplot.

I know where every character is introduced, where they leave the book (under their own steam or on a medic's gurney), where every clue is planted, where the payoff of each one comes, where each reversal appears, and where the surprise endings occur.

At this point I transfer the contents of the Post-its to the computer, and now I organize the outline to represent chapters or, if I divide chapters into sections in which I shift time or perspective, those sections.

Now, I call what I do an "outline," but it doesn't resemble Sister Mary Elizabeth's seventh-grade English class outline:

I.
   A.
      1.
         a.

I use bullets points. I've written a macro in Word (the View tab, easily done) so that when I hit the F9 key, a bullet is inserted automatically. I've found it's helpful to begin each bulleted entry with the location and time of the scene (as is done in movie scripts). I also set custom margins—with the right one being very large (set to four inches), so the outline takes up only the left-hand half of the page. I'll explain why in a moment.

- *Lincoln Rhyme's townhouse, 10 a.m.*
   —*Sachs enters with evidence from tannery.*

—*Suspicious officer (Jones) arrives and reports that a hired
  killer has learned of Rhyme's involvement.*
—*Sellitto reports that the commissioner wants to take
  Rhyme off the case.*

For the next several months I continue this process, adding, removing,
and adjusting entries.

As for subplots, I don't use colored typeface or highlighting—that's too
slow and complicated—so I begin each subplot bullet point with a nota-
tion like this:

• *SSS1. Doctor's office, 11 a.m.*
  —*Rhyme is admitted. Assistant seems suspicious.*

I can easily move right to the subplots by globally searching for "SSS1,"
"SSS2," etc. In this way I can make sure the subplots progress seamlessly
in their own time and place.

When I'm comfortable with the outline, I'll print it out and mount it in
a three-ring binder.

But we're not finished yet.

Let's talk about research. At the same time I'm creating the outline, I'm
doing the research for the novel. I enjoy research and know that readers
love to learn information, whether it's about police procedure, history,
some esoteric trade or business, geography, psychology, or one of thousands of other topics. (I'm writing about outlining here, but I want to add
the caveat that however fascinating you think a subject you've researched
is, you should only include in the novel as much as is necessary to further
the plot and inform the characters. A novel should never groan under the
weight of interesting facts—which become far less interesting if an author
diverts from plot to throw in superfluous details.)

I mount all my research notes and printouts in three-ring binders as
well, all paginated.

I then return to the outline binder and insert to the right of each bullet
point a reference about where to find the research that is to be included in
that section. For instance, let's say there's an important clue in one scene
about eighteenth-century leather-tanning operations. All the research I've
done on tanning in New York City in that era is found on pages 120–22 in

my research notebook. I'll jot that reference in the outline to tell me where to look when I write that scene.

- *Lincoln Rhyme's townhouse, 10 a.m.*
  - *—Sachs enters with evidence from tannery.*   **Research 120–122**
  - *—Suspicious officer (Jones) arrives and reports that a hired killer has learned of Rhyme's involvement.*
  - *—Sellitto reports that the commissioner wants to take Rhyme off the case.*

Now it's time to make a book.

I decide what scene I want to write and put the outline and research notebooks in front of me. I read through them and begin.

You can write the book quite quickly this way. I can write a 110,000-word novel in two months, because I know where the story's going.

I'm often asked whether the final book varies from the outline. Only in small, not structural, ways. Usually I find I've killed too many people (hate it when that happens). Too many corpses results in a lessening of the emotional impact of the story. So I pull back. Occasionally I might have an unexpected moment of inspiration and go in a slightly different direction.

One final word: A criticism I've heard leveled at us plotters is that using an outline means taking a mechanical approach to what should be a fluid creative experience.

I disagree, for two reasons. First, you can see from my sample outline entries above that they are very sparse directions as to what needs to be in the scene. You will bring your considerable creative talents to deciding exactly how to craft that scene, what language to use, what metaphors and other figures of speech will work, whose point of view to inhabit, what details will make it come alive.

And second, coming up with the organization of the story is every bit as creative as deciding what words, grammar, syntax, and punctuation to use in telling it. All art works best when the left brain complements the right.

Let me leave you with another of my favorite quotations apropos of outlining:

ALWAYS OUTLINE!

Books aren't made in the way that babies are: they are made like pyramids. There's some long-pondered plan, and then great blocks of stone are placed one on top of the other, and it's back-breaking, sweaty, time-consuming work.

—Gustave Flaubert

ROB HART

The art of forgetting, and how it relates to writing stronger outlines and not getting lost:

Allow yourself the space to forget things. I use this specifically for outlining. When outlining a new novel, I write the outline, then trash it. A few days later I do it again, and trash that. I do this three or four times until I feel good about it. The idea is that, in the time in between, I always remember the good stuff, I forget the stuff that doesn't really work or interest me, and the shaky stuff will work itself out. . . .

During the editing phase I always do one pass starting with the last chapter and moving backward through the book. The idea being—you start a draft with a ton of fresh energy and by the time you get to the end you just want to be done, which is why endings can sometimes just trail off. This way you're putting fresh energy into the ending, *plus* you're seeing things out of order, which can sometimes help with plot and pacing issues.

HALLIE EPHRON

"Story is what happened. Plot is the order in which it's revealed to the reader." I was the panel moderator at the 2019 New England Crime Bake when I heard Walter Mosley use those words. That simple statement stopped me in my tracks. I repeated them. Wrote them down. And I've been pondering them ever since. One of the biggest challenges in writing a mystery involves reconciling the sequence of events ("story") with the order in which they're revealed to the reader ("plot"). The story should be obvious and logically airtight, but only in retrospect. The pleasure in reading a mystery comes from seeing past the characters' lies and obfuscations, past the author's clever misdirection, and sussing out each character's true motivations and actions.

Never Outline!

The argument for spontaneity.

LEE CHILD

The task is to write a novel. Preferably a good novel. Possibly a great novel. In your dreams, a novel so luminous it will be remembered with affection for a hundred years.

How do you even start on a thing like that? It's a big, complicated question. Ask ten different writers, you'll get seventeen different answers. And all seventeen matter, as do many dozens more. The handbook this essay appears in is packed with answers—hard-won practical advice, scalpel-sharp analysis, late-in-the-day epiphanies, and gnarled wisdom passed down from the greats, probably in a bar, maybe in the afterglow of an award ceremony. A diligent student could spend months sifting through the text, making notes, making connections, making lists, preparing.

But the diligent student shouldn't do that.

I'm going to argue in favor of spontaneity. And against overthinking, and overplanning, and certainly against making lists. Specifically I'm going to suggest: no plan, no outline. That's what I like to see. Although that four-word description is only the bumper-sticker version of something much more complex. But no less risky.

Think of the good novels you've read. What was it you liked about them? Probably many things. A strong and confident voice, no doubt, telling the tale with aplomb and authority. Through characters who for no obvious reason seem more real than made-up. Whose plight could be yours. Whose end could be yours. And so on. Many reasons, and many braids of reasons, all different, all combining and recombining in different weaves and proportions.

Very few of them concern plot.

Which is not to say great plots are not truly wonderful things. They are. We can all remember dozens of deliciously twisty stories. Especially the endings. The perfect ending is both surprising and inevitable, and we can all nominate a top five. Or ten. But be accurate. Were any of those stories not principally carried by the aforementioned voice and people and emotional arc?

It's very rare to remember a book for plot alone. Again, great characters with great voices enmeshed in a great plot make a book memorable. Absolutely. But the characters and the voices come first. They're the necessary prior condition. Without them, the plot won't even happen. Because the reader will stop reading. Or carry on, at some level grudgingly, which will make the clever twists feel manipulative, and in the end irritating, not delightful.

Character, voice, plot. Which takes the most planning? Plot, obviously, except it's a trick question. Plot is the only element of the three capable of *being* planned. Voice can't be planned. Character shouldn't be planned. Characters should just . . . *be*. But what does that really mean? It's not as airy-fairy as it sounds. Characters are—must be, can only be— based on everyone the author has ever known, met, seen, talked to, listened to, or read about, and on every fear and joy and feeling the author has ever had. If they are so based, then characters will be organic, and they will ring true. For no obvious reason they will seem more real than made-up.

Voice and character are instinctive, mined from the deep subconscious database every author carries around. No planning. Only plot requires planning. Which can subtly distort voice and character, inevitably to their detriment. If an author is leading the protagonist—or the antagonist, or both—toward a planned reveal on page 300, they run the risk of making the preceding 299 pages less natural and less authentic. In the real world, no one knows what's going to happen three weeks ahead. And if someone actually does—planning a surprise party, perhaps—it proves hard to act entirely natural as the day gets closer. The same is true of writing. Characters can start to—can be forced to—become less like people and more like pawns on a board. Voice can suffer, too. The aplomb and the authority can wobble. A tiny taint of apology can intrude, as if the author is saying, *Yeah, I know, but I need to crowbar this idiosyncrasy in now, so he has a reason to do the thing he does on page 250, which leads him directly to the thing on page 300. Otherwise I can't get him there. See?*

Ditch the plan. Ditch the plot.

Just start writing. Something will happen, sooner or later. Which sounds scary, absolutely. To quote myself from the introduction to this handbook: *The way I picture my process is this: The novel is a movie stuntman, about to get pushed off a sixty-story building. The prop guys have a square fire-department airbag ready on the sidewalk below.* The point in the introduction was not to worry about subgenres, but the image works equally well here. Jumping off a sixty-story building sounds undeniably scary, even though the guy is well paid, he's done it before, and there's an airbag waiting. Writing without an outline sounds undeniably scary, even though those authors who do it are well paid, have done it before—and I suppose the airbag metaphor translates as inevitable eventual safety: the stakes are, after all, reassuringly low. No one goes to prison for writing a bad novel.

Except really, no one ever needs that ultimate consolation, because writing without an outline is actually not scary at all. Because actually, you never do it. You're never without an outline. It's built in. Where exactly? The clues have been scattered above: *Think of the good novels you've read. . . . We can all remember dozens of deliciously twisty stories. . . . We can all nominate a top five. Or ten . . .*

You're a reader. You love this genre. You've read thousands of books. Therefore just as in: *Characters are—must be, can only be—based on everyone the author has ever known, met, seen, talked to, listened to, or read about, and on every fear and joy and feeling the author has ever had,* your internal sense of outline is already deeply baked in, based on every book you have ever read, every movie you have ever seen, every TV show, every play, and every reaction you've ever had.

It's not a sixty-story free fall, tumbling helplessly through the air. Instead it's an elegant dive, cossetted and guided and nudged left and right by the deep subconscious database every author carries around. Not scary at all. Something will happen, sooner or later. Easy enough. Because after all, how many plots are there? I remember reading Ovid's *Life of Theseus* in grammar school, in Latin. On the bus home I was reading Ian Fleming's *Dr. No,* in English. They're the same story. Two great powers are in an uneasy truce; a young man of rank volunteers for a crucial mission; he enlists the help of a young woman from the other side; he uses a technological device to prepare his exit from an underground lair, where he fights a grotesque sidekick before completing the mission; he returns home to a welcome that is partly grateful and partly scandalized.

You know all the plots already. You could plan for a thousand years and not come up with a new one. What you should do instead is trust your voice, and let your characters do what they want. By all means have a vague idea—as in, *Moby-Dick* is about a whale, and *War and Peace* is about Russia. But don't sweat the details. The reader part of your brain will tell you what needs to happen and when. Trust it. It will be busy combining and recombining all the best bits from a thousand books. Follow it. Let your characters retain their organic integrity. Let page 250 take care of itself. Take off the straitjacket. Take out the artifice. Feel the cool currents of air on your face, pushing you here, tempting you there, into sudden random connections, sudden new ideas, and wide new avenues the front part of your brain never saw at all. Try it at least once. If it doesn't work, no big deal. But if you've read enough books, and you're as bold as a stunt-man, it will.

SHELLY FROME

Perhaps the novelist E. L. Doctorow put it best when he said that writing fiction was like driving at night with only the headlight beams to guide you. You know where you're headed but have no idea what turns you'll make, who you'll meet along the way, and what influence they'll have on your journey. For my part, after I create an intriguing springboard and open-ended structure, I rely on a set of vital characters to surprise me and keep me going. Or, as Rilke, the Bohemian novelist and poet, wrote, "All art is the result of being in danger, of going as far as one can go and beyond."

The Art of the Rewrite

Turning your raw first draft into a clear, compelling story.

LAURIE R. KING

There are—rumor has it—some writers whose first draft is their final one. If you are that person, congratulations, your brain was crafted on a different planet than mine was. For most of us, the rewrite stage is an essential part of making a tight and compelling narrative from a string of ideas and character sketches. For some, it's where the fun lies.

How a writer approaches the rewrite depends a lot on what kind of writer they are. For example, outliners want a full map of the territory ahead before they set off, and happily spend large portions of their professional life working up to the actual writing, so they can visualize precisely what they're going to find as they go. Other brave souls—the "pantsers" or organic writers—plunge into the dark armed only with a flashlight and faith. For them (. . . us), outlining is a largely incomprehensible process, and they learn what the book is by letting it grow.

Q: Which is the Right Way? A: The one that keeps you writing.

For an outliner, the rewrite may amount to a survey checking that the plan worked and all the details of plot, character development, setting, mood, timeline, speech patterns, research, and so on mesh smoothly. For the non-outliner, the rewrite may take longer than the first draft did.

Another consideration is, do you write long or short? Do you blithely produce a sprawling, 800-page first draft for a cozy mystery? You'll need to get out your machete. Or is your first draft little more than 150 pages of well-developed outline? You, my friend, need to bring on the fertilizer.

Then there's the question of publication. If you're traditionally published, your house provides backup, other sets of eyes to check plot development, continuity problems, typos, and the rest. On the other hand, if you are DIY from the writing to the promotion, every bit of polish is up to you.

But no matter your situation—outliner or organic, verbose or pared-down, self- or full-service—you absolutely want to do as much as you can for your book before you turn it over to the world. Self-pub or Big Five, this is your baby, your reputation, your pride and joy. You want to give it the best possible start before you turn it out into the cold world.

Where to Begin?

Let's say you're an outliner, either by nature or by hard-won habit. You spent weeks shaping your characters, researching every setting, choosing the direction your protagonist's choices will take them. Only when you knew exactly what you were dealing with did you open a doc on your computer and type in "Chapter 1." That means when you reach the end, it's all finished, right? After all, you followed your plan closely all the way through . . . isn't that enough?

Well, no. Step one is to go do something else for a while so you can come back to your manuscript with a fresh mind. Then, read your manuscript straight through, looking at the story it actually tells instead of the one you assume is there. Does it follow the outline? Are some scenes and subplots more substantial than you'd intended, while others are thinner? If the story does follow your original plan, do you still agree with it, now that you see the results? As you read your first draft cold, trying to picture its world as if for the first time, you may notice that the story would be stronger if you shifted some emphasis from this character to that one, or that developing a formerly minor subplot would lead to some really interesting character insight.

Perhaps you didn't plan but grew your book in pure organic soil. Fine—but now is the time to make an outline, as a valuable analytical tool. Pulling your first draft to pieces lets you see the stark bones of it: when your characters are present and how they interact; the overall arc and any hesitations, distractions, and thin areas in plot development; the story's balance and internal rhythm. Does the tension build, fall away, build again, relax a little, then keep its momentum to the climax? Is there a heavy load of backstory anywhere? Is there a long stretch where the central mystery gets pushed aside?

Outlines, whether for initial planning or after-the-fact analysis, do not have to follow the classic tiered structure of *I. A. 1. a.* You can use a whiteboard with arrows, color-coded Post-its, three-by-five cards, a giant calendar page, Scrivener—whatever gives you a clear illustration of what is actually in your story, rather than what you think you put there. If you've been doing everything on-screen, sacrifice a tree branch here and print your draft out. Conversely, if you work on paper, going through your draft on a screen can show it in a new way.

The Stages

The rewrite process has stages, which again will change according to your writing style. If you've done nine-tenths of the work in the outline, much of your editorial focus will be on honing. Or if your manuscript is fluid, here is where everything becomes firm.

In any event, even if you feel certain that the structure is perfect, let your first read-through look at big structure, major adjustments, personality changes. Read without a pencil in reach, since what you're looking for is overall impressions. Are the story's bones good? Are its people real? Is its situation believable? Is its overall mood clear? Do you, the reader, *care* about it?

If the reply to any of these is "not really," then where do you need to focus? Does the plot work but the people feel shallow? Work on making them lively, distinct, idiosyncratic, strong. Are the characters great but the plot circles and dithers and wastes their time and ours? You need to dig around under the hood and fix that: What are they after? What blocks can you throw in their way? How can you build the importance of the central concern? Or perhaps you're left with the feeling that the story takes forever to get going, or it sags in the middle, or ends abruptly? Make some notes on where the flaws lie.

Now is the time for major surgery such as moving chapters around or deleting key characters. Here is where you slash and burn portions of that oversize first draft, or conversely, develop the major subplot that your brief manuscript needs. Keep cutting, moving, building until it is vaguely the size and shape you want—like a watercolor painter's background wash or a sculptor's rough cuts of a marble block. Only then, when you can see the correct outlines, do you pick up that editorial pencil and dive in.

Personally, I prefer to make all my notes, corrections, and queries on a physical printout. In part, that's because I'm old-school, but it also forces me to consider any changes twice—once when I mark the page, then again when I return to put it into the manuscript. This guarantees that if I added something on page 34, then realized a better way to do it when I hit page 119, I've had the delay for reflection, gaining perspective as to which is better for the overall story.

How many drafts? That depends on what you consider a draft. Key portions of the story may need to be reworked a number of times, others merely polished. Ideally, you will need only three or four: the raw first draft (organic writers, consider this your outline); a second that follows any major surgery; the third, where you dive deeply into the balance and readability of the story; and a final draft that you read aloud for grammar, awkward wording, pacing details, missing bits of research, and the like.

(Inevitably, a traditionally published writer will later face the comments of their editor and copyeditor, but if you've done your rewrite thoroughly, much of their work will be done.)

So, what are you looking for in this close, pencil-in-hand edit? If the major problems of structure and pacing have been trimmed away, what remains is to hone the story from plot to dialogue, smoothing away any rough patches, leaving a final draft that is clear, compelling, and direct.

The comments below are merely pointers, and are not intended to act as full editorial instructions. Most of the areas covered—genre rules, characters, plotting, rhythm, and so on—have their own essays in this volume. My task here is to guide your rewrite, and suggest where your focus should be.

What Do I Look For?

Genre awareness and consistency. Great books ignore the rules. Unfortunately, so do a lot of bad ones. Even a genius writer should be aware of expectations when it comes to length, complexity, focus, pace, and language. Is my story about a cat-owning bakery owner, or a middle-grade kid who investigates bike thefts, or a mad academic who plans to blow up the Vatican? No one kind of book is inherently "better"—but just as a middle-grade reader might blanch at a 150,000-word volume, an adult who has shelled out thirty dollars for a thriller might be irritated by a side-track into frosting. Decide what your book is, and keep every page true to its home territory in size, tone, language, and the rest.

Plot. Does the plot make sense? Do all the pieces of this complex machine turn smoothly, or are there some places where the first draft tries to cover over its uncertainty? Mystery readers are both smart and experienced, and if there are holes in your plot, if you have forced things into line so they end up where you want them, if your characters simply couldn't have done what you have them do, then the story will unravel for the reader. Map out your timeline; go over your sequence of clues, reactions, and realizations. Watch for which character knows what, and when a fact is learned. Keep all the relationships clear, and all the actions believable. And beware of coincidences, anywhere in the entire book except maybe its inciting incident.

Pacing. This is related to length, but also to what keeps a reader's attention. The slow burn of a police procedural is not the hard push of a thriller or the deceptive chattiness of a traditional mystery. Even within the style of your chosen subgenre, the pacing needs to vary, tightening and letting loose, as the reader is inexorably pulled toward the conclusion. If there are too many detours, pare them down or bring them closer to the main path.

Characters. Your protagonist may be heroic or ordinary; they may change enormously in the course of the story or remain the same person, but every step along their path needs to be clear and understood. Similarly, the antagonist—whether a Bond-world villain or a person who has simply made terrible choices—needs to be clear-cut, believable, and in some way personal to the protagonist. Supporting characters should be varied, distinct, and necessary. Can a reader tell them apart instantly, in background, personality, appearance? There's no need for close detail, especially when it comes to physical appearance, but deft touches that tie together looks with personality can make them memorable. And what about their function in the story? If two characters feel similar, could they be merged into a single more vivid one? If some of the people in your story have a background that is not your own, are they believable, or is there a whiff of cliché? A beta reader, even a sensitivity reader, from your publisher or your circle could be helpful.

Language. Are the story's grammar, vocabulary, and punctuation absolutely correct? Do you choose specific and expressive verbs, or fall back too often on adverbs, modifiers, and the verb "to be"? Is the writing simple and clean, or is it cluttered with the passive voice, unnecessary conjunctions, cumbersome phrases like "It was Mary who . . ." and words that bleed away vitality, such as "of course," "somewhat," and "very"? Is every paragraph its own unit, beginning to end, or does it contain convoluted sentences (the sign of a writer thinking her way along) and too many changes of direction? Worse, are there places where the point of view shifts with no clear signal? And what about the tone: Is the language—the words and sentences—of an action sequence different from that in a contemplative scene, or an angry one, or a silly one?

Facts. Know them. Check them. If you're writing a PI novel, it might matter to you that revolvers don't have safeties, autopsy test results can take weeks, and motorcycles don't have a reverse gear. If your book is set in 1919 England, please don't have your *teenagers* dressed in *crinolines* and taking *high tea* instead of the genteel *afternoon* variety. Mistakes undermine a reader's trust. If you are not certain, ask someone who knows, whether that involves Googling vintage car museums, buying a dictionary of historical slang, or putting out a call for courtroom expertise on your mystery writers group forum.

Background. The story's background, whether setting, situation, or characters, should be invisible, woven into the fabric of the story, not glued on in a solid block of exposition. Look very closely at any background information—the backstory—contained in your first couple of chapters, and see what can be moved or cut entirely. Perhaps that chapter 3 action sequence makes a stronger beginning, anyway. On any page, no matter where in the book, a solid block of prose can be the sign of too much exposition—also known as an info dump. Look for an unobtrusive, less detailed and more spread-out way to present key facts. And speaking of fewer details, if the book is in a series, less explanation is definitely more compelling.

Dialogue. Does your dialogue feel real? Does each character have a distinctive speech pattern that says something about their personality, whether slow and formal or in quick sentence fragments? Do any facts, clues, and pieces of background information that you've put into dialogue feel natural, like something that person might actually say? Or is it an info dump that you haven't been able to work in elsewhere?

The sound. Read your story aloud, even if you're not concerned with the peculiarities of audiobooks, where words that look fine on the page can create odd echoes or blatant misunderstandings. In the editorial stage, listening to the shape of Every. Single. Word is a tool that no writer should neglect. Whether reading it aloud (full-voiced) or following along with your writing software's audio-review function, there is nothing like hearing the words to catch missing phrases, out-of-place clues, and surviving traces of earlier drafts. And while you're at it, do keep that audiobook in mind, and see how many of your *he said*s and *she replied*s you can cut. Speech tags grow tiresome six or eight hours into a novel.

Final Draft

So like most of us, you've determined that your first draft was not your final one. We're all human, and take some tries to make things right in this very human business of writing. But setting a mess straight can be deeply satisfying, as satisfying as creating a clear, compelling story out of a rough first attempt. The rewrite is how we turn a book from a story that speaks to its author into a story that touches the world.

RAE FRANKLIN JAMES

I'm a hybrid writer.

I'm a plotter only up to a point. When I start out writing, I outline the book by chapter, and within each chapter—one-sentence scenes. I used to outline the whole book. But I discovered, for me anyway, a more effective way. I outline to what feels like the middle of the book.

Now, this is when I turn pantser.

Once I outline to the "middle," I jump ahead and actually write the last chapter. By writing the last chapter, I know who did it, why they did it, and how they did it. Then I start writing from the beginning, pretty much following my outline. With this approach, I not only know where I need to go, but what clues (and red herrings) I can plant. I connect the dots from the beginning, to the middle, to the end.

I never have writer's block.

LESLIE BUDEWITZ

Every project will hit a roadblock. Whether you're a new writer or a veteran, a planner or a pantser, whether this is a story you've labored on for years or one you're writing on a tight deadline, you will come to a point where you truly, honestly do not know what to do next.

Remember this: the same brain that created the problem can create the solution—but not if you keep thinking the same way.

So do something different. Write the next scene from the antagonist's POV, even if you don't intend to use it. Write longhand with a pen you found in the bottom of your desk drawer instead of at your keyboard, or at the communal table in the library instead of in your cozy home office. (Yes, put on shoes. Maybe your character wants to take a walk or go out for coffee.) If you write in first person, try third. If you write in third, let your character rip in a private diary only she—and you—will ever see. You're certain you know what happened three years ago that brought your characters to this point? What if you've held on to your first idea, the one that started the wheels spinning in your brain, or the one you built your synopsis on when you pitched the proposal to your editor, but it doesn't quite fit with the story as it's playing out? Toss those preconceptions. Don't know what your character does next? Make a list of ten possibilities. The sixth thing, or the tenth, the thing they would never do as a matter of principle—that's the one that's new and fresh and so exactly, perfectly right.

Whatever you've been doing, do something else. Your brain, your beautiful creative brain, will find another way, if you give it a chance.

Plot and the Bones of a Mystery

Bringing together all the elements of your novel
so it stands strong.

DEBORAH CROMBIE

When I first decided to embark on writing a mystery, I was perplexed—and terrified—by the concept of PLOT. I had an idea for a setting, a beautiful timeshare in the Yorkshire moors. I added a detective, a Scotland Yard superintendent named Duncan Kincaid on a much-needed holiday, and his colleague in London, Detective Sergeant Gemma James. But then what? Something had to happen—a plot! But what on earth was a plot, and how did you get one?

I found all kinds of definitions in books and articles. Some were contradictory—E. M. Forster's famous "plot" and "story" definitions ("The king died and then the queen died" is story; "The king died and then the queen died of grief" is plot) seemed the reverse of how I thought of things. Some theories said there was only one plot. Some said there were three, and some said there were seven, or these five:

- The Quest (think *The Lord of the Rings*)
- Rags to Riches (*Great Expectations*)
- Overcoming the Monster (*Beowulf*)
- Rebirth (*The Secret Garden*)
- Voyage and Return (*The Hobbit*)

But you can see from just these examples that most stories fit into more than one category. Frodo's journey is a classic quest, but it is also a voyage and return.

Author and literary critic John Gardner once said that there are only two stories in the world: a man goes on a journey, and a stranger comes to town. While I suppose you could shoehorn most books into a variation of those stories, neither seemed very helpful in regard to my budding novel, and none of these plot theories seemed particularly germane to a mystery. A few points did stand out for me, however.

A plot is *not* the story. A plot is a merely a *framework* for the story, a structure to hang your story on. The story is characters and setting and theme and voice, all carried along in concert by the vehicle of the plot. Plots require some sort of conflict, whether it's between characters, within the characters, or between the character(s) and the world. A plot must have forward motion. And in every plot, you have a protagonist in conflict with an antagonist while struggling to reach a goal. All of those elements are necessary. (The antagonist can be a situation as well as a person.)

There are five stages common to any plot.

1. Exposition, which introduces the characters and their situation
2. Rising action, in which a series of events (usually triggered by an inciting incident) moves the story forward
3. Climax, in which the story's tension reaches a peak
4. Falling action, which bridges the climax and the resolution
5. Denouement, which wraps everything up

Obviously, the lines between these stages are blurry, and the share each stage occupies in the novel is inexact. But generally the first two stages take up the majority of the book, while the last three can be fairly short—or, sometimes, non-existent. If a book ends with a cliffhanger, for instance, there is no resolution.

A simpler structure is the time-tested three acts:

1. Dramatic opening
2. Major plot developments
3. Resolution

But how to apply all these general tips to mystery? In the most traditional of mysteries, a crime, usually a murder, is committed, either before or after the beginning of the story. A protagonist, usually either an amateur sleuth or a professional detective, must discover the perpetrator. Eventually, all is revealed, and justice is (perhaps) done.

Here, for example, is a plot: A woman is in an unhappy marriage. Her husband dies suddenly. She must come to terms with his death and decide how she will live her life going forward. There is conflict (she is unhappy, she must deal with her feelings and make decisions) and a resolution (she sees a future for herself).

But how does this become a mystery? Let's try again, throwing in a lot more questions: A woman is in an unhappy marriage. Her husband dies suddenly. But was his death an accident? If not, was he murdered? If so, why? And by whom? The woman (or a sleuth) must discover the truth, then confront the killer and bring them to justice. You have your classic conflict and resolution, but you have added *how*, *why*, and *who*. It's now a mystery! And there are more possibilities. If the widow is the viewpoint character, and might herself be responsible for her husband's death, your plot may become psychological suspense. If the widow now fears for her own life and must try to avert her fate, you have the makings of a thriller.

To put these theories in perspective, I reread some of my favorite mysteries and took careful notes. What I discovered was that when you break the most complicated-seeming stories down to their essence, they are, in fact—once you strip away the distractions—quite simple. Murder disrupts the status quo. When the crime is solved, order is restored. It's the clothing in which you dress the body of your plot that makes a novel memorable. That clothing includes character development, setting, dialogue, and, in a mystery, the famous red herrings, or misdirections.

However, when I'm working out the initial idea for a novel, I don't plan red herrings. They flow naturally out of the progression of the story as I consider alternate possibilities, and the assumptions that the characters, especially the detectives, would make, given each set of circumstances.

Which brings us to the question of whether you are a plotter or a pantser, as these two modes of writing a mystery are often called. Plotters know where the book is going. Pantsers write by the seat of their pants, or as I like to think of it, the headlight method, where you can see only what's illuminated right in front of you. I know a number of talented and successful writers who say they are pantsers—they begin a book with a basic idea and allow the story to unfold as they write, often not knowing more than their viewpoint character does. And then there are writers who cover their walls with color-coded index cards that not only lay out the entire plot arc but fill in the details for each scene and chapter in the book. In truth, I think most writers are hybrids, falling somewhere on the plotter-pantser spectrum.

As my writing progressed, I discovered that I fall somewhat into the plotter camp. I've never begun a novel without having an idea of where I intended it to end, but I've also never outlined an entire book before starting to write. However, knowing how you want a novel to end is not the same as getting there!

You may know that there is a logical underpinning to the events in the story, but your detective—and your reader—has to get to that truth in a way that doesn't engender disbelief. This dangerous middle is what my late writing teacher, Warren Norwood, called the foggy valley. From your mountaintop (the beginning) you can see the next mountaintop (the end). But everything in between is shrouded in the swirling fog of the valley below.

How do you navigate the valley?

Over the course of writing multiple novels, I've come up with a method I think of as "story lines." I see a novel as having multiple threads. For example, there is the investigation of the crime. This is normally the driving force of the mystery novel, and one thread. But perhaps you also have the sleuth's relationship with a professional partner, which should progress in some way. That's two threads. Does the sleuth also have a romantic interest? That's three threads. Perhaps the detective has a child who is trying to deal with the complications of her parent's new relationship or job. That's four threads. And what if there is a backstory essential to understanding what is happening in the present? That's five threads. And so on—you get the picture. And I do mean literally a picture, because I make a chart. For my early books, I used big pads of blank newsprint. These days I usually just tape sheets of printer paper together to get the size I need for a particular book.

Admittedly, I write complex books, always with multiple viewpoints, sometimes with multiple timelines, so for each book I might have eight to ten threads. Each thread gets a labeled column in a different color. At the top of each column is the status of that story thread at the beginning of the novel.

For example, in my novel *No Mark Upon Her*, a female police officer goes missing while rowing on the Thames. I labeled the first column of my plot chart *Rebecca Meredith's Murder*, and began it with a bullet point that said "Becca Meredith takes a scull out alone at dusk." At the very bottom of that column, after a huge, scary blank space, I filled in "Murderer revealed." I then made a bullet point for each incident that had to occur in order to logically get from the first thing on the column to the last.

The second column was *Duncan's investigation, Henley*. The third, *Gemma's investigation, London*, as my two detectives are working different aspects of the same case. The fourth was *Backstory*, because of course I had to know all the characters' histories, and how things that happened in the past led up to their current situations. I added more columns that had to do with the subsidiary characters, and with Duncan and Gemma's children. Each column had its own start and end points, with the relevant incidents filled in between. (I've tried mind-mapping software, but it doesn't work nearly as well for me as plain old pen and paper.)

Many of these plot points overlap, which is fine. The chart still allows me to see what is necessary to move the story forward (not to mention have lots of fun drawing crisscrosses between the columns). It also may seem a bit juvenile, like playing a game—but then that's exactly what making up stories is, even if the stories contain serious material and themes.

None of these plot points in a column needs to be fixed in stone. It's just a way of kick-starting the creative process, of generating some signposts in the foggy valley. Characters will develop as you write, and they may direct the plot in a direction you couldn't have foreseen.

Does that mean that your plot should be controlled by the characters, rather than by the structure you've given it? Again, I think most novels are a hybrid, part plot-driven and part character-driven. If you don't listen to your characters, your plot, no matter how well-planned, will feel flat. On the other hand, you don't want your characters to run off to Mars (unless you're writing science fiction).

So, now you have this messy but fun chart. What do you do with it?

Taking the incidents from the beginnings of the columns on the chart and interweaving them allows me to block out the first few chapters of a book. From there I can see how things are developing, what I've already covered, what needs to happen next. This is simpler, but just as applicable, for a single narrative viewpoint. It also lets you see if you've left out points that are necessary for the logical conclusion of your story. If, for instance, in order to solve the crime, your detective must learn early in the story that one suspect drinks only black coffee, you will be sure to include that.

I write in filmic, discrete scenes—a slice of action, then a break—which is one device that can boost your story's narrative tension. If a scene ends on a high point, the reader will want to turn the page to see what happens next. Narrative tension, however, is not the same as plot—it is a means of pulling your reader *through* your plot. Think of it as your novel's connective tissue, holding the bones together. Narrative tension is of course produced by your big questions, who did it or why, but it can also be generated by many small things. Will your character be late for an important meeting? Will a lost dog come home? Will Reacher find a toothbrush and a change of clothes?

But what if you've done all of these things and you reach the middle of the book and you're still . . . stuck? It's easy to write yourself into a box where the ideas you've developed about your story seem like the only options. It helps to remind yourself that this is *fiction*, not reality, and that it's *your* story. Play a little game of "What if? And then?" with yourself. Go back to the major turning points in your story, and sketch out a different alternative. Maybe there was another reason the baby was left on the church doorstep, or maybe your original murderer is not the culprit at all. Just allowing yourself to push the boundaries you yourself have set can open things up and get your story going again.

And when all else fails, remember to *raise the stakes*! Readers don't read mysteries just for the puzzle. You have to give them emotional engagement. How does the solution of the case impact your protagonist, and what are the consequences for your characters? If your reader stays up until the wee hours to finish your book, it will be because they care what happens to the characters you've created.

So get out your map, and remember to enjoy the journey through your novel! Because if you are having fun, you can be sure that your reader will be, too.

TIM MALEENY

A great plot isn't propelled by things going as planned, but by things going horribly wrong.

Great opening lines, like great stories, don't start at the beginning. They start in the middle of the action and dare the reader to catch up.

Suspense is what happens when ordinary people find themselves in extraordinary circumstances.

Love your characters, but treat them like dirt.

ROBERT LOPRESTI

When a new friend learned that I have a full-time job and also write fiction, she asked: "How do you find the time?" I gave my usual answer with a shrug: "If you write a page a day, at the end of the year you have a novel." That does *not* mean you have a first draft ready to send to a publisher. My stuff tends to go through at least five edits, and more often ten. Because I know that no sentence in my first draft is likely to go through the editing process unscathed, I give myself permission to write in a rush, dumping words from my brain onto the keyboard as fast as possible. As bestselling mystery writer Harlan Coben said: "You can fix bad pages. You can't fix no pages." . . .

Should I outline my book or fly by the seat of my trousers? I'd like to offer an alternative. I call it the Rising Island method. Picture a mountain range stretching for many miles, but all of it underwater. Now the mountains start to rise. A few peaks start breaking the surface, appearing as isolated islands. Time passes and more islands break the surface, and they start to link together until finally the entire mountain range is visible. The mountain range is my novel. The highest peaks are the parts I know best. I start by writing the book's high points (ha ha) and each new chapter teaches me about the sections still to come. The islands slowly begin to show their shapes. . . .

If you write fiction you have probably considered the motives of your characters. But what about the motives of your *readers*? If you want them to finish your book—and especially if you want them to buy your next one—you have to make them care about what you write. You have to give them a reason to turn the page. You have a lot of competition for their attention.

Diversity in Crime Fiction

Enriching your novel by writing characters,
not categories.

FRANKIE Y. BAILEY

Let me be candid: If you write crime fiction with diverse characters, you are opening yourself up to criticism. Sooner or later you are going to put your foot in it, and someone—a reader or another writer—will call you out on what you "got wrong." This complaint may not be about a factual error. Instead, you may be accused of being tone-deaf or too lacking in understanding to provide nuance or cultural context. This may happen even if you have done your research.

As writers, we find "doing diversity" challenging, because our desire to have control over our characters and to tell a good story doesn't make us omniscient. Neither are we above the fray. We have our own agendas. We bring all of our conscious and unconscious (implicit) biases, all our irrational beliefs and feelings about other people, to our work. Writers— good writers—are curious about other people and their lives. But we may still feel superior or uneasy or repulsed. We make choices about whether we will deal with our feelings on the page or ignore the existence of the people we find problematic.

You may consider the whole "diversity thing" a made-up, left-leaning political issue that creates unnecessary tension between groups. In that case, you are probably going to skip the rest of this chapter.

On the other hand, you could accept the challenge of meeting the issue head-on and working with other writers to normalize fiction that reflects the world we live in. What I am inviting you to do in this chapter is to look around you and listen and think about how you might be more inclusive in your fiction. If nothing else, it may get you out of any writing rut that you've fallen into.

With that said, let's turn to some suggestions about how you might approach the issue of diversity. Diversity takes many forms—including race/ethnicity, nationality, gender, class, sexuality, age, physical and mental status, education, religion, politics, region of the country, and military status. Often, we stumble even trying to find the language to describe these differences.

But when we write, we have characters, setting, and a plot. We need to weave aspects of diversity through all of these elements of our stories.

Intersections

Humans are complex creatures. No single inherent or acquired trait defines us. We are the products of nature and nurture. How people view us and how we view other people can be understood from the perspective of what law professor Kimberlé Williams Crenshaw describes as "intersectionality." That is, how we interact with and perceive one another is based on overlapping systems of privilege and oppression. Concepts such as race, gender, and class are socially constructed in the course of human interaction. However, such concepts both reflect and sustain the power of dominant groups to ascribe traits to others from a position of privilege. In our society, to describe someone as "a white, suburban wife and mother" speaks not only to demographic categories but to assumptions that those categories have meaning. That meaning is in contrast to "a Black single mother from an inner-city neighborhood." Although the two women are both mothers, one is viewed through the lens of her "whiteness" and her suburban setting, the other through the lens of her "mother-headed household" in a neighborhood that was once known as a "ghetto" but is now described in coded language. Most of us have stereotypes about who these two women are and how they live. We have a problem in real life and in our fiction when these stereotypes lead us to view people who are unlike ourselves as an unknowable and threatening "other," as "them" or "those people."

That is the challenge we face as writers. Crime fiction is one of the genres—along with historical fiction, horror fiction, sci-fi, inspirational fiction, and romance—that has much to say about how we interact with one another. As writers, we explore issues of "crime" and "justice," both slippery concepts dependent on time and place. Recognizing diversity and normalizing inclusiveness in our works may be a difficult process for some of us. We can begin by simply embracing awareness.

Characters and Subgenres

When you begin to populate your short story or novel, there will be some obvious characters based on the subgenre. Characters in a cozy novel will differ from those in a hard-boiled noir or police procedural or thriller. In the 1920s and '30s, during the "golden age" of the classic detective story and the birth of tough-guy crime fiction, the characters who were not white males or females were often walk-ons. These characters were so minor that they were often nameless. They were "invisible" as they performed a function such as serving a meal. They also sometimes appeared as thugs and criminals. Sometimes these minor characters were not physically present as individuals. Instead, their group was referenced in the form of an artifact or a turn of phrase. For example, in Agatha Christie's 1939 novel, now known as *And Then There Were None*, all the characters are white. But this is the third title the book has carried: the first two referenced racially offensive children's rhymes. The first edition of the book also contained a racial slur used by two of the characters to refer to something suspicious. Of course, Christie was not alone. See Raymond Chandler and other hard-boiled writers. During this era, blackface was still acceptable in films, and characters casually thanked one another for being generous, gracious, or honorable by saying "That's mighty white of you."

This is our legacy, but you now have options as you cast your short story or book. We'll get to setting and plot in a moment, but let's begin with subgenre. If this is your first venture into the idea of diversity, no one expects you to jump in feet first. In fact, that would probably be a risky thing to do. But you can take a cue from television shows and movies and introduce diverse characters in secondary roles—the guy in the forensics lab, the judge who presides over the trial, the neighbor who drops by, the math teacher—and in bystander roles—a woman on the subway reading a book, the man pushing a baby in a carriage, the student putting up a poster about a rally, the cabdriver who suggests a restaurant.

To come up with your cast of characters, you can figuratively and literally draw from a hat. Suppose you're writing a cozy, and your protagonist is a dog walker. You feel comfortable writing from her point of view. She is like you and the people you know well. Fine. But she has clients who pay her to walk their dogs. Who are these people? Toss some diversity options into your hat. Yes, I do mean this literally. Write some casting options down on slips of papers. Put the slips of paper in a container, shake, and draw out one at a time.

I know this sounds like a less than elegant approach to incorporating diversity. But it is easy, and it will get you started. Or keep you going when you start to overthink this and panic.

Okay, you pull out one of the slips. A Black male. You don't know anything else about him yet, but you do know that he has a dog and it needs walking. You also know that stereotypes are the death of good fiction. So, maybe he's at home but he doesn't have the time or ability to walk his dog during the day. Maybe he has a home office and is seeing his tax clients, or he's writing his tell-all memoir, or he has a chronic illness. Maybe all your protagonist knows is that he isn't at home during the day, but she doesn't know what he does. If your dog walker's clients are among the victims or suspects, then you will need to learn more about him. But you might also want to think about his dog. Certain breeds of dogs are stigmatized, too. For example, a pit bull or Rottweiler. In books, these dogs are often the bad guy's dog of choice. But maybe your character is like the bodybuilder who was featured in a news article talking about the Chihuahuas that he loves—since a Chihuahua saved his life. Maybe your protagonist's Black rap musician client has a collie because he grew up watching *Lassie*. Or, if he does own a Rottweiler, is his dog vicious, or a well-socialized canine that he adopted as a puppy?

Remember, you don't need to announce what you're doing or have your dog walker lecture your reader. Cast your characters matter-of-factly, allow all of them to have a range of possibilities, and then keep moving.

Of course, if you want to point out a character's implicit biases, you can do that. For example, there is a moment in the 1974 film adaptation of *The Taking of Pelham One Two Three* when Walter Matthau, the Transit Authority protagonist, goes to meet the NYPD inspector he has been communicating with over the phone about the hijacking of a subway train. Matthau looks surprised when the door of the police car opens, and he sees that the inspector is African American. He stammers, "I thought . . . I don't know what I thought." That's it. No response from the inspector—and they get down to business. But the scriptwriters have given the audience an opportunity to check their own assumptions.

Are there types of clients that your dog walker avoids? Clients she takes only because she really needs the money? Clients she has come to believe are unreasonably demanding?

Who are her other clients? Back to the hat. A veteran whose wife has died? A mother with an autistic child? A rabbi? The possibilities are endless, but you don't need to make every character a nod at diversity casting. You can start small—a character or two—as you begin to explore opening up the world of your fiction.

Settings and Diversity

There are some settings that limit the diversity of your characters. For example, a male maximum-security prison, an Arctic expedition, a Navy SEAL team, and a SWAT team are all more likely to have males than females. How would the presence of a woman change the dynamics? What about Harlem in the 1920s and '30s? This was the Jazz Age and the Great Depression. What characters might your protagonist encounter on a trip uptown to Harlem one evening?

In many stories, in genres from westerns to mystery, sci-fi to mainstream literature, an "outsider" arrives. Having your protagonist visit a place as a tourist or as someone who has taken a job or come to find someone or something offers an opportunity to have your character interact with people who are different from them.

Depicting settings by focusing on the details rather than with generic descriptions can be powerful. Suppose your protagonist is driving up to a "trailer park." What he focuses on tells us as much about him as about the people who live there. Walking downtown, does he "see" the homeless woman who calls out to him? Does he pause because he notices the kitten curled up in her lap or the little boy huddled beside her? What does he do? If you're clever, what he sees in a setting could even jog his memory or send his thoughts about the case off in another direction.

Plotting and Research

If you are a plotter, you will have thought about how diversity fits into your plot before you begin to write. If you are a pantser who plunges in and powers through your first draft, you may go with whoever walks through the door. In either case, writing with awareness that you want to find opportunities to diversify your cast of characters and settings makes it more likely that this will happen. This may mean that in the beginning, you will have to spend more time preparing to write if you are a plotter, or more time revising your first draft if you are a pantser. In either case, you may need to do some research.

Social scientists often quote C. Wright Mills about the "sociological imagination." Mills made the argument that we exist within a social world. Who we are and who we become is shaped not only by our personal characteristics but also by what occurs in the world around us. For example, if we talk to our grandparents, we might discover that their beliefs about thrift and waste were similar to those of other men and women who survived the Great Depression. If we look at women who came of age during the women's movement of the 1960s, we might find that even those who did not take part in marches or protests describe themselves as feminists. Therefore, Mills encouraged us to exercise our imagination in understanding how social forces shape our lives.

Biographies and autobiographies of real people illustrate how the events of an era affect the lives of individuals. You can incorporate this into your fiction writing. Whether your book is set in the present, the recent past, or long ago, a timeline of major events during that era (available online, library, or bookstore) will also be a useful reminder of what you might have forgotten. You can begin with a list of world events—then move closer to country, region, state, city. Maybe you're interested in specific events. There are timelines for those as well—music, culture, riots. Where were your characters during 9/11 or Hurricane Katrina or the Covid-19 pandemic? How did this affect their lives? Your police officer? The man she is arresting? What are they bringing to the encounter?

When you have your list of events, go and do some research. The internet is helpful for a first look. You may dig deeper later, but right now you are looking at events that your characters would remember—because they were traumatized, or excited, or it was the best day of their life. What about the family or the community that your characters are or were a part of?

How did those people feel about this event?

Suppose you find one event that had a local impact in a real place. Could you use what happened in that place as inspiration for an event in your fictional setting? Were people involved who might inspire your depiction of your fictional character? Newspaper and magazine articles are a valuable resource.

Even with minor characters, there are opportunities to comment on their social world. A car's bumper sticker (STOP DOMESTIC VIOLENCE) or a runner's T-shirt (BOSTON STRONG), observed in passing, is a nod to a much larger reality.

As you do more research, you'll be reminded that humans—whatever our backgrounds—have much in common. Do you remember hearing of Abraham Maslow's "hierarchy of needs" in a psychology class? Maslow argued that satisfying our needs motivates our behavior. To reach the higher-level needs, we must first resolve the more basic needs we all have. According to Maslow, in order of immediacy, our needs are:

Physiological Needs
Safety
Love and Belonging
Self-Esteem
Self-Actualization

If you think about your characters in their social world, trying to satisfy their needs, you can begin to develop empathy for them. You can begin to perceive the world from their standpoint.

If your new and more diverse characters will play pivotal roles in your short story or book, or will be recurring characters, you should know more about them. You might begin by identifying the issues about which they might have strong opinions. Your character is an individual, a member of a category but not defined by it. For example, not all African Americans are liberals. All groups have generational differences with regard to politics and religion. You are not required to take a side. You can have characters with different points of view who discuss and argue. That's what happens in the real world.

However, you should think about "cultures of memory"—the collective memories of a group who share cultural experiences. In the United States, the Fourth of July is a summer holiday, a weekend when (in normal times) many people barbecue or attend parades or go to an amusement park. But it is a less than inspirational holiday for African Americans who remember that when European Americans were celebrating the birth of a new nation, the slaves were still in bondage. This is why Frederick Douglass, escaped slave and abolitionist, began a speech he was invited to make by wondering, "What to the Slave is the Fourth of July?" This cultural memory of slavery in the midst of freedom might seem irrelevant to your story. But if your story is set in July, you might want to know if your character intends to celebrate "Independence Day" on July 4 or already did so on Juneteenth (June 19).

All groups have a culture of memory. For example:

Native Americans: Trail of Tears, Ghost Dancing, and the Wounded Knee Massacre
Mexican Americans: Bracero program, Zoot Suit Riots, Sleepy Lagoon murder case
Chinese Americans: Chinese Exclusion Act, murder of Vincent Chin
Japanese Americans: Executive Order 9066 and the internment camps
White southerners: Sherman's March to the Sea

Not to worry. Much of this information is readily available. There are experts who will be happy to answer your questions at colleges and universities and in local and state libraries. The Library of Congress is also an important resource.

Readers and Feedback

If you are writing a story with a character who is a forensic scientist, you might try to arrange an interview with a real person who works in a crime lab. Similarly, if you're creating a character who has a background different from your own, you might want to reach out to someone who can tell you if you're "getting it right."

You may have heard someone mention hiring a sensitivity reader to have a look at a manuscript. This professional reader is usually a member of a marginalized group and/or someone with experience in the area of diversity and inclusion, They will advise you about aspects of your characterizations, settings, and/or plot that might be problematic. Working with a sensitivity reader may allay your concerns. However, as when hiring any professional, you should seek information about the process from trusted sources (e.g., writers' organizations).

More often writers will seek out a member of a marginalized group and ask that person to serve as an unpaid beta reader. But even when you feel that you are ready for feedback, you should not assume that you can simply ask someone who is a member of a group you've written about to read your manuscript and provide suggestions. The person you ask may be delighted to hear that you are working to be more inclusive. This reader and/or fellow writer might be happy to help you in your journey. Or this person may resent being asked to educate you about "diverse characters" just because they happen to be a member of that group. This person might be thinking that if you can educate yourself about serial killers, you should be able to learn about other people who have normal lives. They may be having a bad day and just not up to dealing with what you need to know so that you can write your book. So, as in the case of anyone you are asking to provide "expert" insight, please practice good manners. Pause to take a breath and gauge the reaction of the person with whom you're talking about your work in progress.

Rather than asking for a seal of approval for what you have written, you might instead ask your informant (in the social science usage of the term) to tell you how readers with various viewpoints might perceive this character. You might also ask for recommendations of nonfiction books and documentaries that you may not have come across. Your questions should reflect the research you have already done, and demonstrate that you are willing to do the work required for authenticity.

Ideally, you will find beta readers from a variety of backgrounds who are willing to provide you with feedback. Finding and connecting with people from diverse backgrounds will be good for your writing—and might change your life.

ELAINE VIETS

My grandfather was a security guard. He worked weekends, holidays, and nights when temperatures plummeted below zero and frozen winds blasted the empty parking lots. He never said, "I don't feel like guarding the warehouse tonight. I'm blocked." My grandmother babysat. She never said, "I'm not watching those brats today. I'm blocked." So when I spoke at a high school, a student asked, "What do you do about writer's block?"

"Writer's block doesn't exist," I said. "It's an indulgence."

The Protagonist

Your hero: the one we relate to, the one who drives the story.

ALLISON BRENNAN

Character Is Story

One of my best friends told me early in my writing career that "story = character + conflict." This phrase stuck with me first because I didn't want to believe that the core of fiction could be summarized in five words: *story equals character plus conflict*. Yet the more I tried to disprove the theory, the more I proved it was true.

The key point here is that your characters—and, specifically, your protagonists—are the primary drivers of the story. That, in fact, *all* stories are character-driven.

I don't know who said this, but it's a quote that has stuck in my head for many years: *The truth of character is expressed through the choice of your actions.* Consider this the gospel for *your* fictional characters. Your character will reveal himself *through* his actions. This is how readers identify the good guy, the bad guy, the victim, the mentor, and other important characters. Just like a picture says a thousand words, so do actions.

A Compelling Protagonist

Characters make or break your story. You can have a complex plot with a cool twist and write dialogue better than Elmore Leonard, but without great characters, your story will flop. *All* stories are character-driven.

No character is more important than your protagonist.

A protagonist, by definition, is "the leading character or one of the major characters in a drama, movie, novel, or other fictional text."

What you *really* want in a compelling protagonist is a "real" person. Real people have flaws. They might drink too much, or have a difficult relationship with their parents, or have made a mistake in their past (a *believable* mistake, like drunk driving or cheating or stealing) that they struggle with—either because of guilt or because they are pulled to go back to their old ways.

Readers need characters they can root for—characters they want to see overcome their flaws.

Readers also want characters who do things they might not do, say things they would never say. Essentially, characters who are "larger than life" . . . but *realistically* so. (Of course, this need for realism applies less to the popular superhero genre. But even superheroes have flaws.)

Flaws aren't physical or things done *to* the character. It's not a flaw to use a wheelchair, to be the victim of crime, or to be overweight. A flaw is a *character trait* that the character wants to fix, or should fix, because it's preventing them from becoming the person they want to be.

Some of the best flaws are also attributes. For example, if your character is naturally distrustful (likely because of some past event), ask yourself: How does that hurt her? How does that help her? Any flaw should be a positive *and* a negative.

A great protagonist can be rough around the edges and flawed, but they will generally do the right thing (or the wrong thing for the right reasons). For example, in the movie *Romancing the Stone*, Michael Douglas's character is rude and threatening, but you know pretty much from the beginning that, at his core, he's a good guy, because of a pivotal scene: he has the chance to kill the bad guy (shooting him in the back as he's running away), but he doesn't. (Of course, that decision comes back to put him and others in jeopardy—which makes it a great plot point!)

A protagonist is also going to care about others—even if just a family member. They could be a teacher who works with special-needs children, or a soldier who is loyal to his band of brothers. A nurse who works with the terminally ill, or a lawyer who fights to help the elderly who've been scammed. A protagonist has a care, love, or commitment deeper than the love of self. While this may or may not be an important part of the story itself, it will show the protagonist in a positive light.

When writing a compelling protagonist, keep these points in mind:

- A protagonist or hero should drive the story (remember: story = character + conflict).
- They possess common traits that we admire and that set them apart from other characters, such as intelligence, loyalty, duty, courage, and perseverance.
- They have a relatable flaw—they can't be perfect, but their flaw should be something they are aware of (or will become aware of) and that we, as a reader, can understand or relate to.
- Even when they make mistakes, in the end they will always do the right or just thing.
- In crime fiction especially, the protagonist is often driven by the need for truth, answers, justice—find out why.

Many authors write compelling, interesting protagonists. Below are two series I read that illustrate exceptional attention to the main character and how their flaws both help and hurt them:

Mickey Haller, a workaholic lawyer created by Michael Connelly, is a borderline antihero protagonist. He's kind of sleazy, he often represents low-life criminals, but he has a noble strength. His commitment to his clients and job (and making money) has cost him his relationship with his wife and son. He wants to be better, he *wants* his family, but has to battle himself to be better not only for them but for *him*. The complexity of his character, coupled with his desire to find the truth, makes us want him to overcome his very real flaws and achieve his goals.

Eve Dallas, the determined futuristic cop created by J. D. Robb, is clearly a hero protagonist. Her background is complex and violent, and we feel for her . . . but her violent background isn't a *flaw*. It's part of who she is and creates situations that she has to overcome, such as nightmares. She has trouble befriending and trusting people. She views the world literally. It takes her many, many books to learn to trust, to understand the value of friendship, to see nuances in relationships. These are the flaws that she struggles with—and while they stem from her past, they clearly impact her present.

Protagonist as Villain

David Baldacci said, "But protagonists are protagonists and heroes are heroes."

It's important to recognize that while in crime fiction the protagonist is *usually* also the hero, by definition, the protagonist doesn't *have* to be the hero.

There are two primary types of villain protagonist. The first is the "unreliable narrator," which has become popular in crime fiction. While Gillian Flynn was certainly not the first to use this technique, she's one modern author who popularized it today. Readers generally love or hate the unreliable narrator, and this type of protagonist is difficult to do well because readers will often feel cheated if they learn they are being lied to. You need to give them enough clues so they can figure it out along the way, rather than pulling the rug out from under them at the end of the book. I, personally, am not a fan of unreliable narrators. The stories don't satisfy me in the same way that those with traditional protagonists do. But it is a valid storytelling trope.

The other type of villain protagonist is like Joe in the *You* series by Caroline Kepnes (also a Netflix series). Joe is the protagonist—the story is told through his eyes. He is also a villain—he's a stalker, a killer, obsessed with the fact that he has left evidence of his crimes.

A good villain protagonist will also have one or more redeeming qualities. (In fact, any compelling villain—protagonist or antagonist—will have a redeeming quality. It's what makes them complex and interesting and makes them more relatable, sympathetic, and at times even scarier.) In the *You* series, Joe has a strong attachment to children. He helps an abused child *even though* by doing so, he risks being caught for his crimes.

I teach a workshop called "The Villain's Journey" that is built on the premise that the "villain is the hero of his own journey," discussed by Christopher Vogler in *The Writer's Journey*. If you're writing a villain protagonist, this is a good point to keep in mind.

The Antihero

By definition, an antihero is "a central character in a story, movie, or drama who lacks conventional heroic attributes." An antihero *can* be your protagonist. They are very popular in superhero fiction and comics—think Jessica Jones, Daredevil, Batman, Harley Quinn. More literary examples might include Jack Reacher, Jay Gatsby, Huckleberry Finn, and Tom Ripley (though he might be considered a villain protagonist). Han Solo is initially portrayed as an antihero in the original *Star Wars* movie, but he grows over the course of the story into a heroic role and never wavers from there.

Some people consider Walter White from the TV series *Breaking Bad* to be the epitome of an antihero. I would argue that while he started that way, he devolved into the villain protagonist. Compare him to Walter's young partner in crime, Jesse Pinkman, who I consider to be a true antihero. Every time Walter is faced with a clear moral choice, he chooses the immoral or evil action—[**Spoiler alert!**] letting Jesse's girlfriend die; poisoning a child; plotting to kill Gale. Every time Jesse is faced with a clear moral choice, he chooses the moral or just action (saving the little boy, going to the DEA when he learns that Walter poisoned a kid). When Jesse actually commits a crime that goes against his moral core (killing Gale) he spirals down into despair, while whenever Walter commits a crime, he justifies it—and, in fact, glorifies his decision.

When writing an antihero protagonist, keep in mind the primary reasons why they are successful in fiction:

- They are flawed (usually in bigger/deeper ways than a traditional hero protagonist).
- Their moral complexity mirrors our own.
- They are unpredictable.
- They have a moral code (it may be different from ours, but it is important to them).
- We root for them—we want them to be redeemed, and we ache when they fall.

Strengths versus Weaknesses

I started this essay by talking about flaws because this is the area that I see most new writers struggle with—either giving their characters physical attributes that are treated as flaws (like a woman struggling with her weight) or heaping on the tragedy (a guy loses his parents, then his family, then his girlfriend, then his job, and is framed for murder . . .). What is most important to me is that the flaw needs to show readers your character is *real*. That they *could* exist in the world you have created.

As important as flaws—and maybe more important—are your protagonist's strengths.

What *you* consider a strength is important, because you'll be better able to convey that strength to readers through your protagonist.

Donald Maass, in his book *Writing the Breakout Novel*, asks this:

What does "strength" mean to you? Cunning? Stamina? Insight? Intuition? Wisdom? Outspokenness? Cultural pride? Leadership? Knowledge? Open-mindedness? Reverence? Humor? Mercy? Hope? Evenhandedness? Thrift? Gambling for a good cause? Perseverance? Humility? Trust? Loyalty?

His point is that your protagonist's strength needs to be something that not only *you* find admirable but readers will find admirable. He goes on later to say that there are two particular qualities that leave a lasting impression on readers: forgiveness and self-sacrifice.

Your readers will be drawn to your protagonist *because of his strength and in spite of his flaws.* This means his strength is what makes him "better"—makes him someone they aspire to be, doing things they wish they could do—while his flaw makes him feel real and believable.

Avoid Stereotypical Flaws

- A prostitute with a "heart of gold"
- A cop who drinks too much
- An angry crime survivor

This isn't to say that your jaded detective can't drink one too many or be a recovering alcoholic—both perfectly acceptable tropes in crime fiction. It's to say that a stereotype shouldn't be your protagonist's primary flaw or character trait. Consider flaws that average people can relate to, and give your protagonist the ability to address, fix, or at least understand their flaws.

Food for Thought

As you think about your protagonist, ask yourself some basic questions:

- What type of protagonist are you writing and why (hero, antihero, villain)?
- Why do they do what they do? For example, why is she a cop? Why is he a psychiatrist? Don't limit this question to career choice, but ask it every time the character makes a decision, especially if the decision has consequences (good or bad or both). *Why does your protagonist make that decision?* This will help you understand them better. (Remember: action conveys character!)
- Consider how the protagonist interacts with people (friends, neighbors, colleagues, family, strangers). Does she treat one group differently than another? Why?
- What is your protagonist's primary flaw? How is that flaw a weakness? How is that flaw also a strength? Does your character see this as a flaw, and if so, do they want to fix it?
- What is your protagonist's primary strength? How is that strength also a weakness? How does that strength impact the story, both good and bad?

Great writing and storytelling draw in your readers, but a compelling protagonist keeps them turning the page.

Whenever I run into a nagging problem of plotting or motivation that won't go away, I find that sleeping on it helps, particularly when I follow a certain path. First, I try to define the problem in a sentence, such as "Why doesn't Amanda call the police right away?" or "Why does Ben resent his son so much?" I find that when I'm awake, such questions often inspire answers that are unsatisfying and predictable. Letting my subconscious solve the problem often works for me.

The Villain of the Piece

Your hero in reverse:
the forces that create a vivid villain.

T. JEFFERSON PARKER

Villains, whether real or fictional, don't just pop up into our imaginations. They are products of specific times and places, as are the stories and headlines in which they appear. They are shaped by history and the hard facts of time and geography.

So, it's the author's job to understand the time and place in which the story unfolds, which, dauntingly, can be any time and any place. You as a writer have—just for starters—all of planet Earth from which to choose your beat and commence your assignment. Such freedom can be intimidating. Should I tell a story about pre-Columbian Mesoamerica or 1930s Berlin? Stone Age Australia or twenty-first-century San Diego? These are weighty questions for anyone beginning a journey that may easily take years to complete. But once you've decided on the where and when, the *what* can begin to grow, and with that, your villain can be born. Time and place inform character.

Which means that a villain reacts to the pressures that are forming them, as does an oak tree or a car tire or a volcano. In my first published book I wrote about a young artist—a painter—framed for and convicted of a murder he didn't commit. Of course, he gets out of prison and proceeds to set things right. His notion of setting things right is extreme and vivid, always good qualities in a villain.

This Newton-like law of fictional action and reaction keeps you, the author, true to your villain. Because you understand the forces that have shaped them, you can accurately create their reactions. Which leads to another action—often by a protagonist—thus continuing the physics-like chain of events that is the story.

Probing a little deeper, I see two types of villain: the private and the public. The private ones seek no acknowledgment for their deeds (Raskolnikov, Hannibal Lecter, Edgar Allan Poe's guilt-riddled murderers). In fact, they shun the spotlight and avoid detection. The public villains, on the other hand (Richard III, the Joker, terrorists) proclaim themselves, trumpet their wickedness, and revel in the calamity.

Both kinds of villain can work in fiction, sometimes beautifully, as the examples cited above show. But whether private or public, your antagonist must absolutely have two things: a clearly motivated program, and specific, detailed results. All the better if their programs are diabolically clever and utterly within their skills. And better yet if their results are specific and horrendous.

I've written plenty of both kinds of villains. Back in the eighties, when I began to be published, the serial killer was in vogue. Thomas Harris had given us a "new" kind of private villain—maybe the apex of the type. The serial killer entered us like a virus. And is still very much inside us today.

For a few years I resisted, but finally, inspired by this fresh villainy, I built three novels around three very private psychosexual killers. They were good enough crime novels—credible, atmospheric, and very, very dark. I wrote hard. I wrote those three books with the same intention with which I write all my novels—for each to be better than the last. I do remember feeling somehow infected by those villains by the end of my workday. After so much time inside the heads of these characters I needed a brisk physical workout or bike ride, a hot shower, and a strong drink. Sometimes, enough really is enough. I asked myself: Do we need more villains like these? Is there *more* I should be doing? Well—no and yes. And that was the end of my serial killer days.

Some rich years followed. *California Girl*, *Silent Joe*, the Merci Rayborn series—all featured private villains of a less psychopathic variety, including a deceitful U.S. congressman; a young, conscience-less Little Saigon gangster; a Russian strongman out strictly for profit in the United States; a brutal husband covering up the deeds of his even more brutal wife.

Then came a series of private villains in my Charlie Hood books: an

MS-13 henchman; a corrupt young sheriff's deputy; a violent young man with a nearly uncontrollable temper. Again, these were men who were operating on a strictly personal, private level. They were not political or religious extremists. Each one had a different birthplace, upbringing, and history.

You can begin writing a novel with only a partially worked-up villain, so long as you are able to convincingly create the character as you go. Deadline pressure has its upside. As long as you have solid basics on this character, you can trust your imagination and skill to put the right words in her mouth and give her appropriate actions and reactions—back to that Newtonian push-pull that, when applied to fiction, gives a novel tensile strength and logic. When you come to a scene in which your villain appears, picture her walking into it as an actor would, entering the stage. She strides in. She sizes up the competition. Now she only has to say and do what would spring naturally and convincingly from her character *as you understand it so far.* Listen for her voice. Try to capture it. If you fail, lean into that delete key, then try again. And again. You are creating on the spot. When you understand your villain wholly, her authentic words will come. You'll know them when you hear them.

Lately I've been hatching public villains again, likely in response to our publicity-mad, social media–driven times. Not many secrets out there, and not many people who even *want* secrets. Not even the bad guys. So I've chosen villains such as a celebrity torturer who writes a book about his black-site "enhanced interrogation techniques"; a native-born terrorist who publicly pledges himself to Islamic State; a white supremacist sect that is planning to infect thousands of U.S. Muslims with a deadly poison; and American anarchists who perform their violence live on television and post it on Facebook. I haven't had to dig very deep to find these players and to understand what makes them tick: they do most of my work for me. Just read your papers and watch your news and follow your feeds and they'll tell you exactly who they are and what they're trying to accomplish.

These public villains aren't as devious and aberrant as the old-fashioned thrill killers but what they lack in sullen creepiness they make up for in scope and volume: mass murders, explosives, hijackings. And don't forget motive, which is why they've gone public in the first place: religion, race, cultural grievance, national advancement, political bias. They represent the time and place in which we live.

Private or public, villains are inverted heroes. Start with an upright character, then replace generosity, selflessness, honesty, and bravery with greed, narcissism, amorality, and cowardice. As noted throughout, most villains are reflections of their time and place. And reflections are reversals. You look at yourself in that mirror, or in the blacked-out window of a passing limo, or in that still, clear pool of a trout stream, and you see your perfect opposite. Touch your right ear, and the person in the mirror touches their left ear. That's why villains—optically faithful inversions of the good—can be, in real life, very hard to spot. Until it's too late.

A good fictional villain should be not only clearly drawn, motivated, and capable, but *fun*. And by "fun," I mean steeped in the flamboyant colors of ego and self-delusion into which a villain—like a hummingbird seen in the right light at the right time—can burst with such sudden luminosity. Let your villain surprise, terrify, disgust, and infuriate your audience. Let the character be pitied, defeated, obliterated. That's part of why people are reading your story in the first place. Don't be squeamish. Leave some blood on the keyboard. Just enough.

If the villain of your piece is revealed late in the book, then keeping them compelling but obscured until the end can be very tricky. Which is why writing a good villain requires more legerdemain and is often harder than writing a good protagonist. The answer to this is to give your bad actor *a reason to be in the story other than merely as a suspect*. Easier said than done, but when it's done well, you'll get gasps of surprise and recognition when your villain steps into the light.

For those of you who don't outline your stories, there's plenty to be said for allowing your villain—and the other dramatis personae—to develop over the course of the writing. This not only allows you the time and freedom to create the best villain, it also allows the story itself to change, evolve, and improve as you create it. In this sense, your novel is a living and breathing thing, and you must not only give it life but tend to its needs and raise it up to be the best story it can be. I often don't outline, or do so only minimally and with many disclaimers. Way back in my third book, *Pacific Beat* (1991), I became fascinated by a character who jumped into my mind about a third of the way through the outline-less manuscript. For the life of me, I couldn't figure out why he was there or what he was doing. More important, I was aware at the end of the first draft that this novel was really *not* working. So I wrote it again. And halfway through, I saw that this character—one Horton Goins, a weird but apparently harmless young man—wasn't just essential to the book, he was the *key* to why the story had fallen flat. I'd failed to see him clearly until then. Yes, I'd subconsciously understood that Horton was valuable all along, it just took me a few months and another draft to see how.

Another reason why the villains are hard to write is because to understand them, you as a writer need to enter their dark interiors and help them execute their often bloody plans. I mentioned earlier the desire for exercise, a hot shower, and a strong drink after writing those serial killer novels. Fine and good, but if you really want to get to the core of the wickedness/evil/darkness of your bad guy, you might have to get your psyche dirtier than sweat, water, and alcohol can cleanse.

For my 2017 thriller, *The Room of White Fire*, I dug about as deep as a civilian could get into the subject of U.S. torture chambers (black-site prisons) during our "war on terror." I started with the Senate Intelligence Committee's 2014 report on torture, courtesy of Senator Dianne Feinstein's office (a 549-page synopsis of the full 6,700-page report, which is still classified). I read accounts of torturers and the tortured, of guards and other observers, watched video simulations of "enhanced interrogation techniques," and followed at some distance the trials of suspected terrorists (still ongoing). I was sickened by the torture, ashamed of my government for using it, angered that its hideous existence had been so arrogantly obscured for so long, disgusted that two American privateers had profited handsomely for running the prisons (making $80 million by most estimates, plus bonuses for "useful intelligence"). That fury is why I wrote the novel. When I finally crossed the finish line on it, I took a deep breath and looked forward to more chipper subjects. Of course, a book tour came along and I found myself trying my best to interest my audiences in the horrors I'd found, and also trying my best to *sell* torture as entertainment. Where does that leave me in the cast of players in this very dark American drama? I'm not sure.

My literary amigos and I go back and forth on this. We know we traffic in violence and heartless behavior. We ride and write on the backs of victims. We suspect that our fictional appropriations of the world's pain do little to assuage it. Worse, we wonder if we might just be feeding the worst in human nature by putting it center stage. Do we inspire heartless violence by portraying it?

So choose your villains carefully. They're as much a part of you as your heroes, and like your heroes, they will never go away once that book of yours hits the shelves.

A final thought on the villains, both fictional and real: They are to be respected and thanked, because they willingly do what the rest of us will not do. They shoulder the burden of wickedness so that the upright can pursue better things. They bring the dark into which we carry the fire.

KRIS NERI

Before you start writing a mystery, work out the villain's behind-the-scenes actions: how they commit the crime, how they set up an alibi or direct suspicion to someone else, as well as how they counter the protagonist's actions as the novel progresses. Though the villain's identity is typically kept secret until near the end of the mystery, the writer should be able to switch from on-the-page mode to behind-the-scenes mode to avoid plot holes. You also need to know where the villain is at all times. You can't put them off somewhere committing a second murder when they're also in full view of the protagonist (and the reader) in on-the-page mode.

Supporting Characters

The chorus of voices that backs up your protagonist.

CRAIG JOHNSON

An analogy I use when talking about one of the more important aspects of writing a novel is that its construction is akin to a choral group, in that all those voices should be there for a specific purpose. If you make the mistake of using the wrong voice or eliminating it altogether, the whole thing can get out of tune pretty quick.

We all love the idea of sitting at the keyboard and composing witty dialogue and breathtaking descriptions, but first comes the hard work of outfitting a novel for success, an outline that affords you the ability to find a balance and the voices that will allow you to explore the meaning and message of your book.

I've told students before, and I don't think it can be emphasized enough, that you only get to describe a character once in a book, but they speak throughout it, so the individuality of voice becomes imperative, perhaps even more so for supporting characters, owing to their limited appearances.

Support characters aren't there simply to provide a background but rather are there to advance the plot and to accentuate the passions, desires, tragedies, and triumphs of your writing. No man is an island, and no character can be, either. One character can't carry the weight of the world, nor should they, so the supporting characters are important in showing a diversity not only of character but of thought. As an example, take your antagonists—there is an old Cheyenne proverb that says you can judge a man by his enemies, and I think there's a lot to be said for using that formula while writing. The bad guy has to be as fully developed as the hero, or we haven't provided enough of a challenge to bother writing a novel in the first place. After all, Richard III doesn't think he's one of those bad guys, just maligned and deeply misunderstood.

One has to remember, support characters (villains included) may be walk-ons in your protagonist's story, but in their own story, they're the star.

When I wrote my first novel, *The Cold Dish*, I was fortunate enough to stumble onto not only a protagonist but an ensemble of characters who allowed me the opportunity to go beyond one novel into a continuing series. I think part of the success of the books came from that ensemble, a collection of characters varied enough to carry some of the weight that my protagonist, Sheriff Walt Longmire, couldn't carry alone.

It was a risky proposition writing a clinically depressed protagonist, simply because the book could become, well, depressing. I thought about how the voice of the books would be that of the sheriff and that there would likely be a propensity of masculinity, and decided I needed to find some way to balance that out with some strong female characters. One of the things that saved the novel was surrounding the sheriff with what I've referred to as a pride of lionesses, a ring of characters who would support the main narrator in spite of himself.

The first was Ruby, Walt's dispatcher and the person responsible for the structure as he navigates his day-to-day life. She became a sounding board for Walt and provides a physical road map for him by way of the Post-its she leaves on his office doorjamb. Next was Dorothy, the owner of the Busy Bee Café, because if left to his own devices Walt was likely to starve to death. Dorothy also provides a conduit to the community. Ask any small-town cop or deputy where to get information and they'll tell you the cafés and bars, because that's where people talk.

The next was Walt's daughter, who was introduced in the first novel only through the medium of phone messages, reaffirming the isolation that Walt had felt since the death of his wife. She was also the last lifeline to the humanity he still possessed.

Then there's Victoria Moretti, Walt's undersheriff, a transplant from Philadelphia who provides a more specific counterpoint to the sheriff. I figured that Walt's strengths in law enforcement would be more socially oriented, with a knowledge of the people in his county and their histories. Vic, having graduated from the fifth-largest police academy in the country, would be infinitely more knowledgeable in the fields of forensic science, DNA, ballistics, and so forth. She would be with him on a daily basis, providing information about the things he wasn't acquainted with. She would also give the story what I refer to as the introduction of the innocent, the person not acquainted with the highly contextualized environment. I knew that for the book to be a success, it was going to have to appeal to more than just the people in Wyoming (although sales of half a million doesn't sound bad, if every resident bought a copy . . .). Most of the readers would be from somewhere else, so I was going to have to afford them a character as an access point to a possibly alien culture, which Vic provided.

I think that when you summon up the support characters for your novel, you need to think of them as a checklist of strengths and weaknesses, of opposing personalities. For instance, Vic has forensic skills and an urban outlook, in contrast to Santiago Saizarbitoria, who knows more about the people in the county—especially since he speaks Basque, the language of a group of people who figure predominantly in my novels.

Speaking of separate cultures, one of the big issues I was going to have to deal with was another major society, the Native community. As a side note, I suppose I should say something about the current battle cry of cultural appropriation that suggests none of us has a right to compose outside our own personal makeup. I think that's rather foolish. In accepting his Nobel Prize for literature, John Steinbeck said, "Good writing approaches a universality of the human condition." Well, how can we approach one another with empathy and understanding if we're galvanized in our separate little camps? Does that mean that I can't write about Natives, that they can't write about whites, that I can't write about women, women can't write about horses, and so on? Obviously, any kind of writing that stretches outside of one's own community requires a foundation of respect, knowledge, and understanding, but a blanket ban gets kind of silly, pretty quick.

Anyway, I knew I was going to need a character who would be emblematic of the Native culture here on the high plains, and that's when I came up with Henry Standing Bear. The folks up on the Crow and Northern Cheyenne Indian Reservations are my friends, neighbors, and family. I knew Henry was going to have to be a strong character in the novel, someone capable of giving voice to an entire people.

One of the tricks I used to develop that character was one that's been used by authors for centuries, and I think is encapsulated by one of the greatest writing teachers of all time, Wallace Stegner. In his *On Writing and Teaching Fiction*, a compilation of his lectures at the writing program at Stanford University, Stegner talks about the fact that the greatest piece of fiction is the disclaimer at the beginning of every novel that says any person or persons depicted in this novel are entirely fictional. Hogwash. That's your job as a writer, to go out and find interesting people and populate your novels with them.

It's been said that you should be able to take any given character, even the doorman who opens the hotel door for the protagonist one time, and write an entire novel about that character. I agree. There's a fleshing-out that carries the weight of a novel, and the devil is in the details, especially when the details are the supporting characters.

Like I said, no man is an island, and no character is, either, but sometimes you find the support characters in the strengths and weaknesses of your protagonist.

One of the things readers enjoy doing is telling me which characters they like best, and I'm consistently surprised when Walt Longmire isn't on the list. Maybe I shouldn't be. I write in first person, so Walt carries the load of the narrative, to the point that he sometimes disappears into the story, leaving the guest-star roles to the support characters. I'm always getting asked why I don't write a novel with Vic or Henry as the storyteller, but I doubt I ever will, and I'll tell you why: it would be too much of a good thing.

You can turn any virtue into a vice simply by giving it too much head. As the old writing saying goes, you have to kill your darlings. If seduced by your support characters, you run the risk of having the same amount of the same characters in all your novels, which leads to a form of nepotistic repetition, the stone-cold death of any series. Better to have an ebb and flow that allows these characters to go with the story's demands.

Support characters have a magic all their own, and a lot of that resides in leaving the reader wanting more. It's very easy for Henry or Vic to walk into my novels when I need them, take the stage, and then disappear, without the burdens of having to actually carry the story. There was a Shakespeare expert who was once asked why the Bard killed off Mercutio in act 3, scene 1 of *Romeo and Juliet* when it's obvious he's the funniest, most entertaining character in the play. His answer: "Shakespeare had to kill Mercutio before he killed Romeo and Juliet." Telling a story is a balanced affair, and it's easy to be drawn out onto thin ice by charismatic characters, but you do so at your own risk as it's quite possible they'll kill your book.

There needs to be an ebb and flow with the characters, allowing them their time onstage and then giving them the opportunity to shine. This shining can exhibit itself in a number of ways; with continual appearances, support characters can capture the attention of readers . . . and you can always promote them from support to main characters in a future novel.

GAY TOLTL KINMAN

In his book *The Hero with a Thousand Faces*, Joseph Campbell talks about the hero having a mentor. A mentor gives advice and direction but does not solve the mystery for the sleuth. The mentor is also a sounding board. *The sleuth needs a sounding board.* It seems like a simple solution, but to me it was a revelation. A "partner" is better than a mentor because they are on equal terms with the protagonist. That's why there are characters like Dr. Watson. There's no better way to get information out, to show the thought process of the sleuth. And a partner can trigger that thought process.

Writing the Talk

Dialogue that sounds true, reveals character,
and draws in the reader.

GREG HERREN

We all remember great lines of dialogue from films and television shows—frequently, they wind up as memes or GIFs on social media. Whether it be Bette Davis on the staircase in *All About Eve*, archly stating that it's going to be a bumpy night, or Meryl Streep as Miranda Priestly belittling any of her underlings in *The Devil Wears Prada*, or Gloria Swanson ready for her close-up in *Sunset Boulevard*, great dialogue not only is memorable but can also bookmark the work in which it appears in the memory of the viewer or reader.

But films are almost entirely dialogue. How do we use that same element of storytelling in a piece of writing?

The word "dialogue" comes from the Greek words "*dia*" ("through") and "*logos*" ("word" or "meaning"): essentially, the back-and-forth exchange of information between two people. "Conversation," on the other hand (from the Latin "*vers*," to do with turning) is less formal, more about the interaction than what we learn from it.

In its simplest form, dialogue is what characters tell us—about themselves, about their relationships with the people they speak to, about their situation and its dangers and the mood of the world in the story.

Dialogue might seem like the easiest part of writing fiction. After all, everyone talks, even those who are nonverbal. And we spend a great deal of our day *listening* to other people speak—friends, coworkers, television programs, service personnel.

However, hasn't your mind wandered while listening to someone talk? The last thing you want is to have that happen with your reader—once their mind starts wandering, you've lost them.

Everyday conversation is often unmemorable, but dialogue in fiction must have a purpose: it either advances the plot, imparts information necessary for the reader's understanding of the story, or reveals something new about the character who is speaking.

Or all of the above.

Eavesdropping and Taking Notes in Public

A common piece of advice about dialogue is often misinterpreted: *Listen to people talking and use that as your basis.*

That sounds incredibly simple, right?

The problem is that most people do not speak in a way that makes sense on a page. Several years ago, I worked on a research project that required me to transcribe recorded focus groups and interviews with members of the community being studied. For the sake of accuracy, every recording had to be transcribed word for word, including hems and haws and pauses, every sigh and break in speaking. It was an eye-opening experience—and made me realize that you can't, in fiction, write dialogue the way people actually speak.

People have a tendency to talk in run-on sentences and say "um" a lot— oh, and use figures of speech like "you know what I mean" or "blah, blah, blah," and frequently fumble for words (and sometimes use the wrong word or say the right word incorrectly, or their verb tenses don't match and their grammar is wrong and they use dialect that some people might not understand) and then there is the whole aspect of accents and regionalisms and colloquialisms—

No editor would ever let that perfectly natural, utterly run-on sentence I just constructed get past them.

Conversations are not only more disconnected than dialogue in fiction, they also aren't as focused. Actual, real-life conversations bounce from one subject to another and then back again. People frequently interrupt and the topics veer all over the place.

Dialogue in fiction needs to be clear and focused—and yet it needs to *feel* natural. To *sound* real, not to *be* real. Interruptions or changes of subject must either matter to the story or serve as character development. ("She was always cutting me off, never letting me finish a sentence. It wasn't just annoying, but also made me feel like nothing I had to say mattered.")

Dialogue as Character

However, listening to people speak—especially in a setting you don't know really well—can be valuable for a writer. Speech is like a fingerprint: no two people use the same words and phrases, the same grammar and vocabulary, the same rhythm and flow of words. Listening to how others give themselves away through their speech can show us how to do that on the page.

Dialogue needs to illuminate the character. For example, if your protagonist is walking down a street and is stopped by a homeless man who asks for spare change in Shakespearean English, there has to be a reason. And you don't have to explain it right away, but like Chekhov's gun (that is, if a gun is introduced in the first act, it must go off by the third), at some point it needs to pay off: we need to find out this man's story—or at least, you have to use this experience to get your main character to explore their own prejudices and assumptions about the homeless. In either case, having the homeless man speak in an unexpected way is, in essence, a way to build either his character or the character of your protagonist—if not both.

Then there's the rhythm of each person's speech, the almost singsong way the subconscious finds the music in words and language and sends it out through the throat. An important part of building a character is finding the rhythm in the way that person speaks.

Creative use of punctuation in dialogue is a valuable way to indicate those peculiar speech patterns: "I wasn't sure . . . I—I didn't know, you see . . . how to bring it up . . . um, and I'm still not entirely sure if it's the *smart* thing to do; but *someone* has to do *something*, you know?"

Case in point: in my novel *Timothy,* I show one character's idiosyncrasies by capitalizing the words that she emphasizes when she speaks:

> "DON'T mind the way I'm dressed—don't judge ME!" she warned
> with mock severity, wagging an index finger with a perfect French

manicure at me. . . . "I HAVE to play tennis this afternoon, and I didn't WANT to cut my visit ONE minute short to have to run home and CHANGE. Oh, dear, you're SPEECHLESS in HORROR at my CLOTHES." She looked stricken.

This habit of emphasis defines the character in the book, and tells the reader who she is as a person: her background, her relationships, and how she views not only her life but the world around her.

Howdy Pardner: Accents and Regionalisms

Overheard conversations lead us into the question of how best to present those regionalisms and colloquial phrases we pick up.

Again, we are aiming less at exact transcription than at the *impression* we give our reader. A close mirroring of accents and dialects is one of the reasons Faulkner can be so difficult to read. In Faulkner's case, he was showing the differences in speech patterns between different classes and castes of people, to show the effects of education and poverty. Faulkner accomplished this by sounding out phonetically the speech of his working class, less-educated characters, while having his upper class, better educated characters speak standard English.

And while it is true that a southerner would see the way they speak as "normal," a reader from the other end of the country might like the occasional reminder. Not that you want something as literal as:

"Ah doan know," she said, rubbing her forehead. "Ah jess cain't think about thayat raht now, kay?"

I find that hard to read. Isn't this easier?—

"I don't know," she said, rubbing her forehead. "I jess can't think about that right now, 'kay?"

Similarly, if you're introducing a British character in a manuscript that is primarily about Americans, or a teenager into a room of adults, the very first time they speak I would not ding you for putting the exact words and pronunciation, as long as you call attention to what you are doing:

It took me a few moments to realize what he was actually saying, but once I got the hang of his accent [her slang, etc.], it was easy to understand him.

But once you've established that the person speaks with an accent, the need to reference it or spell out words phonetically isn't as necessary as it was to begin with. The occasional touch is plenty.

Drawing In Your Reader

In addition to sounding like the real world and giving insight to the character, dialogue is an excellent way to make the reader feel as if they are participating in the story and figuring things out. Being handed an "info dump" (which could be a lengthy recitation, or simply a piece of information unnecessarily given to a person who knows it already) can take your reader right out of the story.

Readers, especially mystery readers, are bright. An offhand reference to someone's wheelchair or their hard shift on night patrol is a more immediate way to draw the reader into the character than a mere description of physical condition or job. It's a great way for the writer to show rather than tell.

And of course, the mystery reader is always alert for hints and red herrings. Does a character's speech—what she says, and what she *doesn't* say—contain a clue that she might have been in the vicinity of the murder? Does another's uncharacteristically rude interruption hide his anxiety that the speaker might give him away? Is there some relationship that the investigator hasn't yet guessed that the reader might pick up on from two people talking?

Use those!

Said or Shouted? Dialogue Tags and Adverbs

This is not the place for a detailed primer on formatting dialogue (in general, format it in a standard, therefore invisible, manner, with quotation marks, one speaker per paragraph, etc.). But it is worth looking at the all-essential dialogue tag or speech tag, the verb used to show who is talking:

"Where are you going?" Joey **asked.**

Many editors and writing instructors believe that the only dialogue tag necessary is "said"; that if you need an adverb—"softly," "belligerently," "wildly"—or a dialogue tag other than "said"—"retorted," "bellowed," "purred"—to make your meaning clear, it's a sign that your dialogue needs work. The words, the rhythm, the breaks, the punctuation should render most adverbs superfluous.

You often find an outright contempt for adverbs—everyone from Mark Twain to Elmore Leonard and Stephen King advises killing them on sight. But as with all rules, there are exceptions, and to have nothing but a string of "he said," "she saids" on the page can irritate the reader—to say nothing of the audiobook listener. Let's take a simple line of dialogue and look at some alternative ways to present it.

"I hate you!" she said. "How could you do that? How?"

By itself, "said" isn't very strong. What about adding an adverb?

"I hate you!" she said angrily. "How could you do that? How?"

The addition of "angrily" makes her emotion clearer, although a more specific adverb like "furiously" might be more vivid. However, perhaps you can use description rather than adverbs and dialogue tags:

"I hate you!" Her voice shook with anger. "How could you do that? How?"

Or vary the words spoken to convey a more intense emotion:

"I—God, I just HATE you!" she said. "How could YOU, of all people, do that? HOW?"

Or you can use my personal favorite, the action tag:

"I hate you!" She slammed her hands down on the desk. "How could you do that? How?"

Sometimes you only want a dialogue tag to remind the reader which character is speaking. But as these examples show, the more specific the verb, the more detailed the words spoken and action taken, the more of a chance you'll have to give the reader subliminal information about the character and the situation.

Just take care whenever you get away from a basic "said." The verb should have to do with talking: your character can whisper, scream, yell, shout, ask, or reply without problems, but you should think carefully before using a verb that has little to do with human speech—like "laugh" or "pout," "roar" or "explode." And you should hesitate to bring in a fifty-cent word such as "retorted," "declared," or "opined." Those verbs are not wrong, but they stick out, and so risk kicking the reader out of your story.

And please remember: your character can't "hiss" a phrase that contains no S.

You Must Remember This

Always read your dialogue out loud. If you stumble over words or the rhythm sounds wrong, keep talking it out until you get the words right. Get *inside* the head of the character speaking—why would they say this? What is their goal? What is the purpose of this conversation? Can you plant a clue here? Thinking about these things will help you work out how the dialogue should sound and how precisely your character would say what you need them to say—and how the other characters will respond.

Some of the best examples of dialogue writing in crime fiction are Gregory Mcdonald's *Fletch* novels. The stories are told, from beginning to end, almost entirely in dialogue—practically no setting or sense of place or speech tags: the books are mostly the characters talking. They are a master class in writing dialogue. Try writing your scene that way and see if it still works.

Another great exercise is to simply write the dialogue in your scene as if you are writing a play, but with no stage directions or staging details. The goal is to get across everything you need to get across with simply the words the characters are speaking.

Good dialogue is one of the pillars holding up any story. Making that pillar strong will not only place your story firmly in the real world, it will tell your reader all they need to know about your characters, ensure that the pages keep turning, and guarantee that your story will stay in that reader's mind for a long time.

BRADLEY HARPER

Dialogue is an ancient Greek stage direction, meaning "action through words." One of the first critiques I got from an agent, looking at my neatly printed manuscript, was "There's not enough white space," meaning there was too much narrative description and not enough dialogue.

Dialogue opens up the tight-knit block of words we are accustomed to in textbooks, and allows your story to breathe through verbal exchanges between your characters. Frequent doses of white space make your work less intimidating and help your reader speed along through your story.

STEPHEN ROSS

Subtext is your friend.

Subtext is not written, it is implied. It is the *underneath*, the feelings and intuition, the unspoken meaning. Even a shopping list can have subtext.

- Milk
- Bread
- Eggs
- Hammer
- Shovel
- Quicklime
- Champagne

Subtext is one of the writer's tools of magic.

Setting

Your most versatile element: backdrop,
player, and the all-pervading sense of place.

WILLIAM KENT KRUEGER

I'm not easily won over. But I confess that I'm in love with James Lee Burke and his New Iberia. I'm also in love with Tony Hillerman and his Navajo country. And with Margaret Coel and her Wind River territory of Wyoming. And Cara Black and her Paris. And Walter Mosley and his Watts. A visceral sense of place is the key to my heart.

In my own work, I write profoundly out of a sense of place. Setting is the cornerstone of so much of what occurs in my stories and in the stories of those authors whose work I most admire. What we all have come to understand, I believe, is that setting is one of the most powerful and versatile elements in a story. I try to think of the setting not just as a backdrop for what's going to occur, but also as an integral player in the action, motivation, atmosphere, and emotion of a story.

But first, let's take a look at what I'm talking about when I use the word "setting."

Setting Is Place

Broadly speaking, setting is the whole of the environment in which a story takes place. It's Raymond Chandler's L.A., Carl Hiaasen's Florida, J. A. Jance's Cochise County. It's the stage on which most of the action is going to be played out. As such, it will be created with both broad strokes and specific, telling details. Take a look at how Tony Hillerman suggests the vast reaches of the northern Arizona landscape in his classic novel *Dance Hall of the Dead*:

> The sun was low now. The clouds in the west had risen up the horizon and were fringed with violent yellows. Slanting light was turning the alkali and alichi flats in the valley below from white and gray into rose and pink. Seventy miles southwestward, another cloud formation had formed over the dim blue shape of the White Mountains. This great vacant landscape reminded him of Susanne's remark about it being hard to be a Navajo if you minded being lonely.

On another level, setting is where the current scene, the immediate action of a story, is occurring: a booth in a busy diner, a clearing in a dark forest, a kitchen in a quiet home, a sterile interview room in a police station. Each scene will have its own unique character apart from the larger stage and most probably require a closer eye to specific detail. Check out this bar scene from Craig Johnson's *The Dark Horse*, in which he suggests much of the timbre of the place through a depiction of its clientele:

> There were a couple of old ranchers sitting in the gloom at one of the tables, two younger fellows playing eight-ball near the boxing ring, and a large, surly-looking individual in a two-day beard, sunglasses, and a stylish black straw hat at the other end of the bar. He was talking to an elaborately tattooed young woman who held his arm and pressed her hip against his. I smiled and nodded toward them, and they smirked at me.

On the most basic level, setting is the constant grounding of your reader in the immediate moment: a waitress refilling a coffee cup, the jostle in a subway car that interrupts a conversation, the cries of children from a playground that takes a character out of some reverie and back to the present action in a park.

So, first and foremost, setting is a sense of place.

Setting Is Character

Setting is an essential character in a story. Like any human character, it involves a unique physicality. The physique of Nancy Pickard's Kansas is very different from that of Sara Paretsky's Chicago—the one a vast undulating landscape, the other an imposing wall of concrete, steel, and glass. Settings have individual faces, just as humans do. The Bighorns of Craig Johnson's Absaroka County present a ruggedly beautiful countenance, well in keeping with the mythic ideal of a western hero's chiseled profile, while the face of Savannah, Georgia, in John Berendt's *Midnight in the Garden of Good and Evil* is as genteel as a powdered southern belle.

Human characters have voices. It's no surprise that settings do, too. I'm positive that if you blindfolded a reasonably intelligent person and set them down in Tony Hillerman's Navajo country, the voice of that place would give it away. The whisper of the wind across a wide-open landscape. The scratch of tumbleweed across a lonely road. The howl of a coyote or the screech of a desert owl. Now think about the voice of a place like Dennis Lehane's Dorchester. Consider what that voice would be like and how uniquely different from Hillerman's desert. These voices communicate very quickly the nature of the setting.

People have a scent to them, sometimes pleasant, sometimes not so much. So do settings. The clean, high desert air of Michael McGarrity's New Mexico is very different from the heavy, humid air of Randy Wayne White's Florida, laden as it is with the salty scent of the ocean and the fetid backwater bouquet of swampland.

And here's an important one: settings have personality, just like humans. Consider the difference between Michael Connelly's Los Angeles and James Lee Burke's New Orleans. Connelly's L.A. is new, glitzy, fast-paced, cutting-edge, and oh so cool, man. Burke's New Orleans is old, laid-back, calm, and patient, though in a menacing sort of way.

Every attribute that we ascribe to the human characters in a story applies as well to the setting.

Setting Is Motivation

Used correctly, setting ought to contribute to the "why" of a story. The actions should rise naturally out of the place in which they occur, and that place ought to have a part in the reason for the story. The snuff movie industry in Lawrence Block's *A Dance at the Slaughterhouse* exists in large measure because of the complex and often corrupt nature of New York City. The child abduction in Dennis Lehane's *Gone, Baby, Gone* takes place because of parental neglect in working-class Dorchester. Many of my stories rise out of issues that occur in the interface of two cultures in northern Minnesota, white and Ojibwe. I've written about Indian gaming casinos, about the battle over hunting and fishing treaty rights, the influx of the drug and gang cultures on the reservation, the sexual trafficking of vulnerable Native women and children. Think of the stories of Tony Hillerman, Margaret Coel, C. J. Box. The nature of these stories depends enormously on that quintessential western setting. Do you remember the final moment at the end of *Chinatown*? The cop turns Jake Giddis away from the horrific scene of the brutal shooting and says to him, "Forget it, Jake. It's Chinatown." That says it all.

Setting Is Atmosphere

I love Daphne du Maurier's *Rebecca* for many reasons, but perhaps most of all for the heaviness of the story, its moodiness, and for the pervading sense of menace, which is due in large measure to the nature of Manderley, the isolated estate of Maxim de Winter. The place itself casts a pall across every thought, every action. Without that atmosphere, the story would be as flat as a glass of day-old champagne. Think about Hiaasen's Florida. Only within the surreal atmosphere of the landscape Hiaasen paints can a character like Skink, the roadkill-eating former governor of the state, believably exist.

Creating a Sense of Place

First, the one huge don't: don't deliver a travelogue. Nothing will kill the pace of a story as quickly as that. Think of creating your setting in the same way you create every other character in your story. Generally speaking, when you introduce a character, you're not going to give your reader a long paragraph or two of description. You're more likely to take your time and spread out the salient details over many pages until you've gradually revealed the full nature of that character. It's the same with setting.

In creating a sense of place, less is often more. Let the telling detail suggest the larger whole. Take a look at Walter Mosley's description of Bone Street in Watts, in his novel *White Butterfly*:

Bone Street was local history. A crooked spine down the center of Watts's jazz heyday, it was four long and jagged blocks. West of Central Avenue and north of 103rd Street, Bone Street was broken and desolate to look at by day, with its two-story tenementlike apartment buildings and its mangy hotels. But by night Bones, as it was called, was a center for late-night blues, and whiskey so strong that it could grow hairs on the glass it was served in. When a man said he was going to get down to the bare Bones he meant he was going to lose himself in the music and the booze and the women down there.

With a very few succinct details, Mosley offers not only a telling physical description but also a keen sense of the unique character of the place and its atmosphere.

As much as possible, use all the senses in what you offer a reader—and here again we get to the idea of place as a character. Think about the voice of the setting, the unique scent, the textures. Pull the reader in not just visually but sensually as well.

Using Sense of Place

As I said earlier, setting is one of the most versatile elements in any story. It can be employed to accomplish any number of necessary tasks.

- Setting can be an effective way in which to enter a story. I modestly offer one of my own openings, this from my novel *Blood Hollow*:

> January, as usual, was meat locker cold, and the girl had already been missing nearly two days. Corcoran O'Connor couldn't ignore the first circumstance. The second he tried not to think about.
>
> He stood in snow up to his ass, more than two feet of drifted powder blinding white in the afternoon sun. He lifted his tinted goggles and glanced at the sky, a blue ceiling held up by green walls of pine. He stood on a ridge that overlooked a small oval of ice called Needle Lake, five miles from the nearest maintained road. Aside from the track his snowmobile had pressed into the powder, there was no sign of human life. A rugged vista lay before him—an uplifted ridge, a jagged shoreline, a bare granite pinnacle that jutted from the ice and that gave the lake its name—but the recent snowfall had softened the look of the land. In his time, Cork had seen nearly fifty winters come and go. Sometimes the snow fell softly, sometimes it came in a rage. Always it changed the face of whatever it touched. Cork couldn't help thinking that in this respect, snow was a little like death. Except that death, when it changed a thing, changed it forever.

What I hoped to accomplish with this opening was threefold: to introduce the motivating situation—a girl is lost in the wilderness in deep winter; the setting itself—the great Northwoods of Minnesota; and the emotional timbre of story.

- Setting can also be a wonderful way to end a story. Here's one of my favorite endings of all time, from James Lee Burke's *Black Cherry Blues*:

> Neither sleep nor late-night thunderstorms bring them back now, and I rise each day into the sunlight that breaks through the pecan trees in my front yard. But sometimes at dusk, when the farmers burn the sugarcane stubble off their fields and cinders and smoke lift in the wind and settle on the bayou, when red leaves float in piles past my dock and the air is cold and bittersweet with the smell of burnt sugar, I think of Indians and water people, of voices that can speak through the rain and tease us into yesterday, and in that moment I scoop Alafair up on my shoulders and we gallop down the road through the oaks like horse and rider toward my house, where Batist is barbecuing *gaspagoo* on the gallery and paper jack-o-lanterns are taped to the lighted windows, and the dragons become as stuffed toys, abandoned and ignored, like the shadows of the heart that one fine morning have gone with the season.

You don't need to have read everything that precedes this ending to appreciate the power of the prose and the profound emotional sense of place with which it leaves the reader.

- Setting grounds the reader. A novel is composed of scenes, so it's important to ground the reader in each scene, to bring the setting down from the global to the specific. You don't need to waste a lot of time on this, just offer the reader very specific and telling details. Here's a great example from Raymond Chandler's *The Little Sister*, suggesting the nature of Marlowe's office:

> The pebbled glass door panel is lettered in flaked black paint: "*Phillip Marlowe. . . . Investigations.*" It is a reasonably shabby door at the end of a reasonably shabby corridor in the sort of building that was new about the year the all-tile bathroom became the basis for civilization.

- Setting can reinforce or underline a character's emotional or psychological state. Fog, rain, sun, or wind can suggest a great deal more than just the weather. An empty street or a dark alley or a silent house can be more than just the space through which your character moves physically. It can suggest the emotional landscape as well.
- Setting helps create suspense. In the genre, this is a classic use of setting. In my novels characters often find themselves isolated in a forest, with every shadow suggesting menace. In a city, there are the dark corridors of the alleyways, or there's the fog that obscures the street. There's the empty house with the sounds that suggest it's not so empty. It's difficult to imagine creating suspense without using the setting to full advantage.

In summary, setting is the most versatile element in any story. It contributes significantly to a reader's whole experience. In addition to unique characters or clever plot, a powerful setting, that sense of having actually been there, will linger in the reader's memory a long while. A story without a solid sense of place is like a ship lost in some anonymous sea, and who would want to embark on that kind of journey?

THOMAS B. SAWYER

Dashiell Hammett's *The Maltese Falcon* is *the* paradigm, still the seminal modern detective novel, for several reasons—most significantly in that unlike the more traditional mysteries (and *Falcon* is indeed a mystery—*who* killed Sam Spade's partner, Miles Archer, as well as Captain Jacobi of the *La Paloma*, and gunsel Floyd Thursby?) *there were no clues, and almost no emphasis on suspects.* Instead, Hammett took the reader on a journey, involving a bunch of marvelously colorful characters in pursuit of a MacGuffin, and at the end, and happily *without* the tedious old-hat convention of the drawing-room climax, we did indeed get our closure about who did what to whom. But—and this further differentiated it from all the others—*we almost didn't care who the murderer was,* so interesting were the journey, the people, and their stories. That was our approach to *Murder She Wrote*, which ran for 264 episodes over 12 years.

Humor in Crime Fiction

Funny mystery, or mystery with fun:
why, how, and when to stop?

CATRIONA McPHERSON

This essay is not funny. I will be quoting what I believe to be funny lines and referencing what I believe to be funny ideas, but when you dissect these things they deflate from giggly bubbles of delight to flat slabs of fact. It's inevitable. Forgive me.

Why Be Funny?

The first question is whether to have humor in your mystery at all. It is still perfectly respectable to write serious, even solemn crime fiction. Unlike writers of action movie scripts, we have had no *Die Hard* to change the game forever. In fact, if your aim is to make a *living* as a writer, avoiding humor is a good start. Comic mysteries are not, generally, the big breakout *New York Times* bestselling books. But neither are most of the somber ones.

Since an attempt at comedy that misses is a great deal worse than a book with no planned laughs at all, the next question to ask yourself—and answer honestly—is "Can I do it?" Ask someone else if you don't know. But hope you don't get the feedback Cassandra Mortmain receives in Dodie Smith's *I Capture the Castle*, from her father no less: that her writing "combined stateliness with a desperate effort to be funny." Ouch. (Incidentally, that novel is one of the best accounts of writing and writer's block you could wish for.)

Finally, at this planning stage you need to ask yourself what the humor—should you choose to include it—is for. Does this seem too obvious to need an answer? Would that it were so. Wide reading in the genre indicates otherwise. Humor is supposed to make you laugh. Out loud. Make you wreck your mascara with helpless tears and snort so hard you hurt your uvula. Humorous mysteries should be embarrassing to read on the bus, and annoying for the people who live with you and get sick of having bits read out to them while they're trying to read a book of their own. In short, humor is not the same thing as whimsy. It's not comfort. It's not cute. It doesn't make readers feel warm inside. Ideally it makes them feel warm outside, because it makes them pee.

What's Funny and What's Not

So you've decided to be funny and you're sure you can pull it off. Here comes a big decision, though perhaps not the one you think. You can write farce, satire, or slapstick. You can be broad, goofy, or dry. You can use epigrams, absurdities, or irony. Or all nine. And more. But you don't need to know what your humor is, except funny. Someone else—a loved one, beta reader, developmental editor—will tell you after it's written. If *they* don't know, call it "quirky." (It's worth noting that the hardest humor to pull off in writing is slapstick. Descriptions of physical comedy are not reliably funny. If yours are, I tip my hat to you.)

The decision you do need to make at this stage is the location of your line. We're not all Ricky Gervais, thank God. But neither are we all Mr. Rogers, thank God. I'm a medium-size fan of warm humor that celebrates shared experience and invites everyone to see life's lighter side, but I laugh hardest at humor with a bite. And the truth is that any joke that makes one person laugh hard is going to offend another. If you're going to write this stuff, you need to be okay with offending people and taking your lumps, without argument, if they complain.

Note that I'm saying "offend," not "hurt." I'll happily offend anyone's sensitivities about politics, sex, or superstition; I'll puncture vanity and blow a raspberry at pomposity. But I won't—knowingly—hurt anyone by reminding them of their powerlessness in the face of bigotry or oppression. That's my own borderline. Yours might be different. You might find it hilarious to degrade the powerless and bully the weak. If so, and even though we've never met, I don't like you.

Where Does the Funny Go?

Once you've identified your personal line between comedy and cruelty, there are still questions of taste to be addressed. When is it a good idea to introduce laughs and when should we resist it? Can a death scene be funny? A murder? Absolutely. Elmore Leonard wouldn't write them any other way and Oyinkan Braithwaite has taken up the baton in her biting black comedy *My Sister, the Serial Killer*. You have to park most, perhaps all, of your empathy to appreciate wit this scabrous—but it's worth it.

A morgue scene and for sure a funeral scene lend themselves to comedy even more easily. Any time there's an expectation of dignified solemnity, humor becomes almost unavoidable, in writing as in life. (This is why the only good sex scenes are about bad sex, whereas good sex causes some of the worst writing ever published.) Again there's a difference between giving offense and causing pain. Personally, I can't imagine a funny rape scene and think squeezing a laugh from an account of child abuse would be the ultimate punching down. As before, though, you find your line and you take your lumps.

There's a second aspect of locating the humor in your book: Is the book funny or is the stuff the book's about funny? Jeff Cohen's Asperger's Mysteries are funny books about serious stuff. No one in his fictional world is laughing, even though we the readers are wearing our coffee. The danger with locating the humor outside the world of the book in this way is that it can tip into cruelty in less skilled, or less knowledgeable, hands than Cohen's.

But a far greater danger comes when the humor is inside the world of the book—when the characters themselves find their own lives funny. At worst, this can end up like those skits and bits where the only people enjoying themselves are on the stage, laughing too hard to notice the audience squirming. One simple way to avoid that is never to refer to your characters laughing. It's a specific and well-advised application of good old "show, don't tell": show us what's cracking them up, by all means, but don't tell us about it. If *we're* laughing, we'll work out that *they* are. A related "show, don't tell"—and even more of a classic—forbids us to signal a funny line of dialogue via the speech tag.

"Do you shave under your arms?" he asked.
"Well, I shave under one of them," she quipped.

is a sad waste of a decent joke.

How to Help the Funny Happen

So, you've decided whether, and you believe you can. You've pledged to cause actual laughter, you've found your tone and your line, you've got a bead on where humor would best fit, and you've positioned it inside or outside your fictional world. Now what? What are the basic tricks of the trade to have in your tool kit?

Surprise!

Laughter is our response to pleasurable surprise. Humor lies in misdirection, in the subversion of expectations, in the act of leading someone up a path that ends not at all where they were expecting to go. One of my favorite jokes from one of my favorite comics is Paul O'Grady, as Lily Savage, saying, "We were poor, but we were shoplifters." Such a neat switchback on the last word in that short sentence. "I haven't dated in a while; it's time to dip my toe back in the socket" is another one. A great way to get humor in your writing, then, is to search for clichés and subvert them.

It's as Easy as One, Two, Guess What

Our dedication to trinities is so strong that even when we've only got two things to say, we make up a third one: *sex and violence and all that fun stuff; dogs and cats and what have you.* The little word "etc." wouldn't get a quarter of the work without our commitment to threes. Inevitably then, humor needs threesomes. A priest and a rabbi in a bar are wasting their time and ours. So if you're going for funny and one line alone seems to be missing the mark, add another two. The examples of this are so numerous that picking one is a challenge, but here's Kellye Garrett introducing her heroine in the debut Detective by Day Mystery, *Hollywood Homicide*:

> My skin was what Maybelline called Cocoa and L'Oréal deemed Nut Brown, while MAC had bypassed all food groups to call it NC50.

This follows the rule of threes, "NC50" is a good twist, and Garrett—an African American woman—gets in that nice upward punch at white writers who still describe characters of color by cracking out the cookbook.

The rule of three plays a part in running gags as well. If you want one of these to work, you need to time the first three hits to get the gag lodged in the reader's mind without annoying them. The first hit needs to be early on in the book. The second hit should be not too far behind, before the memory of the first one fades. But then, ideally, you'll have a pause. Because the third time a running gag turns up should be a surprise, one that leaves the reader laughing not only at the joke but also at themselves for not seeing it coming. The memory of being satisfactorily hoodwinked buys goodwill for later hits. In my last book, I set up a running gag on page 36, revisited it briefly on page 54, then landed it on pages 108, 138, 176, 209, 256, and 260 in a 280-page book, making the gags shorter and, I hope, funnier each time.

Finally, on the subject of threes: a trio of characters talking to one another is a great boost to humor. A head-to-head dialogue can be funny, of course, but with three participants the scope is greater for non sequiturs, misunderstandings, and parallel conversations, wildly at odds. If your humorous dialogue in some scene or other feels a bit flat, and the story allows it, try adding a third voice, with a different agenda, to derail the other two.

The Old Ones Are Okay

I'm going to go right ahead and assume you've already parked your ego and donated your dignity before you started writing humorous mysteries. So perhaps you're not too proud to use traditional setup lines. I'm a big fan of them:

I wouldn't say he was dead . . . I'd say the great-grand-maggots of the first generation of blowflies who'd feasted on his corpse were dead too.
Not to be hyperbolic . . . but that restaurant has such poor ambience, I usually get it to go and eat at the DMV.
Narco said it was the biggest bust since . . . [I'm going to leave that one for you to complete. I went straight to Dolly Parton.]

These hoary old lines are good news for two reasons. They're familiar and comfortable; if you're going for laughs of recognition based on shared experience, they can help you. But, more important, they telegraph cheese. The very fact that they *are* hoary sets the reader up for a bad joke to follow. If you manage to land a *good* joke—twice the twist for your money.

Leave on the Laugh

It occurred to me that I might have put this section—on timing—too late in the essay and perhaps I should move it up. But that made me laugh, so here it is. Good timing is essential to humor. We all know that. In writing, one of the most important elements of timing is to make sure the final bit of the funny sentence—the last word, or at least the last phrase—is where the laugh comes. This is because when we're interpreting language, spoken or written, we hold ourselves in check until we've got the whole thing to work on. So, if the joke's in the middle and the sentence trails on after it, the laugh might die unlaughed. Watch out particularly if the funny line is dialogue and you've got a speech tag. That little "he said" will kill the joke deader than disco. Consider ditching the tag, if you can. If you can't, try splitting the line so the tag isn't at the end. This overrides the usual advice to "omit needless words." Full disclosure—I don't think that's good advice anyway: it pays no attention to rhythm. Compare:

"How many people have you slept with?" the therapist asked.
"It depends what you mean by 'people,'" she replied.

with:

"How many people have you slept with?" the therapist asked.
"Um, lemme see," she said. "It depends what you mean by 'people.'"

Forty-Nine Shades of Grey
and One That's More Taupe, Actually

My final piece of advice about finding the funny is to commit to detail, detail, detail. Writing in general terms instead of specifics is one of the worst manifestations of one of the worst writing habits. You want your readers to know that your (white) detective hero ate Mexican food for lunch? Don't tell them that; *show* them that. Say he ordered menudo because he thought it was pozole and had to hide the tripe in his jacket pocket because he didn't want to look like a wimp in front of the pretty waitress. If only he hadn't visited a suspect with a dog that afternoon . . .

Another way detail is your friend is that all that extra material—include needed words!—pushes the punch line further from the setup, creating space for expectations to grow, thus making the payoff funnier (as long as you're clear on what the funniest element is so you can place it last). Compare these two versions of the same joke:

This murderer was worse than most. He'd stabbed a guy to death on
a white rug and that's just rude.
This murderer was worse than most. He'd stabbed a guy to death on
a rug that cost five thousand dollars plus out-of-state tax and shipping and only came in white. That's just rude.

So the bad news is nothing's easy. Even the rule of three is a guide, not a guarantee. You need to balance it with the competing rule that sometimes more is more and far too much is barely enough. I'm going to leave you with a quote from Lane Stone's debut, *Current Affairs*, where she's discussing what her trio of retired Georgia beauty queens agree are the rules of golf:

You can pick up your ball if you have to go to the bathroom, if you
make a bad shot, if the snack cart comes by, if you're too hot and

you wish the snack cart would come by, if you either get or remember you need to make a phone call and you have to sneak your cell phone out of your bag, if you forget how many strokes you've taken, if you have taken too many strokes, if you thought you had taken your turn and you hadn't, if you just then notice another player is wearing a new outfit, if a famous actress dies, or if the stock market dips.

I read that seven years ago and laughed my teeth out. I laughed them out again copying it right now. The only written joke that makes me laugh more is P. G. Wodehouse—and who else could finish off an essay on literary humor?—describing a hangover by saying "a cat stamped into the room."

JAMES W. ZISKIN

Over the years, I've learned a few lessons about writing. They might be of use to you:

1. On motivation:

- Scheherazade told stories because her life depended on it. What motivates you?

2. On craft:

- Make "realism" in your fiction an illusion of realism. If your story is "realistic," your main character is probably circling the block three times before finding a parking spot.
- Make it memorable or make it economical.
- Challenge every sentence, every noun, every verb, every adjective, and every adverb.

3. On research:

- Know what you don't know.

4. On writing sex:

- As in real life, a lot of people do it, but not everyone does it well.
- Remember that your mother is going to read your book.

Writing in Partnership

Two writers with one voice:
how we learned to collaborate.

CAROLINE & CHARLES TODD

We considered a writing partnership because we had different interests but share a love of the mystery and of history, and wanted to see if we could actually write a mystery together, combining our talents. The idea began when we stumbled across a real historical mystery while visiting a battlefield, and we were intrigued by it.

It took us more than a year to learn *how* to collaborate.

We quickly discovered that there isn't a simple, single way to go about it, no one-size-fits-all. Instead, each partnership must work out their own method.

That said, there are certain things that are common to every collaboration.

Before we talk about those, we need to touch briefly on different forms of collaboration. For instance, there's a professional agreement such as those between James Patterson and another established author, with a body of contracts and legal considerations with established precedents. Nonfiction collaboration can fall into another category, where expertise of a different sort is involved, often depending on the professional standing each partner may bring to the table and how this background will be used in writing the book. *A History of Forensics*, for instance, might be written by two professionals in the field, a pathologist and a police officer who give different points of view. True crime could fit into this category, where an author and, say, a police officer collaborate on the description of a crime. Two writers might work together to write about an event in military history, or it might be one soldier's experience in a war and the collaborator's knowledge of that war's background.

Then there is ghostwriting, where a celebrity or war vet or sports figure tells their story to someone who writes it from interviews. Often the name of the celebrity takes precedence, while the writer is either listed as "with" or not recognized at all. Again, this involves a very different agreement and process. The ghostwriter makes the story coherent, knowing how to bring the most interesting material to light in exciting and marketable fashion. The collaborators might share in the royalties, or the writer could be paid a fee. Sometimes this work is arranged through publishing houses eager to capitalize on a newsworthy personality. In short, these are generally arranged, for specific purposes.

But let us return to two people who decide to write a mystery together. They could have some experience as writers, or none at all. They could be husband and wife, sisters, cousins—or even strangers who find they have enough in common to work together. This is what we have been doing for some twenty-five years without killing each other.

In their *Dutchman* series, "Maan Meyers" used one method of collaboration—Martin was a terrific researcher, while Annette was the writer. Husband and wife, they put their individual skills to work. Martin did the research and helped with the outline, while Annette did most of the writing. "Emma Lathen," who incidentally kept their collaboration a secret early on, wrote about Wall Street banker John Thatcher, but divided their duties. One of the pair, who knew more about banking and loans, did the Thatcher arc of the story, while the other told the story of the client coming to Thatcher for help. Where these overlapped, they worked out the scenes to suit. These are just two examples of the way others have chosen to divide their partnership.

Both of us wanted to write, not divide duties, and so we came up with a scene-by-scene method of talking, testing, then putting down what we visualize as the way a scene would take shape. Once satisfied there, we move on to the next scene, deciding what it's about, who is in it, where it should take place, and how it advances the plot. Since we don't outline, that keeps the process manageable. Throughout the book, we have shared research, character development, plot and plotting, even the writing of dialogue. It is truly a two-person effort from start to finish. Our library consists of duplicates of every book we have found on our subject and every bit of information we've collected. We can both write battle scenes and we can both describe the emotional problems of our characters, because we have shared the setting and the backstory of those characters.

Oddly enough, because we started working when we lived five hundred miles apart, it is still easier for us to work in different rooms, even when we are in the same house. The reason for this appears to be the fact that we get off track when in the same room. We use text, emails, and phone calls to discuss and test various aspects of a given book, sending material back and forth until both parties are satisfied. Sometimes that goes quickly, and at other times it could take several days of exchanging viewpoints.

One helpful technique often used by collaborators is a storyboard. They agree first on the information they post there: pictures of the setting, information about the characters, how they dress if historical, what they might look like. Clues might go up on the board, along with the murder weapon, the rooms and their furnishings, where the characters live, or venues where the action takes place. This makes it possible for each person to draw on the same material. Others keep a notebook with similar information, or even a file of three-by-five cards. This also helps the collaborators to keep the single-person point of view.

It comes down, really, to finding out early on what your individual strengths and weaknesses are, and how best to share your individual talents. Using a system that isn't comfortable as you work together will create unnecessary problems, both in the writing and in the atmosphere in which you write. This should be your first priority.

Next, we learned very quickly that ego is unhelpful. Where there was a deadlock, we ended it by figuring out what was best for the story. After all, it's the book you are writing that matters: that's why it's called collaborating. When ego creeps in, the reader hears two voices. And ego rearing its head can bring pressures to bear that will affect the partnership. You are supposed to be working toward a common goal, and it really isn't important who had the best idea or thought of the best ending. When one partner wants to impose their will on any part of the process, either because they feel they know best or they feel their prose is too brilliant to cut, it is no longer a collaboration.

Another of the early lessons we learned was to let the characters make decisions, rather than imposing choices on them. That led to unexpected pathways we hadn't foreseen in our plotting. It gave the book life. And this applies to writing in general, not just collaboration. But there is sometimes a natural tendency in collaborating to control the characters, because two people are sharing in their creation. "Let's have her do this, while he does that." When we look instead at the characters as people, their own characteristics, personalities, and yes, even their secrets begin to surface.

We've mentioned single voice and two voices, but we should say more about that. Books written by one person have a single voice: that of the author. In collaborations, the goal should be the same: to come across as one writer, not two. Two voices feel like two points of view, and distracts from the impact your story ought to be having. When readers begin to guess which of you is speaking at any given time, they're no longer concentrating on the book itself. More to the point, when an editor is distracted, you could lose a sale.

A word on plot and plotting: These have to be as tight for two people working together as they must be for a writer working alone. Tangents can be very tempting. But again, the end goal is the story, and while one partner really wants to throw in Mallorca because they just got back from there, does it really suit the story you are trying to tell? It isn't ego so much as excitement about a holiday, but it can cause as much trouble. A plot *can* be adjusted as you learn more about where it is going, and it's okay to try out an idea in the plotting, to see if the bow and arrow could have killed the victim when originally you'd considered poison. But these must be tested, to be sure the change works and doesn't cause trouble closer to the end. A single author often develops an inner editor, who can warn, "Great idea, but save it for the next book." This objectivity is even more important for two writers, for the simple reason that sometimes one can persuade the other too easily when in fact the change isn't for the best. There's a big difference between improving and straying off target. Again, your mantra should be: What is best for the book?

Never assume that you don't need a written agreement until that book contract is signed. Single writers have only themselves to consider. When there are two working together, whatever your relationship, it's surprising how quickly difficulties can arise—and having already-agreed-upon rules will make resolving these issues easier. What the copyright will show, what name to use, how the royalties will be distributed, what financial allowance you will give to research, travel, and promotion, how expenses will be met, even what will happen to the partnership if one of you dies. Do residual royalties go to the surviving partner, or are they shared with the heirs of the deceased? These questions matter.

And don't forget to consider what will happen to earnings—and to your pen name—if you *stop* writing together. Or if one wants to do something on their own as well as collaborate, and the other doesn't. It can happen.

There's something else that counts: respect for one's partner. Whatever is going on behind the scenes, never broadcast it in public, or worse still, hint at it. You have a brand here, just as a single writer does, and you want to protect that brand. Even after a privately acrimonious split, the public face mustn't change. What purpose is served by damaging the reputation of the name on the cover or the work itself?

Remember, too, that you are running a business, not a hobby. Both parties need to read contracts, understand them, and learn how publishing, publicity, and marketing actually work. These should never be left to your agent, no matter how good that agent may be—and they shouldn't be left to just one partner, either. Contracts are the rules you have agreed upon with the publishing house and therefore are essential to how you work and how you are paid.

All in all, collaboration can be very satisfying—and a challenge as well as a lot of fun. On the other hand, it isn't for everybody. The time to find that out is sooner rather than later. The idea can be appealing, it can seem to be quite workable—but the personalities of the two people considering it may be all wrong. If that happens, better to acknowledge it and stop. The book you are expecting to write won't work out, because you will be pulling apart on issues rather than pulling together. That's the whole point of collaborating—finding a way of working as smoothly as possible together toward the creation of a great mystery.

BRADLEY HARPER

Chekhov's advice, "Don't tell me the moon was full. Tell me of the moonlight's reflection from the shattered glass," is so powerful. It gives my brain a sharp image that transports me into the story.

Sounds. Sounds are universal, transcending all language (other than spoken words themselves). A baby's cry or a door squeaking open on a dark night needs no translation. I got it.

Smells. Often overlooked. As a retired physician, I can tell you that smell is our most primitive sense and goes directly to the basic animal brain that reigns over our strongest emotions. Think of cookies coming out of the oven on a cold winter afternoon and you're back in your grandmother's kitchen with pigtails, begging to lick the bowl. Smells have powerful emotional context, and as the olfactory nerve has no intermediate stops, it is a highway to our emotional bank vault. Use smells sparingly, but they can be a powerful ace in the hole when you want your reader nailed to a scene until you're done with them.

Touch and taste. Taste is a wingman to smell, but touch has a wealth of opportunities, and not just in sixty shades of purple prose. Like smell, it should be used sparingly or it loses its punch. Our body is sheathed in this exquisitely sensitive organ called skin. One drop of cold water on the back of your neck sends a shock wave through you, no matter how thick your jacket. One of my favorite words is "frisson," a sudden shiver of excitement. Provide an apt description of a light touch and your reader will lean into the book. They're there.

Tie-Ins and Continuing a Character

Playing in someone else's sandbox.

MAX ALLAN COLLINS

The novelization is perhaps the least recognized, most-often derided form of professional fiction writing; it's also one of the most difficult to do well. Only slightly more respected is the original novel based on a TV show or a movie franchise.

Both novelizations and original licensed novels are considered "tie-in" books. This includes novels or short stories using characters from a TV show or film, but also continuing the work of a deceased author, often with an arrangement with the estate.

An organization of professional writers who find themselves "playing in someone else's sandbox" was founded by myself and television writer and producer Lee Goldberg (who wrote both scripts and tie-in novels for *Monk* and *Diagnosis: Murder*). The International Association of Media Tie-In Writers gives annual awards, in the fashion of the Mystery Writers of America Edgars and the Private Eye Writers of America Shamuses, in various categories. The reason for these awards is that, quality aside, such books are seldom honored elsewhere.

In recent years, a more respectable aspect of tie-in writing has seen the likes of Robert B. Parker continuing Raymond Chandler's Philip Marlowe, and top talents Reed Farrel Coleman and Ace Atkins among those continuing Parker's own work on Jesse Stone and Spenser, respectively. Anthony Horowitz and Jeffery Deaver are among big names taking on James Bond, the Ian Fleming series having been previously continued by Raymond Benson and John Gardner, among others. Listing Sherlock

Holmes authors (beyond Arthur Conan Doyle) is a task I won't attempt, but certainly Nicholas Meyer was instrumental in reviving mainstream interest in the Great Detective.

Major names continuing major series by major deceased authors is surprising only because more of it didn't happen sooner. Gaining entry to that club comes about chiefly when some high-powered editor makes a phone call and—in a refreshing change of pace—pitches the author. Most practitioners of mystery writing should understand that approaching an editor about, say, continuing Miss Marple or Lew Archer is not going to get much out of that editor beyond an eye roll.

Even the often-looked-down-upon tie-in field itself is a fairly exclusive club . . . or at least one that's hard to get into without an invite. A handful of specialists are known to editors as go-to tie-in writers, particularly in science fiction. Other writers, again largely in the s-f field, have networked at fan conventions to talk to editors and agents and get a shot at submitting proposals.

If you are a published writer with at least a little success, you might approach an editor you work with and inquire about getting in touch with another editor at their publisher about your interest in writing a tie-in. But mostly you get a phone call out of the blue, from an editor or your agent, after an editor has read something of yours that makes you seem just right for doing a novel based on one famous TV show or another.

Copyright will be held by the license holder—in the case of TV and movies, often the studio; in the case of continuation of a late author's series, their estate. Whether you receive a royalty or not is to be negotiated, but often you'll be paid a flat fee.

My path into tie-in writing demonstrates the kind of circuitous route that can take *you* into tie-in writing. I was the writer of the *Dick Tracy* comic strip when Warren Beatty adapted it into a movie; as a consultant on the film, I heard a tie-in novel was going to happen. I lobbied through my agent to get the novel, and did, though the experience was a trial by fire, to say the least. I learned that the licensor has the muscle—my pedigree as the writer of the strip carried no weight. I had to "follow the script out the door" and add nothing to it.

(I had a similar experience writing a novelization of the screenplay of *Road to Perdition*, even though the film was based on my own graphic novel.)

239

In 1992, an editor at the Tribune Syndicate I'd clashed with fired me from the *Tracy* strip, which I'd been writing for fifteen years. I called my agent and said, "Get the word out that I am available for movie novelizations." The *Dick Tracy* novel had sold 800,000 copies, after all.

Nothing happened for a while, but finally my agent called me and said, "The good news is Berkley wants you to write a novelization of the next Clint Eastwood movie, *In the Line of Fire*. The bad news is that they need it in ten days."

"Yes" is the only word in the freelancer's vocabulary, much as "no" is the only word in an editor's vocabulary. This was before the internet was much help, and the screenplay (*faxed* to me) included multiple real locations. My wife, Barb, also a writer, made research trips to the library for me and phone calls to friends around the country for info about their localities. I hunkered down and came out only for meals, briefly. If I recall, I did three chapters a day. Later, when we listened to the audiobook of *In the Line of Fire*, I realized the amount of profanity increased in tandem with the hero's own anxiety. So here's a writing tip: if you're having a nervous breakdown, have your protagonist experience one, too.

Word got around that I was reliable and fast. The latter became a problem, because having a reputation as someone to call in a pinch can make for a harrowing writing life. But for the next decade and a half, I would get one or two novelizations per annum. I was extremely lucky—most of the scripts I novelized were well-written and became major movies, among them *Saving Private Ryan*, *Air Force One*, and *American Gangster*.

Others were just plain fun—I did all three *Mummy* movies, for example, which were a combination of Indiana Jones and Universal Studios horror. As a mystery writer, I am somewhat typed, which is fine—being a known quantity has its advantages. But as a tie-in writer, I've been able to write science fiction (*Waterworld*), war stories (*Windtalkers*), espionage (*I Spy*), and sword and sorcery (*The Scorpion King*). I learned a lot, working in different genres, which is one of the joys and advantages of tie-in writing (although you can become typecast there as well).

Movie tie-in writing requires you to find something in the material that can excite you as much as if you had come up with it yourself. In *The Pink Panther*, I wrote about Inspector Clouseau as if Peter Sellers were starring, not Steve Martin. In *Maverick*, I pictured James Garner as young Bret Maverick, not Mel Gibson. In *U.S. Marshals*, a sequel to the film version of TV's *The Fugitive*, I started chapters in the omniscient voice of the narrator (William Conrad—"Fate moves its huge hand"). As a big *X-Files* fan, I was delighted to land the second *X-Files* film and work with the show's creators (a rarity).

Finding a way in, with a movie novel, is crucial. I had turned down several jobs, not liking the scripts, when another dog came in. I asked my agent, "Do I dare turn this one down?" He said, "Sure. You'll just never get anything offered to you again." So I did it. The movie was *Daylight*, a disaster film about a tunnel collapsing. I approached it as a documentary with alternating first-person sections, as if the survivors were talking to an off-camera narrator. I did not use the hero's POV, to give the illusion that he may not have survived (spoiler alert: he does). *Daylight* turned out to be possibly my best movie novel.

My approach has always been to try to make the novelization seem like the book the movie was based on. I vary from some writers of movie novelizations in that I don't follow the dialogue in the screenplay religiously. I use it, but I expand and reshape it (and, frankly, sometimes ignore it). Screenplay writing isn't novel writing. You have to add backstory and interior monologue because (a) it needs to read like a book, not a transcribed screenplay, and (b) it needs to be book length, say three hundred manuscript pages minimum, where a screenplay is closer to one hundred pages. A screenplay may jump from A to C and get away with it, but the novelist must provide the missing B.

More rewarding, at least artistically, was the chance to write original novels. My *CSI* books were bestsellers and got my name out to a wider audience. My agent had initially advised me not to put my real name on any tie-in books, novelizations included. Just having a byline on a tie-in was potentially career damaging. But I saw no reason not to have my name on a book tied to a big Hollywood movie—what's the downside of writing *Saving Private Ryan*?

A lot of the audience for tie-in novels is young—middle school, mostly. Though these books aren't sold as young adult, many young adults read them. As an author of several award-winning juvenile books—a guy named Spillane—once told me, "If you get a reader at a young age, you have 'em forever." I believe that. I also believe in putting my own name on tie-ins—it keeps me honest.

Writing original novels based on TV series requires having real familiarity with the show or bingeing it on DVD or streaming services until you do. Also necessary is resourcefulness.

I signed on to *CSI* early in its first season, and was provided scripts and screeners, which led to long sessions of notetaking. Many shows have "bibles," with background info on characters and general material about the series, but *CSI* didn't have that. Early on, the show was about the crimes and the forensics, with the recurring cast secondary. Soon the actors and the public conspired to flip that dynamic, but initially the TV characters were fairly blank. I had to latch on to every morsel about the people that the series deigned to give me.

Dark Angel, an s-f series, had been on the air two years when I got the call. I'd never seen it, and again had to hit the ground running. Not having time to watch two years' worth of episodes, I watched the pilot movie several times and wrote a prequel to the show. Oddly, the series—fairly popular and already picked up for season three—was unexpectedly canceled. I had two books left on the contract, and was asked to wrap up the series, one novel resolving the second season's closing cliffhanger, the other tying a bow on the show's entire story arc. So, as it happened, I wrote the first and last episodes of *Dark Angel*.

I encounter in the tie-in field a lot of writers who want to write novels about a certain TV series. Some come from the fan fiction community, which didn't exist when I was starting out. Having written fan fiction can be helpful, particularly if *Star Trek* or *Star Wars*, for example, are favorites of yours, but those jobs are hard to land. And writing your own book about one of those franchises and submitting it is almost always a bad idea.

In my view, a professional writer should be able to take on an assignment without having a fannish interest in the material. Going in with that interest can break your heart when you realize how little control you have over these characters you care so much about.

The continuation of famous mystery series by other hands is the most rarefied strata of tie-in writing, deriving not from a TV show or a movie but a body of work by a writer who has put something so personal into it that readers want more even though Elvis has left the building. That requires a respect and probably a love for the work of the writer who created the series.

Bob Goldsborough wrote a Nero Wolfe novel to read to his elderly mother, who was such a Rex Stout fan that the absence of an annual visit from Archie and his boss was too much to bear. And that led to Bob continuing the series for others in permanent Stout withdrawal to enjoy.

It's clear that talents like Atkins and Coleman bring a love of Parker's work to the table, and Deaver and Horowitz (among others) clearly admire the much-underrated Fleming. Those who have successfully continued Ludlum and Clancy also have obvious respect for the creators.

I have had the unique privilege of finishing work left behind by Mickey Spillane, who inspired me to want to become a mystery writer when I was thirteen. I became friends with Mickey in the early eighties and we did numerous projects together, including a dozen anthologies, a comic book series, and a documentary. On a visit to his home in Murrells Inlet, South Carolina, in the late eighties, he sent two unfinished Mike Hammer novels home with me. These were substantial manuscripts of a hundred pages each.

"Maybe we'll do something with these someday," he said.

We grew close over the years—Mickey was my son Nate's godfather. In 2006, Mickey was diagnosed with pancreatic cancer. Not long before his passing, he called about the Mike Hammer novel he was working on, *The Goliath Bone*. He said that though he was deep into it, he might not get it finished. If need be, would I do that for him?

It was both the greatest and saddest honor I've ever been paid. A day or so later, Mickey told his wife, Jane, that after he was gone, there'd be "a treasure hunt around here." For various reasons having to do with everything from disputes with his publisher to objections by his church, Mickey had begun a dizzying number of novels—many of them featuring his world-famous detective, Mike Hammer—only to set them aside. Barb and I went to South Carolina for a tribute to Mickey and stayed behind for that treasure hunt with Jane, going through material in Mickey's three offices.

Since then, I have completed six substantial Hammer manuscripts and two non-Hammer novels—working from one hundred Spillane pages, sometimes with plot and character notes, including at times endings—and another six Hammer novels from shorter manuscripts and/or Spillane synopses. Additionally, a short story collection—*A Long Time Dead*—adds eight short stories from Spillane fragments to the Hammer canon. Mickey published only thirteen Hammer novels in his lifetime—a relative handful compared to other detective characters of similar stature—which means this has doubled the number of Hammer books.

These books all have Spillane content, and he shares, quite legitimately, the byline with me. These are not continuations but completions, not pastiches but collaborations.

I prepare for each one, doing some detective work to figure out when Mickey wrote the available material so that I can place it properly in the canon. Unlike most of the popular series detectives of the twentieth century, Mike Hammer grows and changes and even gets older. For prep, I read several novels in close proximity to the time period of the book at hand. From my perspective, while continuation writers should drench themselves in the original novels, capturing the characterizations of the detective and the rest of the recurring cast is far more important than mimicking the author's style.

Still, my greatest pleasure is when a reviewer quotes lines from one of these novels as examples of pure Spillane, and half of the lines are Mickey's and the other half mine.

This is in keeping with the best of tie-in writing: when you make a novel based on a film script seem like the book the movie was based on, or write a novel that convinces fans that it's a valid "episode" of their favorite show.

HAL BODNER

Less-experienced writers often introduce their characters with vast paragraphs of background exposition detailing their fictional creation's entire life to date. We may read pages and pages about how the infant Amelia was cruelly ripped from her mother's breast, spent her formative years slaving in the copper mines until, finally, the sight of a free-flying bluebird inspires her to spark a revolution and journey across the sea to freedom, where she devotes her life to teaching macramé in a leper colony. Often, the author believes that the exposition is necessary to give the reader something to latch on to so that the plot can move forward. They believe that the reader needs to have Amelia's motivations laid out for them in order to understand why she does whatever it is she ends up doing.

In most cases, this is a flawed technique. It usually ends up boring the reader with information that they do not really need. In the worst cases, the information dump is simply too massive for the reader to digest. It's far more interesting and effective to *show* your audience how Amelia responds to the obstacles and plot twists that you throw in her way. If you're not able to create believable situations to which your character can react truthfully, if you're not able to use words to sculpt a character that leaps off the page with vitality, then no amount of background explanation is going to help you.

After the Writing

Oline H. Cogdill—Secrets of a Book Critic
Reviews and reviewers: what to learn from them, and what to ignore.

Liliana Hart—Self-Publishing
How to flourish as an independently published writer.

Maddee James—Authors Online
Building your author identity and reaching out to readers, online.

Louise Penny—Building Your Community
It's the writer, not the book: finding a home in the virtual village.

Daniel Steven—Legal Considerations
What every mystery writer needs to know about publishing law.

Secrets of a Book Critic

*Reviews and reviewers: what to learn from them,
and what to ignore.*

OLINE H. COGDILL

For many of us who review books, especially mysteries, critiques are both an art and a craft, and, more important, a mission to let readers know about new titles.

That certainly is the case with me. On average, I review about 100 to 125 mysteries a year. That may seem like a lot, but it is a mere drop in the bucket compared to the more than 1,500 mysteries published annually.

For many authors, a review is the first time that word of their new book finally reaches beyond the safe boundaries of family and friends. Now strangers will weigh in on what they think about a book, and their unbiased opinions may not always be as kind as your inner circle's impressions.

But book reviewing is at a crossroads.

Today, more people than ever are giving their opinions—from paid professional critics, to bloggers who write for their own websites or online or print publications, to amateur reviewers who write for sites such as Goodreads.

At the same time, fewer newspapers and magazines publish reviews in print; most are posting these critiques online. Fortunately, reviews are finding a home in publications that cover the mystery genre, such as *Mystery Scene*, *Strand Magazine*, *Crimespree*, and *Deadly Pleasures*.

(Want to see more reviews? Make sure to tell your newspaper or favorite magazine! Respond to these reviews, talk about them on social media, and let the publications know that books coverage is one of the reasons you're a subscriber.)

Ethically Speaking

Book critiquing is in the midst of an ethical crisis.

First, there are still a good number of professional book critics and thoughtful bloggers who care about reviewing and believe in analyzing books ethically and fairly. But many people are pretending to be reviewers to receive free books or to get attention from authors; some have agendas—they hate the author or the genre or believe that reviewing is a license to be nasty.

Even more bothersome is the flux of paid reviews.

As a professional critic, I am paid by the venue for which I write. I am not paid by the author, the publisher, or a bookstore. Bloggers may not be paid; ethical ones do it strictly for the love of the genre.

Unfortunately, an author can buy a review. For years, legitimate publications have been offering book reviews for sale in addition to their authentic coverage. Writers can pay $600, or even more, to be guaranteed a review. While these are presented in a specific part of the magazine and labeled as paid, they are designed to look like legitimate reviews. And writers often try to brag about these glowing reviews.

Websites keep popping up offering review packages. As soon as one site shuts down, another starts.

Let me be blunt: Any author who buys a review is a fool. Buying a review goes against every ethical and professional standard that real critics and reviewers hold. Media outlets such as newspapers, magazines, and some review websites will not touch these reviews—yet these businesses thrive because enough venues will pick up their reviews regardless of the provenance.

Fairness Is No Mystery

As a journalist, I am trained to be objective in coverage.

But being a critic also means one is subjective about what one reviews. And this is where the conundrum comes in—a critic must be both objective and subjective. One should be reviewing the book solely for the reader. We are not doing it to curry favor, or to strike up a friendship with the author, publisher, or bookstore, or to launch our own writing career. We have to be honest and fair with integrity.

And while it can be fun to write a totally negative review, being nasty for nasty's sake is not acceptable. One can give an honest negative review without trashing the book or taking pot shots at the author. A critic reviews the book, not what they personally think about the author.

Reviewers who are consistently mean-spirited are more in love with their own voices than giving solid evaluations of books.

Writers—and readers—also should not pay attention to reviews that contain multiple errors, such as the names of characters and major plot points. Yes, the occasional error can creep into a review—and the critic should feel terrible when that happens. But many errors are the sign of an amateur, and an undisciplined one.

Do Reviews Work?

By calling attention to a book, reviews work for the author. Murder on the Beach Mystery Bookstore in Florida makes a prominent display of my annual list of top mysteries. Buyers respond to it. The store's manager also said that customers often come in with copies of my reviews, looking to buy the books.

Several publicists at major publishing houses say that reviews often result in an uptick in sales. As one publicist said, "As a reader, if you're seeing a book get reviewed in multiple media outlets within a six- to eight-week time frame, it's on your radar and you might be curious to buy it or mention it to someone else who might buy it. Publicity and reviews definitely are a tool to help build sales for a book."

Another added that "for literary fiction and mysteries and thrillers, reviews still seem to really matter. Some are definitely more effective than others—*People* magazine, a daily review [in the *New York Times*]—they can really give sales a lift."

But not every reader buys national magazines or lives in New York. Writers may think the gold standards for reviews are the *New York Times*, the *Los Angeles Times*, and the *Chicago Tribune*. And that is true—to a certain extent. But writers receive more coverage from the Associated Press because those reviews may run in more than three hundred newspapers and websites, as well as from regional newspapers with a strong commitment to books coverage. More readers rely on their local publications or genre magazines or links to reviews on legitimate sites posted on social media.

And more is definitely more in terms of reader response. Added another publicist, "In general, quantity is better—more reviews equal better sales, but it's far from a hard and fast rule."

Privately, several authors have mentioned how reviews helped them. One author, who was being considered to continue a deceased author's series, said that my review was the deciding factor in his favor. Several authors said they felt reviews came just in time when they were about to negotiate a new contract.

(However, let me caution authors that these days it takes so much more than just a review to make a book work, so being creative and having a varied marketing campaign is very important. That's where a publicist is invaluable.)

The Dreaded Amazon Review

Reviews on Amazon and other websites are among the most controversial. While Amazon has tried to weed out fake reviews, some with agendas have slipped through.

An average of four- or five-star reviews is good news, and maybe worth the author and readers paying attention. But writers, especially new authors or those with a thin skin, might want to avoid reading reviews with one star or less.

Writers often are at the mercy of unscrupulous reviewers. One "reviewer" trashed a book because he had heard the author discuss the work in progress. At the time of that discussion, the book was to be set against the backdrop of World War II, but the finished book ended up set in a different era. The "reviewer" gave the book a low score because it wasn't the book he was expecting. A review should focus on the book that is there, not the one the reviewer anticipated.

We've seen negative reviews because a person didn't like the cover, was shocked that a book called *The Death of X* does indeed contain the death of a protagonist, or the author cursed or put sex in the book. A self-published author I know once received glowing reviews from five different people—all of which were his wife using fake names. When the two got divorced, an avalanche of negative reviews appeared, the work of the ex-wife.

Writers should ignore these reviews, as did a famous author who remembers the one-star Amazon review where the text read, "The book never arrived—I'm not sure if I even ordered it." That says it all.

Men versus Women

Complaints have arisen during the past several years that reviews give preference to male writers over women writers and that authors of color or gay and lesbian writers are further marginalized.

Having read countless reviews by other critics through the years, I fear this may be true.

On one hand, an author's gender, race, or sexual orientation should not matter when choosing a book to review. But on a much greater plain, it matters immensely. Critics should strive for balance in the books they choose to review, taking into account the types of stories and genres. A mix of different types of authors and different types of mysteries (hard-boiled, cozy, historical, etc.) makes for a better critic and more interesting reviews.

We live in a multicultural world and that makes for better stories.

A reviewer who refuses to read female writers or dismisses those of color or gay and lesbian authors is unprofessional. Mystery readers love to discover new worlds and will follow a good story no matter where it takes them or who is telling the tale.

Convincing a critic to read outside their comfort level is difficult but not impossible. I recommend publicists continue to write convincing releases to critics—and even copy their editors—about how good a story is. Posts on social media about this inequity has, in a way, shamed critics into looking at the rich variety of stories available. And that's a good thing.

Cozies and paperback originals also are often ignored by mainstream reviewers. For cozies, it generally boils down to a matter of taste—many critics just prefer harder-edged novels, although regional critics will more often review cozies if the author is local or has scheduled a local event. Paperback originals used to be reviewed with other paperback originals, usually in a roundup column. But paperback originals now are often ignored, another victim of space cutbacks. These authors should look for other venues, blogs and websites that will review these books.

Attention Must Be Paid

Authors should allow publicists to pitch books to critics. Publicists have accumulated years of knowing how to promote a book, how to approach a critic, and, just as important, how to accept rejection.

Whether writers hire a private publicist or utilize the one who works for a publisher, these are professionals. They know that turning down a book for review may have nothing to do with the quality of the book; it may be that the critic already has too many books of that category planned for review.

An author who believes that constantly asking for a review will eventually work is wrong. You cannot wear us down. Keep in mind—you are not the only author vying for that review spot. An author who sends a postcard every day for a year—yes, this happened—is just being irritating, not effective. The book, not the author, has to speak to us.

Self-published authors, as well as writers of cozies and paperback originals, have other challenges. Many newspapers and magazines will not review self-published books, but many blogs and websites will. Authors, or their publicists, should contact these venues directly.

For more coverage, be creative. Suggest a story on your background, your novel's unusual backstory, or innovative research, and tie that into a speaking engagement at a local bookstore, library, or organization that is open to the public. That would get you the much-needed publicity.

How Authors Should Use Reviews

Maximize that review for everything it's worth, and do it often. Post it on your website and every social media platform you subscribe to. Post it on your own Facebook page but also the pages of every bookstore, library, or venue at which you've scheduled an event, and your publisher's page. Ask your friends, acquaintances, and fans to do the same. Pluck out a pithy quote that you refer to on social media, your website, and so forth. Even a negative review probably has at least one positive word or phrase you can use. (And be sure to keep that website up to date!)

Writers shouldn't think of reviews as adversarial, but as a learning opportunity. A good review points out the positive and, if necessary, the negative aspects of a book. A review discusses patterns that can help writers hone their craft. If several reviews point out the overuse of the same plot or character tropes, the author might want to pay attention when writing the next book. Chances are the reader also is noticing these deficiencies.

But authors shouldn't write with visions of glowing reviews or awards. Instead, focus on the story you want to tell. Your passion will show in the book.

While I think it is perfectly fine to drop a note thanking a critic for a positive review, it is not necessary, and will not influence the critic when your next book comes out.

While it may be tempting to respond to a negative review with a nasty note or worse, resist. Please resist. Better to complain to your friends and family. No matter how you phrase it, your response to a negative review will come off as whiny and immature. Do not try to humiliate a critic on social media or launch an angry writing campaign, or, as one British writer did, start stalking the critic. None of this will do any good. The review will not be changed.

Publishers also frown on authors who go after critics.

Unfortunately, critics should develop a thick skin as well. A colleague once received a box of human waste after a negative review. I had at least two authors try to get me fired for daring to dislike their work. Neither of those actions are the conduct of a professional author. Yes, a writer is upset because the critic has just called their "baby" ugly. But they need to move on. A negative review for one book doesn't mean a negative review for the next; nor does a positive review ensure a career of accolades.

A critic should never be influenced if an author has been rude or condescending or has a different political agenda. All that needs to be put aside to concentrate on the book.

A good critic reviews the book, not the author. Just as authors—and readers—review the critic for the fairness they show.

Are We Friends?

If Facebook has taught us anything, it's that not all friendships are created equal. Being Facebook friends doesn't translate to being real friends.

I am a friendly person who attends many mystery writers' conferences and often moderates or participates in panels with authors. But that doesn't mean we are all going shoe shopping and then taking a cruise together. Being friends on social media and following an author or a critic are professional situations. By all means, feel free to like a comment, share a post, or even thank a critic for a review that's posted. That is welcomed and further gets out the word about the book. But don't ask why a critic hasn't reviewed your book.

What I Owe the Reader and the Writer

With each review, I make a pact with the reader: I won't give away plot points. If a twist is a surprise to me, I want that twist to be a surprise to the reader. I will look at the book as it is, not what it could have been. I'll view the characters with an open mind.

And finally, I'll just be honest for the reader and to the author.

MARILYN STASIO
(THE NEW YORK TIMES BOOK REVIEW)

How Not to Get Reviewed:
Send multiple copies of your book to the reviewer's home and keep bugging her by email.

—Marilyn

Self-Publishing

How to flourish as an independently published writer.

LILIANA HART

At the time of this publication, I'll have sustained a successful self-publishing career for a decade. Anyone who's been in publishing for more than a minute knows two things: first, success is defined differently by different people, and second, publishing (no matter how you do it) is hard.

If you're reading this, I'm going to make a couple of assumptions. The first is that you're a writer—that you've learned to cope with the voices in your head, felt the rush as fatigue and boundless energy wage war with each other as you get closer to typing "The end," and fallen into the pit of despair when the story isn't right or your career has taken a nose dive, even though you've done everything you're supposed to.

Let's be honest. Publishing is weird. We never know why one book resonates and others don't. Or why one book becomes a bestseller over another. Believe me, self-publishing is just as weird and unpredictable as traditional publishing.

The second assumption I'm making is that you want to write *and* make a living. It's important to have dreams. Twenty years ago, I fantasized about the day when I'd be able to quit teaching and write full-time. I had vivid Technicolor dreams about becoming an eccentric recluse who lived in soft pajamas and toiled away at my computer like Kathleen Turner's character in *Romancing the Stone*. I'm not going to lie: I'm living my dreams. And it's fabulous. But still hard, because writing is hard.

Publishing (no matter how you do it) isn't for wimps.

I get asked often about the "secret sauce of success" for self-publishing, as if there's a switch you can flip or a genre you can change to, and *KA-*

BOOM! You're an immediate bestseller. It used to drive me crazy when I first started giving keynotes and workshops, because people would introduce me as an "overnight success." But I'd get up to the podium and remind them that just because readers discovered me seemingly overnight didn't mean I hatched from an egg the day before. I wrote for thirteen years before I ever saw a dime from one of the books that I put blood, sweat, and tears into.

I do want to give a word of encouragement for anyone who wants to self-publish or who is currently self-publishing. I do believe you can still be successful in self-publishing. Yes, even after the "gold rush" of the early years. There is no such thing as easy publishing, and publishing never has been, and never will be, a get-rich-quick scheme. Just write great books and put in the work. You can do it!

Which leads to my first tip for successful self-publishing.

1. There Is No Secret Sauce

You've got to write a good book. Period. That was the truth ten years ago, it's the truth today, and it'll be the truth ten years from now. The longevity of your career depends on the content you create.

2. Write More Than One Book

Self-publishing is not the model you want to use if your goal is to write one book. Or even one book every couple of years. I like to think of self-publishing as a machine that needs constant maintenance. When I first started self-publishing I wrote like an insane person. I wrote full-length novels and novellas. I wrote a romantic suspense series and two different mystery series. I'm a data nerd. I wanted to see what readers wanted to read, how long it was taking them to read it, and which series they bought more of.

You don't have to do that. It's just what I did because I realized the potential of self-publishing once I started doing it. And logic dictated that I'd make more money if I wrote more books. Just write.

I'm currently writing three books a year, and maybe a novella or two if the whim strikes me. I'm perfectly happy with that production pace, so if you're a slower writer than I am, you can still be successful self-publishing.

3. Write a Series

I still believe this is the best way to hook readers, especially when you're a new author and you're looking to establish a reader base. One of the amazing things about self-publishing is that it's only about you, your book, and the reader. Want to write cross-genre? Do it! Want to write shorter or longer lengths? Do it! There are no rules. Only good books.

Getting readers to keep reading is what every author wants. If you write a great series with great characters that keep readers coming back for more, you'll have done your job *and* you'll benefit by getting a much higher royalty rate through direct sales channels than through traditional publishing.

I gave this advice when I first saw success, and I still believe it today. There's strategy to self-publishing, and one of the best strategies that worked for me—and dozens of authors I've mentored through the process—is to write at least three books in your series before you hit the publish button. Writing one book in a series and leaving readers hanging, especially when you're first starting out, does two things: it irritates your readers, and it gives them time to forget you while you're writing the next book (especially if it takes too long).

Patience in self-publishing is key, and in my experience, it's something that most authors who try it lack. There's a reason there are a lot fewer self-published authors now than there were over the past few years. They want things to happen fast—fast money, fast books, fast readers. And if you really want a career as a writer, you've got to have a vision that extends past the most recent deposit that dropped in your bank account.

4. Don't Quit Your Day Job

You'd be surprised how often this happens. Again, patience is key. You've got to make a living if writing is not making the living for you. Yes, it's hard to be creative and write while holding down a full-time job. During those thirteen years while I was becoming an "overnight success," I moonlighted as a high school band director, and I still managed to write three books a year.

And before you say it, you do have time. One of my biggest pet peeves is listening to someone expound on how busy they are and how they wish they had time to write. You can go ahead and insert a giant eye roll here. Bruh, *everyone* is busy. I worked ninety-hour weeks and was a single mom to four kids. If you want something bad enough (whether it's scrolling through social media or watching episodes of your favorite TV show), you'll find a way to do it. If you want to write, you'll write. Period.

When you start making a consistent income as a writer and you can meet your financial goals, then quit your day job.

5. Don't Chase Shiny Objects

There are a couple of things I mean by this. Write what you love to write. Your genre might not be popular right now. Or maybe your genre was selling like hotcakes and now it's dead in the water. Don't jump ship and write something you're not comfortable with or don't love just to chase the current trend. Be patient. Publishing is cyclical and you'll see your genre rise in popularity again.

The second part of this is for those of you who may already have found success in self-publishing: It's possible to drown in opportunity. The more books you sell, the more things you're able to do. You make more money, so you can spend dollars on advertising or something like audiobooks, where you're making more of an investment. But remember that the book is the core of your business. It's easy to get caught up in doing everything but writing your next book. Focus on what you're good at. Focus on the core of what's going to make you money.

6. Marketing and Promotion

Here are a few tips I've learned to keep momentum going in your business and increase visibility:

- Your next book is the best promotion. Write the next book and stop worrying about promoting your one book to death.
- Cultivate a newsletter list. Social media is fickle. Don't rely on people seeing your posts or following what you're doing. Social media changes constantly. People who sign up for your newsletter want to hear from you. You're not bothering them. They asked to be kept informed about your books.
- Advertising and marketing are for visibility, not for sales. A lot of people get disappointed when they invest in an ad campaign and they don't see immediate sales results. Marketing is about visibility. It doesn't equate to sales. So when you invest your money, keep that in mind.
- The days of books getting visibility in retail stores through algorithms is gone. Invest in Amazon ads. It took some time, but we've learned how to do them. This is another one of those things that takes lots of trial and error. And patience. That word keeps resurfacing. There are a lot of companies that charge a lot of money to do ads for you. I've used them. You can do just as good of a job, if not better, learning to do it yourself. No one will care about your business and your product like you do. Getting readers to follow you on BookBub is also time well spent, as well as getting BookBub featured deals. Those are the three main marketing tools I use that I know have gotten my books into the hands of new readers—new readers who are going to invest their time in the entire series. (See "Write a Series" above.)

7. It's a Business

I'm going to repeat that. Self-publishing is a business. I've found that some people don't like to hear that. They want to be creative, write beautiful words on the page, let people discover them, and blah, blah, blah, blah, blah. Whatever. If you don't want to treat self-publishing as a business, then you shouldn't do it. Unless you're publishing so your mom and your third-grade teacher can read your art.

It's a business. Have a business plan. How many books do you want to write a year? What genre? Do you have business hours *and* writing hours?

What's your budget? Do your covers represent your genre and who you are as an author? Are your books identifiable to the reader through your covers or how your name appears on the cover?

Seriously, I can't stress this enough. I hear from authors all the time who are frustrated and angry that their book sales aren't better. The first thing I ask them to do is to describe their business to me. You can't just write a book and expect the fairies to magically transform it into a million sales. I know I'm probably preaching to the choir for most of you, but I get *a lot* of questions about how to make sales better, and I come to find out the people asking often aren't putting in any of the work on the business side of things.

I love having an end-of-year vision meeting. I look at what book sales did for the past year, and I make goals for the upcoming year. I set budgets for everything. I have a release schedule and know what books I'll be working on in which series for the next twenty-four months. I get editors and cover designers scheduled. *It's a business.* The things that a traditional publishing house does to get books out (with a few exceptions) are the things you should be doing.

I do want to talk a bit about covers. We've already established that you have to write a good book. But you also need to invest in a great cover. It's the first thing readers see as they're scrolling through the store, which means it not only needs to be a great cover, it needs to be a *recognizable* cover in thumbnail size. You want them to click on your book. They'll do that before they ever read your blurb, reviews, or sample pages.

As long as we're talking about self-publishing being a business, professionalism should be in evidence in every aspect of your work—not only covers, but also editing, formatting, graphics, social media posts, and newsletters. It's a business. You're the CEO and president of your own publishing house.

8. Don't Sell Yourself Short

There are a lot of ways to publish your book and get it out to readers. I'm a big fan of experimenting and testing the waters. Do what works, and when it doesn't work, change it and move forward. I've published more than sixty books and I've done it in every way possible. I've self-published,

I've been published with a small press, and I've signed big contracts with major publishers. I've distributed my self-published titles among every possible vendor, and I've strategically moved an older series into Kindle Unlimited.

Try everything. And stick with what works. You don't have to reinvent the wheel. I make the most money in three areas:

1. My mysteries sell well across all platforms, and most specifically at Apple Books. They sell well at Amazon, too, but Amazon is not the be-all and end-all for these types of books. There are a lot of readers using a lot of different devices to read. Take advantage of that.

2. My romantic suspense series sells better on Amazon, so I put it in Kindle Unlimited. This is where I use Amazon ads to boost page reads, and then I amplify that by using my free days and rotating my Kindle Countdown Deals.

3. I highly recommend audiobooks. They're worth it. I started doing audiobooks for self-published works back in the early days, and I can tell you the sales have more than doubled every year. Audiobooks are huge, and if you're looking for a good investment, then look no further.

9. Don't Be a Jerk . . .

Seriously, don't. You'd think this would be a given, but I've seen a lot of crazy things happening in the self-publishing world over the last ten years. When I first started writing, back in the day when you had to mail out all your manuscripts and query letters with an SASE, the writing community was extremely professional. It's not a huge community. Word gets out about behavior. Especially bad behavior.

Unfortunately, I've seen a lot of bad behavior from self-published authors who didn't have the advantage of belonging to professional writing organizations. And it's sad. I've seen bar fights, blackball lists, and just plain nastiness. The internet has made creative introverts keyboard warriors. It's not pretty. And it's not professional. Kindness never costs anyone anything.

If you're not part of a professional writing organization, then join one. Writing is a very insular world. Worry about yourself, your product, and your career. Don't compare yourself to others, and be happy for others' successes. Negativity in any capacity (anger, hatred, disappointment, jealousy, frustration) is a creativity killer.

10. Self-Care and Balance

Speaking from experience, there's such a thing as too much success. Find your balance. Find what kind of production schedule makes you comfortable. Write what makes you happy. Find something to do that's not writing or managing the business of writing. It's easy to work eighteen-hour days when you own your own publishing house. It's also very easy to burn out and not be able to produce anything.

Take care of yourself, love yourself, and your writing will reap all the rewards.

In the old days, it was a death knell when your series got canceled. A new publisher wouldn't pick it up because they didn't have control over your backlist. Even if your sales were steady, that didn't count in the blockbuster mentality. With nowhere else to turn, you had to start fresh and create a new concept to attract another traditional publisher. This isn't the case anymore. You have choices now. A small press may take on your series, or you might decide to indie publish your work. You can become a hybrid author, self-publishing your ongoing series while submitting a different project to a new publisher. The end no longer has to be the end. One caveat here: make sure you retain the rights to your characters and series.

If you want to conclude the series and move on, write a book or novella or even a short story to tie up the loose ends with your characters. Or consider creating a spin-off series, with new characters but in the same world readers have come to love. Writers have many more options today when a series is canceled. It's only the end if you say it is.

Authors Online

Building your author identity and reaching out
to readers, online.

MADDEE JAMES

You've written a book: congratulations! Now, whether you've found an editor/agent/publisher or you've decided to self-publish, the vital question is: How do you get your book out into the world, and more specifically, how do you use the internet to market yourself and your book? Here are the most essential things you need to know.

Good Writing Comes First

The most important thing any author can do is write a good book. Focus on that first. Everything else comes second.

Writing the book is the fun part for many authors, and what comes next—the branding, marketing, promotion, website building, social media—can feel overwhelming. But this chapter should make you feel less stressed, because the simple answer is that you don't actually have to do everything you hear others talk about. While you definitely need to establish an online platform, once you get the basic needs down, you can focus on what works best for you—and then get back to the joy of writing the next book.

Build Your Author Identity

It's important to put forth a clear conception of you and your writing, and one of the best ways to do that is through building your author identity—your *brand*. There are many different names for the genre(s) you may write in: mysteries, thrillers, historical fiction, psychological suspense, gothic mysteries, cozies, and so on. Figure out what "theme" or "feel/style" best describes your books. While you may write more than one type of book, there is most likely a theme that unites your work.

How do you want potential readers to perceive you and your books? Suspenseful, dark, atmospheric, frightening, humorous, romantic? That's the first thing you have to figure out. Try to come up with a brief elevator pitch that describes all your books, and then use that to build your author brand. Your brand should clearly show your readers what you and your writing are about and what they can expect when they read your books and come across you online. Your brand is . . . *you*.

Along with your theme, make sure you know your target audience. You may write for adults, young adults, or middle-grade readers. These are very different kinds of readers, particularly in the online universe. Note that if you write across genres and for multiple age levels, your theme should still allow you to have a focus . . . you just may have to work at it a little harder.

Once you know your brand and target audience, you're ready to get more into the nitty-gritty of what's next: building your website, your newsletter list, and your social media presence.

Your Author Website: The Epicenter of Your Professional Online Presence

Your author website is the hub of your online identity because it's the number one place you can control your message. It should include information about you, your books (including buy links, of course), the social media you participate in, a way to contact you, and a clear form for readers to sign up for your newsletter, among many other things.

Domain names

Reserve your domain name regardless of where you are in the publishing process. Your domain name is your very own home on the internet. If yourname.com isn't available, add "author" or "books" to it, as in yournamebooks.com. Get a .com name if at all possible.

If you want to get additional domain names, like your book titles, feel free, but your author name is most important and is the one the other domains should point to.

Website design (theme and branding)

Starting with the home page, your website should make it immediately clear what your theme is and who your target audience is. It's not just about the content; it's also about the colors, the logo, the font, the style, the imagery . . . viewers should be able to get an idea of your author brand the second they view your website.

It's worth every penny to have a website that looks and feels professional. If this is something you can do yourself, go for it. But there are many author website designers to choose from, at a wide range of costs. It's well worth your time and money to get a site that shows your work in the best light.

Website responsiveness

Responsive websites that adapt to all screen sizes (desktops, laptops, tablets, phones) are extremely important for both viewer visibility and search engine optimization. Make sure your website stays current on all devices.

Website platform

There are many choices for platforms on which to build your website. Choose one that has stood the test of time, like WordPress. Other companies have come and gone, but WordPress has been around forever. There are many, many WordPress themes to choose from that allow websites to look very different.

Website hosting

Choose a website hosting service based on longevity (again, some of these companies come and go), good customer service, site speed, automated backups, etc. Have an SSL certificate (this is a protocol for web browsers and servers that allows for the authentication, encryption, and decryption of data sent over the internet) on your website, regardless of whether you plan to do e-commerce, for two reasons. First, Google gives preference in its rankings to websites that use SSL certificates, which could affect your search query position. Second, site visitors who see "not secure" in the address bar might not feel comfortable viewing your site—even though there's no security threat. Seeing the padlock or the word "secure" will make these visitors feel safe.

Website analytics

All sites should have analytics code installed to monitor site traffic. Delving into your website analytics allows you to figure out marketing strategies to help drive people to your site.

Search engine optimization

Search engine optimization, or SEO, is the practice of optimizing your website to make it reach a high position in the search results of Google or other search engines. In the simplest terms, it means adding keywords and specific content so that a search engine might show it as a top result when users search for certain keywords. However, with billions of websites online, rising to the top of a search engine is close to an impossible task. Along with doing the basics of SEO (using your name as your domain and adding keywords, title, and description in the head section of your website), your goal should be to build a website with clear navigation and unique, interesting content about you and your books.

Navigation and content

The most important content on an author website is as follows:

- Home page
- Bio
- Books
- Contact and social media links
- Newsletter sign-up
- Media downloads

Home page: The opening page of your website should have, at a minimum, your latest (and/or upcoming) book, buy links, and a newsletter signup. As previously stated, it should be immediately clear what you write about. Viewers should be able to get an instant idea of your author brand, who you are, and what kind of books you write.

Make sure to update your home page at least several times a year, and ideally more, as keeping your website fresh is very important for SEO.

Bio: Every author website should have both a personal bio and a shorter professional bio (the latter is described in the media downloads section below). The personal bio is important in that it tells the reader who you are, or at least the author brand that you want to project. While authenticity is extremely important, it doesn't mean you need to tell the reader too much personal information. Figure out what kind of author persona you want to express, and make this clear in style and feel.

Books: This is obviously the most important part of an author website. The books section should show all your latest covers, clearly indicating which are stand-alones and which are in series, with the latter showing the order. If your series books don't need to be read in order, state that in this section, but still show the order, as this is important to many readers.

The book page(s) should have synopses and links to purchase the books, along with both professional and reader reviews. Excerpts and other bonus material about each book can also be included (book club questions, author Q&As, background information, book inspiration, etc.). Note that buy links should include direct links to all major book retailers along with a link to independent bookstores when possible. You can give links for ebooks, print, audiobooks, etc. Also be aware that many online retailers have affiliate programs you might want to sign up for.

Contact and social media links: There should be a contact form visitors can use to reach you and information on how to reach your agent or publicist, if you have them. Include links to all the social media platforms you are active on (more on this in the following section).

Newsletter sign-up: Set up a newsletter sign-up with a mailing list service such as MailerLite or Mailchimp as soon as possible so that you can start collecting the email addresses of readers. The folks who sign up for your newsletter list should be considered your superfans—those who always want to order your book the second it is available, talk about you to others, and so forth. You need to cultivate this list and treat your superfans like gold.

Make sure your newsletter sign-up is on a prominent spot on every page of your website (without being obnoxious about it). You'll find more on newsletters in a following section.

Media downloads: This section should include images available for download: at least one professional author photo along with the latest book cover(s). This is also where your short professional bio (100 to 300 words) should go. The purpose of this section is to make it easy for anyone in the online or print media to get what they need if they are writing an article about you or your books.

Social Media Platforms Are Where You Build Your Online Community

If your website is your professional hub, your social media platforms are your social hub, where you can interact with readers, other authors, and industry professionals on a more personal level.

But: choose only the platforms that you actually *want* to engage on. Many authors (and publishers) will tell you that you have to be part of all major social media platforms in order to best market your book. They are wrong. You shouldn't have a social media presence somewhere you don't want to be. The whole point is to be social, to have fun, to interact with people. If you don't like a platform, you won't have fun and, in turn, you won't be authentic. It will all just become a huge frustration and time suck.

The second most important thing, once you decide which platforms you *want* to join, is to think about which platforms best fit you from your author branding standpoint. Different platforms appeal to different types of audiences. Make sure to research this before you begin.

Always keep your author brand in mind for consistency. Through the use of headers, and of course what you choose to post, what you are all about should shine through. It's also important to use the same name on your social platforms that you do in your website URL.

This brings us to another crucial point: what you should post. A well-established rule is the 80:20 ratio, meaning 80 percent of your social media posts should be fun and personal, and only 20 percent should be promotional. What you will hear more often than anything else is to be authentic. Show people who you are as a person and a writer and it will naturally move them toward wanting to check out your books.

You can do "hidden" promotion by posting about things that have to do with your books, like amusing videos of yourself reading from them or photos of locations in them . . . in other words, you can promote your books without being direct about it. But the key here is to have fun with it. Become known for something like silly pet photos or videos, inspirational quotes, stories about your goofy partner, your love of history or nature or peacocks or muffins—unique things about you and your life that keep people coming back for more. And leave the sales on your author website, where they belong.

Video is fantastic for creating an instant connection. Some ideas for videos you can post include you reading an exciting (or humorous) excerpt from your book, music clips that inspire your writing, you reading reviews of your own books (including the bad or ridiculous ones!) or other authors' books, interviews with other authors, and book trailers.

Last, post consistently (not only when you have a new book out). Stay engaged with your followers by commenting on their posts, at least occasionally. Make sure to respond when they ask you questions or comment on your posts. Remember that you are building a community around your author brand.

Newsletters Are the Best Way to Keep in Touch with Your Readers

Your mailing list, which you use to send monthly or semiregular newsletters, is one of the foundations of your online presence. Newsletters allow you to reach your biggest fans directly. They are also more of a long-term, stable way to reach readers than social media channels, which may come and go.

You want to let your newsletter subscribers know when you have a new book coming out or an event coming up, but you also want to give them an exclusive look into your writing world. If you consistently engage your subscribers with fun and interesting newsletters, you will have fans for life. So treat your subscribers as you would your dear friends, with great care. Make them feel special. Let your personality shine through (as long as it's consistent with your author brand). Be funny, be engaging. Tell them things they can't find anywhere else. That will keep them reading your books, coming back to your website, connecting with you on social media, and telling their friends about you.

Support Other Authors

Authors supporting each other is one of the joys of the mystery/thriller community. We see it all the time on social media and blogs, in newsletters, and at conferences. It's a simple fact: nurturing relationships with other authors online helps you, too.

Ideas for this include posting about books you're excited about, sharing others' good news like award nominations, recommending new releases by other authors, and doing giveaways for their books in your newsletters, blogs, and social media platforms. What helps one helps all.

Another good idea is to start a blog or social media page with a group of like-minded authors who are similar to you in theme or genre. This is an almost effortless way to support and cross-promote one another. Some of the best group blogs are like being part of a coffee talk with the authors; it's very personal and makes readers feel like they are in the authors' circle of friends. Make sure to throw in questions so people have a reason to comment. Like with newsletters, be amusing, interesting, and engaging. Draw readers into your world.

You Can Do It!

So, the basics: write a good book, figure out your brand, build a website, sign up with a mailing list company, engage in social media that appeals to you, and support other authors. Simple, right? You can do it!

MYSTI BERRY

Five Ways to Tame the Social Media Monster:

1. Spend more time on writing than you do on marketing.
2. Social media channels are NOT DIRECT SALES CHANNELS. Yes, I'm shouting. It's important.
3. Expect to spend a lot of time and money on just getting people to discover you. Only a fraction of the people who notice you will be interested, and only a fraction of the interested people will buy what you are selling. Approaching every channel as a direct-sales channel will alienate people before they have a chance to evaluate you, your brand, and your products.
4. The best ways to get attention and engagement can change rapidly in social media contexts, so anything that anyone tells you today may be mostly true, partly true, or totally false tomorrow.
5. Social media channels are great ways for you to invest in social capital—to support the community of writers that you most admire or identify with. That means shout-outs for great books you've read (reviews on Amazon or random blurts on your favorite channels or both!), especially those by marginalized writers; following writers you admire; and following writers you want to encourage. All this sharing builds a positive community that includes you. After you have established a personality and paid it forward ("it" being your social capital investments), your funny, charming, or humble blurts about this or that accomplishment will be welcomed by the people who follow you.

Building Your Community

It's the writer, not the book: finding a home
in the virtual village.

LOUISE PENNY

After my first book was written but before it was published, my husband, Michael, and I went to a panel of crime writers in Montréal.

As the chairs were being put out for the smattering of onlookers, mostly family and friends of the writers, I stood by the refreshment table, trying to look like I belonged. As I reached for another cookie, I overheard a snippet of conversation that changed my life.

A veteran writer (I honestly can't remember who it was) was talking to someone whose first novel had just come out, and who was having an anxiety attack about the upcoming panel.

The debut author admitted he had no idea how to promote his book.

"I'll tell you how," said the vet.

I leaned closer.

"Don't promote your book," he said. "Promote yourself."

"Huh?" said the new writer.

Exactly what I was thinking. *Huh?*

"If they like you, they'll probably buy your book, and will probably like it," the vet explained. "And will probably tell others about it."

Wait a minute, I thought. *That doesn't make sense. Liking a book has nothing to do with liking the writer. If a book's bad, no amount of liking the writer will change that.*

And that's generally true. And yet . . .

Over the following weeks, as I sat with that simple statement and looked at my own reactions to things, I began to see the truth in what that veteran writer said.

The fact is, I am more inclined to like something if I like the person who created it. I want their book, their painting, their meal, their design to be good. I want to believe it's good. It's a kind of alchemy that comes with affection.

The idea here isn't to manipulate (no one likes that). It's to make it easy for people to come to your book. To pick it up. To spend precious money, precious time on it. To be predisposed toward liking it (though I'm sure it really is brilliant).

To tell others about it and create that mystical word of mouth.

And, in so doing, you build a following: readers who will join your virtual community.

That panel discussion in Montréal was many years ago. Before Facebook and Twitter. Before Instagram.

Before anything called "social media," there were blogs and newsletters and websites. So much has changed, and yet the fundamentals have not. People are still people. We have the same needs that we always did. And the same needs as others.

That piece of overheard advice has become the heart of what I try to do. Not sell books, at least not overtly. Certainly not sell myself.

In my posts and newsletters, I simply talk about the world around me—both literary and personal. I talk about my life. As a woman. As a writer. The successes, but also my vast collection of insecurities. My at times almost crippling fears.

The failures. And the triumphs.

What it's like to be both a published writer and a human being. I have never, ever told anyone to buy my books. I've told readers that they're available, and left it at that. They can take the next step, if they want.

I initially saw the posts as a sort of diary, left open for others to read.

But then something unexpected happened. Over the years, with each event, each blog post, each newsletter, each book, more and more people came not just to the books, but to the blog, and later the Facebook page.

More and more signed up for the monthly newsletter.

And they wrote back, telling me about their lives. Their families, their jobs. Their struggles. Sometimes they wrote about my books, but often they didn't.

On Facebook, they began to discuss their favorite authors. They shared devastating medical news and talked about their journeys through cancer and dementia. They told us about recent births. And job promotions. About the weather.

They wrote about their lives.

And their messages didn't just sit there. I'd respond when possible, but so did others. Independent of me. It became a conversation. A virtual bistro.

It reminded me of the allegory (I'm not sure if it's true or not) of the gorillas who, when the group is threatened, advance to meet that threat. Screaming, beating their chests, baring their teeth and glaring at the aggressors.

But every now and then they'll reach out and, without looking, touch the gorilla next to them. To make sure they're not alone.

That's a bit what this felt like. Without, thankfully, the aggression.

We couldn't see each other, but when we reached out, we knew someone was there. We were not alone.

What else is community, if not that?

Where Do I Start?

I'd like to give you my thoughts on how to create your own literary community. To balance the practical purpose as a writer, to sell books, and the human rewards of being among, in the words of Anne Shirley, "kindred spirits."

One way to meet other writers, and readers, is in person: book tours, library talks, crime conventions. When you go, force yourself to chat with strangers. Most writers I know, myself included, would just as soon hide in the hotel room. Do not do that. Unless you want to reach out and discover there is no gorilla beside you.

For most writers, the web is where connections lie. However, if your social media presence doesn't impart a sense of belonging, you haven't created a community, just a marketing ploy. A sort of Disney World, fun for a while but fake and ultimately callow. It may sell books, but we're talking here about community—or rather, communities.

There are several different, and often intersecting, types of communities for a writer.

There's the company of other writers. Writers do not compete with one another, not really. Indeed, the most successful, certainly the happiest, among us are those who help and support and promote each other. With writer friends, you'll know you're not going crazy when you hate your editor or publicist, or get lost in the "muddle in the middle" of your latest manuscript. You'll know you're not the only one to have no one come to a book signing or to be certain that your book is a dog's breakfast.

There are practical benefits, too. We introduce one another to favorite booksellers and librarians. Promote each other's books on our social media.

We champion each other.

When you're starting out, you might consider joining, or forming, a collective of writers who will take turns posting on social media. There are quite a few of those groups. Their readers will discover you, and vice versa.

But ultimately what you want to do is create a community of your own readers.

First, you need a road in, some way they can find not just you and your books, but one another. You need a platform.

Before I go further and you invest any more time in this, I need to tell you that I am no specialist in social media. I have no statistics about which platform is the most effective or how often you should post. (Enough so that people are happy to see you pop up, and not so often that they want to throw up?) Is Twitter better than Facebook? How about Instagram? No idea. You'll figure out what is the best fit for you.

Pick your outlet, and once you start posting, consider adding value: holding contests, doing giveaways, even forming a book club. Make it attractive for people to visit and revisit your site. And to tell their friends about it.

But once they're in your "world," why would someone stay? How do you turn a literary tourist into a resident and a booster?

Why do any of us, if we have a choice, live where we live? Convenience, perhaps, though other places are probably just as convenient. Friends? For sure. Familiarity? Absolutely. Laziness? Guilty.

But finally, it comes down to that ineffable knowing. In your heart. You belong.

How powerful is that? What a great gift. To belong. To find home.

Building a Literary Home

Creating a literary home for our readers is one of the great goals. We try to do it in our books, in the worlds and characters we create between the covers. But if it can cross that fourth wall so that it also becomes a place of belonging in real life, what an experience.

Readers are attracted to your characters, your setting, your world. You. But for it to be vibrant and alive, a community must take on a life of its own.

That happens with time. With care. With trust.

That happens when people know they are not simply being manipulated into buying books, but that there is something far more profound, more meaningful, at work. They see that this community may be virtual, but it is also genuine.

This is a creation that goes far beyond people enjoying your books. It can change lives. It can change your life, in ways more meaningful and lasting than any bestseller list.

There are, of course, boundaries. You need to find for yourself where the lines are. Sometimes they shift, or are hard to define.

What is an inappropriate post? What happens when people are rude to each other? When a disagreement becomes an argument becomes a fight?

For the most part, you set the tone. People look to you for leadership on what is acceptable comment.

And then there are the personal boundaries. How far do you let people into your life?

I needed, through trial and error, to make the distinction between what is private and what is personal. What to post and what not to.

I've made mistakes, of course. Oversharing. Undersharing. But eventually I found an equilibrium. I will tell people quite a lot about my personal life, my home, my routine. Often, with permission, about my family and friends. They become fixtures in the "village."

But I do not talk about topics I consider private.

You must know, too, that there are flash points, issues that you feel strongly about that others will not agree with. Only you can decide how open you want to be about those.

Just know that if you do take a stand, some people will disagree. Which, of course, is fine. You probably don't want to create a fascist state.

But the result, when your views are known, could be a certain migration out of your virtual village. When I have taken stands, those losses, while sad, were a price I was willing to pay. And, interestingly, they were almost always offset by new people finding our little village because of the controversy.

It's not, in all honesty, something I do often, or lightly. But it happens.

I have only ever asked one person to leave. Which they did. I can't now remember the exact post, but it clearly crossed the line into hate speech.

It's important to know that your community revolves around not just your books, but you. And what you write in your posts, how you write, has an impact.

Community Goals

You, and any online assistant you may depend on, need to keep some goals in mind.

- Try to be good stewards: respectful, genuine, warm, and tolerant.
- As much as possible, write all the content—the posts, the tweets, the text on your website and in your newsletters, etc.—yourself. If you can't, then make it clear when it's not you writing.
- It's vital to have your "voice" known and recognized. It must be sincere and consistent.
- Treat each "villager" as a person and not as a potential sale.
- When you are starting out, much of your effort can appear to sink into a void. It's a little heartbreaking when you post and no one responds. When you have ten followers on social media, all with your own last name. When few, if any, show up at a book signing. We've all been there. And the fact is, these efforts are never wasted.
- Don't be discouraged. You are making important contacts. Laying the foundation for a literary home, open to all. With you at the heart of it.

Of course, there is a reason no reality TV show has followed the life of a writer. We pretty much just stare into space most of the time. And mutter. Expletives. Often, there isn't that much to say, if you're trying to post every day.

As time went on, I'd talk about writing. About the weather (I am Canadian, after all). About something funny that happened. About the terror of handing in a new book and the writhing that comes with reading the editor's notes. (How dare she not see that every word is genius. Genius, I say!)

About the upcoming tour. Or being on tour. I'd post photos of the snow. Of the dogs. Of my life with Michael. All was going swimmingly.

And then . . . something happened.

Michael was diagnosed with dementia.

Should I mention it? (That was not my first reaction.)

Where's that undulating line between private and personal?

Michael and I discussed it. He was a doctor and felt strongly that disease of any sort was nothing to be ashamed of. He did not want to be hidden away, and he sure didn't want his dementia to be seen as embarrassing.

It was just something that was happening to us.

And so after we told family and friends, and had the time we needed to absorb the news ourselves, I posted on Facebook.

By then, readers had gotten to know Michael—his smile, his bright blue eyes, his humor, and his steadfast support. We went on tour together and to conventions where he met and bonded with readers and booksellers. He had become a personality in the virtual village.

To be honest, up until the time he was diagnosed, I had seen social media as something that helped my career. That all changed with Michael's dementia.

People responded by writing about their own experiences. They wrote with support. With suggestions. With encouragement and understanding. With generosity and courage, they opened their lives to us. And gave us strength.

Slowly I lifted my head and saw what others in the virtual village already knew.

We were not alone. This community I'd created for others was there for us, and was as real as any brick-and-mortar town.

We had a circle of friends around us physically, thank God. But we also had these people who were not simply followers. What had begun as an audience I was trying to reach had become my wider circle of friends.

I will tell you, sincerely, if you can be involved in the creation of that kind of community, you are fortunate indeed.

It's just possible that book sales are not the end product, not the purpose or the prize.

The community is the reward.

BEV VINCENT

Story is what characters do when confronted with a situation. . . .

I took a gamble a few years ago and decided I would not only promote my work on Twitter but also embrace my political opinions. It was a calculated risk—I knew I could turn potential readers off. However, much to my surprise and delight, once I turned into a Twitter activist, my following exploded.

Legal Considerations

What every mystery writer should know
about publishing law

DANIEL STEVEN

Ask a mystery writer about criminal law or police procedures and you'll likely get a lecture. But ask that writer about copyright, defamation, or privacy claims—and you'll get a blank look.

Every writer is capable of understanding business and legal issues, but writers often don't know what they don't know. This article will focus on what is important—and what you generally don't have to worry about. **This is not a substitute for and shouldn't be used as legal advice—you should of course consult an attorney to assess your specific situation—but it is provided to give you a baseline understanding of some of the issues to consider.**

What You Should Know about Copyright

A writer's stock in trade is copyright. It prevents others from copying or publishing all or a substantial part of your original work.

How do I get copyright? You become the owner of your original work the instant it is fixed on paper, saved to disk, or recorded for the first time. Publication is not required. Copyright is intellectual property: a "bundle" of various rights you can transfer, sell, assign, and leave in your will. The U.S. Copyright Act specifically gives the copyright owner the exclusive right to do and to authorize others to do the following:

- Reproduce the work in copies or electronic form
- Prepare derivative works based upon the work
- Distribute copies (electronic or paper) of the work to the public by sale, rental, lease, or lending
- Perform or display the work publicly

What can be copyrighted? Copyrighted material must be an "original work of authorship" fixed in tangible form. "Original" obviously means it was created independently, not copied from someone else. "Work of authorship" means it fits within certain broad categories in the Copyright Act: literary works, musical works, choreography, graphic and sculptural works, motion pictures and audiovisual works, and sound recordings. (A letter, for example, is a literary work for copyright purposes.)

What cannot be copyrighted? You can't copyright ideas, titles, names, short phrases, slogans, concepts, discoveries, procedures, lists of contents, or facts, no matter how original or unique. That's why so many books and movies have the same title. Some titles can be trademarked, but that's another story.

How do I secure my copyright? Despite what many believe, a formal registration of a work with the U.S. Copyright Office is *not* required—as noted above, copyright is instant when the work becomes "fixed." But you *should* register, no later than the date of publication. I don't think it is necessary for you to register unpublished works when sending your manuscript to agents or publishers. A reputable agent or publisher won't risk its reputation by stealing your work, and a disreputable agent or publisher will typically be interested only in getting fees from you. Once your work is published, however, registration is essential. It establishes a public, searchable record of your ownership and is a prerequisite to filing a lawsuit against an infringer. More important, if registration is made *before* the infringement or within three months of first publication, the law confers significant additional benefits, such as statutory damages (compensation without a showing of actual loss) and reimbursement of your attorney's fees. You can register online for a thirty-five-dollar fee (at www.copyright .gov). Your publishing agreement may require your publisher to register the work for you upon publication.

How long does a copyright last? For works originally created on or after January 1, 1978, copyright protection in the United States lasts for the author's life plus 70 years. The term of copyright protection of a "work made for hire" is 95 years from the date of publication or 120 years from the date of creation, whichever expires first. "Works for hire" are those created by an employee as part of their regular duties or created as a result of an express written agreement between the creator and the party commissioning the work.

Do I need a copyright notice? No—and yes. A copyright notice is *not* required to obtain protection, but it still serves an important purpose. The notice informs the public that your work is protected, identifies you, and shows the year of first publication. If your work is infringed, the infringer may not claim "innocent infringement" to limit the damages you claim. You don't need permission from the Copyright Office to use the notice, but to be effective it must contain three elements:

- The symbol © (the letter C in a circle), the word "Copyright," or the abbreviation "Copr."
- The year of first publication
- Your name, an abbreviation by which your name can be recognized, or a pseudonym

For example, an effective copyright notice might read: © 2020 Jane Doe.

When can I use the work of others? Despite claims of "fair use," the answer is generally never—without permission. Many writers hold the mistaken belief that reproducing short excerpts of someone's copyrighted work without their permission qualifies as fair use. But "fair use" has a very limited meaning as defined in Section 107 of the U.S. Copyright Act, and applies far less often than writers think. There is no rigid test, and courts will apply the very specific and narrow exceptions in the law on a case-by-case basis. Section 107 gives four factors to determine whether a specific use is to be considered a "fair use":

- The purpose and character of the use, including whether such use is of commercial nature or is for nonprofit educational purposes

- The nature of the copyrighted work
- The amount and substantiality of the portion used in relation to the copyrighted work as a whole
- The effect of the use upon the potential market for or value of the copyrighted work

Accordingly, fair use typically is a *short* excerpt used in connection with genuine criticism, news reporting, parody, or teaching.

Writers love to use song lyrics as part of setting a scene. Although novels are expressive works, the fair use analysis may not be as generous to that kind of use as it might be to, by way of example, a critical discussion of a lyricist's use of meter in a song. Even a few lines of lyrics can comprise a significant percentage of a whole song—or a few lines of a poem can be a significant percentage of the whole—and so their use might not be "fair use" under the copyright law. Music companies aggressively protect their rights, and will quickly send a "cease and desist" letter to you and your publisher even if the use might qualify as fair use, which is why publishers generally disfavor even the inclusion of just a few lines.

You should also be cautious before using characters from other novels, movies, or plays to avoid having your work constitute a "derivative work" of a work belonging exclusively to another copyright owner. There are limited situations in which referential use to other works is acceptable, but it's best to err on the side of safety and avoid it entirely.

What You Should Know about Defamation, Privacy, and Right of Publicity

Hundreds of thousands of books are published every year, and only a tiny percentage result in lawsuits. So relax. Novelists use real people in their writing all the time, either as characters or as models for fictitious characters. But when you write about real, live people, you may expose yourself to legal liability for defamation, breach of privacy, and publicity claims. This is because American law protects three types of "real persons": living ordinary people; living public figures (celebrities); and, in some states, dead public figures (really).

Defamation. Defamation is written or spoken injury to a *living* person's or an organization's reputation (you can't defame the dead). Libel is the written act of defamation, whereas slander is the spoken act. The injury—exposure to hatred, contempt, ridicule, or pecuniary loss—must directly affect the reputation of a living person or an organization. It must be "published," revealed to someone other than the subject of the defamation.

In modern American law, truth is an absolute defense to defamation; a true statement cannot be defamatory. But what if it isn't true, or is only partly true? A plaintiff in a defamatory lawsuit against a novelist must show that a "fictionalized" character was objectively identifiable as a real person, and that there was a defamatory statement of and concerning such person that the reader would impute to such real person. The inquiry would then be to assess whether the author was negligent in publishing such a statement (or, if it's concerning a public figure, whether the defamatory statement was published with "actual malice").

Right of privacy. Privacy law is a broad area and varies from state to state. In general, only public disclosure of private facts is relevant for novelists. This can occur when a writer discloses private and embarrassing facts about a living person that most people would find "highly offensive" and that are not of public concern. (First Amendment rights protect publication of items of legitimate public concern, such as the details of a crime.) So, what is "highly offensive"? A subjective standard, it is whatever a judge or jury decides is offensive. Typically, however, the disclosed information must be very private and very damaging.

Simply changing the name of a real person in your novel is no solution if the person can be identified by circumstances, appearance, or setting, but you can minimize your risks. Novelists should mask distinguishing characteristics and avoid retelling life stories too closely. The more villainous the character, the more the writer should change the characteristics.

To protect themselves, many publishers and writers use disclaimers, such as the standard "This book is a work of fiction. Any resemblance to actual events or persons, living or dead, is entirely coincidental." But this disclaimer doesn't provide any guarantee of protection. If a court finds that an author or publisher should have known the subject was identifiable, and private facts were revealed, the use of a disclaimer will be disregarded.

Right of publicity. Most states now have laws that protect living celebrities from commercial exploitation of their name, likeness, or persona, and some states do the same for recently dead celebrities, like Elvis Presley. News stories, biographies, and fiction, however, are protected by the First Amendment. To the extent that you portray celebrities in your novel for editorial purposes *without* defaming them or their family, you need not seek the celebrities' permission. Books are generally considered editorial rather than commercial use. Such protections might not extend, however, to purely commercial "merchandise" of your work, such as T-shirts or posters that use a celebrity's name to promote your book in a noneditorial context.

Liability for violating right of publicity in a novel is rare; it typically occurs only when an author uses someone's name or image for advertising or promotional purposes. Beware of using a real person's name or image on a book cover, in an advertisement, or in any way that implies an endorsement without that person's express permission.

About the Contributors

Beth Amos is a recently retired emergency room nurse in Wisconsin. In contrast to her nursing career, where she worked toward saving lives, her writing career involves coming up with clever ways to kill people.

Beth has twenty-five published novels, including the Mattie Winston Mystery series and the Helping Hands Mystery series (written as Annelise Ryan), and the Mack's Bar Mystery series (written as Allyson K. Abbott), all with Kensington Books.

Beth is a *USA Today* bestselling author, the recipient of the 2017 Wisconsin Library Association's Notable Author Award, and a member of Mystery Writers of America.

Kelley Armstrong believes experience is the best teacher, though she's been told this shouldn't apply to writing her murder scenes. To craft her books, she has studied aikido, archery, and fencing. She sucks at all of them. She has also crawled through very shallow cave systems and climbed half a mountain before chickening out. She is, however, an expert coffee drinker and a true connoisseur of chocolate chip cookies. Visit her online at www.KelleyArmstrong.com.

Frankie Y. Bailey is a professor in the School of Criminal Justice, University at Albany (SUNY). She specializes in mass media/popular culture, and crime history. Her nonfiction books include *African American Mystery Writers*. Frankie's mystery novels feature southern crime historian Lizzie Stuart, and Albany, New York, police detective Hannah McCabe. Her short stories have been published in *EQMM* and in several anthologies. She is working on her sixth Lizzie Stuart novel. She is also working on a historical thriller set in 1939. Frankie is a past executive vice president of Mystery Writers of America and a past president of Sisters in Crime National.

Linwood Barclay is the author of more than twenty novels, including *No Time for Goodbye*, *A Noise Downstairs*, and *Elevator Pitch*. His novel *The Accident* was made into a TV series in France, and he wrote the screenplay for the film *Never Saw It Coming*, based on his novel. He lives in Toronto with his wife, Neetha.

Stephanie Kay Bendel has been a member of Mystery Writers of America since 1973. She is the author of *Making Crime Pay*, a textbook on mystery and suspense writing; *A Scream Away* (as Andrea Harris), a romantic thriller; and *Exit the Labyrinth*, a memoir, as well as numerous short stories and articles on writing. She has taught writing classes for college and adult education students and run several writing workshops since 1989.

She lives in Westminster, Colorado, with her husband, Bill.

Dale W. Berry has been creating independent comics professionally since 1986. A San Francisco–based writer and illustrator, his graphic short stories have appeared in *Alfred Hitchcock's Mystery Magazine* (the first comics creator to do so), and he is the author of five books in the *Tales of the Moonlight Cutter* graphic novel series. In 2019, *The Be-Bop Barbarians*, in collaboration with writer Gary Phillips, was published by Pegasus Books to much critical acclaim. Dale's life has also included stints as a carnival barker, concert stagehand, rock radio DJ, and fencing instructor. For more info visit: http//www.myriadpubs.com.

Mysti Berry has an MFA in writing from the University of San Francisco but never lets that get in the way of a good story. She lives in a forgotten corner of San Francisco with graphic novelist husband Dale W. Berry. Her short stories have appeared in *EQMM*, *Alfred Hitchcock's Mystery Magazine*, and a variety of anthologies, and she is the editor of *Low Down Dirty Vote* (two volumes), charity crime-fiction anthologies.

Hal Bodner is a multiple Bram Stoker Award–nominated author whose freshman vampire novel, *Bite Club*, made him one of the top-selling LGBT authors in the country. The royalties continue to keep him in "cigarettes and nylons"—even though he quit smoking and never did drag. He subsequently authored several paranormal romances, which, to his agent's chagrin, he refers to as "supernatural smut." He is currently working on a series of comic thrillers that paints classic noir fiction with a lavender glaze. Hal is married to a wonderful man, half his age, who never knew that Liza Minnelli was Judy Garland's daughter.

Allison Brennan is a *New York Times* and *USA Today* bestselling author of more than three dozen books and numerous short stories, including the Lucy Kincaid series and the new Quinn & Costa thrillers. She lives in Arizona with her family and assorted pets. For more information, visit allisonbrennan.com.

Leslie Budewitz blends her passion for food, great mysteries, and the Northwest in two cozy mystery series, the Spice Shop mysteries set in Seattle's Pike Place Market and the Food Lovers' Village mysteries set in northwest Montana, where she lives. She'll make her suspense debut with *Bitterroot Lake*, written as Alicia Beckman, in April 2021. A three-time Agatha Award winner (2011, Best Nonfiction; 2013, Best First Novel; 2018, Best Short Story), she is a past president of Sisters in Crime and a current board member of Mystery Writers of America.

Carole Buggé (C. E. Lawrence, Carole Lawrence, Elizabeth Blake) has too many pen names. She is the author of fourteen published novels, award-winning plays, musicals, poetry, and short fiction. Her most recent novel is the third Ian Hamilton historical thriller, *Edinburgh Midnight*, under the pen name Carole Lawrence. Also recent is *Pride, Prejudice and Poison*, under the pen name Elizabeth Blake. Her Silent series (*Silent Screams* and its sequels) follows NYPD profiler Lee Campbell in his pursuit of serial killers. Her plays and musicals have been performed internationally, including an original Sherlock Holmes musical. Her most recent musical is *Murder on Bond Street*, based on a true story. In another life, she was a professional actor, singer, and improvisational comedian. A self-described science geek, she likes to hunt wild mushrooms. Visit her website: CELawrence.com.

Suzanne Chazin is the author of two thriller series. Her first stars Georgia Skeehan. a scrappy firefighter turned fire marshal investigating arsons in the macho world of the FDNY. Her second stars Jimmy Vega, a Bronx-born Puerto Rican cop navigating the new suburban melting pot and his own complicated place in it. Find her at www.suzannechazin.com.

Oline H. Cogdill reviews mystery fiction for *Publishers Weekly*, *Shelf Awareness*, Associated Press, *Mystery Scene* magazine, and the *Sun Sentinel* in Fort Lauderdale/Tribune Publishing Wire. She also blogs regularly at mysteryscenemag.com. She has received the 2013 Raven Award from Mystery Writers of America, the 1999 Ellen Nehr Award by the American Crime Writers League, and the 1997 *Sun Sentinel's* Fred Pettijohn Award. Oline is a judge for the 2020 and 2021 Los Angeles Times Book Prize in the mystery/thriller category.

Nancy J. Cohen writes the Bad Hair Day Mysteries featuring South Florida hairstylist Marla Vail. Her series has won numerous awards, along with *A Bad Hair Day Cookbook* and her instructional guide, *Writing the Cozy Mystery*. Active in the writing community, Nancy is a past president of Florida Romance Writers and Mystery Writers of America, Florida Chapter. When not busy writing, she enjoys cooking, fine dining, cruising, and visiting Walt Disney World. Visit her at NancyJCohen.com.

Max Allan Collins is an MWA Grand Master. He is the author of the Shamus Award–winning Nathan Heller historical thrillers (*Do No Harm*) and the graphic novel *Road to Perdition*, basis of the Academy Award–winning film. His innovative seventies series, Quarry, revived by Hard Case Crime (*Killing Quarry*), became a Cinemax TV series. He has completed thirteen posthumous Mickey Spillane novels (*Masquerade for Murder*) and is the coauthor (with his wife, Barbara Collins) of the Trash 'n' Treasures mystery series (*Antiques Carry On*).

New York Times best-selling author **Deborah Crombie** is a native Texan who writes crime novels set in the United Kingdom. Her Superintendent Duncan Kincaid and Inspector Gemma James series has received numerous awards, including Edgar, Macavity, and Agatha nominations, and is published in more than a dozen countries to international acclaim.

Crombie lives in North Texas with her husband, German shepherds, and cats, and divides her time between Texas and Great Britain. Her latest novel, *A Bitter Feast*, is available from William Morrow. She is currently working on her nineteenth Kincaid-James novel.

Lindsey Davis is best known for her Roman detective, Marcus Didius Falco, and her new series about his adopted daughter, Flavia Albia. She has also written standalones, novellas, and short stories.

Her awards include the Premio Colosseo (from the city of Rome) and the Crimewriters' Cartier Diamond Dagger.

She has been chair of the UK Crimewriters Association and the UK Society of Authors.www.lindseydavis.co.uk

Jeffery Deaver is an internationally number one bestselling author. His novels have appeared on bestseller lists around the world. His books are sold in 150 countries and translated into 25 languages. He has served two terms as president of Mystery Writers of America.

The author of forty-three novels, three collections of short stories, and a nonfiction law book, he's received or been short-listed for dozens of awards. His *The Bodies Left Behind* was named Novel of the Year by the International Thriller Writers association, and his Lincoln Rhyme thriller *The Broken Window* and a stand-alone, *Edge*, were also nominated for that prize. He's been nominated for eight Edgar Awards.

Hallie Ephron is the *New York Times* bestselling author of eleven suspense novels that reviewers call "deliciously creepy." Her *Careful What You Wish For* (William Morrow) received a starred review in *Publishers Weekly*. In a review in *Time* magazine, Jamie Lee Curtis called it "thrilling and suspenseful." Her *Never Tell a Lie* was made into a Lifetime movie. A five-time finalist for the Mary Higgins Clark Award, her *Writing and Selling Your Mystery Novel* was an Edgar Award finalist. Hallie is a popular presenter at events and writing conferences. She blogs daily on the Anthony Award–winning blog *Jungle Red Writers* (www.jungleredwriters.com).

Lyndsay Faye is the internationally bestselling author of the Edgar Award–nominated Timothy Wilde trilogy and *Jane Steele*, in addition to three other critically acclaimed novels. An avid Sherlock Holmes enthusiast, her short stories are published in numerous magazines and anthologies and collected in *The Whole Art of Detection*. She has been translated into more than a dozen languages and is delighted, humbled, and thankful to be part of this essay collection. Lyndsay is a proud member of numerous Sherlockian organizations and has served several terms on both the local and national MWA boards. She lives in Queens, New York.

Shelly Frome is a member of Mystery Writers of America, a professor of dramatic arts emeritus at University of Connecticut, a former professional actor, and a writer of crime novels and books on theater and film. His fiction includes *Sun Dance for Andy Horn*, *Lilac Moon*, *Twilight of the Drifter*, *Tinseltown Riff*, *Murder Run*, *Moon Games*, and *The Secluded Village Murders*. Among his works of nonfiction is *The Actors Studio: A History*. *Miranda and the D-Day Caper* is his latest foray into the world of crime and the amateur sleuth. He lives in Black Mountain, North Carolina.

Meg Gardiner is the award-winning author of fifteen thrillers. Her novels have been bestsellers in the United States and internationally and have been translated into more than twenty languages. *China Lake* won the 2009 Edgar Award for Best Paperback Original. *UNSUB* won the 2018 Barry Award for Best Thriller. She taught in the Writing Program at the University of California, Santa Barbara, has presented master classes for Curtis Brown Creative and HarperCollins UK, and teaches seminars for the nonprofit organization Texas Writes. She served as the 2019 and 2020 president of Mystery Writers of America. Gardiner lives in Austin.

Trained as a medical doctor, **Tess Gerritsen** built a second career as a thriller writer. Her twenty-nine novels include the Rizzoli and Isles crime series, on which the TV show *Rizzoli & Isles* is based. Among her titles are *Harvest*, *Gravity*, *The Surgeon*, *Playing with Fire*, and *The Shape of Night*. Her books are translated into forty languages and more than thirty million copies have been sold. She lives in Maine.

Chris Grabenstein is the number one *New York Times* bestselling author of the award-winning Mr. Lemoncello books as well as four dozen other books for young readers, including several fast-paced and funny page-turners coauthored with James Patterson, such as the I Funny, Jacky Ha-Ha, and Max Einstein series.

Rachel Howzell Hall, author of the critically acclaimed novel *And Now She's Gone* and the Anthony Award–, Lefty Award– and Thriller Award–nominated *They All Fall Down* (Forge), writes the acclaimed Lou Norton series, including *Land of Shadows*, *Skies of Ash*, *Trail of Echoes*, and *City of Saviors*. She is also the coauthor of *The Good Sister* with James Patterson, which was included in the *New York Times* bestseller *The Family Lawyer*. She is currently on the board of directors for the Southern California chapter of Mystery Writers of America and is a Pitch Wars mentor for 2020. She lives in Los Angeles. You can find her at www.rachelhowzell.com and Twitter @RachelHowzell.

Bradley Harper began writing at sixty-three after thirty-seven years in the U.S. Army, first as an infantry officer, then as a physician/pathologist. With more than two hundred autopsies and twenty forensic death investigations to his credit, he uses his clinical experience to inform his writing.

Harper's debut novel, *A Knife in the Fog*, pitted Arthur Conan Doyle against Jack the Ripper and was a Finalist for the 2019 Edgar Award for Best First Novel by an American. The sequel, *Queen's Gambit*, won Killer Nashville's Silver Falchion as Best Suspense and Book of the Year. His website is www.BHarperAuthor.com.

Charlaine Harris is a true daughter of the South. Born in Mississippi, she has lived in Tennessee, South Carolina, Arkansas, and Texas. Her career as a novelist began in 1981 with her first book, a conventional mystery. Since then, she's written urban fantasy, science fiction, and horror. In addition to more than thirty full-length books, she has written numerous short stories and three graphic novels in collaboration with Christopher Golden. She has featured on bestseller lists many times, and her works have been adapted for three (soon to be five) television shows. Charlaine now lives at the top of a cliff on the Brazos River with her husband and two rescue dogs. She has three children and two grandchildren.

Carolyn Hart, an MWA Grand Master, is the author of sixty-two mystery and suspense novels, including the Death on Demand, Henrie O, and Bailey Ruth series. Her stand-alone novels include the WWII novels *Escape from Paris*, *Brave Hearts*, and *Letter from Home*. She is a past president of Sisters in Crime and a member of MWA since 1964.

Liliana Hart is a *New York Times* and *USA Today* bestselling author of more than sixty titles. After starting her first novel her freshman year of college, she became addicted to writing and knew she'd found what she was meant to do with her life. She has no idea why she majored in music.

Since publishing in 2011, Liliana has appeared at number one on lists all over the world, and all three of her series have appeared on the *New York Times* list. Liliana can usually be found at her computer or hanging out with her real-life hero, Scott.

Rob Hart is the author of *The Warehouse*, which sold in more than twenty languages and was optioned for film. He also wrote the Ash McKenna crime series, the short story collection *Take-Out*, and he cowrote *Scott Free* with James Patterson. His short stories have been published in places like *Thuglit*, *Needle*, *Mystery Tribune*, and *Joyland*. He's received a Derringer Award nomination for best flash fiction story, and his short story "Take-Out" appeared in *Best American Mystery Stories 2018*. He also received honorable mention in both *Best American Mystery Stories 2015* and *2017*. He lives in Staten Island, New York.

Greg Herren is the award-winning author of thirty-three novels, two novellas, and three short story collections. He has published over fifty short stories, in markets as varied as *Ellery Queen's Mystery Magazine*, *Mystery Tribune*, *Mystery Weekly*, *Men*, and numerous anthologies. He has edited twenty anthologies, including *Blood on the Bayou* and *Florida Happens*. He has won two Lambda Literary Awards (out of fourteen nominations), an Anthony Award, and two Moonbeam medals for Young Adult Fiction. He has been short-listed for countless other awards, including the Shirley Jackson Award and the Macavity.

Naomi Hirahara is an Edgar Award–winning author of multiple traditional mystery series and noir short stories. Her Mas Arai mysteries, which have been published in Japanese, Korean, and French, feature a Los

Angeles gardener and Hiroshima survivor who solves crimes. The seventh and final Mas Arai mystery is *Hiroshima Boy*, which was nominated for an Edgar Award for best paperback original. Her first historical mystery standalone is *Clark and Division*, which follows a Japanese American family's move to Chicago in 1944 after being released from a California wartime detention center. For more information, go to her website, www. naomihirahara.com.

Steve Hockensmith is the author of two finalists for the Edgar Award (the mystery-Western hybrid *Holmes on the Range* and the middle-grade adventure *Nick and Tesla's Secret Agent Gadget Battle*) as well as a *New York Times* bestseller, *Pride and Prejudice and Zombies: Dawn of the Dreadfuls*. In addition to writing more than a dozen other novels, he contributes short stories regularly to MWA anthologies and both *Ellery Queen's Mystery Magazine* and *Alfred Hitchcock's Mystery Magazine*. You can download free samples of his fiction at stevehockensmith.com/steves-stories.

Maddee James is the owner of xuni.com, a small, dynamic website development company that has created, designed, and maintained author websites for more than twenty years. Though xuni.com clients span across all genres, we specialize in customized Wordpress sites for mystery and thriller writers. We also support author branding through print and online ads, social media design, custom newsletters and other promotional materials. While we are in the business of creating functional beauty, we are best known for our individualized attention to clients and details, along with amazing responsiveness. Check out our work, client list, and much more at xuni.com.

Rae Franklin James was raised in the San Francisco Bay Area. The first book in her award-winning, five-star Hollis Morgan Mysteries, *The Fallen Angels Book Club*, was released by Camel Press. The last book in the series, *The Identity Thief*, was released in 2018. Book one in her new series, *The Appraiser*, was released in 2019. James sits on the board of Bouchercon Mystery Convention. She is a member of Mystery Writers of America, Sisters in Crime, and Northern California Publishers and Authors. She resides in Northern California. Her website link is www.rfranklinjames.com.

Craig Johnson is the *New York Times* bestselling author of the Walt Longmire mystery novels, which are the basis for *Longmire*, the hit Netflix original drama. The books have won multiple awards: Le Prix du Polar Nouvel Observateur/BibliObs, the Wyoming Historical Association's Book of the Year, Le Prix 813, the Western Writers of America's Spur Award, the Mountains & Plains Book of the Year, the SNCF Prix de Polar, *Publishers Weekly* Best Book of the Year, the Watson Award, *Library Journal*'s Best Mystery of the Year, the Rocky, and the Will Rogers Award for Fiction. Johnson lives in Ucross, Wyoming, population twenty-five.

Stephanie Kane is a lawyer and award-winning author of six crime novels and a blog about how storytelling shaped a true cold case. She has owned and run a karate studio, lectured on money laundering and white-collar crime in Eastern Europe, and given writing workshops across the country. Her thrillers starring dyslexic defense lawyer Jackie Flowers won a Colorado Book Award and two Colorado Authors League Awards. Her latest heroine, paintings conservator Lily Sparks, debuted in *A Perfect Eye* and continues with *Automat*. She lives in Denver with her husband and two black cats. Visit her at www.writerkane.com.

Gay Toltl Kinman has nine award nominations for her writing, several short stories in American and English magazines and anthologies, twelve children's books and stories, a YA gothic novel, eight adult mysteries, and collections of short stories. Several of her short plays were produced—now in a collection of twenty plays, *The Play's the Thing*; many articles in professional journals and newspapers; and has coedited two nonfiction books. Kinman has library and law degrees.

William Kent Krueger is the author of the *New York Times* bestselling Cork O'Connor mystery series, set in the great Northwoods of Minnesota. His work has received the Edgar Award, Macavity Award, multiple Anthony, Barry, and Dilys Awards, the Friends of the American Writers Prize, and has been translated into more than twenty languages. He lives in Saint Paul and does all his creative writing in local, author-friendly coffee shops. His most recent novel, *This Tender Land*, has spent several months on the *New York Times* bestseller list.

Robert Lopresti is a retired librarian. He has been a published author for more than forty years. His stories have appeared in the major mystery magazines and been reprinted in *Best American Mystery Stories* and *Year's Best Dark Fantasy and Horror*. He has won the Derringer Award (three times) as well as the Black Orchid Novella Award, and been nominated for the Anthony. His most recent novel, *Greenfellas*, is a comic caper about the Mafia trying to save the environment.

Gayle Lynds is the *New York Times* and internationally bestselling author of ten spy novels, including *The Book of Spies*, *The Assassins*, and *Masquerade*. *Library Journal* calls her "the reigning queen of espionage fiction." Her books have been published in thirty languages and have sold millions of copies worldwide. Among her many awards is the Military Writers Society of America Award for Best Novel. With Robert Ludlum, she created the Covert-One series. The first book, *The Hades Factor*, was a CBS miniseries. With David Morrell, she cofounded International Thriller Writers and ThrillerFest. You can visit her at www.GayleLynds.com.

Tim Maleeny is the bestselling author of the award-winning Cape Weathers mysteries and the comedic thriller *Jump*, which *Publishers Weekly* described as "a perfectly blended cocktail of escapism." Tim's short fiction appears in several major anthologies and has won the prestigious Macavity Award for best story of the year. *The Irish Times* says, "If comic crime fiction is your thing, Maleeny delivers in spades." He lives and writes at an undisclosed location in New York City.

Catriona McPherson was born in Scotland in 1965 and lived there until immigrating to the United States in 2010. She is the national bestselling and multi award–wining author of the Dandy Gilver series of preposterous 1930s detective stories, set in the old country, the Last Ditch Motel series of crime comedies, set in the new country, and a strand of somewhat darker psychological suspense novels. A former academic, she now writes full-time and lives in Northern California.

Catriona is a member of MWA, CWA, SoA, and a former national president of Sisters in Crime.

ABOUT THE CONTRIBUTORS

Kris Neri's latest novel, *Hopscotch Life*, featuring quirky protagonist Plum Tardy, is a New Mexico–Arizona Book Award winner. She also writes the Tracy Eaton mysteries, with the daughter of eccentric Hollywood stars, and the Samantha Brennan and Annabelle Haggerty magical series, featuring a questionable psychic who teams up with a goddess/FBI agent. Kris's novels have been finalists for such prestigious awards as the Agatha, Anthony, Macavity, Lefty, and others. She teaches writing for the Writers' Program of the UCLA Extension School and other organizations. Readers are welcome to visit her website: krisneri.com.

Neil Nyren retired at the end of 2017 as executive vice president, associate publisher, and editor in chief of G. P. Putnam's Sons, and is the winner of the 2017 Ellery Queen Award from Mystery Writers of America. Among the writers of crime and suspense with whom he has worked are Tom Clancy, Clive Cussler, John Sandford, C. J. Box, Robert Crais, Carl Hiaasen, Daniel Silva, Jack Higgins, Frederick Forsyth, Ken Follett, Jonathan Kellerman, Ed McBain, and Ace Atkins. He now writes about crime fiction and publishing for CrimeReads, The Big Thrill, The Third Degree, BookTrib, and *Publishers Weekly*, among other publications.

Dag Öhrlund is a bestselling Swedish author and award-winning photographer who has written twenty-four successful crime novels and seventeen other books. He has also participated in another thirty-five other books—anthologies, photo books, etc. His spine-tingling books have been sold to several countries.

He began his career as a journalist and photographer forty-eight years ago. He has traveled and worked in thirty countries, his articles and photographs have been published in more than 150 magazines around the world.

In his adventurous life, Dag has had multiple brushes with death. He has been shot at, arrested, survived a terrorist attack, been paralyzed and had to use a wheelchair, events that have had a profound impact on his writing.

Dag lives in Sollentuna, Sweden, and Cape Coral, Florida.

Gigi Pandian is a *USA Today* bestselling and award-winning mystery author, breast cancer survivor, and accidental almost-vegan. The child of anthropologists from New Mexico and the southern tip of India, she spent her childhood traveling around the world on their research trips, and now lives outside San Francisco with her husband and a gargoyle who watches over the garden. Gigi writes lighthearted traditional mysteries including the Accidental Alchemist mysteries and Jaya Jones Treasure Hunt mysteries, and she loves locked-room mystery stories. Her debut novel won the Malice Domestic Grant, and she's been awarded the Anthony, Agatha, Lefty, and Derringer. www.gigipandian.com

T. Jefferson Parker is the author of twenty-six novels and numerous short stories and essays. He's been a member of MWA since 1990 and has won three Edgar Awards. He was born in Los Angeles and now lives near San Diego. When not at work he enjoys fishing, hiking, gardening, hunting sea glass, and a good bottle of Bordeaux.

Louise Penny is the author of the number one *New York Times* bestselling Chief Inspector Gamache crime novels. She lives in a small village in Quebec.

Gary Phillips has published various novels, comics, more than sixty-five short stories, and edited or coedited several anthologies including the Anthony Award–winning *The Obama Inheritance: Fifteen Stories of Conspiracy Noir*. *Violent Spring*, his first mystery published in the mid-nineties, was recently named one of the essential crime novels of Los Angeles. He was also a story editor on *Snowfall*, an FX show about crack and the CIA in 1980s South Central where he grew up.

Stephen Ross's short stories and novelettes have appeared in *Ellery Queen's Mystery Magazine*, *Alfred Hitchcock's Mystery Magazine*, several MWA anthologies, and many other magazines and anthologies. He has been nominated for an Edgar Award, a Derringer Award, and a Thriller Award. He was a 2010 Ellery Queen Readers' Award finalist and the 2018 winner of the Rose Trophy for Best Short Story. Stephen has lived in London and Germany, and he currently makes his home on the scenic Hibiscus Coast of New Zealand. His favorite thing in the world is going for coffee and bagels in Manhattan. www.StephenRoss.net

Hank Phillippi Ryan is the *USA Today* bestselling author of twelve thrillers, winning five Agathas, three Anthonys, and the Mary Higgins Clark

Award. She's also an on-air TV investigative reporter in Boston, where she's won thirty-seven Emmy Awards for groundbreaking journalism. Her 2019 novel, *The Murder List*, was an Agatha, Anthony, and Mary Higgins Clark Award nominee. Of her 2020 psychological standalone *The First to Lie*, the *Publishers Weekly* starred review said: "Stellar. Ryan could win a sixth Agatha with this one." Hank is a former board member of MWA and a past president of national Sisters in Crime.

Charles Salzberg, a former magazine journalist and nonfiction book writer is the author of the Shamus Award–nominated *Swann's Last Song* and *Second Story Man*, which is also the winner of the Beverly Hills Book Award. His novel *Devil in the Hole* was named one of the best crime novels of 2013 by *Suspense* magazine. He is a founding member of New York Writers Workshop and he serves on the MWA-NY Board.

Emmy and Edgar Award–nominated **Thomas B. Sawyer** was head writer, showrunner, and producer of the classic series *Murder, She Wrote*, for which he wrote twenty-four episodes. He wrote, directed, and produced the cult film-comedy *Alice Goodbody*; was the colibrettist and lyricist of *JACK*, an opera about JFK; and authored *Fiction Writing Demystified*. His latest thriller is *A Major Production!*, his memoir is *The Adventures of the REAL Tom Sawyer*, and its companion book is *9 Badass Secrets for Putting Yourself in Luck's Way*. www.ThomasBSawyer.com

Alex Segura is a writer of novels, comics, and podcasts, including *Star Wars Poe Dameron: Free Fall*, the Anthony Award–nominated Pete Fernandez Mystery series, *The Black Ghost*, *The Archies*, *Lethal Lit*, and more. He is a Miami native and lives in New York with his family.

Elizabeth Sims is the author of the Rita Farmer Mysteries, the Lambda and GCLS Goldie Award–winning Lillian Byrd Crime Series, and other fiction, including the standalone novel *Crimes in a Second Language*, which won the Florida Book Awards silver medal. An internationally recognized authority on writing, Elizabeth has written dozens of feature articles for *Writer's Digest* magazine, where she's a contributing editor. Her instructional title, *You've Got a Book in You: A Stress-Free Guide to Writing the Book of Your Dreams* (Writer's Digest Books) has helped thousands of aspiring authors find their wings.

Daniel Stashower, a three-time Edgar Award winner, has been a member of MWA for more than thirty years. His true crime books include *The Beautiful Cigar Girl: Mary Rogers, Edgar Allan Poe, and the Invention of Murder*, and *The Hour of Peril: The Secret Plot to Murder Lincoln Before the Civil War*.

For the record, my name is **Marilyn Stasio**, and I am the crime and mystery reviewer for the Sunday *New York Times Book Review*.

Daniel Steven is an attorney practicing publishing and media law. He has published prize-winning short fiction, two suspense novels, *Final Remedy* and *Clinical Trials*, a legal reference book, coauthored *The Street Smart Writer*, and articles in writer's publications, including *The Writer* and *Writer's Digest*. He has worked as an editor, counsel, and executive at a major publishing house; is a frequent speaker to writer's groups; teaches creative writing; and is chairman of the Contracts and Grievances Committee of the Mystery Writers of America, Inc.

C. M. Surrisi was nominated for a 2019 Agatha for her cozy middle-grade mystery *A Side of Sabotage*, the third book in her series, The Quinnie Boyd Mysteries. She is the author of short stories: "Actresses are Like That," published in Malice Domestic's Anthology *Mystery Most Theatrical*" (2020); "The Bequest," published in TC Sisters In Crime's Anthology *Minnesota Not So Nice* (2020); and "Know Nothing," published in the Guppy Anthology *The Fish That Got Away* (2021). She is the president of Minnesota Sisters In Crime.

Art Taylor is the author of *The Boy Detective & The Summer of '74 and Other Tales of Suspense* and *On the Road with Del & Louise: A Novel in Stories*. His story "English 398: Fiction Workshop," originally published in *Ellery Queen's Mystery Magazine*, won the 2019 Edgar Award for Best Short Story. His short fiction has also won the Agatha, Anthony, Derringer, and Macavity Awards. He is an associate professor of English at George Mason University. www.arttaylorwriter.com

Caroline & Charles Todd are a mother and son writing team who live on the east coast of the United States. They are the *New York Times* bestselling authors of the Inspector Ian Rutledge series and the Bess Crawford series. They have published more than thirty titles, including two stand-alone novels, an anthology of short stories, and more than twenty short stories appearing in mystery magazines and anthologies worldwide. Their works have received the Mary Higgins Clark, Agatha, and Barry Awards along with nominations for the Anthony, Edgar, and Dagger Awards.

Susan Vaught (www.susanvaught.com) is the two-time Edgar Award–winning author of *Footer Davis Probably Is Crazy* and *Me and Sam-Sam Handle the Apocalypse*. *Things Too Huge to Fix by Saying Sorry* received three starred reviews and an Edgar Award nomination, and *Super Max and the Mystery of Thornwood's Revenge* was called "an excellent addition to middle grade shelves" by *School Library Journal*. Her debut picture book, *Together We Grow*, received four starred reviews and was called a "picture book worth owning and cherishing" by *Kirkus Reviews*. She works as a neuropsychologist at a state psychiatric facility and lives on a farm with her wife and son in rural western Kentucky.

Elaine Viets returned to her hard-boiled roots with *Brain Storm*, the debut novel in her Angela Richman, Death Investigator series. Charlaine Harris calls *Brain Storm* "a complex novel of crime, punishment, and medical malfeasance." *Brain Storm* was followed by *Fire and Ashes*, *Ice Blonde*, and *A Star Is Dead*. She's written thirty-three bestselling mysteries in four series: hard-boiled Francesca Vierling, traditional Dead-End Job, cozy Josie Marcus Mystery Shopper, and Angela Richman, Death Investigator. Elaine's *A Deal with the Devil and 13 Short Stories* was published by Crippen & Landru. She's been toastmaster and guest of honor at Malice Domestic Mystery Conference. Elaine passed the Medicolegal Death Investigator Training Course for forensic professionals. She's won the Agatha, Anthony, and Lefty Awards. www.elaineviets.com

Bev Vincent has been a contributing editor with *Cemetery Dance* magazine for twenty years. He is the author of the Edgar-nominated *Stephen King Illustrated Companion* and other nonfiction books. In 2018, he co-edited the anthology *Flight or Fright* with Stephen King, available in more than a dozen languages. He has also published nearly a hundred short stories, including appearances in two MWA anthologies, as well as *EQMM* and *AHMM*. He lives in Texas with his wife, and can be found online at bevvincent.com.

Pat Gallant Weich is a Manhattan-based writer. She is a widow and mother of a son. Her work can be found in anthologies, magazines, and newspapers. Ms. Gallant Weich has just completed a book of literary non-fiction shorts called *Holding On to Right-Side Up*, which made the Finals in the 2019 William Faulkner/William Wisdom Literary Competition. Ms. Gallant Weich is currently working on a "how dunnit" mystery novel *Revenge Is Sweet*. She has her own company, Edit Write Away.

Kate White is the *New York Times* bestselling author of seven standalone psychological thrillers, including *The Fiancée* and *Have You Seen Me?*, and eight Bailey Weggins mysteries, including *Such a Perfect Wife*. The former editor in chief of *Cosmopolitan* magazine, she is also the editor of *The Mystery Writers of America Cookbook*.

Jacqueline Winspear is the author of the *New York Times* bestsellers *The American Agent*, *To Die But Once*, and *In This Grave Hour*, as well as twelve other bestselling Maisie Dobbs novels. Her standalone novel, *The Care and Management of Lies*, was a *New York Times* bestseller and a finalist for the Dayton Literary Peace Prize. In addition, Jacqueline is the author of two works of nonfiction: a memoir, *This Time Next Year We'll Be Laughing*, and *What Would Maisie Do?*, a companion to the series. Jacqueline's next novel, *The Consequences of Fear*, will be published in March 2021.

James W. Ziskin, Jim to his friends, is the author of the Anthony and Macavity Award–winning Ellie Stone mysteries. His books have also been finalists for the Edgar, Barry, and Lefty Awards. Jim worked in New York as a photo-news producer and writer, and then as director of NYU's Casa Italiana. He spent fifteen years in the Hollywood postproduction industry, running large international subtitling and visual effects operations. His international experience includes two years working and studying in France, extensive time in Italy, and more than three years in India. He speaks Italian and French.

Contributor Permissions

Extract from "Maintaining Suspense in Your Mystery: The Poker Game" Copyright © 2017 by Beth Amos, Used by permission.

"Diversity in Crime Fiction" Copyright © by Frankie Y. Bailey. Used by permission.

"When I Write a Book" Copyright © by Linwood Barclay. Used by permission

"Whenever I run into a nagging problem" Copyright from *The 101 Habits of Successful Novelists* used by permission of Stephanie Kay Bendel and Andrew McAleer.

"Graphic Novels" Copyright © by Dale W. Berry and Gary Phillips.

"Five Ways to Tame the Social Media Monster" Copyright © by Mysti Berry. Used by permission.

"Less-experienced writers" reprinted from *Writers on Writing*, in 2016, by Crystal Lake Publishing. Used by permission of Hal Bodner.

"The Protagonist" Copyright © by Allison Brennan. Used by permission.

"Every project will hit a roadblock" Copyright © by Leslie Ann Budewitz. Used by permission.

"Often our best characters" Copyright © by Carole Buggé. Used by permission

"I write because" Copyright © by Suzanne Chazin. Used by permission.

Introduction and "*Never* Outline!" by Lee Child. Used by permission.

"Secrets of a Book Critic" Copyright © by Oline H. Cogdill. Used by permission.

CONTRIBUTOR PERMISSIONS

"In the old days" Copyright © by Nancy J. Cohen. Used by permission.

"Tie-ins and Continuing a Character" Copyright © by Max Allan Collins. Used by permission.

"Plot and the Bones of a Mystery" Copyright © by Deborah Crombie. Used by permission.

"Lindsey's Top Ten Essentials for Aspiring Writers" Copyright © by Lindsey Davis. Used by permission.

"*Always* Outline!" Copyright © by Jeffery Deaver. Used by permission.

"Assess the Mess" Copyright © by Hallie Ephron. Used by permission.

"On Style" Copyright © by Lyndsay Faye. Used by permission.

"The Young Adult Mystery" Copyright © by K.L.A. Fricke Inc. Used by permission.

"Story and the Characters Freedom" Copyright © by Shelly Frome. Used by permission

"The Medical Thriller" Copyright © by Tess Gerritsen. Used by permission.

"Keeping it Thrilling" Copyright 2021 © by Meg Gardiner. Used by permission.

"Unleash Your Inner Child" Copyright © by Chris Grabenstein. Used by permission.

"Finding Lou: The Police Procedural" Copyright © by Rachel Howzell Hall. Used by permission.

"Dialogue is an ancient Greek stage direction" and "Chekhov's Advice" Copyright © by Bradley Harper. Used by permission.

"Crossing the Genres" Copyright © by Charlaine Harris. Used by permission.

"A traditional mystery" Copyright © by Carolyn G. Hart. Used by permission.

"Self-Publishing" Copyright © by Liliana Hart. Used by permission.

"The art of forgetting" Copyright © by Rob Hart. Used by permission.

311

CONTRIBUTOR PERMISSIONS

"The Villain of the Piece" Copyright © by T. Jefferson Parker. Used by permission.

"Building Your Community" Copyright © by Louise Penny. Used by permission.

"The Be-Bop Barbarians" Script Copyright © by Gary Phillips and Artwork Copyright © by Dale W. Berry.

"Subtext" Copyright © by Stephen Ross. Used by permission.

"You stare at your blank page" Copyright @ by Hank Phillippi Ryan. Used by permission.

"It's something you hear over and over" Copyright © by Charles Salzberg. Used by permission.

"Writing For MURDER, SHE WROTE or Creating 264+ Murders Using Three Motives—and No Blood, Violence, Crazy People or Forensics" Copyright © by Tom Sawyer Productions, Inc. Used by permission.

"The Mindset of Darkness: Writing Noir" Copyright © by Alex Segura. Used by permission.

"Occasionally I talk to schoolchildren about writing" Copyright © by Elizabeth Sims. Used by permission.

"Ten Stupid Questions about True Crime" Copyright © by Daniel Stashower. Used by permission.

"How Not to Get Reviewed" Copyright © by Marilyn Stasio. Used by permission.

"Legal Considerations" Copyright © 2020 by Daniel Steven. Used by permission.

"If you are writing a mystery for kids" Copyright © by C. M. Surrisi. Used by permission.

"The Short Mystery" Copyright © by Art Taylor. Used by permission.

"Writing in Partnership" Copyright © by Charles Todd. Used by permission.

"Mysteries for Children: An Introduction" Copyright © by Susan Vaught. Used by permission.

CONTRIBUTOR PERMISSIONS

Index

INDEX

INDEX

INDEX

INDEX

INDEX

INDEX

INDEX

INDEX